‾ores

'Keely is one of the most convinci st d
in Winton's work but in recent ficti^d
questing novelist of estrangement from
appears to have considered the themes ᴜhat have dominated his
career since *An Open Swimmer* and, for all the honours he has
gathered, has written his finest novel to date. The nostalgic heroes
of beautiful early works have here become beaten, weary and vulnerable if no less heroic and even more profound. For all its harsh-
ness – and it is a tough, at times shocking narrative – *Eyrie* is also
wise without becoming knowing'   Eileen Battersby, *Irish Times*

'Some readers will be surprised that a novel from the twice-
Booker-shortlisted author takes place around a tower block, so
successfully has he made himself the poet laureate of the wide sky,
the red dirt, the salt and thick estuarine mud of Western Australia
in his previous work. But it is in many ways the logical end point
of tensions between the natural world and human exploitation of
it that have been present in his work from the beginning . . . In the
hands of a lesser writer, the novel's allegorical intensity could feel
stagy, but Winton is in absolute command of his story. The pace
and tension is unremitting, the language unfussy while retaining
Winton's trademark lyricism'   Evie Wyld, *Guardian*

'Tim Winton is one of the world's leading novelists . . . Written in
Australian English and liberally studded with words and phrases
that make Standard English feel limp and drab, it crackles with
caustic energy'   *Glasgow Herald*

'Winton comes vividly and vigorously into his own in his novel's
blazingly immediate portrayal of Fremantle and Perth . . . *Eyrie*
consolidates his status as a matchlessly exhilarating and excoriating
fictional chronicler'   *Sunday Times*

'Time and again I found myself panting admiringly at Winton's imagery . . . I also can't think of any other contemporary writer who can sustain a story with just three main characters in it for more than 400 pages'   *Evening Standard*

'Winton writes with all five senses'   *Intelligent Life*

'By turns bleak and uplifting, but always compassionate and funny, this is an enthralling novel about renewal and the sheer mess of being human. Winton is always well worth reading. Here he is on top form'   *Mail on Sunday*

'Winton's latest novel is one of his best. Visceral, wry, emotionally complex . . . This is a tale packed with black humour, tragedy and pathos, driven by the fast-moving prose of its unreliable narrator and an exceptional ear for dialogue . . . Winton once compared writing to surfing. When the waves show up, he said, you must turn around and ride that energy to the shore. Winton's caught big waves before, with *Cloudstreet*, *The Riders* and *Dirt Music* to name a few. With *Eyrie* he's hanging ten'   *Scotland on Sunday*

'*Eyrie* is a clear-eyed yet compassionate depiction of the under-class that lives off the crumbs of the resource boom . . . However elaborate your analysis of *Eyrie*, the novel stands, like all of the author's work, on its ability to marry sophistication and simpli-city. Page by page it is an engrossing novel; the reader is moved and enraged in equal measure by the plain human story of Keely and his beautiful, battered adoptive family. You long for the good guy to win. You pray and ache for a fresh start for them all. And, as ever, it is couched in the prose of a writer on whom nothing is lost, for whom the tiniest local detail bears an epiphanic charge'   *Australian*

EYRIE

TIM WINTON

EYRIE

PICADOR

First published 2013 by Hamish Hamilton, Penguin Group (Australia)
707 Collins Street, Melbourne, Victoria 3008, Australia (a division of Penguin Australia Pty Ltd)

First published in the UK 2014 by Picador

This edition published 2015 by Picador
an imprint of Pan Macmillan, a division of Macmillan Publishers Limited
Pan Macmillan, 20 New Wharf Road, London N1 9RR
Basingstoke and Oxford
Associated companies throughout the world
www.panmacmillan.com

ISBN 978-1-4472-5347-1

Copyright © Tim Winton 2013

The author acknowledges cultural reference on page 6 to Bob Dylan's 'All Along the Watchtower'.
The song adapted from Isaiah 40 referred to on page 140 was written by Ken Kelso. The reference to
'despair's boutiques' on page 213 is from Les Murray's poem 'The New Moreton Bay'. Mention on page
307 of the inquest into the death of Aboriginal elder, Mr Ward, is made in sorrow, with respect.

1 3 5 7 9 8 6 4 2

A CIP catalogue record for this book is available from the British Library.

Printed and bound by CPI Group (UK) Ltd, Croydon, CR0 4YY

FOR DENISE, ALWAYS

they shall mount up with wings as eagles;
they shall run, and not be weary;
and they shall walk, and not faint.

ISAIAH 40:31

I

So.

Here was this stain on the carpet, a wet patch big as a coffee table. He had no idea what it was or how it got there. But the sight of it put the wind right up him.

Until now Thursday hadn't seemed quite so threatening.

It was a simple enough thing, waking late and at liberty to the peals of the town hall clock below. Eight, nine, maybe ten in the a.m. – Keely lacked the will to count. All that stern, Calvinist tolling gave him the yips. Even closed, his eyes felt wine-sapped. He hung on a while delaying the inevitable, wondering just how much grief lay in wait. The tiny flat was hot already. Thick and heady with the fags and showers and fry-ups and dish-suds of others. The smells of his good neighbours. Which is to say the stench of strangers, for his fellow tower-dwellers were alien to him in the most satisfying way imaginable, anonymous and reassuringly disconnected, mere thuds and throat-clearings behind bare brick walls, laugh tracks and pongs he needn't put a face to. Least of all – and strangest of any – the madwoman next door. In all these months he'd never seen her. All he knew was that she invested a good portion of each day fending off the wiles of Satan. Which was honest work, granted, but hard on the nerves. Especially his. For the moment she was mercifully silent, asleep or maybe holding Beelzebub to a nil-all draw between breakfast and lunch, and God bless her for that. Also for keeping it down while the poisonous afterglow of all that Barossa shiraz had its wicked way with him.

The building twitched in the wind, gave off its perpetual clank and moan of pipes, letting out the odd muffled scream. Ah, *Mirador*, what a homely pile she was.

He peeled back the lids with a gospel gasp and levered himself upright and bipedal if not immediately ambulatory. Teetered a moment in the bad weather and shapeless mortification of some-thing like waking consciousness. Which was heinous. Though in the scheme of things today's discomfort was the least of his troubles. He should be glad of the distraction. This little malaise was only fleeting. Well, temporary. Just a bloody hangover. But for all that a pearler anyway, a real swine-choker. Even his feet hurt. And one leg was still intoxicated.

The real pain was yet to stir. A pillar of dust in the distance.

In the bathroom, before a scalding block of sunlight, he tilted at the mirror to see how far the eyes had retreated from the battlefield of his face. Above the wildman beard he was all gullies and flaky shale. Badlands. His wine-blackened teeth the ruins of a scorched-earth retreat.

He took himself hand over hand to the mouldy shower recess,

stood under a cold and profligate cataract until all prospects of revival were exhausted.

The towel not remotely fresh. Pressed to his face, it brought to mind the honest, plain, mildewy scent of hippies. Not to be judgemental, comrades. But while definitely on the nose, it hadn't quite graduated to the full gorgonzola. Life in it yet. If you were a man unmolested by romance. Having let yourself go to this extent.

He tied the rag about his softening waist, sloped into the livingroom with its floor-to-ceiling window, and beheld the unstinting clarity of the western frontier: the shining sea, iron rooftops, flagpoles, Norfolk Island pines. All gathering up their cruel, wince-making sheen in the dregs of morning.

Port of Fremantle, gateway to the booming state of Western Australia. Which was, you could say, like Texas. Only it was big. Not to mention thin-skinned. And rich beyond dreaming. The greatest ore deposit in the world. The nation's quarry, China's swaggering enabler. A philistine giant eager to pass off its good fortune as virtue, quick to explain its shortcomings as east-coast conspiracies, always at the point of seceding from the Federation. Leviathan with an irritable bowel.

The great beast's shining teeth were visible in the east, through the kitchen window. Not that he was looking. But he could feel it at his back, the state capital looming out there on the plain in its sterile Windexed penumbra. It was only half an hour up the Swan River, as close and as incomprehensible as a sibling. For while Perth had bulldozed its past and buried its doubts in bluster, Fremantle nursed its grievances and scratched its arse.

And there she was at his feet. Good old Freo. Lying dazed and forsaken at the rivermouth, the addled wharfside slapper whose good bones showed through despite the ravages of age and bad living. She was low-rise but high-rent, defiant and deluded in equal measure, her Georgian warehouses, Victorian pubs, limestone cottages and lacy verandahs spared only by a century of political neglect. Hunkered in the desert wind, cowering beneath the austral sun.

By God, didn't a man come over all prosy the morning after. These days he was pure bullshit and noise, just another flannel-tongued Jeremiah with neither mission nor prophecy, no tribe to claim him but family. His thoughts spluttered on, maudlin, grievous, fitful, lacking proper administration, useless for anything more than goading the pain the vicious light had set off already. And, Christ, it was beyond anything the booze could induce. Here it came, the smoke and thunder, the welling percussion in his skull. Like hoofbeats. Two riders approaching. And the wind set to howl.

In the kitchen he scrabbled for ammunition, pre-emptive relief. Any bottle or packet would do. Said the joker to the thief. Lucky dip and rattle them blind from the knife drawer. Gurn them down like bullets. And reload. Or at least stand to. Sprawled against the countertop. Sweating through his soapy freshness in a few seconds. Think of something else.

He reached for the radio. Checked himself. Many, many months now, and he still struggled to master the impulse, as if some ruined bit of him yearned for the ritual of the pre-dawn recce, scouting for bad news before the phone began pinging. Because there'd always be a whisper, a Cabinet leak, a buried press release about another government cave-in, fresh permission to drill, strip, fill or blast. The industrial momentum was feverish. Oil, gas, iron, gold, lead, bauxite and nickel – it was the boom of all booms, and in a decade it had taken hostage every institution from government to education. The media were bedazzled. There was pentecostal ecstasy in the air, and to resist it was heresy. But that had been his gig, to meet the stampede head-on every morning, beginning in the dark, trolling across the frequencies half asleep while the basin filled with shave water and the still functional face took shape in the mirror at roughly the same speed as his thoughts. Part of it was simple triage, belching out soundbites like a spiv's PR flak. All the while trying to hold to the long view, the greater hopes he'd begun with. Like appealing to people's higher nature. And getting Nature itself a fair hearing. Which was, of course, in this state, at such a moment in history, like catching farts in a butterfly net.

No easy thing to unwind from. The toxic adrenaline, the ceaseless performance, the monastic discipline. Sucking in trouble every day before sun-up, preparing a full day's strategy in the shower. Finding yourself in the office at midnight, after the final, five-way phone hook-up, shaking with rage, caffeine and fatigue. But a year's bitter liberty should have done the trick. Really. For a bloke who was half smart. Getting sacked? That was a mercy, a cold-turkey intervention. For which a man should be grateful. He was well out of it. What had it all been anyway but one long fighting retreat? Mere pageantry and panto. He'd just been something for the cowboys and their wild-eyed cattle to wheel past, a procedural obstacle set in their path while they yahooed on towards the spoils.

So screw it. Don't touch that dial. Not the radio, nor the telly. Least of all the laptop. Leave it shut there on the table like a silt-sifting mussel beside the mobile. He was no longer relevant. And he didn't give a shit about any of it now. He just couldn't. Would not. Didn't even read the papers anymore. Tried not to, at least. Had no need of more stories about 'clean coal'. The national daily prosecuting its long war against climate science. Didn't matter which rag you read, it would be another instalment about the triumph of capital. One more fawning profile of a self-made iron heiress and he'd mix himself a Harpic Wallbanger and be done with it. Just to get the fucking taste out of his mouth. You didn't even need to look. You knew what to expect. The summer ration of shark stories and prissy scandals about the same coked-up footballer between episodes of soul-searching about shopping hours. Made your kidneys boil for shame.

Nah, the news only upheld what you understood already. What you feared and hated. How things were and would be. It was no help. Neither was the plonk, of course – only fair to concede that. Like the news, drinking offered more confirmation than consolation. And it was so much easier to fill a void than to contemplate it.

Still gnashing at that meatless bone. Let it go. Concentrate on choking down the morning's free-range analgesics. And stay vertical. Think up.

Well, the upside was he hadn't died in the night. He was free and unencumbered. Which is to say alone and unemployed. And he was in urgent need of a healing breakfast. Soon as all his bits booted up. Just give it a mo.

At the sliding door to the balcony he looked down beyond the forecourt across the flaring iron rooftops to the harbour. Cranes, containers on the quay in savage yellows, reds, blues; the hectic green superstructure of a tanker's bridge. Searing flash of sun on canted glass. Everything vivid enough to bring on an ambush.

The sea beyond the breakwater was flat, the islands suspended in brothy haze. An orange pilot boat surged past the moles and out into open water, twin plumes of diesel smoke flagging from its stacks, the wake like a whitening wound on the skin of the sea. Which seemed all very lyrical and seafaring until you cracked the door a little and felt the red-plain wind. More hellish updraught than pastoral uplift. Harsh, pitiless. Laden with grit sharp enough to flay a baby-boomer to the bone.

Retreat. Snap the slider back in its slot. And stand there like a mouth-breathing moron. In your rancid towel.

Still. The real estate agent was right: it was a hell of a view for the money. *That* was the upside. Not just surviving the night but waking to this, an unparalleled prospect of the great Indian

Ocean. The champagne outlook for a homebrew outlay. The Mirador wasn't just the tallest building in town, it was the ugliest by quite a margin. You had to smile at the lovely deluded aspirational romance of the name. When local worthies could have just settled for Aqua Vista or Island Vue they plumped for Mirador: bolthole for the quaking matador, the sex-free paramour, sad, sorry and head-sore. Where you had, despite your fears, the unsought luxury of looking out from on high. Out and down. Like a prince. From your seedy little eyrie. On all the strange doings and stranger beings below. All those folks, booted and suited, still in the game. Trying to give a shit. While keeping the wolf from the door. As if that were even possible.

Keely rested his brow against the warm glass of the door. A ship's horn set the pane thrumming against his skull. The first blast sent a zizz through his brainpan, down his jaw to the base of his neck. The second was longer and stronger, rooting so deeply into him he recoiled and backpedalled with a grunt.

And that was when he registered the strange sensation underfoot. The carpet. It was wet. And not just wet, it was sodden.

The stain was a metre long. It squelched as he stepped out of it. He noted, for what it was worth, that there were two distinct wet patches – one large, the other small – like the elements of an exclamation mark. Like two blasts of a horn, which at least had the courtesy of signifying something.

Keely's place was ten storeys up, top floor; this was unlikely to be a plumbing issue or an overflowing bath. A leak in the roof? The last time a decent spot of rain graced this city, he'd been in a job and not quite so comprehensively divorced. Anyhow, there were no watermarks on the nasty stucco ceiling. It was low enough to reach on tiptoe. The surface wasn't simply arid, it felt powdery, left white grit on his fingertips. And the rest of the flat – galley kitchen, bedroom – was normal. Floor, walls, ceiling. Even the kitchen sink was dry. The only other wet surface in the place was the grout-sick shower stall he'd just left.

Keely slumped into the solitary armchair and looked out across the balcony with its coralline aggregations of dove shit. No reason to panic about a bit of damp carpet, he knew that, but his heart knocked like a sick diesel. And it was with him again, that evil shimmer. Fucking head. All these weeks. Mersyndols, codeines the size of bullsharks; they'd kick in soon. Surely. But he couldn't even feel them in the water yet. Swim, you bastards. It was an effort to think straight, to glance past his hairy knees at the gun-metal carpet and find a reason for such provocation as this wet floor, to reason on it and not panic.

With a single big toe, he dabbed at the nylon weave. Positively marshy. He stood again. Pressed his foot into the disturbing lushness of it. The towel fell away and there he was, naked, flabby, heat-blotched. He was a long way up, but knowing his luck some unsuspecting ratepayer was getting an eyeful. Hoary morning glory, ahoy! He kicked the towel against the wall, swayed a moment from the effort. And then an awful thought reached him, as if on relay. The room swam a little.

What if he'd made this stain himself? Had he done things last night he didn't remember? Had it come to that? He'd hit it hard lately but he didn't drink to the point of passing out. Well, not *blacking* out, that wasn't his form. He got hammered, not crazy. But who else could have spilt something here in his livingroom? And spilt what, exactly? He hoped to Heaven, and by all that was green and holy, that he hadn't found a new means of disgracing himself. Couldn't endure it.

But he had to know.

So he knelt on the carpet and sniffed. He dabbed at the fibres, smelt his fingers – delicately, tentatively at first, and then more boldly – pressing his palms into the dampness, snuffling, rubbing, squinting. Until he thought of the picture he made, truffling about on all fours, date in the air, tackle adrift, whiffing out his own spoor like a lost mutt in full view of whichever bionic parking inspector happened to look skyward at this awful moment. Which – yes – seemed funny enough in its way, just didn't feel very amusing. Not yet, not while he was trapped in the dread of not knowing, with shame looming behind the flashes of colour in his head. He'd laugh later. Right now he had to make sure.

Safe. All he wanted. Was to be safe. In his flat. In himself. So he kept at it. Until he was satisfied. Reasonably, moderately sure. Unable, at least, to detect a hint of urine. Or faint notes of puke. Or any other bodily fluid.

Thank God. Thank Ralph Nader, Peter Singer – the entire sandal-wearing pantheon. Comrades, he was in the clear. Which solved nothing, of course, but you had to hold onto any little triumph that came your way, didn't you? Yes. Yes, yes, yes. For three seconds Keely was exultant. Until the thought sank in. There he was. A middle-aged man of moderate intelligence, nuddied up and egregiously hungover. Almost high-kicking and spangle-tossing at the prospect that he had *probably* not gotten up in the night, off his chops on the fruit of the Barossa, and pissed on his own floor.

So. Elation departed in haste. And dear God. Here it was. Whatever it happened to be. There on the carpet. Evidence that his inner Elvis had surely left the building.

And now, next door, as if feeling his misery in the ether, the demoniac started up for the day. No you don't, she said through the thin wall. No, you won't. Never!

No, he muttered bitterly. Probably not.

He was hungry.

He poured himself a bowl of muesli and champed away penitently, not taking his eyes from the stain. Nah, that wasn't urine. But if he was wrong, on a February day like this, his sanctuary would soon reek like a Marseilles pissoir.

After two spoonfuls of Swiss chaff he gagged and conceded defeat. He required an improper breakfast.

Regardless.

Immediately.

Along the open walkway of the tenth floor, on the eastern face of the building, all doors were shut and most curtains drawn against the sun, so there was no one to greet, nothing to be said as Keely made his way towards the lifts in the roasting wind. To steady himself he gripped the iron balustrade. The metal was lumpy from decades of paint, as scaled and lime-caked as the taffrail of a tramp steamer. Hauling himself along it he felt the full span of uprights begin to vibrate in weird sympathy, humming louder with every step until it seemed the building and the surrounding streets were speaking across each other. Down there it was a mash of idling buses, cooling stacks, car alarms and feral screamers. Behind, below, before him, the air sawed and seethed. Good Christ, the heat, the cacophony – they were insupportable.

But he had to get out, pull his mind away from what he didn't understand, couldn't fix, had to let slide.

At the lifts he hunted a bit of shade, which meant the grungy stairwell. While he waited, the croon and chirp of little kids rose from the convent playground across the side street. Rugrats having at it – this was the sort of noise a man should never tire of. But in truth it was getting old. Even child's play sounded sinister after a while, something else to steel yourself against.

And now his heart was in his neck again.

And where was the bloody lift?

He wondered if it was possible he'd left his door open last night, just flaked out and left it ajar in the smothering heat. Maybe some nutjob had snuck in for a laugh, to mess with him, give him a fright. No shortage of scumbags in the building. But the door was closed when he went to bed. Wasn't it? Pissed or sober, he was very particular about locking up. Anyway, it was shut when he woke. If someone had crept in, seizing the moment, taking advantage of his temporary lapse or possible derangement, they'd pulled the door to on their way out. From what – good breeding, pity, regret? There was no sign of any other mischief. They'd taken nothing. Not that there was much to take. He had no enemies here. That he knew of. He kept to himself. Studiously. No one, not even family, had crossed the threshold. So the thought of a lurker there while he slept, someone hovering in the hot darkness, watching – it went through him like a colonic twitch.

The lift was mercifully empty. He travelled unseen and uninterrupted to the ground floor. Let the lobby doors roll back. Took it full in the face. All that hideous light. Walked out like a halfwit into a bushfire.

He didn't even know where he was headed. Discovered himself walking the wrong way, for one thing. It was hot enough to kill an asbestos sparrow. The concrete forecourt livid, the street branding, blinding, breath-sucking. Acid light plashed white underfoot, swashing wall to wall, window upon window, and he waded in it a moment, tilting spastic and helpless, so suddenly porous and chalky it was all behind his eyes in an instant, fizzing within his skull until it rendered everything outside him in flashes and flickers. No gentling tones out here, only abyssal shadows or colours so saturated they looked carcinogenic. Keely glimpsed, gasped, fought off the dread and gimped on gamely, but he didn't see the bodies on the pavement outside the Chinese joint until he'd almost trampled them.

A girl hunkered in the busy foot-traffic beneath an audience of women who bickered with such conviction they had to be relatives. All of them fat and angry, red-faced, sniping. The girl herself was changing a baby's nappy in the street; a hot, shrieking girl-child on the bare concrete. And as he pulled up, sculling a moment, disoriented as much as obstructed, he felt the clan stiffen, saw them scowl as if preparing to fend him off. He hesitated, sought a course around them, as the oldest, a stout and ugly woman, bunched a Kmart bag and shoved it beneath the infant's head. In nearly the same moment the squatting mother shot a glance upwards that seemed directed solely at him. It may only have been a glance of shame or even defiance but to Keely it felt like hatred and he turned aside as if struck.

He angled away into an oncoming torrent of pedestrians, all boiled faces and beetling sunglasses, a surge of elbows, phones, smoke-puckers and semi-syllables within a fug of sweat and warring perfumes. He yielded towards the road's edge where buses shuddered and gulped at the kerb. A skateboarder swept past. The street pulsed and roared as he fought for a bearing. Target, pharmacy, real estate agent, bank. Fuck, he was listing, yawing, hopelessly self-correcting. It was more than he could manage. Any second he'd capsize.

So he lurched into the closest entry. Coles. Safe harbour. Obedi-ent glass doors, airconditioning, muzak. Went deep, headed instinctively for the fluorescent headwaters, seeking cool air and cooler still, until he found himself in the produce section, staring at spears of Peruvian asparagus in slender, uniform lines of pale green. They were only cut vegetables, for Christ's sake, and cheap imports at that, but there was something lovely and clement about their serried ranks and pastel colour, and now that he noticed it, the entire refrigerated colonnade had over it a misty sheen cool enough to make a Celt weep. Moist, clean, unending blur. Beneath the muzak, a special kind of quiet. Silent gusts of respite. And such calm, such unpeopled order. He caught himself fighting the urge to lie down there in the lee of these wafting cabinets and sleep till dark. Just him and poor Karen Carpenter. Him and the clean pine crates and the Pine O Cleen disinfectant and those vegetables to which clung the last faint odour of something like life itself. He imagined it, thought better of it, then discovered himself on the lino, being stood over by a woman with spectacles and brown fists. She seemed distressed, even angry, but she was being perturbed in a language he didn't speak yet. She pointed at him excitedly, bleating and toothbaring a little before she began to hammer with some emphasis at the steel cradle of the impressive tomato display. But his cheek was cool against the floor and he couldn't quite feel the immediacy of her concern. And then she was yanking at him without fear or favour, and he was on his feet, alone.

Maybe this was what it was like to die a little, to feel shriven, rescued, redeemed. Having your collar pulled, your fucking beard tugged by the roots until there you were, upright and guiltless, watching your irritated saviour scuff away in Third World foot-wear, pushing a loaded trolley.

Becalmed. Adrift. Summoning a bit of puff.

He ghosted through the aisles accompanied by the sad, sweet

Carpenters – who he hoped were now both safely dead. For his peace of mind. For their own good.

Finally, for the sake of propriety, to feel in charge of himself once more, he made a few purchases. The steadying force of retail.

This. This. That, whatever it was. Couldn't afford any but he bought them all.

Going through the motions at the checkout helped a little, but it occurred to him – winked like an oil light on the dash – that he really could be losing his mind. And that couldn't be all his fault. Surely.

The change. Which he accepted graciously. Along with the girl's limp smile of boredom.

And there he was, successfully transacted, having paid dearly for his little digression, his minutes of stunned mullethood, hoisting this clammy bag of unnecessaries, suddenly aware again of how eerily hungry he was and why he'd ventured out in the first place.

He craved a couple of Bub's fluffy double-shots. But he'd never make it to the Strip. He lacked the loins, pure and simple. Only a trek of three hundred metres or so, but out of range today. He was rogered. Unless he chanced his arm somewhere here in the refrigerated mini-mall. There was a nook of sorts beside the Cut and Blow. Yes, here it was. With malarial bain-marie and plastic tables. Open to the polished concourse, so the muzak was free and endless, and the smells of burning cheese and scorched hair roiled like confluences about the vinyl palm tree separating the two establishments. What the hell. Time to experiment. Necessity being the motherfucker of whatever is in its way.

Took a little round table. Pressed his thumbs, like his very own executioner, to his temples. Ordered something that sounded safe enough. And took stock.

Usually – on his standard wasted day – he'd walk an hour, take a swim, lounge at Bub's and dodge certain faces by judicious use of the menu or a reiki tract left by some wide-eyed chump. All the while convincing himself that despite appearances his days retained a certain functional coherence. That was an effort, and today such feats were beyond him. He felt peeled, without defences. He was not himself, not even the remnant self he'd been yesterday afternoon. Maybe it was just the bad start. The nasty fright. Which, of course, would turn out to have a simple explanation. But the town felt hostile this morning and the world past its modest boundaries without pity. He could feel it pressing hot and breathless against the glass doors in the distance. Or perhaps that was just weather.

Besides, it was pension day. The fortnightly full moon. Twelve hours of tidal chaos. So if he really wanted to press on further from home in search of better fare and more congenial surrounds, then he'd have to run the payday gauntlet between this little granny mall and Bub's. And that was a lot of crazy shit to get through. For that you needed skin. Ramrod will. And funds. Because before you even got to the corner there were toothless winos and humbugging Aborigines, each with a case to make and a cloud of misery and body odour to drive it home. Once you'd fought your way clear of the bottlo and the junkie park, you'd need to penetrate the phalanx of charity-tin rattlers skulking soulfully in the trinket alleys and shady arcades. And what could you do but honour their efforts, sign their petitions, fork out the shekels while seething? He gave bogus addresses, snail and email, and hated himself for it. Their causes were just but doomed.

Thank God they were all so fresh and endlessly replaceable, these kids, because they almost never recognized him. What could you tell them, these smiley elves from Oxfam, Greenpeace, or Friends of the Forest, what could you honestly say? It killed you, the bright-eyed marsupial innocence of their faces. No. No sir. Not today.

And even if he did make it that far without falling over again or yacking on someone, he'd still have the buskers to deal with. They were worse than any charity picket, more offensive and evil-smelling than any derro or waistcoated do-gooder. These talentless nitwits were the final obstacle between you and a fistful of arabica beans. And by the time you reached them you were already punch-drunk and desperate. Without discrimination or pride. So there you went, most days, creeping past the tattoo dens and incense emporia where they lurked, steeling yourself to stride by solemnly but almost always ending up shelling out like a man envious of the higher gifts. Just to get by, just to be left alone, just because you felt sorry for the same three chords about the usual damage done.

After all that he'd finally totter onto the little avenue of self-congratulation that everyone called the Cappuccino Strip. Fifty umbrellas around which a certain civic pride once rallied. In the seventies the Strip had been a beacon of homely cosmopolitan-ism, a refuge from the desolate franchise dispensation stretching from sea to hazy hills. But that was before it calcified into smugness. Somewhere along the way the good folks of the port settled in the wisdom that coffee was all the culture and industry a town required. Butcher shops, hardware stores, chandlers and bakeries had steadily been squeezed out and surplanted by yet more cafés, new spaghetti barns. Rents were extortionate, house prices absurd. The city had become a boho theme park perched on a real estate bubble, and behind every neglected goldrush façade and vacant shopfront was a slum landlord counting pennies, lord-ing it over family and bitching about refugees.

Freo, *mon amour*. It gave him five kinds of sulphuric reflux to think of it. Didn't know how he could still love it so. Tried to tell himself at least it wasn't Perth, that pastel toy town upriver. But, Christ, that wasn't saying much, was it?

No, this sad little caff would have to be it today. He was physically infirm and psychically unable to go any further. He'd sit tight and watch the trolley-boys trundle by, the parched oldsters wheezing in from Centrelink and Culley's on their walkers, the rat-tailed infants chucking tantrums on the shiny tiles. He could bear this. Couldn't he? He was here already, he'd made his order. He was all set. And yet he could not rest. For the mind charged on, cataloguing the horrors he'd spared himself. The manky footpath jewellers, the already drunk Irish backpackers, the mouthy schoolkids.

Still, when he beheld his breakfast on its sunny yellow plate, his resolve began to decay. He couldn't help but think of properly fried bacon, of hash browns and fluffy free-rangers, of a coffee upon whose bronzed *crema* a spoonful of sugar might wallow, like a cherub upon a cloud. As he struggled with some aberrant species of ham-and-cheese croissant that clung to his gums like denture glue, he began to wonder if he might just man up after all and make a dash to Bub's. Well, perhaps not a dash. A power shuffle, a wilful creep.

Hell, yes. And he was bracing against the sticky plastic in preparation for a slow-motion getaway when he remembered the time. It was witching hour on the Strip. That meant yummy mummies. Über-matrons. He couldn't abide them. Or resist them. They'd see him off in a heartbeat. Without even noticing him. Without registering his feeble presence. With their hulking all-terrain strollers and jogging sheen, their kooky ethnic headscarves and gleaming thighs, they were enough to make a man kick a Buddhist. Late morning they ran in packs, descending upon the quarter to circle their wagons and colonize entire cafés for cistern-sized lattes and teeny-cutesy babycinos. There was something loathsome and luscious about their fruity chirrups, their sweet-smelling sweat, their mist of satisfaction. Not content to be healthy and handsome, they had to be cruelly ravishing. And Jesus, even Leni Riefenstahl had spared us lycra.

Keely's contempt and lust were no match for them. Which was why he usually went early. To save himself the suffering. So that was that. Here he stood. Sat. Wrestling his greasy bolus. Sipping this bituminous brew. Having barely gotten change from a tenner. Let no man say he didn't keep an open mind.

Nothing for it but to suck it up and beat a ginger retreat.

Home was only forty metres away, sixty at the most. But something of a challenge given the blurred vision and the intermittent sparks of lightning in his head. Twice he needed to steady himself. First against a jacaranda. Then by high-tackling a molten parking meter. And in these restorative pauses he leaned back like a tranquilized pole-dancer to take in the brutal monolith that rose above trees, chimneys and whining wires.

The Mirador. Not much of the winsome Spanish turret about it, that's for sure. It was a classic shitbox: beige bricks, raw concrete galleries, ironbar railings, doors and windows like prison slots. Hard to credit that fifty years ago some nabob thought it a grand idea, a harbinger of progress. The place had grown old and grim within months of its completion and the subsequent years had not been gentle. Locals despised it. But it had been a haven for old folks, retired lumpers and clerks, invalid pensioners, transients, drunks and welfare mothers. They were still there, many of them, lately joined by the first gentrifying hopefuls and middle-class casualties like himself. Keely looked up at its meagre balconies. The drying mop, the ruined telly, the Dockers flag, the jaunty sunflower in a pot, the wheelchair flashing in the sun.

He swayed against the meter and felt a little flutter of affection for the old hulk. Like him, the building was a product of the sixties. And like him it was too large a mistake to be undone.

I'm not much, he told himself on the caustic forecourt, but I'm home.

The lobby stank of laundry soap, fresh paint, and mopped floors. As he entered, Keely fell in behind a woman and child heading for the lifts. He would have preferred to peel off into the laundromat a moment until they were gone, and then go on up alone when the coast was clear, but he was desperate to lie down; he felt faint and the headache was evil in him. Besides, the lift door rolled open as he approached; he'd only look like a wally backing away now. So he followed them in, careful to arrange himself and his morally unflattering plastic bag in the farthest corner of the carriage. When the woman punched the key for the tenth floor his heart sank.

You? she asked without looking his way.

Oh, he murmured. Same.

Neighbours, then, she said with a hint of scepticism.

He grunted. She sighed as if she'd already discounted his presence.

Keely snatched a look at the boy as he laid his head against the woman's hip. The kid avoided his gaze. As they were hauled up slowly Keely fixed on the woozy stippled pattern of the car's stainless-steel lining.

No good? the woman asked the boy.

I'm not right in myself, said the kid.

Did you sick up? The teacher didn't say.

No, said the boy. But I'm not well.

You're hot.

Yes, hot in the temperature.

The woman made a gentle laughing sound through her nose and repeated it without mockery: *Hot in the temperature.*

Keely sensed the pale flare of the woman's face turning his way.

When he was really little, she said, he thought his forrid was his temperature. You know, *let me check your temperature* and everythin. Little smartarse.

Am not.

Are so.

Keely assembled a makeshift grin but spared himself the eye contact. There he was in monstrous outline, distorted by the shiny pressed steel, radiating fluorescent light from a hundred welts and dints. When he moved, his head swam. God, he thought, all the stoners in the building – do they take the stairs?

He dug a thumb into his temple, closed his eyes.

And now, she said. Now, he's *not right in himself.*

Well, said the boy. I'm not.

You never get crook of a weekend, do ya?

I was once.

That was Easter, you dill. All that chocolate. Eyes bigger'n yer belly.

He felt the woman's attention, the full force of her gaze. It was all he could do not to cringe. Inside his shirt the sweat began to run; he could feel panic rising in him like nausea and only the bounce of their arrival delivered him. As the door opened he lunged forward, hoisting his clammy supermarket bag after him, and took in a hot draught of air. Out on the walkway he stepped aside so they could pass, and the woman brushed by smelling of cigarettes and body spray. But the boy lingered. And when Keely looked back he saw him planted in the gap, fending the closing door off with hip and shoulder like a little half-back. His gaze was intense but removed and without the boy actually looking his way Keely sensed himself being registered, sized up. And it was awkward. Standing there, suspended. The woman waiting beside him with no pretence at patience. As if she blamed him as much as the kid for this delay.

Keely prepared to walk away but there was something about the boy that intrigued him. Perhaps the dark rings beneath his eyes. Or the pale blue irises. Such a round face. And they did something odd, those shadows, made the kid seem older than he was, older than he could be. His hair fell white and straight to his shoulders. He licked his lower lip, which was chapped, and bunted the door away again as the woman jangled her keys. The boy wore a little polo shirt, shorts, sneakers. Just an ordinary Mirador kid trying it on with his longsuffering mother. So what was it that made Keely's stomach flip, standing here watching him gaze across the rooftops while the hot wind rose from the shaft at their feet? He had no experience with kids; he didn't know what this was. But it felt a bit like being cased by a dog too wary to come right up and sniff.

When you're ready, said the woman.

I'm ready, said the kid, stepping out, letting the door roll to.

Hope you feel better, Keely said to the boy.

You too, said the kid.

The woman snorted and fished for something in her bag. She'd been pretty once. In her denim skirt and sleeveless top she seemed puffy, almost bruised. Her dirty-blonde hair was dry and she had the kippered complexion of the lifelong smoker, but any man would still look twice.

You look familiar, she said.

She seemed to be about his age. One of her front teeth was chipped and discoloured, as though it were dying.

Well, he said. Same floor, I guess. Like you said, neighbours.

Where are you again?

It occurred to him she was only being careful, that she suspected him of having followed them up from the street through the security door.

Ten-oh-seven, he said.

Huh, she murmured, taking the serious little boy's hand. Don't think I seen you here before. Know you from somewhere, but.

Keely tried to bring it to a close by setting off along the walkway. Well, he said over his shoulder – a little more abruptly than he intended – I keep to myself.

He heard her grunt; it could have meant anything. When he pulled up at his door he saw her strolling along hand in hand with the boy, no longer in quite such a hurry. She was making sure. Which said something about the way he looked, no doubt, so he made a performance of digging out his key like the hunter home from the hill and all. But he was running out of puff now, listing against the gritty bricks, and as he hauled back the security screen and shoved the key in the lock, he saw the kid surge ahead of the woman, dart towards the iron balustrade and mount the bottom rung with a suddenness that sent a spasm of apprehension through him. He fumbled the key, dropped it, but couldn't stoop to pick it up with the kid perched there on tiptoe, right outside the door, two metres away. The child's skinny arms were knitted over the iron rail, head suspended in a roasting updraught, hair ripped back like the tail of a comet. As if he were speeding, hurtling, falling already. Brutal silver rooftops, far below. Traffic noise. Playground cries. A ship's horn signalling imminent departure. Keely didn't dare take his eyes off him. Too stunned, at first. Terrified he'd startle him disastrously by moving, by lunging, calling out. And then, for two, three, four whole seconds he was convinced his steady gaze was vital, that he was the only force securing the kid to the building. Sneakered heels tipped up, laces snickering in the wind. Keely heard the woman, clocked the peripheral blur of her ambling. Could not believe she was so lax, so sanguine about the child being this close to the edge, ten storeys high with his feet off the mottled concrete. He just locked onto the slight frame with his last fading energy, growing angrier with every slow-moving moment, furious at both of them for being so careless and such a cruel interruption. Until the little boy's throat began to work and he looked as if he were about to puke. And in the instant Keely tensed himself to spring, to haul him back to safety, when it seemed the kid would retch and lose his grip, the boy hawked and sent a shining gob of spit out into space. And then the woman was there, cuffing the back of his neck goodnaturedly.

Don't spit, ya dirty bugger, she said. Some poor mug'll think it's rain.

One drop? said the kid.

That was a joke, ya knucklehead.

Was it funny?

Thanks a lot.

Keely subsided against his door. Like a badly wrapped parcel, a side of beef on the turn, wrappers sodden, every exposed patch of him livid and unwholesome. Christ, he reeked. He snatched up the key, fell through the door and left the pair of them bantering away as if he'd never been there.

Git down off that, said the woman. Carn, it's hot.

Keely shut the door, pitched his pointless shopping onto the bench and lurched towards the bedroom. Fell to the mattress like a burning man into a swimming pool.

Thank God. Or whoever. Just, thank you. And in that first flush of deliverance Keely felt feverish relief. Before the blood rushed to his head and the ceiling blurred horribly, pressing down against his eyes, chest, tongue. Nothing for it but to lie there. Taking it. Giving it time to resolve. Willing the distorted sensation to back off enough for him to get his wits together, breathe easy again.

But there was a knock at the door.

Not now! he called.

The rapping continued. The fridge kicked in so hard he felt it in the neck. And a voice, like something through water. Burbling. Ramping up the pain. Every knock at the door was like a thudding heartbeat out of sync, needling through his teeth. For pity's sake!

He got to his feet seeing double, slammed his hip against the kitchen bench heading for the door and was too consumed by all the competing sensations to even say anything when he reefed it open and saw them still there, backlit into fuzzy silhouettes on the other side of the insect screen.

Tommy Keely, she said.

He blinked. It was nasty, hearing his name uttered. Here in the building. Out in the open. Through his own screen door.

It took a while, she said. But I knew it was you.

Well, he croaked, congratulations. I guess.

It's you, though, isn't it? I'm right, aren't I?

Maybe. Who cares?

Sorta bloody question's that?

I dunno. I'm sorry. I'm. I dunno.

Keely sagged against the fridge a moment, his head ready to split like a melon. When he looked back, the boy was gone. The air outside danced with bubbles of light, camera flashes, a violet pulse.

You alright? she asked.

Yeah. Nah. Yeah.

You don't remember?

Yes, he said. I remember who I am.

Not you, ya fuckwit. Me.

He stared at her through the flyscreen. Saw little more than the flaring nimbus around her head.

I'm sorry?

Blackboy Crescent, she said.

Shit. Really?

I thought you'd remember.

I remember Blackboy Crescent.

But not me.

It occurred to him that this was the point at which he was supposed to throw all caution aside and ask her in, but he'd lived too long in wary isolation. And already regretted admitting who he was. But Blackboy Crescent, that set him back. And where was the kid? What was she doing about the kid scampering somewhere along the open gallery?

Your little boy, he rasped.

Watchin telly. Bloody scam-artist.

He tried to straighten up. He could feel her peering in. Feel her scoping out his entire ruined carcase.

Your sister's name is Faith.

Okay, he said, pressing against the screen door for a closer look. The woman chuckled. He could not truly see her for turbulent, twitching lights.

Mate, you're off your chops.

No. Headache.

Right, she said sceptically.

So, he said. So. So, how d'you know Faith?

Same way I know your mum's Doris and your dad's Neville.

He's dead.

Oh. Jesus. Sorry. Fuck. I forgot.

Doesn't matter.

You look different, she said. Maybe it's the beard.

I guess so, he muttered, finding the thought distantly amusing, as if it could only be the whiskers that were rubbish and the rest of him was in showroom nick.

She stood there a few moments more in hazy outline. He thought he might fall. For a moment he wanted to be sick. No nausea, just the urge, which was a recent thing and perplexing. Yet he could still feel her disappointment, the sense of something curdling. Blackboy Crescent. The swamp, corrugated-iron canoes, tuart trees, yellow dirt, the engine-oil smell of his father.

Anyway, she murmured.

Right.

I'll let you go before you fall over.

Okay.

It's Gemma, by the way, in case you were actually wondering.

Gemma? Gemma Buck? Are you serious?

No, I'm bloody makin it up, what d'you think?

I'm, I —

And then she was gone.

The bed came halfway across the flat to meet him.

When he woke it was almost dark. The sea breeze rattled the blinds above his head and the building clanked and gurgled with showering, dinner-making, dishwashing. Weird the way coughs and cries and TV laughter travelled through the bones of the place. Outside, only gulls and the murmur of traffic, everything subdued, as if the fever of payday had broken.

He got up slowly, in stages. He was weak. His headache had retreated to the intensity of a mere hangover and this was as close to relief as he was likely to get. His vision was more or less back to normal.

As ever, somebody was cooking with old-style curry powder – Keen's or Clive of India – the smell of church suppers, student digs. The junkies would be content, on the nod. And, having peaked early, the drunks sleeping it off at home, on the street, in custody. Everyone else treating themselves to a nice chop, a bit of spicy chook. All was well.

On the kitchen bench in a puddle, his bag of groceries. He slung it into the fridge and tried not to think of salmonella. Over by the sliding glass door there was no longer a visible stain on the carpet but when he walked across it he found the area still slightly damp underfoot. At least it didn't stink.

He slid the door open and stepped out onto the balcony to feel the briny wind in his hair, his beard. Out over the sea the western sky was all fading afterglow. Beneath him, the melancholy lights of the wharves, warehouses, streets.

Blackboy Crescent. Gemma Buck.

A festive mob of pink and grey cockatoos settled on the date palms behind the cathedral. Galahs, he thought fondly, they were the backpackers of the skies – rowdy, rooting freeloaders, God love em. For a minute or two he watched them preen and dance for one another, and it was calming. Until the slider next door grated open and he retreated inside as someone stepped out to light a fag and hack up a lungful.

Now he was forced indoors, he thought he should eat. His appetite was all over the place. He felt hollow, so maybe food was the thing. Cooking a meal every night was about the only form of self-discipline he'd been able to maintain of late. Apart from keeping his head down. But tonight he was too spent and shook up to bother. He'd nuke the leftovers of yesterday's stir-fry and make it up to himself tomorrow.

And while the bowl suffered bedspins inside the microwave, he tried to make sense of the Gemma thing. Couldn't even come at the kid on the rail, that whole freaking thirty-second scene, no, not now he'd levelled out. The idea of her, though. Being outside his door, here in the building. That was already more than he could deal with without burning a circuit.

Gemma Buck. Not a girl at all, but a woman – and a pretty ordinary middle-aged woman at that. He couldn't get to grips with it. For in his mind she was still a needy urchin with white-blonde plaits. Someone's irritating little sister.

Inside the machine the bowl of food began to sweat and the flat filled with the earthy scents of shiitake and sesame oil. A reminder that he'd been functional up until the early evening last night, at least. Which didn't quite warm the cockles, but he'd take it as a small success regardless. The box bleated. He set his wholesome vegies free and plonked the bowl on the bench to let them cool. Which made him wonder why he bothered heating food at all. And then he actually was hungry, too urgently hungry to wait. So he burnt his tongue. Of course. Et cetera.

The Buck girls. From up the hill. They were in the house so often, those kids, like permanent fixtures. And actually lived with them for part of one year: 1971, maybe, or '72. He could see it crisply, all of them in the lounge, on their bellies, with the TV flashing in glorious black and white. Little Gemma at one end of the tartan travel rug, and his sister Faith beside her. Then him, next to Baby Buck, the older one. The girls in their flannelette nighties, him in his goofy pyjamas. The old man behind them all, chortling in his recliner-rocker. Flip Wilson, who seemed to look blacker in black and white. Everyone yelling in joyful unison: *Here come de judge!*

Little Gemma Buck. She came to mind along with *McHale's Navy*, Herb Alpert and the Tijuana Brass, primary school. She belonged to the golden time before his world collapsed. When Nev was still with them. And, man, did Nev love that Flip Wilson.

Keely gave the food another crack, chewing his way back.

Gemma was a mouth-breather, now he thought of it. Cute enough in a Cindy Brady way, but clingy, too. She was completely unlike her big sister. And kind of annoying for always being around. But they were a protected species, those girls; they had problems, trouble at home for which you had to make allowances. Faith and he learned to let a whole lot of things slide in order to spare themselves a Disappointed Lecture from the oldies.

Keely thought of the hundred nights the Buck girls came knocking: summer evenings out there on the porch sobbing in their nylon nighties, the sound of glass breaking up the hill behind them. There was always screaming; their place was bedlam after dark. Fridays were the worst, when Johnny Buck drank his pay right up to closing time and did not care to be admonished by the missus when he came home shitfaced and broke with a couple of brown baggers under his arm and a torn shirt hanging off his back. The beltings were fearsome and public. No one ever called the cops. The girls would just be at the Keely door, whimpering on the porch until a light went on and Doris took them in. Then the old man would go looking for his boots, gathering his wits a moment, muttering some prayer or imprecation, before trudging up the hill to deal with it best he could.

In those days the Keelys didn't have trouble, they fixed it. By faith, with thanksgiving. And now and then, when the shit hit the fan, with a judicious bit of biffo.

The oldies were careful to shield his sister and him from the carnage in the street, but some mayhem got past the cordon sanitaire. Keely had flashes of recall that would never fade. They were, he supposed, his first experiences of violence. And it was always strange how foreign they seemed, these memories, for all their lurid immediacy, because although they were inescapably from his old neighbourhood they did not feel as if they belonged to his world, not then, not now. But he could still see it, wild and vivid as a nightmare. He saw Bunny Buck. The girls' mother. Mrs Buck. On her knees on lumpy buffalo grass. In her front yard.

Down on her knees with a sanitary pad pressed to her bleeding face. He didn't even know what a pad was until years later. She had it planted against her swelling jaw as if any form of softness might be a comfort. As shadows flayed her. Two men facing off in the driveway. Johnny Buck in his work duds. Neville Keely in stubbies and a singlet. Plenty of lights on across the road, next door, silhouettes in every front garden, but no help forthcoming. In the porchlight, Nev circling, voice like a horse whisperer, sleep in his eyes and grease in the cracks of his hands. Johnny Buck staggering, squinting to keep him in view. Nev pressing in, smiling, feinting, nattering about Forgiveness, and Letting Go, and Owning Up, and Giving In to Love, a kind of dancing, panting midnight homily brought to a head by a sudden lunge and a half-nelson that had the nasty little prick on his arse in a moment. And it was hard to forget the sight of a big man like Nev blessing Johnny Buck while burying his face in the grass. The faceless neighbours cheered; he remembered that.

So where had *he* been standing that night? Had he snuck away at last to see for himself, left Faith and his mum and the girls in the house and skulked his way from yard to yard to witness what it was that bent their nights out of shape? Or were the girls there, too, shrieking, clutching at Doris, imploring the spineless spectators? He didn't remember. He could only see Johnny Buck struggling and swearing on the grass. His father copping a few in the chops for his trouble. And then Nev abruptly prevailing, kneeling on him, like a man in prayer, pinning the shithead's arms to the earth until the bloke was weeping. A moment later his wife was at his side to comfort him and call Nev a churchy fuckin bully-bastard who should mind his own bloody business.

It was confounding. And it felt wrong that her humiliated fuck-you should remain as indelible as the violence itself. But even now the memory brought a welter of shame along with the pride.

It was the year Harold Holt drowned. Somehow that fact had stuck in his head. But Keely knew it had been happening since Menzies was prime minister. It went on until Whitlam. It was standard procedure in Blackboy Crescent. When some addled boofhead started playing up the neighbours sent for good ole Nev. He was the holy fool with hands like mallee roots and a heart, while it lasted, as big as a beer keg. Night after night, they sent him out and let him bear it all. And hung back in the shadows, urging him on from a cosy distance.

Keely finished the stir-fry. He was still standing. Not quite as calm as he'd been looking down on the birds. Agitated by the memory. But the weight in his head had lifted a little, the disgruntled passenger was dozing.

He felt odd now. But not so terrible. Better, even. As if Gemma's sudden appearance had kicked him out of a spin. Something new, unexpected. Okay, maybe old and unexpected. To take his mind off the five thousand things he was frying his own wiring over. It was kind of nice to go on a fresh tangent. To sieve through the memories.

But what could he really remember? About Gemma, specifically? Not that much, actually, now he thought about it. Apart from the sight of her and her sister huddled beneath Doris's dressing gown, mewling like pups. And those blonde plaits. Not much else at all. Because it was the older girl, Baby, who'd made the impression. She was tough, chubby, kind of clammy, and foulmouthed. He'd copped a flogging from her once at school in front of a dozen boys; he didn't remember why – just recalled the laughter and the exploded feeling in his cheek. Baby gave off a strange current. Boys noticed her, said things to her, and so did men. When she lived with them those months, when her father was in prison and her mother still in hospital, Keely noticed her vaguely horticultural scent and the peculiar formality with which his own father addressed her. Nev was not a cautious man, but around Baby Buck he was careful, almost courtly.

The Buck sisters. They were strays who couldn't be shaken off until the Keelys were gone themselves, swept away by disaster into a new life. For Faith and him those teen years were fogged with grief. The Bucks just fell away with everything and everyone else. After Blackboy Crescent he hardly thought another thing about them.

But had caught sight of them occasionally. Must have been the late seventies when he walked past Baby in Barrack Street one night. Tilted against a wall, one shoe broken. She looked drug-fucked, or just fucked in general. There was an awkward moment of mutual recognition but no greeting. A couple of times he saw Gemma at a distance. At a concert, a pub. Under the arm of one dangerous-looking dude or another. She was all tan and sun-streaked tresses, a leggy provocation, and by then, for the likes of him, a total impossibility. Their gazes met but Keely pretended not to see her. Remembered how his ears glowed for shame.

Last night's dishes were still there on the sink. The heat of the day had baked stains to a glaze and the purple crust in his wine-glass smelt fruity as a bishop. He washed without conviction, buried his bottles deep in the recycling crate and wiped everything down, from restlessness as much as anything.

But he was still a little buzzed. He should bag some laundry. Better still, call Faith. She'd be tickled. Curious at least. Besides, having stumbled into all these memories he felt the need to hear her voice. He looked at the clock. Singapore. Same time zone. He grabbed the landline phone, punched his sister's number.

Faith answered from within a noisy room, a restaurant by the sound of it. He had to repeat his name twice before she understood who was calling.

Are you alright? she asked. Is it Mum?

She's fine, we're fine.

You don't sound it.

Nah, I'm good.

Have you seen someone?

What?

Did you try those numbers?

Quacks and bankers, mate. You know me.

Sometimes I wonder.

Tell you who I *have* seen —

Tom, I'm in a meeting.

Okay, sorry. Just that I thought you'd find it . . . weird.

Everything's weird just at the present. The world as we know it is choking on a bone.

Yeah?

You actually have no idea.

Well, I get the broad picture.

I doubt it.

Anyway, I've got two words for you.

Please tell me they're not Lehman Brothers.

Funny.

Not that funny. Which words, Tom?

Buck. And Gemma.

Gemma Buck?

You're quick, sis.

Blackboy Crescent Gemma Buck?

That's the one.

What about her?

Lives in my building, mate. Same floor.

This is a joke?

Am I that funny a bloke?

Hell. Wow, that's . . . weird. So, what does she look like?

Keely couldn't help but laugh.

What? she asked.

I love that it's the first thing you ask. If a bloke said it you'd serve him his tripe on a platter.

Aw, boohoo.

Actually she looks a bit ground down.

Wasn't she a bit of a stunner?

I spose she was.

Listen, I have to go. Can you call me later?

Alright.

Give me another hour, okay?

Not a problem.

I'll call you.

Don't worry, he said, I'll ring back.

Of course you will. Anyway, I can afford it.

I said I'd call. Didn't I?

Love you, she said with an air of defeat before hanging up.

Yeah, he said to the ether. You too, sis.

For a moment he was buoyed by a fleeting sense of closeness. He thought of the safe mass of her in a sleeping bag beside him in the back of the station wagon. Her asthmatic wheeze, the soapy-vanilla scent of her above the smells of vinyl upholstery and wet grass. The sound of crickets. All those nights parked on front lawns while the oldies ran committees, prayer groups, demo meetings. That wheezy, sweet lump in the car up close. His baby sister, the merchant banker. He kissed the phone like a sap and set it back in its cradle.

Surveyed the empty flat a moment. Snatched up his keys.

He sauntered past shuttered shops in the emptying streets, knowing he should phone his mother. He owed Doris a call anyway and she'd probably be delighted to have news of Gemma. But he knew he wouldn't; he could do without the loving scrutiny, her urging him to see another GP, a new counsellor, some western-suburbs employment guru who'd come highly recommended. He didn't want the telling silences, her withering patience. For a minute or two he was close, once more, to mental uproar. But he talked himself down, the meeting came back to order.

It was still warm. A smattering of joggers and strollers abroad. There were late commuters out on the pavement, loiterers, lost souls, women thumbing phones to summon taxis. Down the main drag, a couple of lycra-free cyclists coasted by, laughing, God

TIM WINTON

bless them. In their wake rumbled Commodores full of local boys lapping the block, windows down, saying ugly things to women. Girls with tatts and skinny dogs told them to go and get fucked. A bloke tried to fly a kite off the balcony of a backpacker joint but the breeze was fluky between buildings.

The evening air was heavy with salt, coffee, exhaust fumes. The vibe in town was weary and benign. It was the same joint he'd shunned this morning, but tonight it felt easier to forgive. It was a village, with all the virtues and vices of intimacy. And he knew the place backwards, had lived here most of his working life. But he had to remind himself daily that it was quite another town to him now; in his new circumstances he lived in it differently, felt its properties anew. These days he was more at its mercy, it acted on him in ways he hadn't really experienced before. You could hate anywhere and anyone that didn't need you. He was skint in every possible sense. Surplus to requirements. But lofting a little this evening, rising as if from a nasty bounce.

Along the Strip Keely bought a beer, drank it quickly and left before he could go on to a soothing second. Felt good about himself a moment, then thought of Doris again.

Under the date palms across from the station, drunks called querulously for taxi fare, train money, two bucks mate. Their goon bags flashed silver beneath the trees, and soon enough those hopeful, matey shouts took on the standard overtone of menace. He pressed on, over the footbridge to the wharf.

Call Doris, he thought, crossing the quay. Don't be a weasel.

Cars streamed away from the ferry landings. At the dockside, tourists struggled to find their landlegs after the trip in from Rottnest. Others wheeled bikes, suitcases, prams writhing with squalling kids.

His mother was a brick, a saint. Which of course made everything so much worse, especially since she'd had ample time to form a view of his situation. Two years since the break-up. A whole year since his catastrophic brain-snap and all its rewards. Doris was a shrewd old bird. She didn't miss much. He did not want to suffer her thoughtful analysis a single moment but he was pretty certain he already understood it in all its loving, pitiless permutations. Her view was undoubtedly this: that by now her only son could reasonably be expected to pick himself up amidst the wreckage of his life and make something new happen. She was, of course, canny enough to refrain from saying so. But she radiated it.

Her faithful presence, her restraint, her carefully calibrated attention said everything for her, and even absent she exerted tectonic moral pressure. She was right to be puzzled, justified in her impatience. Yes, yes, yes, fucking yes, these months *had* been wasted and he probably was a coward getting cosy with his own self-hatred, but he couldn't get past the suspicion of more to come, that something worse was necessary, or at least inevitable, as if he were not yet properly shriven. But it was only a matter of time. And maybe when he struck bottom there'd be certainty, fresh conviction, a sense of immediacy he could no longer feel. She thought this was bullshit, madness even. Though he hadn't breathed a word, didn't need to. Doris could read him in five languages and scan him in Braille. Since his cataclysmic truth-telling, he'd felt the eloquence of her every withheld judgement and longsuffering stare. He didn't have to guess what she thought of his morose passivity, his bitterness and wounded silence, which is why he'd been avoiding her of late. It was no treat embodying something your own mother pitied, probably even despised. She loved him, her compassion seemed boundless, but her disappointment smarted more than any other humiliation. Problem was she thought he was strong, still judged him accordingly, and did not yet know he was lost.

But he wasn't going there tonight.

He had to let it go. Doris's scarifying empathy. The known unknown. All of it.

I have, he told himself, I've let it go.

Which was bullshit, really, but he kept thinking it because it seemed necessary.

I'm okay, he muttered aloud.

Which seemed slightly safer as a proposition but hardly sound.

I'm good! he announced to a startled passer-by.

And yet, righteous as he was in his misanthropic way, goodness was something of a stretch. Misunderstood Keely was. Yes. And it was true his intentions were invariably good. But only when he had them. Some days he struggled to even form an intention.

He teetered at the fulcrum of his lighter mood. Darkness sucking at him.

But the evening air was all salty grace. Close to the water it smelt divine, felt merciful. And whatever bollocks he told himself, however feeble and false the positive lingo was once you stacked it up against shitful reality, the lovely, saving night stole up on him. The rest didn't matter. For reasons he couldn't fathom, the hopelessness suddenly lost ultimate power over him. As if for a moment the chains fell off and his heart was free. Well, on the lam at least.

He ambled along the wharf past rank-smelling sheds where the *Leeuwin* rode the tide on creaking hawsers. On deck, beneath the maze of spars and rigging, a dreadlocked kid stood hosing crates, the lights glancing off piercings in his face. To Keely he looked exultant, like a boy unable to credit his own youth and beauty and good fortune. To be there on a tallship as passing strangers took note – that had to be worth something, worth basking a few minutes in the palpable sense of envy and mystery, worth prolonging a simple task like rinsing dive crates. Barely suppressing the urge to huzzah, Keely bore on past families of low-murmuring Vietnamese as they reeled in minuscule yellow-tail and fingerling trevally. He turned a forgiving eye to their lard buckets of bloody water teeming with fins and white bellies and hundreds of golden tails. He didn't stoop to scowl or tut. They were folks catching a feed: tired, shy, suspicious. They didn't need his purse-lipped concern tonight. The concrete wharf was gummy with pollard, mired with the innards of crushed blow-fish, spangled with scales. Bored schoolgirls sat on milk crates, texting, jiggling, hating to be there while their fathers and grand-fathers squatted in plastic sandals, grey trousers and white singlets to thread maggots onto tiny hooks and press damp pollard into berley cages. Peaceable, calm, purposeful folks. Keely strolled on – living, letting live.

Out towards the end of the quay, in the lee of the shiny new museum, he rested against a bollard to watch a pair of romancing backpackers share a can of beer. Birkenstocks, topknots, golden limbs. They stared across at the otherworldly light of the con-tainer terminal. Their voices were soft and foreign. They sounded Nordic. And they gave off an irrepressible sense of contentment, as if this warm evening at the far end of the earth had been worth the journey. He lingered a moment, riding the swell of the contact high. Until they gave him a look that sent him on his way.

When the lift door opened at the tenth floor Gemma Buck stood waiting in some kind of uniform.

Bloody hell, she said. What's the odds?

Hi again, said Keely as they stepped around each other awkwardly to exchange places.

Out for dinner? she asked, holding the door back with a downy arm.

Just a walk, he said. You?

Work.

In the hard light of the lift's fluorescent he saw the supermarket logo across the breast of her tunic.

Nightshift?

Packin shelves, she said. It's real fulfillin.

Keely smiled. Gemma tugged a bag across her shoulder. In her hand was an unlit cigarette. A moment passed and she gave a wry grin. As the door began to close once more Keely stepped into its path and let it butt his hip.

What'd you forget?

Your boy. I mean, I just . . .

Asleep, said Gemma.

Keely stood there with the door shoving at him, conscious of how much he'd assumed about her with no solid idea of her circumstances. For a moment he'd even thought she was leaving the child unattended.

He's a nice kid.

Yeah. He is.

Listen, sorry about today.

Gemma shrugged.

I was a bit of a mess.

You reckon?

I didn't mean to be rude.

Orright.

I guess we'll talk.

Sorry?

Maybe catch up on things.

Oh. Yeah. Maybe.

Well. Let you go.

Night, she said.

He stepped back and the door finally closed.

For half a minute he stood there as the lift groaned and clanked down the shaft. Tired as he was, he knew he wouldn't sleep. Or call his mother. He wouldn't call Faith back, either, because it'd only set him off on some melancholy tangent. He'd watch some ancient B-movie and hope sleep stole up on him.

As soon as he'd let himself in the phone rang. He hesitated a moment, then snatched it up. Instead of Faith it was Doris.

What's up? he asked.

I'm watching Victor Mature. Could you imagine Samson being quite so wet-lipped and doe-eyed? I don't think so.

So, I take it Faith called you.

Yes, but love set me free.

Very funny, Mum.

I called before, she said.

I went for a walk.

Good idea.

Well, it wasn't a Eureka moment. But yeah, it was nice.

Faith says you ran into one of the Buck girls.

That's right. Gemma.

God, she was a beautiful child. Don't you remember that gorgeous hair?

Hmm.

She was like a little doll.

Whatever happened to them? he said. The parents.

Bunny left him in the end. John died at Port Hedland in the eighties. I used to wonder she didn't kill him herself. Believe me, there were times when I could have done it for her.

You were good to them. I haven't forgotten.

Tommy.

I mean, how it was, what you did.

You okay?

Mum, I went for a walk. I'm fine.

I'm sorry. I didn't mean to —

Not a problem.

Tom, I'm not worried.

He laughed.

Why are you laughing?

Well, Doris dear, not worrying seems to be a special mum-thing.

Okay, she admitted. Caught.

I give you cause, I know.

You're fine, love.

Anyway, tonight you shouldn't fret.

It'll get better, Tom.

Yeah, he murmured. I expect so.

Let's have lunch.

No worries.

Monday?

Alright.

Call you Sunday night?

Sure.

Love you.

You too.

When he hung up, Keely realized his mother had barely asked about Gemma. It was unlike her. Perhaps it was a sign of how worried she was. Or how far she'd left the old days behind her. Maybe he'd figure that out at lunch. But his buoyant mood was gone.

He lingered near the slider, flexed his toes in the nap of the carpet, felt nothing and was not much comforted.

Felt a little thump. From whatever. Like an elbow against the wall of his skull. The tenant turning over in bed.

He gobbed a couple of Nurofen Plus. A bit of sandbagging for good measure.

Turned on the telly. And there he was in his loincloth. Victor Mature, looking camp as a row of tents. Soon to be eyeless in Gaza.

Turned it off. Stared at his sadsack reflection in the window. Knew he'd end up back at the knife drawer any minute. For something to kick him over the edge. Tried to stare himself down. Et cetera. And blinked, of course.

A wrenching gasp and there he was. On the bed in the foetid room. Every surface dancing and flashing. A streetsweeper droned far below. Blood spritzed in his limbs as if he'd only just come off the boil.

Three o'clock. He'd been dreaming – something awful, something that had mercifully evaporated the moment he woke.

In the bathroom he sluiced himself with cool water, stood dripping a while in the half-dark before reaching for the gamy towel. The dim outline in the mirror moved in sympathy. Not really in sync. An approximation.

But when he turned for bed and stepped through the doorway there was a different form in the bedroom window, a shape too small to be his reflection, too distinct to be any kind of reflection at all.

The size of a child. Naked in the strobing, distant light. Pressed against the screen as if held there by wind-shear alone. Bare arms aloft in benediction or flight. He was calm, those moments he lingered; the boy was calm and solemn and terrible.

Then gone, like an unsustainable thought.

Keely knelt on the bed before the suddenly vacant window. Nothing there but breathless night. When his pulse finally subsided he lay down and tried to sleep. But he could feel it returning. Not the image, but the dream. In wisps and fits and flashes. Settling upon him like a dread familiar.

It was the boy. Gemma Buck's kid. In the dream he was out on the balcony – Gemma's, not his. And in the dream Keely was alone, wrapped in a towel in cool, cool air, impossibly cold air, not seeing the boy out there across the way until he moved. The child was three balconies distant. He was bare-chested, squatting on a milk crate, breasting the rail and dipping his head to it. His pale hair shone in the dark as he perched and bobbed, lapping dew off the iron like a thirsty dove.

And that was it. All the dream that would come safely to mind. Even this much frightened him. He sensed that there'd been more than just squatting, but he didn't want to go there; he was practised enough at shelving what could not be borne. But the logic of something worse beat on in him for minutes until he began to feel he'd assimilated it for what it was, a harmless bit of mental indigestion. He was fine. It was all good and there was juice left in the pills, current enough to tug at him so he felt himself leaching away towards delicious sleep. And yet he could feel the pale glow of the boy there, waiting. In the swamp of his ungoverned country. Perched, pigeon-chested. Too high. Unguarded. Only a straightened leg away from toppling.

Keely clawed back, roused himself. Got up. Dragged on some shorts. Blundered through to the dim livingroom, jacked open the slider and stepped outside.

All along the building the balconies were deserted. A few railings were still illuminated by blue flickers of television, but nobody was out there.

The invisible sea revealed itself in throbbing boundaries – red lights, green lights, the distant pulses of the island lighthouses. The port thrummed, the town itself reduced to echoes and murmurs as the streetsweeper trundled out towards the marina.

He went back in. But was too afraid to sleep. Which should have been funny given how much he craved it, what he'd swallowed to get there, how muzzy and ready he felt. He'd just lie here a while, ignore the leg tremors, wait it out.

Dawn. Morning. Day.

Didn't take the bike out. Didn't swim. Eyes like hot pea gravel. The flat was roasting but he holed up there all day. The building trembled with the comings and goings of others. All that purposeful Friday traffic. He tooled about on the laptop, googling aimlessly, squinting, holding his scone like it was an IED.

His inbox was stacked with unread emails, most from bewildered or exasperated friends and comrades, though the most recent were many weeks old. By the boldface subject titles he could see solicitude taper away to hurt silence and worse. Two of the last, from people he'd promised vital briefings on the wetlands strategy, were simply headed, **WTF?** Piled in their aging strata, these unanswered messages were a miserable sort of archaeology, a register of failure. It was absurd and lowering to keep them like this. Sick to pull them up and survey them, scrolling down the list, pausing over one now and then as if daring yourself to open it. It was time to end it.

He got up, strode to the sliding door, looked out at the sea a moment, then returned to the table and closed down the email address, fried everything while he had the will.

Afterwards he felt a glimmer of achievement. But in terms of satisfaction it was hardly more substantial or sustaining than the afterglow of a good shit.

The phone rang twice that day – in the morning, in the afternoon – but he didn't answer. He scrounged leftovers, ate fruit no longer in the first flush of its youth. Market day, but he wasn't going down there. Tourists. Earnest local faces. All that friendly stallholder shouting. The heat. The confined cattle smell of his countrymen. Fuck that.

Still ruined from his dream-stalked night, he napped fitfully in the chair. In the afternoon the woman next door cranked up, fighting off powers and principalities with chants and admonitions. He had to admire it, the way she held herself together with language. The longer she went, the stronger she sounded. He envied her. Which was stupid. And frightening.

Late in the day, bored rather than needy, he dug the last cleanskin from the carton under the bed – a flabby grenache he usually resorted to only as a stopgap sedative – and the first glass he poured was hot and calming. He worked through it unhurriedly, savouring the late arrival of the sea breeze, and at sunset he used the dregs to wash down a few Mersyndols and a hayfever tab for good measure, closing out the day with a certain resolve.

Maybe one last moment on the balcony before bed. To make sure of it, confirm it'd all been in his weary mind. He'd get up in a moment, go out. If only he could swim up against the weight of all that tepid water pressing him into the chair.

But hang on. Wasn't that him? Not even bothering to wait for Keely to doze off. There already. There before him. Just past the pulsing insect mesh of the slider. The kid. Perched atop the rail, braced against a battering sea wind. The boy was motionless. Held there like a kite in the updraught. While the building swayed and rustled like a tuart tree. The sky purple, violent, the child without expression, staring off in profile, hair shining. Keely called out, tried to wave him back to safety, but the kid seemed startled by the sudden movement. Flexed. Pitched forward. And was gone in an instant.

He woke and it was dark. Woke. Actually, fully awake. But trusting nothing. He stood outside in his briefs. Gemma's balcony was empty but he was too rattled to let things go at that. He went back in, unlatched the front door and weaved his way up the walkway to where the dome light burned above the grille at 1010. The door behind the screen was the same dirty beige as his, the warped security mesh furred with corrosion from the salt wind. At the kitchen window the curtain was drawn, but there was a light on inside. He didn't know what to do. He wanted to make sure all was well, but at 11.08 p.m. in his cock-jocks there seemed no easy means of doing so. He lingered, dithering, pressed against the hot bricks.

Down the walkway, a door slammed. A woman in a sari – a deep green sari it was – gathered her keys and handbag. Lustrous dark hair. A bindi red as a camera light on her brow. On that dark brow, that raised face. Which was looking directly his way. Seeing him, recording his semi-nude presence. She stiffened, let out a sudden chirp of alarm, and sent him tilting homeward.

He was late getting up, and bleary along with it, but for the remainder of the morning he kept an eye out for Gemma, even broke his own rule and left the door ajar, but she didn't come by. With the nightshifts he was loath to knock on her door. He paced. He made his grimy bed. Paced a little more.

Flipped open the Mac. Just to pass the time. And then he cracked. Couldn't help himself. He trolled through the newsfeeds, taking in the headlines. Instantly bewildered. Same-same but worse.

Faith was right. The world was indeed choking on a bone. Obama trying for a bail-out. Everyone covering the bankers' arses. Which was heartwarming. But here at home hardly a ripple. Endless reserves of mining loot. Safe as houses. Although when it came to bricks and mortar it seemed the good folks of Perth were stunned to learn that their property prices might flatten out, which would be for them, he imagined, confirmation the world really had slipped its moorings. Still, some bloke in Queensland, clearly refusing to surrender to the lure of introspection, had set a new record by busting forty-seven watermelons over his own head. Go, Australia.

After years of professional habit, or maybe just masochistic impulse, he sieved up the environment story of the day. But it was hardly news. In Hobart, evidently fretting about trade relations, the Feds had raided the Sea Shepherd ship, the *Steve Martin*, or whatever it was this year, *Steve Jobs*, *Steve Buscemi* – what did it matter? Anyway, they were back, those wild-eyed buggers, returned from another season of irritating the Japs. Glamour-hounds and donor-hogs they may be but he loved them. All bluster aside, they were doing what government lacked the balls to do. Had it been a gas field down there in the Southern Ocean the Feds would be sending gunboats. But they left it to these cow-boys. And then pursed their lips in disapproval. Didn't seem so long ago those vegan pirates were tied up here at the end of the street. Another petty imbroglio into which he'd been dragooned. Down on the quay in front of the cameras, facing off against the network girlies with their pancake make-up and Darth Vader hair. Calling in a bunch of favours to broker a deal and shame some dingleberry member of Cabinet into letting the vessel refuel and take on fresh celebs. Thankless Sunday morning's work that'd been.

Anyway, enough. He slapped the laptop shut. Pulling back while he still could. For a clear head, pure mind.

He sat there. Pointlessly alert. And no one came by. Forty-eight hours ago he'd have counted this a blessing, a major domestic success. But now he was unsettled. Fidgeting in gormless anticipation.

It was bloody unnerving.

At noon, hungry and twitchy as a numbat, he gave up and went down into the streets for breakfast. Bub's was only four blocks from home, on a side street off the Strip, but it was a trek getting there, hacking his way through a thicket of sticky tourists and weekend wood ducks. The joint was heaving. Saturday. What was he thinking? The moment he arrived Bub sent him out a sly double-shot and a muffin. Local privileges, that at least was something. And he appreciated it. But the crowd made him leery so he didn't hang about. It was back to the bat cave for him. Sent off with a knowing hitch of the eyebrows by good old Bub who knew what was what.

A block from the Mirador he came upon Gemma and the boy as they emerged from a sports store. The street was hot and snarled with cars idling for a park. Gemma looked frazzled. The kid clicked along on a pair of football boots fresh from the box. The expression on his moony face managed to combine triumph and solemnity. He glanced back at his own heels and watched himself, slightly startled but pleased, in the shop windows.

G'day, said Keely.

Oh, said Gemma. Hi.

Someone got lucky.

His birthday, said Gemma.

Well then, happy birthday.

I know who you are, said the kid.

I'm Tom, he said. What's your name?

You had rats, said the boy.

Rats?

Get out of the sun, said Gemma, hauling them into the lee of an awning.

How old are you? asked Keely.

Six, said the kid. We're having fish and chips. Gonna feed the sea-goals.

Gulls, said Gemma. It's gulls.

Must be the boots, said Keely.

Both of them looked at him blankly.

Goals, he said. Football boots.

Right, she said with a look of cringe-making forbearance.

Hapless, Keely looked to the kid, not really knowing what he expected – fraternal understanding? Weren't pissweak jokes milk and honey to a six-year-old? The boy studied him. Shade or no, Keely felt hotter than he had with the sun beating on his skull.

Can Tom come? For chips?

Well, he said, sensing Gemma's irritation.

Tom's busy, said Gemma.

But it's my birthday.

You mind? she asked, embarrassed or maybe just annoyed.

No, he said, of course not.

But it's your weekend.

Not a problem, he said, startled by the look come over her face. Like she was glad, even grateful.

Not a problem, said Gemma. Your dad used to say that.

Really? I don't remember, he admitted.

Not a problem. Jesus. That's Nev orright. God bless him.

Anyway, he said, fish and chips it is.

The kid kicked the air. He glanced at himself again in the glass, brandished a gleaming boot.

Carn then, you two, said Gemma. Come if you're comin, I'm roastin out here.

No cracks, said the boy, indicating the slabs of the footpath.

Right, said Keely. No cracks.

Crossing town in the direction of the marina, he found it was quite some effort avoiding joins or cracks in the pavement, what with everything else in his head. He was relieved to reach the green swathe of the esplanade, which teemed with picnickers and shirtless youths playing cricket. On the grass beneath the Norfolk pines the boy concentrated on avoiding dog poo, a sport closer to Keely's heart and of which he was already a grizzled veteran. It was fun. Though he began to wonder if the kid wasn't a bit compulsive about it. But who wasn't finicky about dog shit?

Tell about the rats, said the kid as they came to the rail line that formed the last boundary between the town and the water.

Don't start that again, said Gemma.

But Nan, you said.

Nan, thought Keely. Nan?

Quit bugging him, she said. Tom doesn't want to talk about rats.

You told him about my rats?

John, George, Paul and Ringo, she said with a grin that was almost shy.

I'll be damned.

I wanted them rats, she said, shaking out a fag with a laugh. I used to take em outta the cage when you weren't there.

What sorta name is Ringo anyway? asked the boy.

Dunno, said Keely, straight-faced. It just came to me, I spose.

Gemma snorted.

They were good pets, he said. Good rodents all.

As they stepped over the rails at the crossing, the boy took Gemma's hand and moved with a peculiar precision, as if the track were electrified. Left and right, people jounced strollers and wheeled bikes across, but the kid concentrated on avoiding all contact. And when they made the path on the far side he returned his attention to paving cracks. Soon they were on the board-walk whose flashing green slats between planks reduced him to a geisha gait that was comical.

Where are those rats? asked the kid. What happened to them?

Kai, love, yer not gettin a rat, said Gemma. So don't even ask.

I don't really remember what happened to them, said Keely.

Maybe another time, Gemma said darkly. Enough about rats.

They're hard work, said Keely. And they stink a bit. Anyway, they're no good in a flat, sport.

I could keep em on the outside bit.

The balcony?

Kai, said Gemma, I told you. No rats.

Anyway, said Keely. You couldn't just leave them out in the weather. Besides, he said, reaching now, but heeding Gemma's desire to snuff the entire notion, birds might get them.

That's right, said Gemma, busking it.

You know, like owls, kites, hawks. They all eat mice and rats.

And sea-goals? Gulls? asked the kid.

Nah, but maybe a heron'd have a go.

Heron.

That's a waterbird. They mostly hunt fish.

But it's high up, said the boy. Floor ten.

No problem for a bird.

Like . . . like a eagle?

Exactly, said Keely, beginning to enjoy himself. Or an osprey.

The boy tested the word, seemed to like it. Said it again.

That's a sort of eagle, said Keely. Swoops down, snatches up something good to eat, flies off to his nest right up high. He's like, king of the mountain, prince of all he surveys.

The boy glanced up at Gemma for verification. She shrugged, blew smoke sideways as they negotiated the dawdling, icecream-dripping hordes.

Reckon Tom knows his birds, she told the boy. He's a nature nut. Isn't that right?

Keely returned the shrug. Keen on birds, are you, Kai?

The kid said nothing.

Keen on givin his nan the runaround.

Osprey, said the kid.

Keely did the arithmetic. Gemma was barely into her mid-forties. So that was how it'd gone.

Around the northern rim of the marina the chippers were packed, their jetties and terraces aswarm with lunching day-trippers, sunstruck Brits, giggling teens. Enormous white cruisers pulled in to moor alongside, bristling with portly folks in deck-shoes and sun visors anxious to parade their grand success. It was a kind of western-suburbs ritual, casting off from their enclaves upriver in Perth to steam downstream in their ocean-going craft, and the moment they met the open sea they hurled the wheel hard aport to tuck in here and tie up two metres from dry land along-side the plebs who could gawk and chew, rendered dumbstruck, presumably, by the angelic logic of the trickledown economy.

Doesn't that pep you up? he said.

What? What's that?

These floating gin palaces. Give you the can-do feeling, that aspirational awe.

Gemma ignored him, or perhaps she didn't hear, preoccupied as she was with muscling them into a table by the water's edge. She lunged, weaved, saw a party get to its feet and pounced.

Stay here, she told him. Kai'n me'll go inside to order.

Keely obeyed, sat a few minutes in the shade of the umbrella, and breathed in the vapours of fat and diesel and algae. Which were rather homely, now he thought of it. But he felt self-conscious down here with the weekenders, wary of faces too familiar for comfort. Few locals came down anymore, cer-tainly not at the weekend, but there were always the pollies and bureaucrats in their short sleeves and Country Road shorts, the epicene journos relieved of an afternoon's weeding, and he didn't want any sudden encounters.

Gemma and the boy returned with hefty paper parcels of fried goods. And he stuffed himself, soaking chips in harsh white vinegar, slathering his wedge of snapper in the sort of ketchup that probably glowed in the dark. He watched the kid. How he gorged on chips and left his fish so long the batter went soggy. Eventually he peeled it back with meticulous care, as if it were a scab on his knee. Then he ate it, grease leaking from the corners of his mouth, and left the fishmeat naked on the paper. Not completely odd. Just a kid doing more or less what Keely would have done at six.

A few metres away a pelican alighted on a jetty pile, sending Chinese tourists into a frenzy of videography.

What about a pelican? said the boy. Would a pelican eat a rat?

I doubt it, he said.

They catch fish, said Gemma. Like that other thing. What was that other bird, Tom?

Heron, he said, wiping fat from his chin.

The kid's fingers twitched. He blinked. Keely saw him silently count the syllables, then the letters, absorbing the word.

There used to be one round here, said Keely, a heron that pinched my koi, my goldfish. Swooped down, reefed them right out of the pond.

You got a pond? said the kid. At your flat?

No, said Keely with a chuckle. This was when I had a house. Back over there, see? Past the boatsheds, behind the trees.

Gemma turned with the child, looked across the marina to where he was pointing. She chewed, said nothing.

Did ospreys come too? asked the child.

No. But they're around. Sometimes you can hear them. They have a weird sound, like a whingeing noise they make.

The boy looked doubtful, glanced at Gemma.

What? said Keely.

He thinks you're winding him up.

But it's true.

And there's really ospreys? asked the boy. Here?

He nodded. Maybe one day I'll show you. And your nan.

He'll be telling the truth, said Gemma. It's a Keely thing.

What's a Keely thing?

Never mind. Carn, you two, I'm as full as a fat lady's sock. That's us done.

They left the marina and let the kid run across the little beach behind the long stone mole protecting the rivermouth and the shipping harbour. Riding seaward on the other side of the breakwater a reeking sheep carrier loomed like a slum, the hawser of smoke from its stack coiling back upriver to the wharf. Kai seemed happy enough by himself at the water's edge and Keely sat with Gemma on the low wall above the sand, taking what little succour the sea breeze offered. They were quiet a while, the two of them, and awkward. Then, unprompted, Gemma told him about her daughter, the boy's mother. Her name was Carly. She was Gemma's only child and she was doing a stretch in Bandyup for drugs, assault and thieving. Not her first stint by any means. Kai had been with Gemma, off and on, for much of his life.

You're good with him, he said, for something to say. He thought of the dreams. Didn't know why. Tried to focus. Really, he said. You're a champion.

She shrugged, said nothing.

So what's it like? he asked before he could help it.

She pursed her lips. Is what it is.

They watched Kai a moment.

You had a house on the water?

Near it, he said.

Posh.

We both had good jobs, I guess.

And?

Had to sell it, he said. Divorce.

And now you're livin in a one-bedroom flat.

Yep.

What's *that* like?

Feeling the rebuke, he looked at her. She blew smoke into his face and smiled.

Tommy Keely.

Yep.

What's the odds, eh?

The studs of Kai's new boots rapped at the pavement all the way home. Touching neither turd, crack nor rail. The kid was canny. Pedestrians parted before him and if he noticed he didn't let on. Keely wittered on about ospreys and other birds of prey for the pleasure of the kid's attention. He didn't know that much about raptors. Birds weren't really his thing. Which was cute, given he'd gone down in flames for the sake of an endangered species of cockatoo.

I need a wee, Kai announced as they came into the forecourt.

Litre of Coke, I wonder why, said Gemma.

Keely followed them through to the lifts. Thought of the same sequence from a couple of days before. Their meeting in the dim lobby. And felt strangely cheered. They rode up in a companionable lull and at the top floor Gemma gave the jouncing boy the keys, sent him on ahead.

Is it safe?

Is what safe?

Letting him run like that, letting him go on his own.

She fixed him with a smirk. What are you, a kid expert, too?

He shrugged, a bit stung. In the distance the screen door slapped; the kid was inside.

For Gawdsake, aim to please! she bellowed after him.

They were silent a few moments.

So, tell me, he said, what did happen to my rats?

Ah, she said. Me, actually.

What d'you mean?

When you all moved. You left em with me.

Geez, I don't even remember.

I was *that* excited. Almost forgot why you had to go, I was so thrilled.

So how did it go?

Lasted one day. First night I fed em all rum and raisin icecream. Thought I'd spoil em. And in the morning they were cactus. Every one of em. Toes up.

Keely honked with laughter.

Fat as tennis balls, they were. Cried me eyes out.

Oh well. They died happy.

As they reached Keely's door Kai belted back down the walkway.

How do you spell it?

Spell what? said Gemma.

The eagle bird.

Osprey, said Keely, spelling it out for him. I can show you one on the computer. Actually I know where one lives.

For real?

Yeah. True. I can show you.

Today?

Kai —

Well, today's a bit hard.

Tomorrow?

You got school, said Gemma.

Nan, it's Sunday!

Well, Tom's busy.

Actually I'm not.

Well, it's your funeral.

It'd be fun. We can all go.

Terrific, she said without enthusiasm.

I'm gonna get ready, said Kai, turning for home.

It's tomorrow, love, said Gemma with tender exasperation.

The screen door slapped to. Keely bellied up to the rail and looked down at the beetle-backs of the tenants' vehicles below.

Listen, he said. If you need someone to look after him. I mean, I know you work at night.

We're fine, she said. He's used to it.

Sure. And I guess you can't be too careful.

Gemma stood beside him, forearms on the rail. Her hair luffed against his arm in the wind. She smelt like the mums of the old neighbourhood, of smoke and aluminium deodorant, fried food.

Well, she said. I didn't go to any uni, but I'm smart enough to trust a Keely.

I don't even know what that means.

How is she?

Faith? She's in Singapore.

I mean your mum.

Oh. She's great.

Must've been proud.

Yeah?

I used to see you on the telly.

Oh, he said with a grimace.

In a suit. With them greenies.

Yep. That was me.

You their lawyer or somethin?

Campaigner, he said. Spokesperson.

Spoke*person*.

Anyway. Doris is great, he said. I'm calling her right now. About tomorrow.

She's comin?

What? No.

Oh. Right. Well.

Is ten okay?

For what?

Birdwatching.

Christ, she said. Can't wait.

Years ago an old friend from uni told Keely that only two good things ever came out of Fremantle. And both of those were bridges. He thought of her as the train trundled across the Old Traffic Bridge towards the gilded city. The river shining below for a moment and then the farther shore suddenly beneath him. Melissa was from a stolid suburb of Perth. Wembley, if memory served. She'd gone on to teach history and English. Went back and did a master's degree. Or maybe it was a doctorate. But last he heard she was up at the mines along with everybody else, flying in and out in hi-viz every fortnight, making four times the dough for half the hours. As a bus driver. Said it was boring as hell but the money soothed all wounds. The way she said it sounded defensive. And that saddened him. As if she expected a crack about her being another cashed-up bogan. What a pious knob he was.

The train eased through the stops until there was no mistaking the tiny but telling territorial differences. The trophy cars. The pouty boutiques. The irrepressible confidence of life in the dress circle.

He found Doris in the restaurant courtyard with a glass of something newly poured. She was jotting things in a spiral notepad. In the fading light, beneath the trellised vines, his mother was as handsome as ever, perhaps a little less approachable for the self-possession she projected these days. Against the rough pavers and terracotta pots, she was silvery, slim, more noticeable than a son might prefer. Her thick grey hair was twisted into girlish plaits that flapped against her arms and when she hoisted them across her shoulders and stood to greet him, the ethnic confusion of bangles clunked and chimed chaotically – that maddening, reassuring clangour. They were a nightmare at the movies, those hoops, clanking and rattling at every moment of mirth or dramatic intensity, but they'd become the sound of her. She was a calm, quiet person, often so restrained that without the bracelets and baubles you'd never register the intensity of her excitement or agitation. That was the bit of her he remembered most from his bruised adolescence: the chatter and rattle of bangles as she turned pages and made notes, studying late into the night after he and his sister were in bed.

Well, she said, pouring him a glass. What a good idea. Monday really was too long to wait.

You must know somebody. To get a table Saturday night.

Bollocks, she said. I promised we'd arrive early, eat like pokie machines —

And tip like a Haulpak truck, eh?

Money, she said with a sigh.

They're right. It talks.

But wouldn't it be lovely if now and then it had something interesting to say.

Keely smiled, enduring her benevolent glance – yes, he was a ruin – and tried to give his full attention to the riesling she'd ordered. Something from the Porongurups, something new.

Well?

Nice, he said. He swished it round his glass, in his mouth. Beneath its citric charm there was something almost sandy. He felt his temples draw in a little, like windows pressed against their frames by a suddenly opened door. He realized Doris was speaking.

Sorry, he said. What?

Nothing, she said. I was just faffing on about the wine. To impress you.

But her face had fallen and he suspected she'd been talking about something more important. Doris, love, I'm always impressed.

She smiled for him and it smarted.

He drew himself up, took in the rich spillover of kitchen vapours, the briny scent of the river. Saw his right leg twitching waywardly. The house music – some generic World nonsense – was loud. He shot a look at the staff flexing their tatts by the kitchen pass. No use asking them to turn it down; these days restaurant music was not for the paying customer.

Hey, he said into the taut pause in proceedings. I might come by tomorrow and grab the dinghy.

Just in time.

How's that?

I was getting ready to turf it out at the next street collection.

Couldn't blame you.

Well, it's been a while.

I'm thinking of a spin on the river.

Good. Lovely.

Listen – did I sleepwalk as a kid?

I won't even inquire about *that* rapid transition.

Sorry.

Somebody once peed in the linen press, if I recall.

Don't remember *that*.

Well, she said with a laugh. Then you may have your answer.

But you would have said. If it was one of us there'd be an inescapable family legend.

Probably. But I do recall small bodies ghosting about in the night. Having to steer them back to bed.

Kids from the street, he said. Your lame ducks.

Lame ducks? she said with arched brows.

Doris let him marinate a moment. He saw the irony. Now that he was the chief wounded bird in her life, the least functional member of the family. He raised his glass, all the acknowledgement and surrender he could manage.

I remember a lot of sheets on the line, a lot of wet beds. All those kids you took in.

They had their reasons, she said.

I don't doubt it.

But, no. Neither of you wandered or wet the bed.

Huh.

A long moment passed. Doris jingled.

Why d'you ask, love?

Keely sipped his wine, tried not to gulp.

Oh. Nothing, really.

She gave a diffident nod but he knew she wasn't buying it. She hoisted a clacking arm and summoned one of the prowling narcissists for some service.

Keely tried to address the menu but he was preoccupied by

her heightened watchfulness. The flash of her specs coming off and on – clunkitty-click. Every vegetable, every bit of protein on the list had a provenance more complex than a minor Rembrandt. And he didn't know what half of it meant. What the fuck was a *coxcomb of Serrano solar*? Or was he just obtuse? Christ, he was starting to sweat. He was leaving great smudgy fingerprints.

Food, she said. It wasn't always this stressful.

He smiled. What a lovely, impressive old duck his mother was. By some obscure law of nature he was expected to supersede her, yet in her presence he felt like a flake. It wasn't really what she said that made him feel wet and feeble, it was just who she was, what she'd done for Faith and for him, and what she'd achieved for herself. A young widow with two kids, she'd gone back to finish high school, studied social work part-time and kept two jobs as well as a home life. After that, the law degree, and all the quixotic social justice causes. Daughter of a wharfie, wife of a diesel mechanic, Doris may look like Julie Christie but her voice was still pure Blackboy Crescent, as broad and dry as the coastal plain.

As if resisting the catalogue of fetishes on the menu, she ordered briskly, almost offhandedly, and he found himself following suit. The waitperson stalked off as if aggrieved by their want of reverence and after a shared chuckle they fell silent. Doris drank her wine, chewed her lip. Keely felt his pulse quicken. He sensed trouble.

Well, she murmured, setting her glass down carefully, turning it worryingly once or twice. Here's an interesting piece of information I've been wanting to share all day.

Oh dear, he said, tamping down his panic. You're actually looking over your shoulder.

Just being sensible.

You're running for parliament.

Don't be absurd.

Then what?

The Crime and Corruption Commission is about to call before it a certain lobbyist.

Keely rocked back in his seat. Placed his hands gently upon the table.

Relating to certain matters involving the rezoning of a nature reserve and a subsequent real estate development.

Old news, he said, feeling the pulse in his throat. Ancient history.

In the wake of statements by a shire councillor and a town planner, now deceased. Along with the lobbyist, they're hauling in at least one member of parliament and several senior public servants.

Why tell me? he said. I don't even care anymore.

Some methodical drongo kept files, a diarized record. Documenting at least one payment of seventy thousand dollars to a public officer, an inducement from the developer.

One bit of evidence. Hardly a case.

And phone intercepts.

Shit, he said. They knew all along?

Or at least had their suspicions.

Well, whacko, he said bitterly. Put out the flags.

This is just the beginning, Tom. It's all going to come out.

This is Perth, Doris. Nothing ever *comes out*. People keep their heads down. They're shit-scared and they have every right to be. These pricks will string it out forever; they're lawyered up till doomsday, they'll wear the CCC to a nub and walk away.

No. Not this time.

Oh, what does it even matter?

It matters that you told the truth. You were right all along.

Of course I was fucking right, he thought, setting his glass down with monumental care. Had she fallen for the smear like everyone else? Was this why she was so excited, because she'd thought he was the embittered nutter they cast him as?

Tom, are you alright?

Fine, he said through his teeth.

You'll be vindicated.

Re*deemed*.

Those words still mean something to me.

Yes, he conceded.

I know it's been hard.

You're going to tell me it was worth it?

I wish you could have confided in someone. We could have tackled it strategically.

I spent every day for fifteen years doing nothing else, Doris. But we lose. Not because we're rubbish at it. That's just how it works. We're meant to lose. And campaign and calculate all we like, the bulldozers still arrive, the agencies wash their hands, the media get their little flash of colour and it's back to business as usual. We're the soft story wedged in before the sports results. Twice a week in a slow week.

Look, I know it's hard not to be cynical —

Remember the old slogan? *EPA: Every Proposal Accepted.* Used to think it was hyperbole, propaganda. But it's pretty much the truth. Like every other arm of government, it's a servant of industry, 'facilitator of ongoing prosperity'. Bribery isn't even necessary. That's the real insult. The system works beautifully without it.

But in this instance we're talking about a prima facie case of actual corruption. And I think it'll stick.

You really have drunk the Kool-Aid.

Doris blinked. She leant across the table and he knew by the venomous rattle of Third World hardware that he'd crossed a line.

I'm sorry, he said, but it sounded hollow.

Who do you think you're impressing, some doe-eyed intern in a sarong?

Doris —

You think you're the only person who has to live and work in this hothouse? I've been dealing with this little club of red-faced chancers since you were a schoolboy. You think I don't know what it is to be traduced?

Really, he said. I apologize.

Anyway, that's my news. For what it's worth.

It's just that being vindicated —

We needn't talk about it.

There's no job waiting, no welcome back. You saw how fast we settled. The donors were bolting like rats from a housefire. WildForce couldn't get rid of me fast enough. And now no one'll touch me. All for a few trees and fifty birds with faces only a mother could love.

Mothers are like that.

It was stupid. I mean, we've lost so many bigger battles, places more important in the scheme of things. When I saw those trees falling I didn't even feel anything. But that little black cloud of birds. And the wailing hippies and the mums and dads there in their sunsmart hats, and the poor bird-boffin with his specs broken —

Let's not talk about it.

I just lit up. Like a flare.

I know. We all saw.

And you know, it felt great. Five or six minutes. Like, I don't know what. Like vomiting hot coals.

Isaiah, said Doris.

He looked at her. Those glittering eyes. The rueful smile. Saw how afraid she was for him, how long she'd kept herself in check. He was ashamed. But angry, too. That there could only ever be one subject.

Oh well, he said, trying to draw this line of conversation to an end. Too late the hero, eh?

Never too late, she said. Never.

To the good fight, he said, brandishing his glass. And all our lost causes.

Doris didn't reciprocate. She flicked her plaits. A rattle of impatience, irritation.

There was a silence between them. The hectoring music. Falling darkness.

Tell me, she said. Are you married to that beard?

Why, because you used to be?

And what's that supposed to mean?

Someone said it makes me look like Dad.

Who? Who said that?

Gemma Buck.

Hmm.

You're not going to ask about her?

Doris shut down a moment, pushing her glass in circles.

I thought there might be more important things to deal with. Before we got all nostalgic.

Like what, for instance?

Faith. She's worried.

She hasn't even *seen* the beard. She's watching brokers leap from skyscrapers. What I'd like to know is why can't she get more of them to take the plunge. God knows, we need a cull.

Tom, love.

What?

You're being a bit of a nong.

I imagine so.

You can always desist, you know.

But here I am, vindicated and persisting.

I'm sorry. I shouldn't have mentioned the . . . thing.

You want me to shave the beard?

Forget the bloody beard.

I'm sorry.

She took up the bottle, but he covered his glass like a man in regal control of his impulses. She refilled her own, sat back and restored herself.

So tell me about Gemma, then, she said with a wan smile.

Not much to say, really. I just saw her in passing.

What does she do? How does she seem?

Dunno, he said. It was just a chance encounter.

Family?

There's a grandkid. A boy.

Good for her.

He glanced up, saw her appraising stare, felt the lost moment in her false brightness.

I often think about them, Baby and her.

He nodded, wishing he could go back, begin the evening again, but it was hopeless. He lacked the gumption to set things right, he was too accustomed to the logic of defeat. He saw it now, the rest of the meal. They'd eat in fraught politeness and leave the moment the last fork was laid down. She'd insist on driving him home. He'd protest, pile in anyway. And she'd want to come up and see the flat once and for all but refrain from asking. She'd take his kiss on the cheek like a lowball tip and wheel the boxy old Volvo away, looking game as ever, masking her hurt and disappointment as he stood limp and seething on the forecourt.

The task at hand was getting to that final, miserable moment as quickly as possible.

Keely was halfway along the open gallery, digging at his temples, when he noticed something flapping in the security mesh of his door. Some civic announcement, no doubt: a plea for a lost kitten, a notice about building maintenance. But when he pulled it from the grille he saw it was a child's drawing, a crayon outline of a bird. Dumpy, earthbound, like an overfed kiwi.

Once he got inside he clamped the sheet of paper to the fridge with a magnet. At other people's places – friends from work, people with kids – he'd always looked with an inner sneer at their fridge doors plastered in clumsy daubs. Everything their brats committed to paper was so special, so important it required immediate and prolonged display. The kids probably forgot their work the moment they put the brush down, never thinking another thing of it. And now here he was, chuffed to have it there. This peculiar burst of colour, this lovely intrusion.

He banged down a couple of Panadeine Forte with a chaste swish of apple juice. It was ten-thirty but from his balcony he saw that the lights were on over at 1010. A few moments later he was outside her kitchen window, tapping lightly. The curtain ricked aside. Gemma squinted out, tense, alert, annoyed.

She cracked the door but left the chain on. A gust of fried onions and menthol smoke blew past her. In the gap he saw she wore a faded housecoat. She was barefoot.

Sorry, he said. I know it's late.

You orright?

Yeah. Just got home.

Right.

We're all set. Tomorrow.

Fair enough.

Meet you out the front at ten?

Like we said.

Yeah. And hey, I got his drawing.

You what?

Kai's drawing. Of a bird. It was in my door.

Little bugger. I've told him a million times. Jesus. He's not sposed to wander off.

He's okay?

Asleep.

You look tired.

Because I am.

Right. So I'll see you in the morning?

She closed the door on him.

Keely slunk back down to his place. He glanced at the bird on the fridge. Thought of his mother. Knowing Doris, she'd still be up. So he called.

Are you okay? she asked gently.

Sorry about tonight, he murmured. We didn't really get to talk.

I was talking, she said.

I know. Like you said, I was a goose. A stupid mood.

Doris was quiet.

You're working? he said.

Reading, she said. Charles Birch.

So, you're a pantheist now.

After menopause, she said, all bets are off.

Very funny.

If you still need the car, the keys are on the sink. I'll be in church.

You still go?

You know perfectly well I do.

The Anglicans. It's come to that.

Well, I *am* the demographic. Sometimes I'm half the congregation. You should come one day.

What, and spook the poor buggers?

Is this about the beard?

No, Mum, it's not about the beard.

It does make you look like him. It's . . . well, it's a little unnerving.

I hadn't realized. To be perfectly honest. It just grew of its own accord.

Tommy, love, go to bed. You're slurring.

Slurring? I had two glasses, he said truthfully.

My mistake.

But shit, he thought. I'm sober. Slurring?

Tom?

Yeah?

What're you doing? Are you talking to me or thinking aloud?

I'm going to bed, he said, hanging up, rattled.

But to get off he needed help. A sleeper slug. Just the one. And a couple of Valium to ease past that hunted feeling that lingered of late any time he had to entrust his head to the pillow.

It was nine when he woke. So he had to scramble. Burnt his mouth gulping tea. Wasted time searching for a clean shirt. Then, halfway to the station and hopelessly late, he hailed a cab he could sorely afford.

Doris lived in a stately Edwardian weatherboard in a riverside suburb of Perth. From just below her place, at the water's edge, you could see upstream, past the snaking coils of the river, the thousand-eyed towers of the business district with the shimmering red-roofed plain behind. The hills were shrouded with bushfire haze that formed a dirty yellow rampart against the world beyond. At times Perth really did feel like an island, a country unto itself. This brassy little outpost of digging and dealing tilted relentlessly at the future, but these days it lived on life support – desalinated seawater and ancient shrinking aquifers. Behind the veil of smoke lay the wheatbelt and the salt-ravaged badlands that only a century before had been a teeming woodland half the size of Poland.

Up on Doris's verandah, however, there was no view, grand or troubling. Her place was much of a piece with its neighbours but for the telltale wind chimes and the signs of a garden run amok. He dragged the dinghy and trailer down the drive, swept leaves from it hurriedly, stuck the bungs in, then hitched it to the old Volvo. Somehow he still had the presence of mind to check the outboard fuel and when he saw the state of it he poured it guiltily against the wall behind the shed. He'd stop in at a servo along the highway.

Stalking back past the house with the petrol tank, he was startled by his mother standing in her nightie on the deck. She held up a coffee mug and he nodded. While she was indoors he checked the motor, the oars, the mouldy lifejackets.

I thought I was going to have to use it as a fishpond, Doris said, handing him a mug.

I thought you were putting it out on the verge. And shouldn't you be at the nine-thirty?

Late night, she said, blowing across her mug. I'll go to the eleven o'clock. Uproar at Saint Whatsit's, no doubt.

Everything alright?

Hope so, she said, without quite glancing his way. She looked a little frail without the armour of her fabrics and bangles. Her silver hair was loose, fanning in skeins at the whim of the breeze.

Keely said nothing, just sipped his coffee. He wanted to say something kind, conciliatory, but he was stranded. She seemed relieved when he finally passed the empty mug and shook the car keys.

Gemma looked surprised, even concerned, to see the boat in the street beneath the Mirador, but Kai seemed delighted. Keely drove them down to the riverside ramp and shoved the dinghy off its seized rollers. Neither the boy nor his grandmother had the first idea about boats so just getting them aboard was a mission. He had to wrangle the kid into a lifejacket and once she saw him in it, Gemma decided she needed one too. There were slips, tumbles, a shriek or two as he swept them out into the channel and steered upstream with the wind ahead and the tide behind them.

I thought this was a birdwatchin expedition! yelled Gemma, dashing the hair from her eyes, hunched awkwardly beneath the cumbersome roll of the jacket collar.

It is.

On the bloody river?

Exactly. I've got a point to prove.

You blokes, you've all got that, she said, bracing against the smacks and bumps.

It was funny, in its way, seeing her scowl and wince, clutching the child in fear, but after a short while he relented and eased off the throttle to slap along sedately. Kai stared at the tiller, the wake, the scum of rotten leaves at his feet. Was he anxious? Keely thought perhaps he could have launched somewhere closer to where he planned to take them. He hadn't even considered the possibility that the jaunt upstream might be a trial. God, he thought, negotiating the slop from a passing ferry, don't let me make a meal of this.

But by the time he had them round the bend and into the lee of the limestone bluffs of Blackwall Reach, the boy had lifted his head a little and Gemma managed a game smile. Keely pointed to the teenagers jumping from the cliff above them, yodelling as they fell. The water boiled where they speared in.

Keely motored over as a pale youth broke the surface with a hoot and gave Kai a thumbs up. The boy seemed at a loss to respond.

You want to steer? Keely asked.

Kai shook his head.

It's twenty metres deep here, he said. At night you can hear fish down there, big mulloway, croaking in the dark.

The idea did not seem to appeal to the boy.

Is there really a bird? asked Kai.

We're getting there, mate.

But is it true?

You'll see.

You promise?

Hold onto your hat, said Keely, banking out across the channel to the next bay. It'd been months since he'd seen the ospreys he had in mind. Maybe he should have checked first to spare himself a disaster.

Christ, said Gemma. Look at those houses.

Keely grinned. He thought of Balzac's line – *behind every great fortune, a great crime*. Where was Jehovah when you needed Him for a good old-fashioned punitive landslide? And, yea, swept were the wicked unto the darkest deeps.

He steered wide of waterskiers and wankers on jetskis, slowed down to take in the terraces and lawns, the swanky boathouses. Gemma turned in her seat, gazed up, wide-eyed, beginning to enjoy herself. He eased them past a chaotic and giggly regatta of little sailboats at Freshie, rounded the point into the next bay. Here picnickers sprawled on blankets beneath the peppermints, dragged kayaks across the obstacle course of fig roots at the bank. Keely didn't cut the outboard until they were past all of it, deep into the slough where the shore was obscured by a confusion of native cypresses, melaleucas and gnarled gums. Above them a limestone ridge whose brows knitted, hatching everything before it in flickering shadow.

Is everything orright? Gemma asked.

Will be in a moment, he said. Are we looking? Do we have our eyes open?

The breeze wafted them by slabs of stone, blond tablets freshly pupped from the bluff. They lay in a monumental jumble at the water's edge, misted with dancing insects. There were jellyfish all round the boat, big as pumpkins, and Keely breathed in the estuarine miasma of algae, cypress and invertebrate slime that reminded him of holidays, exam week, summers gone. He watched their faces. Gemma wore a look of heroic forbearance but the kid blinked miserably.

I'm no good at this, Kai said in little more than a whisper.

Keely wiggled his eyebrows in encouragement, but the kid didn't appear to appreciate the suspense. He caught Gemma glaring at him, face like a spanked arse. Christ, he thought, how many promises had this kid seen come to nothing? He hadn't thought of that. This better bloody work.

Lie back, he murmured, trying to reassure himself as much as the boy. Both of you. Just lie back and watch.

What for? asked Gemma. What're we lying down in a boat for?

Just for the view, he said with a brightness that already felt thin. Up ahead, the ancient marri upon which all his hopes rested began to emerge from the shadows, more skeleton these days than living tree, a barkless grey column topped by contorted white limbs that towered out across undergrowth, rocks, shadow, water. He'd come here a lot with Harriet, then alone sometimes when he visited Doris. Back when he actually bothered. You could hike down the scree-slope from the road, but the view from the water beat everything. That tree, he thought. It stood before whitefellas even dreamt of this place. It was here when the river was teeming, when cook-fires and dances stitched the banks into coherent song, proper country. Just to see it was a mental correction, a recalibration.

The boat yawed, the tree hung right over them. And Keely realized he'd been seeing it for seconds already, seeing it without taking it in at all. Thank God. There it was on the outermost limb, the same colour as the bleached and weathered wood, motionless, watching them, plotting their drift, not yet deigning to stir. The bird of his married years, the stolen weekends, of even the long puzzled silences near the end.

Still there. What a bird.

But what was *it* seeing? Three bodies in a silver boat? Or just background, faunal wallpaper, nothing of the slightest interest?

The raptor unfurled its wings, propped, let out a scratchy cry. Beside him the boy gasped. His face suddenly open.

There!

Look at that, said Keely. I told you.

Will it get me?

Get you? No. You don't look much like a fish to me.

It's creepy-lookin, said Gemma.

Nah, said Keely. It's beautiful.

And it was. A severe, stately bird, watchful, poised, tensing even now.

Osprey, said Kai.

The creature tilted its head, twisted slightly, then gathered itself. It rose, languid, powerful, to reach into the air.

Osprey, said the boy.

It climbed without effort, wheeled up past the supplicant fingers of clifftop trees and retreated to the shadows, leaving only a harsh cry to signal its presence.

Did we scare it? asked Gemma.

Nothing scares him, said Keely. He's just seen something else, I'd say.

The boat drifted back into the noonday light. The boy blinked skyward. And then the chalky flash blew past them, hit the water in a weltering flare and hauled itself up again, climbing off at a loping tangent with something shining but doomed in its talons.

Keely refrained from commentary. The act itself was enough. The boy and his grandmother craned their necks, watching the sky, waiting for more.

By the time he'd taken the others home, returned to Doris's to park the boat and flush the outboard, left the keys to the Volvo under the mat and caught the train back to Fremantle, it was past mid-afternoon. His exalted mood had decayed somewhat; he was ravenous and the sun had gotten to him, but for all that he felt better than he had in weeks. He showered, gulped a couple of beefy brufens, made a sandwich and sat in his armchair sipping water.

At dusk he was still there. Half the sandwich dry and curled in his lap and the pint-glass capsized on the carpet beside him. He brushed the bread away, glanced an uneasy moment at the new watermark and went out onto the balcony to clear his mind.

Dreams. Feverish sequences. Beyond him now; he didn't care to recall.

In the mild evening breeze he caught a flash of movement at the edge of his vision. Kai. A few balconies down. Dressed only in shorts. Actually, truly there. He smiled but the kid seemed not to notice. Keely felt strangely self-conscious, anxious that something about his being out here wasn't quite right. He was dressed, wasn't he? Awake. And sober. What else could it be unnerving him but the queasy scraps of dreams? But this harried feeling, why wouldn't it let go?

It was none of his business whether the kid was out there or not, but he wished Gemma wouldn't let him do it; it wasn't safe. And he hesitated, reluctant to move for fear of startling him. But Kai was facing his way. Such an odd, affectless gaze. It felt awkward, even creepy, to just stand there, not acknowledging him. Keely raised a hand. Kai lifted an arm from the rail, returned the wave shyly, and went inside.

Keely had promised himself a proper meal that night and he was cooking with the spoils of Thursday's shopping spree in Coles when Faith rang. Once more she was in a crowded room. In the background there were stabs of noise – announcements, exhortations – as if she were at an airport or train station.

You didn't call, she said mildly.

I meant to.

A man of grand intentions.

Where are you?

London.

Hell, that's sudden.

It's freezing. I'm waiting for the driver. Hey, I was thinking about that canoe we used to have. Was it really just the roof off an old car? Am I remembering that right? We used to push it out through the reeds, across the swamp. Am I imagining all this?

Faith, why're you in London?

We used to say I was the only Keely without the rescue instinct. Nah.

And you're always crapping on about backing the vanquished.

Keely laughed and his sister joined in a moment. She sounded uncharacteristically rattled.

Mate, he said. Has something happened?

Nothing I'm allowed to talk about. I guess it's just funny, me mounting a rescue package.

I don't even know what that is.

In my world it's salvation without mercy.

You okay?

I was just thinking about us as kids, that's all. And, you know, just wanted to hear your voice.

It was the roof from an old Holden, he said. The canoe.

But the signal began to falter and Faith seemed to be speaking to someone else, her driver, apparently, and the rest was rushed farewell.

In the wake of the call Keely went on fixing dinner. He thought of Faith at ten in her pink boilersuit and Levi's sneakers. What a game little girl she had been: that measured stare, the straight-cut fringe. Bold as a mudlark, but kind along with it. She'd shared her room with the Buck girls the winter their mother lay in hospital held together by screws and wires and plaster. Maybe she resented it – the sudden disorder, the wet beds, the night terrors, the missing toys. Perhaps his memories of her stalwart decency were not reliable. Because whenever he saw her now, Christmas being the last example, she seemed so cool and withheld. But her world had been flying like shit off a shovel. Tough time. Maybe she needed to project that corporate armour just to survive. And the diffidence?

Probably due to the sight of him, dishevelled, maudlin, strangling the festive cheer from Doris's big day.

Anyway, enough of that.

He mashed potatoes, tooled about with the sauce a while and steamed the snake beans. He put on some music, the Bach fugues Harriet used to like. And it didn't upset him. In fact he felt a rare buoyancy. Faith's memory of their hijinks on the swamp, perhaps. Or the day on the river finally sinking in. That bird, the way it watched them, trying to decide what they were. Just the glorious fact of it being there, like an answered prayer. What a deliverance it had been. He couldn't have borne to disappoint the kid. To screw that up as well. And it was mad, but now he felt like a bloody champion.

He'd only just sat down to eat when there was a knock at the door. He sat chewing a moment, cleaving doggedly to his moment of happiness while it lasted.

Just me, called Gemma.

It was like a soap bubble bursting. The mood was broken. But some slippery film of equanimity clung on as he got slowly to his feet.

He opened the door, still chewing. Freshly showered and in a sleeveless dress, Gemma stood barefoot peering past him.

Everything alright?

Sorry, she said. You got company?

He blinked, shook his head, swallowed.

I could smell it from my place. It's doin me head in.

What is?

Whatever you're cookin.

You want some?

I've eaten, she said.

Okay.

But, Jesus, she said. Smell's bloody beautiful.

Keely was stumped. She had such an avid look on her face, almost febrile, and she just stood there, as if waiting to be invited in.

You mind? she asked. Just for a sec?

He unlocked the security screen and when he stepped back she slipped right by him and went straight to the stovetop.

Chicken, she said. Garlic. Bacon by the looks. And the gravy's what, white wine?

Keely closed the security screen but left the main door open. Mostly.

Aw, she said, looking at his little dining table. You haven't even hardly started. Tommy, sit down. Jesus, I didn't realize.

Sure you don't want some?

Eat, she said.

He sat back down, resumed eating, but he was self-conscious now.

Little bugger wouldn't go to bed, she said, leaning on the bench between them.

He's okay?

Christ, he was that excited.

Keely nodded, his mood lifting a little.

That was a nice thing you did.

Not a problem, he said, smiling around a mouthful.

Not a problem, she said, mimicking him. Hey, maybe I will have some of that.

He motioned for her to help herself and she fished around for cutlery. Paused a moment at the knife drawer, checking out his jumbled pharmacopoeia, which gave him a moment's anxiety. But she didn't even seem to register it, so urgent were her movements, so flighty her disposition. He watched as she forked up something from the pan and turned it over in her mouth experimentally before chewing with gusto. He saw her wipe gravy from her lips with the back of her wrist.

Something I can't pick, she said, hoisting the skillet to the bench as if setting in to polish off the remainder.

Sage, he said. I picked it today at Mum's.

Doris? You saw her today?

Yeah. That was her car. Didn't I tell you? I have to keep the boat at her place.

Gemma straightened a moment, oil glistening on her chin.

So you brought us home before you went back to her place?

Well, yeah.

Right.

I caught the train home, he said, puzzled by the cloudy expression on her face. Kai looked pretty worn out. I thought I'd run you home, save you both another hour of farting about.

Fair enough, she said, crestfallen.

I didn't realize, he said, seeing it now. At least he thought he saw.

I spose it *was* a long time ago.

No. Really. I should have thought.

Just . . . I loved your mum. Guess I thought she might like to see me.

Of course she would. I was just preoccupied, that's all, thinking about the boat, the car, getting you home.

You're embarrassed. Aren'tcha?

About the *car*?

About me, you dickhead. Bein seen with me. In front of yer mum.

I don't know what you're talking about, he said, irritated.

Nah, course ya don't.

Keely bridled at this. He thought of the lengths he'd gone to these past months, for the sake of guarding his privacy, so that no one, friend or foe, could get close enough to commiserate, gloat, accuse, correct, needle or interrogate him. It was the one thing he wasn't gutsick-depressed about. And here was a woman in his kitchen, this person he hardly knew, eating his food and calling him out as some kind of snob. He was angry with himself, furious he'd dropped the ball so comprehensively, let her into the flat, his head, his fucking life.

Whoa, and now yer sulkin, eh.

No, he said with some effort. I'm just surprised, that's all.

Well, it doesn't take much to get you all hot'n bothered.

He pushed his hand through his hair.

Forget it, she muttered.

No, he said, like a twat who'd forgotten every survival instinct he had. What is it you're trying to tell me?

Gemma looked at her fork, shrugged.

These days you're just a bit more . . .

More what?

I dunno. Posh.

Keely laughed; there was nothing else for it. Though it didn't sound as mirthful or unruffled as he'd hoped.

Fuck off, she said mildly.

Posh? Me? You must be on drugs.

Don't talk to me about fuckin drugs.

Gemma, I'm unemployed. This is it, he declared, waving at the armchair, the bookshelf, the TV, the portable CD player, the obsolete iPod. Apart from the battered laptop beside him on the laminated table, there was nothing else to see but a couple of Stanley Spencer reproductions and the Peter Dombrovskis on the wall.

You went to uni and that.

True.

And there you were all the time, on the telly, on the news, in the paper. In ya house by the water in Freo – bet that place had *character*.

He lifted his hands in surrender.

Just cause you don't have a job and you look like shit, doesn't mean you're not flash.

Alright, he said. I hear what you're saying. But I think you've got the wrong idea. If I'd known, if I'd thought of it – Gemma, it's not a problem. I wasn't thinking, that's all.

She looked unconvinced but after a few moments staring him down she did seem slightly mollified. Whether that was a result of having said her piece or seeing him yield he couldn't tell.

You really that broke? she asked.

Pretty broke, yeah. I wasn't very careful with the severance pay.

So, you're renting this joint?

No, he said. I own it.

She grinned without mercy.

You got anything to drink?

There's wine in the fridge, he said, knowing it was rude not to get up and pour her a glass, but he was flustered now and would have preferred her to go away.

Gemma cracked the fridge open, examined its contents as if seeking further confirmation of his lofty status and then hauled the bottle out. She held it at arm's length a moment, found a glass and filled it. She glanced at him inquiringly but he demurred. She sipped at the wine sceptically.

Look, I'm sure Doris'd love to see you, he murmured.

Gemma leant back against the fridge. At her shoulder, pinned to the door by magnets, lay Kai's crayon bird. She raked her hair irritably with her fingers.

She'll think you're on with me. Slummin around.

Don't be ridiculous. She already knows you live in the building.

She ever come here?

I don't *have* anybody here.

Really? How come?

I just prefer it that way.

You really are a bit of an odd-bod, aren't you.

Yes. I spose.

She gulped the rest of her wine. Keely tried to finish his meal but his appetite had gone. He'd made the effort, that was the thing.

So I'm ridiculous, she said.

Mate, I didn't mean it like that – I mean, come on.

Wouldn't have said it when I was younger.

Gemma, I only knew you as a kid.

When we were kids, but, weren't you interested?

No! Geez, you were a little girl.

Didn't stop anyone else.

Well, shit. That's awful. Why are we talking about this?

She propped her elbows on the bench and leaned forward, sizing him up. The tops of her breasts were visible in the vee of her dress.

What about the Snakepit? And the White Sands? We weren't kids then.

No, I guess not.

Wasn't ridiculous then.

Keely didn't know what to say. His nerves were jangling.

Back then we were more the same.

Well, it was so long ago.

And you never even thought about it?

Keely said nothing.

I was always around. I remember being in your room. I got in your bed once, in the night. Pretended I was scared.

I don't remember that.

But you remember I was pretty.

Gemma, he said, trying to steer clear of this perilous current, I was a kid; I didn't even notice girls.

I wasn't the sort you'd notice, then?

Hell, everyone noticed. Later.

So, tell me.

Tell you what? he asked, annoyed at her persistence, the way this conversation was headed, as if she were determined to extract some shred of old glory at his expense. Just because he hadn't thought to present her to Doris, for God's sake. It was moronic, fucking banal. And he was getting a treacherous hard-on, despite himself. Gemma was tipsy. He hadn't paid enough attention; she'd been half cut the moment she arrived.

Garn, she persisted. Tell me what I looked like.

Mate, he said with a resentful sigh, you were beautiful. Alright? And now I'm just an old boiler.

Not that old.

Well, thanks a lot.

I didn't —

Haven't you even thought about it? she asked, cutting him off. Not once?

Bloody hell, what's got into you?

I dunno, she said. I had a few Baileys, that's all. It was a good day, Tommy. You know how many good days I get, livin like this?

Fair enough, he said, shamefaced.

You know?

Yeah, it doesn't look easy. But he's a lovely kid.

Talks about you, now. Day and bloody night. Thinks the sun shines out yer clacker. Never stops askin questions.

So what d'you tell him?

The truth. What I know, what I remember.

Like what? he said, unable to resist.

I dunno. Just old shit. About you'n Nev.

He looked at his hands, felt his spine slump into a defensive curve. At least she'd changed tack; it was something to be grateful for.

You were the only ones.

The only ones *what*?

That didn't fiddle with us.

Shit, he said, shoving his plate across the table. You didn't tell him that, I hope.

Of course not. But that's how I learnt what's what, who to trust and who to steer clear of.

I guess that's something.

Is to me.

I didn't mean to sound so —

You musta wanted kids. Of yer own.

Why d'you say that?

University of hard knocks, mate. Instinct. Like I said, who ya trust and who's trouble. He knows. I can see it.

You've lost me, he said truthfully.

You went to a lot of trouble to impress a kid today. And I have to figure out if it's cause you're a dirty perv or if it's just that you wanna suck up to me, to get into me pants.

Keely looked at her. She was completely serious. If he told her to get out now he'd look guilty; one charge or the other would stick. It was insupportable. And he felt the seconds of silence thud by.

I mean, if it was about me I wouldn't mind so much, she went on. But I've had to learn the hard way, if you know what I mean – about blokes. And I haven't got time for it anymore, tell you the truth. Sorry – I'm just sayin.

Despite his indignation, Keely was trying to imagine the life she'd led since their days as children. He wondered about her scarred hands, the broken tooth, the daughter in prison.

Gemma, there's no agenda. I'm not that sort of person.

Oh, I know that. I'm just sayin. This is the sort of thing I've gotta ask meself.

Okay. I get that. But, really, you don't have to worry.

Gemma nodded slowly. She looked past him. To what – the ocean lights, the wharf? She chewed her lip a moment.

Pity, really, she said, turning to the fridge.

Keely watched in a snarl of conflicted impulses and competing thoughts as she poured herself a refill. She belted the tumbler of wine down in two gulps and set the glass on the bench with a smack. He couldn't read her smile. And he wondered about the kid. It was late. He got to his feet, hoping she'd sense the signal. But she seemed oblivious. He squeezed past her, set his plate on the sink.

You should get rid of that bloody beard, she said. Look like a science teacher, for Chrissake.

Well, I was for a while. More or less.

What'd you teach?

Geography. And biol.

Shoulda known. All them books there. Always liked ya books, eh.

Yes.

And ya little orange bible.

That too, he said, closing off despite himself.

Now you're cranky.

No, he lied.

Don't be cranky, mate – I just need a break. You know what I mean?

I think so.

Do it all on me own.

Yes, I can see that.

It's lonely.

Yeah.

I should get used to it. Like you. You don't even like people, it sticks out like dog's balls.

He shrugged.

But me, I'm stupid, I still like people.

Nothing stupid about that, he said, trying to sound sincere.

Mind if I close the door?

It's hot, Gem.

Open door makes me nervous.

He said nothing. She bumped the door closed with her hip and as she turned back her shoulder brushed the kid's drawing, left it askew on the fridge.

I was thinkin, she said.

About what?

Nothin real complicated.

Okay, he said, feeling corralled there in the narrow galley.

But it's a secret. You can keep a secret, can't you?

I guess, he said, alert to her approach. She was fully lit up now. Her limbs seemed slightly unwound. It was hard to discount the shape of her in that little dress.

Why don't I walk you back? he said, moving slightly towards the door.

But I'll tell you the secret first, she said, taking his arm as he tried to pass. Here, I'll whisper it.

She tugged his collar, drawing him in so close her winy breath filled his ear and he was unravelling before she even whispered it. The simple, blunt declaration was like something spearing deep. It found the softest, neediest part of his being and yet he still tried to separate himself as delicately as he could.

Gemma, mate, I don't think that's a good idea, he said.

Jesus, Tommy, don't make a girl beg.

I mean, I'm flattered, more than flattered —

But you want it. I can see that.

Yeah, but why me? Why now?

Because you're safe, and I'm goin fuckin spare up here. We could both do with cheerin up. Carn, cobber. Old times' sake.

She slipped a hand into his shirt. He felt her belly against his crotch and her tongue was still cool from the wine. He let his hand fall against the curve of her hip, then her arse. And he didn't care anymore about how crazy this was. She tasted of garlic and smoke. She kissed with a kind of smile. A friendly fuck, that's all she said, something safe, and it began that way, awkward and companionable in the slot between the fridge and the kitchen bench, but by the time they'd reached his unmade bed with its grey sheets and its bovine whiff of old spunk and perspiration the upwelling of all that desperation and longing overtook them and they were both fierce, half mad with painful urgency and nothing they wanted or did felt safe.

Afterwards he lay in a sheen of sweat and mortification. It seemed weird, even wrong to be thinking of Harriet. Of that night in the reeking village on Sarawak when a week of hurt silence had broken like a bruised monsoonal sky. The sex had been furious, frightening, and in the aftermath, for the remainder of their coastward trek, he was haunted by the growing sense that their belated passion signified an end and not a renewal, as if the force of that night were from a seal finally, fatally blown. But he'd buried the thought; he was like that, he knew it now, he could carry disaster with him, pressing on as if it might wither in the dark if ignored.

That was nice, said Gemma, head lolling against his chest. Better than a visit to the funny farm.

He tried to smile. At himself, at her directness. Here he was with all his tics and anxieties. He should take this for what it was, a bit of comradely relief. That's all she meant by it. That's all it could be.

What's the matter? she asked.

Nothing. I guess I just didn't see it coming.

You didn't want to?

It's not that.

Cause it didn't feel that way to me.

He pulled her to him, felt her hair spill across him.

Good old Tom. You need to see everythin comin, don't you? You're that sort.

And after it's arrived I'm the kind of sad bugger who has to look a gift horse in the mouth.

Which isn't a real flatterin way to talk about a girl.

Sorry.

Her laugh was low and inflammatory. He wished they could just stop talking and go back to fucking. She felt it. She reached down between his legs.

Aw, Tommy. Tom Keely.

Stupid, he said.

Who?

Me, he said.

I just suddenly wanted to.

Suddenly?

Well, gradually. And then suddenly. Like a *bastard*.

Wow.

Nothing wrong with that, is there?

He shrugged.

What?

Nothing.

Jesus, she said. You really, actually wanna know why, like a list of reasons?

Oh, maybe not, he said.

Right, then, she said briskly, as if drawing the discussion to a close.

It was confounding, delightful, having Gemma Buck here, stroking him idly like this as the building rumbled and clanked. It was unimaginable.

I don't even like birds, she muttered.

What?

Birds.

Oh. Okay.

Like, I had a good day, don't get me wrong.

But you don't fancy birds, he said, finding it hard to concentrate with her thigh slippery against his fingertips.

Fuckin hate em.

Pretty common phobia.

It's not that, she said impatiently.

Well, he said, stuck, aching, distracted.

Shit, you don't know what it was like for me.

What what was like? he said, hearing the weary tone of his voice.

Blackboy Crescent.

Well, I was there, wasn't I?

No, she said, letting him go. I don't think so. Not the same way I was.

What're you talking about?

Different for you.

Because I moved away? Because I went to university? Geez, Gemma, he said, sitting up abruptly. What is it with you?

You want me to go?

No, Keely lied, pulling away, embarrassed now by his uncharacteristically durable hard-on. This whole scene was just too bloody peculiar; an awful mistake.

I think I'll go, she said, turning away.

Kai's alone, he said, as if it mattered more now than it had fifteen minutes ago.

Yeah, she said. Thanks for the reminder.

She reached for her clothes.

Wait, he said. I'm sorry.

No worries. No hard feelins, eh.

What were you saying? What is it I don't know?

Doesn't matter.

Please.

It doesn't. Not anymore. Well, it shouldn't.

He stretched across to where she sat, fingered her hair in a way that seemed to irritate her. He watched the curve of her back, the heavy tilt of her breasts. She smelt of smoke and sweat and come and now she did not want to be touched.

You shoulda used a condom, she said. Jesus, I need a shower.

Shower here.

I should go.

Stay a minute.

You just want to fuck me again.

I thought we could talk, he said, which was half the truth at least.

No, I'll go.

Just tell me, he said. This thing. About birds.

She sighed. She was quiet for a long moment.

They make me feel bad. Sad and guilty, sorta thing.

But they're just birds.

See, when I was a kid, men wanted me.

Yes. It's . . . it's —

Shit, that's what it is. And it wasn't my fault. I thought it was just Baby. She was older. She didn't mind so much. But I didn't want it. Christ, I didn't even know what it was, what it meant. They were always touchin me. Even the way they looked was like they were touchin me.

Oh, mate.

In the end you kinda give in. But before that I still had some fight, you know? But it meant I did somethin rotten, shockin.

Who could blame you? I mean, hell.

When I was eight I set fire to somethin. It wasn't an accident – I planned it. Thought about it for days. Figured out how to do it. In cold blood, you know?

Like a car or something?

It was an aviary.

Keely jerked upright, nearly tipping her off the bed.

Bunker's birdcage, he said. That was you?

I hated him, that grimy old bastard.

He had a bad leg. No, a club foot.

Caught me in his yard once. Lookin at the budgies and the finches and the cockies. Said he wouldn't tell no one. He got me by the hair, the plaits, pushed me up against the wire and all the birds are goin crazy, all claws and beaks and flappin. And he says things to me a little girl shouldn't have to hear. All the time, those birds rushin at me, my face hard in the wire, and he's got his hand right up me, like a bloke pullin the gizzards out of a Christmas turkey.

Keely's gorge rose. He sat beside her, close but not touching.

I shoulda told your mum, she said, her voice flat, almost deadened. Nev woulda fuckin killed him. And I wanted him to. But I was embarrassed, afraid – ashamed, I guess. And I wanted to fight, you know? Fix it meself.

But. Eight years old.

I got petrol from the can near the mower. Nev's mower. Tipped it into a shampoo bottle. Waited till Bunker was out – the races or somethin, down at the pub, I dunno. Went around the back, squirted everythin. Whole cage. Them poor birds goin spare. Just lit the match. And whoof! Lucky I didn't set meself alight. They were like crackers goin off, all those poor birds. Just flames flyin and screamin. Like Catherine wheels, they were. It was fuckin horrible. I wish I'd done his house instead. Wish I never done it.

That was really you?

I used to wonder if they suspected and didn't let on. Nev and Doris, I mean. Protectin me. Sometimes I wish they hadn't. Because afterwards I had no fight left. I just put up with it. Not from Bunker. He didn't dare. But there were other blokes.

Gemma, I had no idea.

Well, I never told, did I?

We should have known. They should have stopped it.

Back then, nobody was lookin the way they look now. Ya mum'n dad, they didn't see it. And I couldn't tell em.

Keely thought of the plume of smoke, the fire engine arriving, the almost festive air in the street, and Faith's pronouncement at dinner that whoever incinerated those poor birds didn't deserve to live. Were the Buck girls there at the table?

He died, y'know. Years later. Old Bunker. And I reckon he always knew. I went to his funeral for a laugh. I was as pissed as a rat, but it felt great.

She reached for her dress on the floor, fished around for her ruined knickers but cast them aside and stepped into the dress.

Look at you, she said. Buyer's remorse.

No.

Doesn't matter. I got what I came for.

Chicken and sage in white wine.

Yeah, she said with a hoarse laugh. Here, zip me up.

You're only a couple of doors down; it's dark out there.

Girl's still got standards.

This evening notwithstanding.

As she presented her back he felt a pang of lust but resisted the urge to pull her to him. He saw that old man with her hair in his fist, pressing up behind her. Keely touched only the zip and stepped back as she turned to survey him in the crooked light.

It's alright, he said. I'm still safe.

Safe enough. Anyway, it was a oncer. There's the boy to think of.

Sure.

But it was fun, eh. I always wondered.

Well, I guess now you know.

She smiled and he followed her through to the door, and heard the bars of the walkway still jangling after she was gone.

It was there again. The stain. Or a dirty great blotch just like it. Right in front of the slider. Only a step or so from the balcony, on perfectly dry carpet. A ghostly macula at a distance, but close up there was no missing it. The size of a sleeping dog, curled in front of the smudged glass. Smelt of nothing but nasty nylon carpet, though underfoot it was crisp, almost crusty. Shit a brick, he didn't need this at the beginning of a new week, staggering bright-eyed and bushy-tailed into the frigging Shroud of Turin. And having woken this early and so clearheaded he wasn't about to squat here all day scratching his head and reading entrails. Rare as rocking-horse turds, these days, feeling halfway to decent, with barely a sick twinge, and he was damned if he'd waste it.

Even though the sheets smelt sweeter this morning, he stripped the bed and bagged them with a couple of other loads he left churning in the laundromat on the ground floor. Walking past the soup kitchens and dosshouses, he considered starting the day at Bub's where he was safest, where there was less to provoke a flare-up, but he felt sturdy enough to sit out on the Strip and watch the weekday circus stir itself into inaction. He didn't know if this was confidence or masochism, but he strode along the avenue of coloured brollies and set himself down on the prime corner where the view was good and the coffee decent. He marked his territory with his sunglasses and a Rupert-rag he filched from an abandoned table. He went indoors, as was the local custom, and queued up to order. You had to love it, the way a cafeteria could still pass itself off as an actual café. Well, so be it, he thought. When not in Rome. Et cetera.

Due to the early hour there were only five or six in line ahead of him at the counter and it wasn't such a long wait by Freo standards. Even at the top of his game, when his social capital was enviable and the glaze of his armour seamless, this procedural ordeal was like being paraded in front of the class, like a perp walk, with the haughty baristas before him and the watchful lurkers at every table behind. Keely focused best he could on the comestibles in their brightly lit cabinets, the delicious oily reek of milled beans. He crabbed his way to the cash register, stood in the receiving line like all the other supplicants, and emerged unmolested with a pretty decent double espresso and a blueberry muffin like a bloated toadstool. His ten-dollar sunglasses were still on the table but the shopsoiled newspaper had been botted by someone else. No matter, it'd served its purpose, which was worth a nod in the great man's direction. Wherever that was. Now that he was ubiquitous, multinational, omniscient, perhaps even eternal.

The sun was out, the shadows black and deep beneath the awnings. The first suited skateboarders were hurtling by with backpacks and briefcases. Women in pencil skirts and four-inch heels minced their way towards the train station. Keely settled in, nursing his mood as much as the coffee, in order to watch and marvel.

He felt a rare and comradely magnanimity as locals arrived to stretch their yogic limbs and kick off their Berserkenstocks.

Here and there, once his eyes adjusted, he recognized the odd face: a chanteuse fiddling with her manky dreads, a couple of Labor Party grifters, the retired QC and his jaunty little mutt. Across the street at safe distance, a Greens claque conferred behind a stockade of bicycles and to his relief followed their daffy MP into the juice joint in the alley beyond. All around him dogged Aquarians discussed positive energy, bodywork, and the Real Causes of Cancer, and it was nothing to him, water off a duck's proverbial. Close by, right at his elbow, a spidery Amazon with a shock of henna began to shout into her phone about social evolution and personal transformation. She'd moved on from revolution, she said, but she still believed passionately in radical change. She was rather fetching in her saffron tanktop. Perhaps she mistook his indulgent grin for something untoward, for she snatched up her towering soy latte and stalked off to another table, sallying on without a comma.

By nine almost anyone who did anything productive in this burg had cast off their lines and steamed out to sea or hustled to the station for the express to Dullsville. Which left quite a crew of idlers like himself who seemed to have nowhere to be and nothing to produce. He wondered how many trust funds kept the bustling Strip in business, how much could be attributed to middle-class welfare. The moment he thought it he began to feel his serenity give way to pangs of unfocused guilt and anxiety. The entire scene was a festival of procrastination. And it was amazing how snugly he fitted.

He couldn't help but think of all the charity kitchens only a few blocks away, the underclass gathered alfresco for a sandwich and an industrial brew. Invalid pensioners, denizens of the dosshouses, park sleepers, wharf rats, outpatients of the failing mental health service. At this rate he'd be joining their number soon enough. He guessed rough-sleepers and drunks had their own resolutions and rituals of deferral. Street shouters were armed with excuses; he'd heard their litanies of grievance and misunderstanding. He'd slot in handsomely. If only he wasn't so soft. The moment would surely come. And then he'd hit the final barrier, the stubborn middle-class conviction that his was a special case. When really he was just a creepy fuckwit poncing through town full of peace and love because he'd got his rocks off. A tipsy grandma desperate for a root had hauled him into bed and given him a blowsy seeing-to. His triumphal glow was pathetic. And that was nothing when you thought of the aftermath. Her confession. To which he'd listened distractedly, still pawing her, like a grimy priest who couldn't distinguish her needs from his own. He disgusted himself. In an instant he felt oblivion stalking, crackling, flashing behind his eyes, and he welcomed it, deserved it.

His glass shattered on the pavement. The saucer wheeled in woozy arcs at the feet of startled loungers. One arm flapped independent of him and as he stood and fled he clawed it into submission with the other, breaking into a shambling run through a wilderness of spots and sparks.

Furious blank.

A kind of.

Kind of.

Kind of turbulence.

Suddenly down by the marina. Standing, walking. Sleepwalking, really. With gulls like empty thought bubbles overhead. How many minutes had he lost? Ten? Twenty? Closer to forty. Jesus!

Okay.

Tamp down the panic.

Okay.

Nothing you can do about it. Well, nothing you'll let yourself do. Being what and who you are.

Alright. Whatever.

So.

Here he was.

The marina. The fishing-boat harbour. Prawn trawlers, cray-boats. Yachts. Boardwalks. Finger jetties.

He must have had something in mind. During his little lapse in transmission, while the test pattern flashed on and on inside. Some destination, a plan, a notional refuge that eluded him for the moment. But here he was. The marina. Where, yes, he had spent a lot of time in better days. Their little sloop that Harriet referred to as *The Folly*. Okay, he thought. This is where you've brought yourself. Old circuits firing. So walk. Walk it out, walk it off.

And as he did he let his safer thoughts unsnarl themselves slowly. Could only think of them as coloured wires now. All brittle, everything ginger. Couldn't get straight, shiny lines anymore, no orderly layout like something fresh from the shop floor. But he could separate them, more or less, even if they were still nested around that awful pulsing void, the dread he'd been hauling about the past few months. It had no size or shape. Its origins obscure. It was his own dark planet. Within him. And there was absolutely no point in giving it direct attention; it was simply there, he accepted it now, thrumming like something about to detonate. But with sufficient will, bending every perilous thought aside, keeping all wires from touching, you could shrink it from something planetary to just a blemish, a fleck, like a tiny bit of shadow-matter tracking momentarily across the sun. Safer, better, not to look. Took such a shitload of energy, though, powering it down by mental force. Just to make some space and turn your thoughts to lesser mysteries. Like how to make a living, first and foremost. Because it really was conceivable that before Easter he could be working on his grimy street tan like those poor buggers lining up outside St Pat's. If he didn't pull up, if he didn't shake this self-pitying jag he was giving into day upon day, it wasn't just possible but inevitable.

He couldn't let Doris keep propping him up. She'd paid his phone bill. He owed it to her to get his shit together.

He shuffled away from the boardwalk and the tourist traps, tailed by a posse of gulls. Busy little pricks, gulls.

He thought about going back to teaching. Still possible, wasn't it? If he could tidy himself up, get his nerves in order. It would weird people out, having him there again, considering what he'd been doing. He was too long out of the game. Things had changed. And now public education was like bearbaiting. He'd faced down proxy thugs of all species, from robber barons to the unions. But he shivered at the prospect of being left alone in a room with thirty 15-year-olds. Maybe something non-contact, a support role? Which had its own complications. Given that he'd probably burnt a few bridges in the bureaucracy over the years. There were heads of department who'd make certain his applications were regrettably unsuccessful.

Which left what – gardening, driving a taxi? For all his skills and achievements these were his best chances and he should bloody well get used to it because to the pollies he was poison, too dangerous, too likely to say something uncomfortable. A decade and a half of supreme self-control and in a few minutes he'd rendered himself a rogue forever. In the media he was a heretic, a traitor to progress.

No NGO could possibly risk hiring him. And in the broader environmental movement he would always be the Great Disappointment. The deepest darkest greens thought he was a hero, but their admiration wouldn't butter his bread.

He wondered, briefly, about the private sector. Consultancies employed all sorts of colourful folks: disgraced premiers, tycoons jailed for massive frauds, sportsmen with blemished records. There was stuff he could do – lucrative, too. But it would be mercenary work.

Of course the resource sector would take him on in a heartbeat. On the quiet. That was his Patty Hearst option – join the revolution. They wouldn't need to parade him like a hostage; they had plenty already. They'd just pump him for intel. Plans, policy positions, databases. All those establishment donors from the Golden Triangle they could woo back to the fold with a little pressure from old school chums. A few discreet threats of a purely social nature. He'd seen it done. And who knew the who-where-what like he did? But just thinking that way made him feel grubby.

This was what happened now. It was occurring everywhere. People reduced to toting up whatever made them valuable to the market. Which was to say the bosses. They'd approached him, well before the blow-up. A big mining corporation looking to spritz up its greenwash. The bastards had more propaganda money at their disposal than most nation states. For every eco-ad from a cash-strapped NGO they'd publish fifty lavish fakes. Top whack. Full pages in broadsheets and sixty-second prime-time TVCs. They stood some tame khaki naturalist in front of a red gorge or a bit of forest. A few lies, a couple of half-truths and there they were, all logo and soaring music. Australian Miners – nature's greatest custodians. And not a hole to be seen. At the time he'd pretended not to understand what they were asking of him. Now he was desperate. And he knew they'd come back. There were unopened emails with jaunty subject headings he'd consigned to the ether. But he'd never do it. Anyhow, his value would only last a few weeks. He'd hardly get through betraying himself and his comrades before he found himself on St Georges Terrace with nothing but a cardboard carton and a non-disclosure agreement.

No, he was a fuckup, but not a turncoat. Which was something to hold onto, wasn't it, Doris? Wasn't that the upside?

The gulls gave him up as a dud prospect. He wandered past the boatlifters where someone was blasting a hull clean. The noise was like a dentist's drill. Made his hair crackle. Sent him on to the sardine jetty with its spangly glitter of scales from the morning's haul. It reeked, but the smell was comforting, homely.

The upside.

Who knew, maybe Doris was right. Perhaps the CCC would vindicate him. He could eventually launch civil action. Years, it would take, during which he'd be grooming his victimhood and paying for the pleasure all the while, and that would be worse than living like he was now. No, let them do their procedural polka – he just sought a bit of order, maybe a low-key job without excitement or stress. A quiet life. As himself. Because he was still largely himself, wasn't he? Perhaps not the Tom Keely of old, but still within reach of him. His principles were intact. He wasn't totally threadbare. Not morally. Was he?

He was staring at the blunt, pitted face of a mooring bollard. As if he'd been addressing it. Beseeching it, even. And maybe he had been. Yes, he had. But, glory, look at this thing. It was massive, bovine, the size of Lang Hancock's head. Like an inscrutable idol shorn of its horns. In the face of Keely's puny human query the iron plug radiated mineral contempt. It was indifferent. Which was as it should be. After all, it wasn't fair on hardware, being expected to dish out spiritual advice.

He stepped away. But for a moment he couldn't walk straight. Too hard to navigate and manage his thoughts at the same time. He settled for a limestone boulder in the lee of a boatshed. Stared at the junk washing against the seawall above the little coomb where the old slipway had been.

No, he wasn't so sure what he was anymore. Didn't feel so righteous. Not after last night. It was one thing to have felt favour at last, however brief. What disturbed him was not the sex but the talk. Gemma telling him about Bunker. That was her mistake and he didn't know how it could be undone. She thought he was safe, as if he'd earnt that kind of trust. But he was just another randy bloke staring at her legs, yearning to touch, and such misplaced trust frightened him. Whole thing was a bloody mess. They had nothing in common, the two of them, just kid stuff and middle-aged loneliness. And now he was stuck with her. Or without her. Whichever. Only three doors from his hideout. Every day from here on in. With the kid. Who set something off in him each time they met.

So now he was doubly bound, trapped like a bug in a jar – addled, livid, dizzy, butting his head and turning circles. Making a damn fool of himself. Wilting in the full shock and awe of the sun, losing minutes like a man shedding dandruff. He should go home, find a hat at least, but he was so restless. And the pain wasn't terrible. He could see fine now. Better. And the boats were everywhere, beautiful, familiar, diverting.

He got up and walked on through the clutter of docks, sheds, jetties and dealerships into the hardstandings where yachts, cruisers and workboats stood on chocks and hung in slings to be scoured and anti-fouled. The air stank of diesel, grease, paint, fibreglass, and Keely tried not to think of all the toxic crap washing into the sea. Someone else's fight now.

He sidled between buffed hulls and scrofulous strakes, beneath stepped masts and exhaust-blackened transoms as drills and sanders wailed in the bellies of launches, ocean racers, gamefishers. He suffered a boyish twinge kicking through teak shavings and bundles of rags, cable-ties, trimmed electrical wire, steel swarf. As he thumbed a burnished bronze prop he thought again of *The Folly*. And was rescued from another sad jag by the sight of Wally Butcher's clapped-out van.

He hadn't seen the old rogue to speak to for a year or more. Wally was always in and out of these yards and in better times Keely had enjoyed running into him. Wally was old-school. But since losing Harriet, the boat and then the job, Keely had dodged him guiltily, waving at a distance or faking preoccupation. From shame. Perhaps even vanity. And it was rotten. Ducking the old coot. Because Wally was loyal as a cattle dog. Forty years of hurt and bafflement and not once had he heard the man offer a harsh word about his father.

He'd only been a boy when things went wobbly between Wally and Nev. In the days when most tradesmen were happy to work for the council or a government works department they'd gone into business together, made a go of it on their own. Just a pair of working-class blokes, they were, but they went hard at it, balls to the wall, and had begun to make some headway. Before Billy Graham and his groupies showed up. Before Nev and Doris went all 'different'. Before Wal was left holding the rag. By all accounts the divergence hadn't been gradual. Not that it was acrimonious, just bewildering. For the Keelys it was a sudden, radical shift, a total explosion of reality. Happened to lots of people those years, often only a momentary enthusiasm, but for Nev and Doris it was deep and lasting. In the wake of their religious conversion they were fundamentally realigned. And even for Wal, who bore the brunt, whose life was overturned in a manner less joyous, it was impressive – even frightening – to witness.

Nev did nothing in half measures. He was an all-out, open-throttle bloke, and in one blinding 'Just as I Am' moment he was letting the dead bury their dead. And the partnership, if not the friendship, was chaff to the winds. He just walked from the business and went out saving souls with Doris. No one could blame Wally for feeling bitter, not after what it cost him to save things singlehandedly and press on. Said it was twice the work and half the fun. He'd survived financially, but without his mate in it with him it was suddenly just work. Nev was lost to Christ. Yet by some miracle of agnostic tolerance the friendship endured. And even if

Wal's teeth were gritted he did his best to give Nev his profane and tender blessing.

Keely remembered him from Saturday afternoons in the garage. His feral sideburns like long streaks of grease as he looked up from the entrails of a Norton. The footy yammering away on the old bakelite radio. Wal was forever urging young Tom to pull his finger, rewarding him with a fart redolent of meat pies and lager. Evenings on the back verandah, the men sat in a pair on the bench seat from a wrecked EH, often speechless in the last light of day. You could sense something solid between them. Despite Jesus. And all the lost Sundays.

Oh, the sight of Wal in church. The only time he ever came. Staring up at Nev in the pulpit. Wal's face blank and closed like the ex at the wedding. That's how he'd looked at the graveside, too. Like a man spurned all over again.

Keely angled up to the familiar van. It was parked alongside an old plank riverboat some fool was busy pouring his savings into. Beneath the scaly transom, a midden of tools, rags, oil filter and sump. Between torrents of Wally's bilious imprecation, snatches of talkback radio rose like the fumes of something noxious from the bilge. Keely stepped onto an upturned milk crate and beheld the hairy arse and the King Gees protruding from the engine hatch.

What's that in there, a Cummins? called Keely in the blokiest voice he could summon.

Perkins, came the gruff reply.

That's all a Perkins needs – a greasy one-eyed butcher. Can't this joker find a proper mechanic?

Wally hauled himself upright and peered evilly over the gunwale. It took a moment for the old bugger's face to rearrange itself.

Tommy bloody Keely, he said with the makings of a grin. How are ya, son?

Ah, I'm alright.

Christ, by the looks of ya I think you might be kiddin yeself.

Keely laughed. Okay, he said. I'm shithouse. How are you?

I'm old, son. If anyone could find a spare paddock they'd lead me out there and put a bullet in me from kindness.

You don't look too bad, said Keely. For an ugly old bastard.

Jesus, you look like your old man with that bloody beard. Where you been?

Oh, I'm still in town.

Don't see you on the telly anymore.

Nah, they rissoled me.

Well, you did call that fat cunt a crook. And on the telly, no less. I did.

So yer old man was wrong, then. The truth won't set you free.

Keely shrugged indulgently.

So, what'll those shit-stirrers do without ya?

They seem to be coping.

Pity, said Wal. Got used to seein ya every other night. In ya fancypants suit. Stirrin the possum.

Constraining our great economy.

Makin us all feel guilty for fuckin the world up.

Traitors to progress, Wal.

Tree-huggin homosexuals, the lottaya. Strippin the hair off a man's chest.

Keely laughed; the old bugger was only half joking.

Need some work done?

Nah, said Keely with a grimace. Boat's gone. Only the tinnie left. Just walking past, really.

Once a victim, eh? They get ya, boats. They're not as much fun, but women are cheaper, son.

I thought you might've retired.

Who can afford not to work? said Wally, looking him up and down appraisingly.

Well, some have greatness thrust upon us.

And how're you enjoyin it?

Don't ask.

Hittin the piss, by the looks. So, how's that girl a yours?

Keely's wince was enough.

Well, shit. You are in the wars.

Nah, that's old news.

Wally wiped his hands on a rag and climbed out over the transom to sit splaylegged on the boat's marlin-board. He was a short, fat man, bald and speckled with sun lesions. He sported a glass eye. And it was immediately evident he did not favour undies.

No bulldust, with that fluff on your face you really do look like him.

Nah, said Keely, basking a little despite himself.

You know, he'd be as old as me now. Think of that, eh? He never got old.

You're not *that* old, Wal.

Well, youth has flown, sunshine. There it is. Unlovely fact.

Keely dipped his head. In this man's presence he felt about fifteen years old.

Just think of it, but. Last time I saw him he was younger'n you.

Yeah, I do think about it. Too much, these days.

Well. We got that in common, then. That and our good looks.

Keely stood there toeing a ravaged drive belt.

He's a hard one to live up to, Wal.

But you're a chip off the old block, son.

No.

Any mug can see it. Out there savin the world from itself. Callin it as ya see it. And gettin ya tit in the wringer for ya trouble. He'd be proud, the mad sod.

Hey, said Keely, trying to break the drift of the conversation. You still ride a bike?

Piles and all.

Never give up the Norton, eh?

'65 Atlas.

Nev swore by the Trumpy.

Hate the Poms, love their bikes, said Wal with a grin. His teeth had not fared well.

Keely felt soft as a chamois, perilously vulnerable. He was suddenly apprehensive about what the old fella might say next.

Your mum orright?

Keely nodded.

Bloody fine woman.

She is.

How old are ya, exactly?

Forty-nine.

Truly, ya do look like him, son. At the end.

Keely felt the jab in his guts.

And I don't say it to make a prick of meself.

No? he asked, smarting.

As a mate, son.

Really.

Him and your mum – they never went soft, didn't fake it, never gave up. If his heart hadn't give out, he'd've been up and back at it. That was him, what I loved about him. He had that boilin thing in him. You know: *Fuck this, let's do somethin about it.* Of all that churchy talk, son, it was the only thing rung true to me. Like he said, believe what ya like. Think what ya like. You'll be judged for what ya do. Even if ya cock it up. Die tryin. You were a kid, I spose. You won't remember.

I remember, Wal.

Well, just bloody make sure ya do.

What're you saying?

I dunno. What would I know? Just don't roll over and go soft.

Show some family pride and stick it up em.

The old man looked at Keely a long moment, eyes lit up. But blinking, too, as if remorseful. Sensing he'd let himself get caught up and had said too much.

There ya go. Advice on life from Wally Butcher. If ya didn't look broke I'd send you an invoice.

Always happy to listen to wisdom, Wal, said Keely tightly. Anything else while I'm down here?

Always pay cash. And try not to piss in the shower.

Shoulda brought a notebook, said Keely.

That's all the nuggets I got, son.

Well, it's plenty to be going on with.

Wally rooted around in his shirt pocket a moment and passed down an oil-stained card.

Give us a call sometime – we'll go crabbin.

No worries.

And say hello to your mother.

I will.

Sure yer orright?

Yeah, he lied.

Here, shake a man's hand, why don'tcha.

Keely shook his big, gnarled, greasy paw and stood gormlessly for a moment until Wally hoisted himself back into the bowels of the boat.

His father.

Once more.

Forever.

The father.

Keely walked homeward stung but more or less coherent, as if Wally's bluntness had momentarily unscrambled him.

Lame that it always came back to this. Faith said he was a man who needed reminding he had a mother, a parent who had not been dead thirty-five years.

Yet there it was. The father-shaped hole in him, hot and deep and realer than any notion he had words for.

Neville Keely. Forever the young bear. How would he have fared, had he survived? This was an era for reptiles, not bears.

Would he have faced down the shellacked bump and grind of the evangelical super-church, the evil sugar-drip of prosperity theology? Imagine him taking his stolid, courageous Bonhoeffer into that swamp of co-option and collaboration. Maybe Wal was right. If not for the heart attack he might have still gone out and kicked some iniquitous arse. Or perhaps he'd have moved on to subtler work like his widow. And it was true, Faith was right, Doris had only become visible to Keely once the old man's gigantic presence was gone. Still, he left a hell of an absence. It was harder all the time to distinguish reality from myth. And he'd known for years that he modelled himself upon a memory. Probably unwise. But impossible to let go, even now.

How could you measure up? There was no longer any grand striding towards justice and equality. In this new managerial dispensation change was incremental or purely notional. Big gestures were extinct. Even on YouTube messianic figures arose and evaporated in hours. And yet he knew his father was not just a man of his time. For all his own triumphs as an activist, the forest coupes spared, the spills exposed and species protected, there'd be no one talking about Tom Keely in thirty years. His father had exceeded the bounds of his class and refused to follow the template of his generation.

He had nine years of school to his name. Married a wharfie's daughter, put in ten hours at the workshop, four in nightschool, enrolled at a provincial bible college and took theology units by correspondence, then waded untimely into parish affairs, bringing a bit of shopfloor pugnacity to matters of the spirit. The man remade himself, then tried to refashion the entire world around him, which was his making and breaking, Keely knew it – and by comparison he felt like a coaster, the inheritor of another man's social and moral capital. From his baby-boom standpoint of generational ease, it was hard to credit just how hard Nev had worked, how far he dragged himself, how wildly he swam against the current.

Keely only had to recall how wrong his father looked in church. He simply wasn't a suit man, wouldn't even consent to wearing the Pelaco shirt or brown brogues of the true evangelical. Doris said that in his jeans and workshirt he looked like a wrestler impersonating Woody Guthrie. He was for the little bloke, the reject, the no-hoper. He bellowed about saving bodies as well as souls. Keely could remember it vividly: the early excitement in the drip-dry congregation at having this rough beast suddenly among them, the parishioners thrilled at being groovy enough to hire him. And the queer cocktail of pride and shame he felt as a boy hearing Nev preach.

It was only a matter of weeks before you could feel the first troubling currents of resistance from the pews. And it came so quickly, that awful Sunday evening when the string-lipped elders froze Nev out, cast him off, sent him packing with his dirty commo outrage to all that was sacred and true. After which, though the times were a-changing, no mainstream outfit would have him. So followed a period when Doris and Nev ran house churches and drop-in centres that were warm and anarchic and better suited to all the Keelys' gifts and temperaments, and it felt, in retrospect, like the sweetest time for all four of them. Just a few good and happy years before the biker church rumbled into town and everything went sour.

They were a glamorous, sinister outfit, those Harley-riding holy rollers, and their local chapter only lasted a year, but for a few months Neville Keely was their front man, their bighearted dupe. Revvin Nev, riding high, open throttle, steering Christ's hog down the highway, imploring easy riders not to blow it. Never knowing what he'd signed up to, how the power was distributed. And it was painful for Keely, recalling how fast his adoration had curdled.

All through his boyhood the old man had been a moral, physical giant who only grew in stature. He was Christ's own viking, all love and thunder. And then, at the cusp of Keely's adolescence, once this biker thing took hold, his father suddenly looked like another goofy old fart on a Triumph spouting peace, love and understanding. It was Keely's guilty secret, this creeping shame, relieved only by Nev's complete humiliation when those octane Jesus freaks turfed him out on his arse and began legal proceedings against him. Nev had discovered and then robustly challenged the bikers' impervious conviction that they were British Israelites, and must be, therefore, a whites-only outfit. He'd signed stuff he hadn't even read, heard arcane wafflings he hadn't bothered to take in. And he didn't understand that he was dealing with a corporation as much as a church. He fought on like a man who believed justice would prevail. And they ground him down until he'd mortgaged half the house to pay the legal fees. He never surrendered. But he wore himself into a ruin. Keely remembered him in a cane chair beneath the almond tree, praying, weeping, his beard full of crumbs. Soon afterwards the heart attack carted him off. And they were alone, his mother, his sister and him, in debt, bewildered.

A good man, his father, but not always smart. It was only when he was gone that Christ's puzzling injunction to be as wise as serpents and innocent as doves began to make brutal sense. Indeed it became a rueful family motto. To which Doris and Faith had been trying to return Keely's attention for several years. And they were right. In both marriage and work he'd become more angry than effective, more impatient than observant and more honest than useful. Wal saw him as a chip off the old block. And maybe Gemma did too. But he was just not that man.

Silent and backlit, the boy stood in the doorway. He was no more substantial than a blur. The minute he ghosted into the frame, filling the space with his peculiar static energy, something about this lack of resolution caused Keely's hackles to rise, as if some unknowable danger hung in the supercharged air about the boy. Keely snapped upright in the kitchen chair, awake now but unsettled. He'd dozed off right there, sunburnt as a ten-pound Pom. Leaving the door open like that. An open invitation to chaos. A week ago he'd never have been so lax.

But it was only him. If indeed he was awake. And if the blur in the doorway was only a child.

He waited for Kai to speak. But the only sounds pouring into the flat were car horns and wattlebirds. A tiny jet of panic. Sudden irrational fear.

Kai?

Keely leapt to his feet. The suddenness of it set off a thud in his head. He was truly awake. He approached the screen door.

Only a boy. Flushed in the face and barefoot. In the ugly little shorts and stretchy polo shirt that passed for school uniform these days. His helmet of hair, fine and fair, riffled in the breeze.

The boy gazed impassively at a point just past Keely's hip.

So, said Keely, clawing back some calm. How's school?

Good.

Well. That's good.

Nan said you're comin tonight. For tea.

Oh, said Keely. Am I?

The boy pressed his hand against the insect screen and it puckered his flesh in rigid patterns.

Alright, said Keely like a man hypnotized. What time?

Tea time.

Well, he said, recovering a moment. That seems fair. You want to come in for a sec?

I've been here before.

Oh. When?

I was stuck, said Kai.

In here?

No words, said the boy in a strange, flat tone. Things didn't work. I wasn't feeling right. Something had to take me.

Keely peered at the kid. None of what he'd said made any sense. And the child's delivery made it queerer still. Kai looked past him, and then a moment later directly at him, only it felt to Keely as if he were looking straight through him, and it rankled.

Just run that by me again, he said, lowering himself to Kai's eye level.

But the kid backed away.

Kai?

He was gone. Seconds later Keely heard the clack of the door along the way.

Gemma's place was smoky and cluttered – a couch, a big TV, some posters on the wall, a potted ficus by the slider, a midden of washed laundry on the coffee table. The layout was identical to his, but her flat felt homelier, more lived-in.

She looked pretty in her denim skirt and sleeveless top, but she was subdued. On the tiny kitchen table Kai had a book on raptors open at a picture and description of the brahminy kite.

He haunts that library, said Gemma, setting some chops into a pan.

I was the same, said Keely, taking in the third chair pulled up to the table.

Don't worry, I remember. Always had your face in a book.

No wonder I never noticed anything, eh?

You want a beer? she said as if she hadn't heard him.

Nah. But you go ahead.

Can't, she said. I'm workin tonight.

The boy seemed content to leaf through his book undisturbed. Keely watched Gemma cook the meal briskly, without flourish or fuss. He didn't quite know where to sit or stand, what the evening was about, how he was placed, but he was glad of the invitation, appreciated the brief sense of propulsion it afforded him, and there was something lovely in the domestic fug of this flat: a woman, a child, food being prepared. This was the life functional people lived and he had to guard against it setting things off in him he couldn't manage. He was nervous. About her more than anything.

He leant against the bench savouring the curve of her butt in its denim skirt. Impersonating a man at his ease.

When the food was ready Gemma set the plates down unceremoniously and they sat, the three of them, around the scuffed little table. Keely made too much of the lamb chops, the mash and the peas. Gemma suffered his praise and directed him to shut up and eat and so they ate shyly, silent but for the low mumbling TV, the burp of the sauce bottle and the scrape of cutlery. The meal was like something from Blackboy Crescent: the three colours on the plate, the dull sheen of laminex, the mist of sheep fat in the hot evening air.

Keely couldn't help but observe Kai. The boy segmented his food with precision, aligned it on the plate by size and category, and chewed gravely, consuming his meal with the unhurried method of a lonely spinster, and it was only when he addressed the wicked finger of fat on his chop that he became, in Keely's eyes, a child in whom he could see himself, a kid – avid, exultant. He tried not to smile, lest it disrupt the boy's hermitic concentration. The adenoidal snuffle, the hunched wings of his shoulders. Here, surely, was a kid without friends, a boy who was an island of self-possession. He was peculiar. Compelling in a way.

Keely felt Gemma watching, and wondered if he was paying the boy too much attention. He smiled at her. She gave him a thin grin of uncertainty, maybe regret. Was she having second thoughts about this, him, last night? For here they were. A woman alone. A friendless child. A man adrift.

You had a sister, said Kai.

Keely saw the boy peering his way, as if emboldened to examine him. Perhaps it was the abruptness of the inquiry or the boy's use of the past tense that left him stranded.

Tom? Gemma said, prompting. Your sister?

Oh, said Keely. Yeah. I do. I still have a sister. Her name's Faith. Your nan used to sleep in her room sometimes.

I don't have a sister, said Kai.

No?

No brother, too.

Still, said Keely. You've got your nan, though, eh?

The boy nodded but appeared to find this fact unimpressive. Now it was one discomfiting moment after the other.

The kid scratched himself. Gemma's irritation flared.

Look at you. Wrigglin around.

Itchy, said Kai. In the underpits.

Cause you're a dirty sweaty little so-and-so.

So-and-so, said the boy. He seemed to be testing the phrase but Gemma took it as mockery.

Into the shower, she said with force.

What about icecream?

We're out.

The boy blinked. Once, twice. It wasn't incomprehension; it was protest. What a thing they had going, these two. Gemma burred up, the kid needling her blankly.

There's no damn icecream, orright? So git.

Kai gazed at Keely a moment as if considering an appeal.

You heard, said Gemma.

The boy retreated to the bathroom. Keely squirmed a little, said nothing.

When the water ran Gemma lit a fag and sat back, cradling an elbow in her spare hand. Smoke coiled towards the open slider, grey, sinuous, reeking, and she squinted a little, following its passage in a manner that seemed studied, the way a smoker can make something out of nothing or, indeed nothing at all from something, with a struck pose and a bit of business. Not that you could blame her. Here he was, surveying her, cataloguing her really, from across the table. And sensing this, why wouldn't a woman arm herself with a little performance? What could she be thinking in the wake of last night, having gone to bed with the ghost of a boy, a wreck like him, out of raw need or the false safety of nostalgia? She had to be wondering what she'd done and how to extricate herself, having him right here in the building. Dinner was probably a gesture of kindness, a gentle kiss-off, the neighbourly thanks-but-no-thanks.

And then as he watched, Gemma's face was overtaken by a crooked grin.

Underpits, she said indulgently. Bugger me.

He's a good kid, Gem.

When he was little he had *eyebrowsers*, too.

Eyebrowsers. I like that.

Keely relaxed a moment. He set his knife and fork together on the plate and sat back. She tilted her head, amused.

Doris taught us to do that.

Do what?

All that table manners stuff. Elbows off, elbows in. Wait for the cook to start, close ya mouth, knife and fork together at the end. *May I please leave the table?*

Geez, he said. Sounds a bit uptight.

She had standards, mate. Nothin wrong with that. She knew shit. She taught me how to read, you know. And about girl things. Showed me how to plait me own hair, used to brush it for me morning and night. I used to sit in her lap and get dreamy. She smelt like apples.

So did you, he said. It was the shampoo.

Thought you didn't remember anythink. About me.

Well. There you are.

It was beautiful, my hair. Inside I was rubbish. But on the outside, them golden plaits, I was a friggin princess. And look at me now.

It was beautiful hair, he said.

Nah, it was just trouble. Honey on a plate.

Oh? he said, as if he didn't know what she meant.

A bloke pulled a hank of it out once. Whole bloody handful. Spose it's one way to express your undyin love. Couple of times I nearly cut it off meself anyway. Wished I was a nun. Not that God's any different. All hard feelins from Him in the end.

Keely had nothing to say to any of this. He was not remotely competent.

Gemma stubbed out her cigarette, raked a hand through her faded hair and gathered up the dishes.

I'll do these, he said. You see to Kai.

Suit yourself.

Keely filled the sink and peered through the curtain. The window could have been his own. Same sink. Same terylene curtains. Same view of the war monument and the date palms on the hill. The human things were unfamiliar: the cheesy knick-knacks, the Blu-Tacked posters, the potted cactus on the bench, the happy snaps in Kmart frames. But the bare brick walls, the mean, low ceiling, the shifty parquet floor in the kitchen – they were no different. For some reason it made him smile. A totally separate life being lived in exactly the same space. That was the Mirador for you. Ten floors of architectural uniformity. And within it, all these folks resisting replication. The thought gave him a stab of fondness, for people, for shambling, ordinary folks. Yes, for just a moment he loved his crooked neighbours with his crooked heart.

Then it occurred to him as he rolled suds like lottery balls through his fingers that she was right. After all, what were the odds? Of his being him instead of Gemma. And the pair of them, decades later, finding themselves here in identical containers like the tools of some finicky technician.

As he dried and set everything on the bench behind him, he listened to Gemma and the boy in the bathroom. Then closer, in the bedroom. She had a gruff way with the kid familiar from Keely's own boyhood but no longer approved of in middle-class circles. Kai's voice was toneless. And Keely wondered what that was about. He could barely imagine the life the boy had endured. Endless uncertainty. Disorder. Probably worse. It'd be cruel for her, seeing her own childhood repeated like this.

On the bench, stood up in a ghastly quilted frame the colour of smoked salmon, was a photo of Kai as an infant in the arms of a girl Keely could only assume was his mother, a pretty-enough blonde partly hidden by the outsized lenses of her sunglasses. The infant Kai stared at the camera as if trying to decide what was necessary. To smile? To stay still? To keep the peace. Looking at him there, with his silky hair adrift, he could have been Gemma in the sixties.

She was sixteen when she had him, said Gemma.

Keely swung about and almost dropped the frypan. He didn't like to think how long she'd been there. Reading his thoughts, all his social judgements, his anthropological musings.

Gem, she looks lovely.

She was. Once.

Like you, he said.

Gemma grunted, displeased.

His Nibs wants you to say goodnight.

Oh? Oh. Sure.

Keely didn't need to be shown the way to the bedroom. But he managed to feel a little lost along the way, for it was suddenly strange territory. Harriet had nieces and nephews but Keely hadn't been in a kid's bedroom in a very long time. He felt a snag of panic. And sensed Gemma watching from the doorway, doubtless smiling, finding his awkwardness comical.

Given its mélange of boy-things and woman-things – Motocross posters and high-heeled boots, face creams, action figures, bras, boxer shorts – the small bedroom was orderly if not strictly tidy, and it smelt a whole lot better than his own, cigarette smoke or no. There was a queen-size bed. A couple of boxy side tables. The standard miserly built-in robe.

Kai sat bare-chested beneath a sheet. His Bart Simpson pillow lay alongside Gemma's flouncy shams. As Keely stood wiping his hands anxiously on the back of his shorts, Gemma came in, snatched a few things from the end of the bed and went through to the bathroom.

No nonsense, she said before closing the door. You hear me?

Keely raised his eyebrows mischievously but the boy did not respond. With the door shut and the shower running, he stood a sheepish moment before sitting at the bed's edge. Perching. The boy smelt of toothpaste. He had a vee-shaped scar just beneath his collarbone. His skin was creamy as if he'd never been outside without a shirt. Perhaps it was the way these days. Safer. But it looked foreign, this ghostly pallor.

The boy shifted beneath his sheet, impatient. Keely didn't like to get too close in case they touched inadvertently. Kai looked over as if assessing him.

Can you tell a story?

A story.

About eagles.

The boy's face was plump and round and serious. Yesterday's sun lingered on his cheeks and along the soft bridge of his nose. To that small degree he was comprehensible to Keely. Just this bit of colour made him an Australian child in a way he recognized.

Um, well. Okay. A story about eagles.

I don't care if it's make-up.

Well, I used to know a song.

About eagles?

Keely wasn't sure about this. He was way out on a drooping

stalk here. Hadn't seen it coming. The sudden memory of the devotional chorus; it had to be about this morning, the memories of Nev and Doris and all those fireside church-camp singalongs.

But I don't know if I can sing it, he said a little desperately. It's been a long time.

Orright, said Kai flatly, as if accustomed to build-ups that went nowhere.

And it stung Keely, spurred him into croaky song. He just lumbered into it. Like a man pitching himself off a ledge.

We will fly with wings of eagles, he warbled in a key too high to sustain. *We will rise and fly away. We will run and not be weary. We will walk and not be faint.*

Okay, said Kai.

That was a song I knew when I was a boy, he said, flushing. It just came to me, that's all.

But have you got a story? asked Kai as if he were prepared to put this embarrassing interlude behind them.

Right, said Keely. Yes. Not a story so much. But I know one interesting thing about raptors.

Nn?

You know from your book an eagle is a raptor, right?

A kind of bird. What hunts.

Pretty much. Well, did you know that when they do hunt, when a raptor grabs something, its talons lock up? Its claws – they kind of go on automatic. Like the osprey. It dives for fish, mostly. Imagine what it's like when it gets hold of something too heavy to lift out of the water. I saw that once, on a documentary, a film on TV. This great big bird underwater, trying to drag itself up with a huge fish way too big to carry. It couldn't heave itself out of the water, couldn't even get to the surface, but couldn't let go. It was locked on. Fighting up through the water with its wings. Like something you've never seen in your life. This great white bird hauling itself up, trying to fly against the ocean.

Kai blinked. Keely sensed, too late, that this was hardly bed-time fare for a child. He'd gotten carried away, florid as a souvenir teatowel.

One day, said the boy. The birds in the world will die.

What? he asked. What did you say?

In the end, said the kid. All of them, the birds. They die.

Well. Yeah. I suppose everything dies eventually.

I saw pictures. All the birds dead. On the beach, in town.

Ah, he said. Right. That. Jesus, he thought, I'm in the weeds here; this is way too close to home.

And then I knew, said the boy. One day all the birds in the world will die.

Kai, he said, trying to keep himself in order. That was lead poisoning. It was an accident. Well, actually a bad mistake. It's just a terrible thing that happened because people were lazy and stupid.

Keely knew it was so much worse than that. But he shouldn't be thinking about it right now. Had to let it alone for his own sake. And yet his mind had already run ahead, flashing on it, dragging him in. Esperance. Ten thousand birds killed. An entire town con-taminated. Vegetable gardens, watertanks, clothing, food. Kids poisoned. Because of how easy it had become to do business in this state. There was nothing in the way of the diggers and dealers but hot air.

Look, he said too brightly. It's over, Kai. It's fixed.

The boy didn't seem convinced.

This is where it begins, Keely thought, the lying to children. He had to stop thinking about this shit. Right now.

Dinosaur birds went extinct, said Kai.

What's that? he said, tamping the tremor in his hands.

Bird dinosaurs, they went extinct.

Yes. Yes. That's right. A long time ago.

The boy yawned.

Now it's just bones.

Yes.

And birds will just be bones.

Well.

Extinct, he said through another yawn. Like us.

But our birds are okay, Kai. And we're okay, too.

Keely could not believe what he was saying. He'd never lied like this in his life. And he'd broken into a sweat.

The boy slid down the pillow, pulled the sheet to his neck. Keely felt a little knee brush his hip as the kid rolled on his side and looked up with drooping lids.

Extinct, he whispered, as if tasting the word, trying it on for size.

Everything's fine, Kai. It's all going to be okay.

Orright, you two, said Gemma in a billow of steam. Lights out.

Keely felt the urge to ruffle the kid's hair, to pat him reassuringly, but he didn't dare. He felt Gemma waiting for him to leave.

Night, mate, he said on his way out.

The light clicked behind him as he went through to the livingroom; he thought he might slip away while he had the chance. But it felt wrong not to stay and thank Gemma for the meal. The mute TV flickered on – another bit of evening trash masquerading as current affairs. He saw his hands trembling, shoved them in the pockets of his shorts.

Gemma came out in her powder-blue tunic. She dropped a cheap pair of gym shoes on the seagrass matting and while he stood there, trying not to look at the chipped paint on her toenails, she spread a towel across the corner of the kitchen bench and set to ironing a fresh pair of school shorts.

How long've you been doing this? he asked, still standing.

Sometimes she dumped him. Other times I took him off her. And now I've had him a coupla years.

The iron swished breathily. The old fridge kicked into life.

Tough, he murmured.

Well. What can you do, eh?

You work at the place on the corner? That's handy.

Did, she said. Now I'm up Canning Highway. They shoved me across a month ago. Bloody buses hardly ever come when I need em. Spend half me pay on taxis. It's shit, really.

Keely was stuck for a moment. For want of something to fill the gap, he gestured at the travel posters gummed to the raw bricks of the wall. Coconut palms and sunset at Kuta. A smiling child feeding the dolphins at Monkey Mia.

Which did you prefer? he asked.

Prefer?

Which place did you like the most?

I do speak English, Tom.

Sorry.

Never been to either of them, she said dismissively. Kai found the posters at the Vinnies.

Wrongfooted, he made the neutral sound any nitwit makes stalling for time. He stared hopelessly at the clunky old Telstra phone and the notepad beside it.

Gemma turned the shorts over, sighed at a paint stain, and finished ironing them.

Listen, he said at last, surrendering to failure. Thanks for dinner.

Just chops.

It was nice.

Gemma set the iron aside and looked him up and down as if considering something. Keely thought he saw an idea retreat from her face. He took up the pencil beside the pad. It seemed that every page had a different bird on it, sketches and doodles Kai had worked on. Many of them bore no resemblance to any bird he knew, but the kid had given all his creatures wings.

I'm just writing down my number, he murmured.

We know where you are.

Right, he said, steadying himself to remember the digits. But you're off to work, he's here on his own. I mean, in case you're worried.

I'm not worried.

I know it's none of my business.

But.

I don't mind looking in on him.

He's fine, she said. He's used to it now.

For a fleeting moment Keely thought he could detect a hint of regret, as if she wanted to take him up but daren't. He wondered if it was last night, the lingering implication of a transaction. Or just pity, having seen how hopeless and awkward he was.

Well, the offer's there.

Sad. That you didn't have em.

Kids?

They fuck you up, anyway.

Every good thing does, doesn't it?

She shrugged and he felt himself gently dismissed.

At the door she patted his arm. He hesitated. Then pecked her on the cheek. And pulling away, saw that it irritated her – the hesitation, or perhaps the kiss itself. She closed the door on him before he'd even turned to go.

With the laundry all done and no dinner dishes to deal with, Keely found himself at a loose end. A stroll perhaps. But he was still tenderfooted from this morning's fugue-walk around the marina. And he hardly had the funds to entertain himself in town. Not at a pub and certainly not the bottleshop. He couldn't afford them, not in any sense. So there was no other choice but to stay in. Which left what? Google? While he still had access. Either that or the rich tapestry of network TV. He'd given up on the Norwegian novel – couldn't concentrate.

He should clean the flat. That'd burn an hour or so. And God knows it needed doing. But just thinking about it made him wilt.

He was tired. His brain felt scorched. Too much sun. Too much happening and too quickly. And he didn't want to think anymore, not tonight. Being with Gemma. Her strange kid. The Esperance fiasco bringing him back to the boil. He needed to break off, cut the frigging circuit before he shorted out. Needed to calm the fuck down. His bloody heart was pelting. So shower again. Clean towel. Brush your teeth. Jesus, that face. Eyes like crushed strawberries.

Just paracetamol. Two. And nothing else.

And lie down. Fucking head. Like there's sand in it. Just lie there. And go to sleep like a normal person. Sparking.

He tried a few of the relaxation exercises Harriet had gone in for. Lying back on the righteously clean pillowslip, endeavouring to ignore the slightly shrunken feel of his sunburnt face. He was tired enough – wasn't he always tired? But getting over the edge was the objective. Once you tilted out you were alright. And there was no feeling so sweet as falling. So over half an hour he huffed and cooed himself into a swoon. And for five, maybe ten minutes he was close, giddily close, projecting, wafting out towards the purple New Age precipice, beyond which only sleep awaited. No thinking, no puzzling or raging. Just sleep. Goneness. Paddocks of sleep, forests of sleep, valleys and rivers and churning gorges of sleep.

And he was almost there, right at the cusp, when he heard it. The whimpering wall. Those cries of fear. The noise that made his arse pucker in horror. His neighbour. So clear, so close. She sounded as if someone were in the flat with her, standing over her, slavering, ready to do something unspeakable. But there was nothing he could do. She was alone in there, duking it out with herself, tormented by something that descended on her like the weather. You could feel her cringing, hiding, balling up, quiet-ening a moment until she gathered herself, became defiant, cried out, cursing whatever it was at her shoulder, commanding it to get behind, and then retreating, finding a rhythm, falling into the grunts and chants that saved or ensnared her, poor beggar. It was horrible to hear: and there she went again, off and riffing, on a roll now, louder, more insistent, uglier, more desperate and distressing every second. Oh, Christ!

Keely sat up.

How could someone so troubled be allowed to live ten storeys in the air? How was it she hadn't hurled herself from her balcony already? And how was it, for that matter, that he hadn't done so himself in order to be free of her? The poor creature – why couldn't they help her, why couldn't they just cart her the hell away and let him sleep?

Get out! she growled. Out! Out-out-out-out-out-out-out-out!

He belted on the wall with a shoe. She fell silent a moment, as if startled by the intrusion, then she muttered darkly, cried out once, plain and shrill, and resumed the chant.

Keely got up, flailed about for the dinky iPod, and shoved the buds in his ears. He tried a bit of Delius to calm himself, but quickly discovered that the first cuckoo in spring was no match for the nutjob next door. Yelping and barking through the wall, she was more cuckoo than anything the London Philharmonic could come up with. What he needed was a fortress of noise, his own sonic Monte Cristo, but Black Sabbath seemed in poor taste in the circumstances. So he chose a bit of Captain Beefheart, despite how perversely it brought Harriet to mind. He shouldn't be thinking about her like this. She hated Beefheart, the opaque melodies, absurd lyrics, the man's savage, grating voice. Keely cranked it up, hoping to match madness with madness, and he blasted the poor woman out of range, cast her into a lake of fiery tumult which gave him wild relief, before the guilt set in and his head began to fizz and his thoughts returned unhelpfully to Harriet.

She needn't have gone. They might have gotten past it eventually, outlived the catastrophe she'd brought down upon them. He could have lived with it, with what had happened; he was convinced of that. Hadn't he forgiven her? She thought he had to be cracking up, just by saying it, but could simple forgiveness be such a threat? Apparently so. She said it frightened her when he was like this. So weird and jerkadelic, like his stupid Beefheart albums. So florid and manic. As if he thought he were a character in a Russian novel. It was creepy. It wasn't normal.

It was no good.

He ripped the buds from his ears, lurched up off the bed with a sickening suddenness and weaved out into the livingroom, tormented afresh by thoughts of Harriet and her baby. The other bloke's baby. He had to get off this jag, stop thinking about it.

So many half-clear weeks on that front and he was back to flaying himself with something he could never fix. It was unsound, unhelpful; it unhinged him and rendered him pathetic, laughable, immobile. Et cetera.

He stood at the open sliding door to watch the orange lights of container cranes strobing across the north quay. Beyond them, like a fence against the darkness, the channel markers flashed red and green without ceasing.

Gemma was right. They fuck you up. Even the ones you don't have. Especially them.

But enough of that. He needed to be asleep, to be gone from this.

As he wrenched the knife drawer open all the matt-plastic bottles rolled away as one. He snatched up the first serious-looking container within reach and got it open and pitched a bunch into his palm. The tap water tasted metallic. And he wondered if that was how a horse tasted the bit, whether it tasted anything at all.

The phone.

Phone.

Phone.

That really was the phone ringing. So far away. So close to his head.

Waking was like clawing his way free of something dark and heavy. But he was, in the end, awake. He lay panting. The phone brayed away on the side table. He craned to see the luminous digits of the clock – 2:15. Not good. If he really was awake, then this wasn't good. Unless it was Faith in London, forgetting the time difference; that was just an accident, that'd be harmless.

He snatched the thing up. There was only breathing.

You're kidding me, right? You're fucking kidding me. Who is this?

Tom?

What is this?

Tom?

Tiny, feeble, fearful voice.

This is Kai.

Kai?

Yes.

What – mate, what are you doing up? It's the middle of the night.

Yes.

Are you okay? Keely asked, gathering himself a little. The building was quiet. Down on the docks a container hit the deck of a ship with a muffled boom.

There's a dream, said the boy.

You had a nightmare?

It's a dream.

Did you call your nan?

She's busy. It's work.

You want me to give her a call? I don't have her mobile number.

It has to be important.

She'd want to know you're alright, Kai. Wouldn't she?

A dream, said the boy, is not an emergency.

Well. Okay.

It's the only job she's got.

I know, mate.

She has to have the job. Or the people take me.

Keely hauled himself up. He pressed his head against the bricks.

Kai, no one's gonna take you. You want me to call your nan? I think I should.

No. You can't.

Okay, Kai. Alright. You want to talk for a bit, until you can get back to sleep?

Yes.

That's fine. We can talk.

Here?

We can't just do it on the phone?

The boy was silent. Stayed silent. Keely tried to steel himself against it. He couldn't be doing this. This would not look good. But the kid held out. Diamond drill-bit silence. Boring into him.

Okay, he said at last. Alright, Kai. I'll be there in a moment.

Keely switched the light on, began casting about for his shorts, maybe a shirt. The wall furred and buckled slightly. He wasn't right. Not even close.

Up at 1010 the kitchen light was on. Through the terylene curtain he saw the wiped bench, a mug, a tin of International Roast. The curtain twitched and Kai's face appeared. Keely gave him a goofy thumbs up and hitched his shorts woozily as the lock clunked and the door sat back. For a moment, the boy was just pale mist in the narrow gap. Keely felt himself being scrutinized, as if the kid needed to make certain it was him. Keely smiled as reassuringly as he could, given the hour. He steadied himself against the gritty wall.

You want me to help you get to sleep?

The boy shook his head.

You want to talk?

Kai scratched his scalp, expressionless. Then he pulled back the door.

Keely hesitated a moment. He was reluctant to cross this threshold but he didn't fancy standing out here in the walkway in full view at this time of the morning.

He stepped in. The flat still smelled richly of lamb fat. The boy closed the door.

What about a glass of milk?

Kai shook his head.

On the table was the battered library book on raptors. Beside it lay the pad with Keely's number on it.

Keely sat at the table. Kai stood opposite, hands pressed against the laminated edge at the height of his bare chest. There were tiny purple anchors in the cotton of his shorty pyjamas. Dockers jarmies. And the kid had brand-new football boots. One day, he thought, one day I must take him for a kick. This season I'll take him to a game.

You had a dream, then?

The boy nodded.

What sort of dream?

Flying, the boy murmured.

I have flying dreams, too, he said scratching his beard. I like them.

The kid looked sceptical.

What happened in your dream?

I crash, said the boy. There's people there. With only eyes showin. And I can't talk.

Hang on a sec. What did you crash?

Just me, said the boy.

You crash to the ground?

But there's people there, with only eyes. All black. And just eyes. Behind them it's . . . fire.

Fire. Like a crashed plane?

No.

So . . . what kind of fire?

Fast. Shooting.

You mean *firing*? Was this like a movie, Kai?

The boy rocked a moment, considering. He nodded, but without conviction.

You're flying. You crash to the ground. And there's people on the ground. And they only have eyes?

They talk, said Kai, eyes clouded with awe. But, not proper words.

Like aliens, like space people or something?

Kai shook his head.

Then what happens?

They go away.

Where do they go?

They're kind, I think.

Wait, Kai – how do they go? How do they leave?

The kid twisted his pyjama bottoms intently.

Everything goes away, he said. Soft.

Soft?

Like, no battery.

Ah. Like a game?

The boy champed his lip. Like I die, he said.

Wow, said Keely, leaving no time for this thought to hang there. Then what?

Kai shrugged. I'm laying there and I die.

Then you woke up, right?

He nodded.

And you were here at home, right as rain.

Kai nodded again.

Well, it's just a dream. You don't have to worry about something like that.

Sometimes it's not me.

You mean you've had this dream before?

The boy nodded, yawned.

How many times?

Kai looked at the backs of his hands as if calculating. Seven? he said uncertainly.

The boy appeared to have wilted a little. Keely wondered if it was prudent to keep asking him questions. He was way out of his depth already.

But you're okay now, he said. You're safe. Everything's good, eh?

The boy blinked. He was clearly exhausted.

Maybe you should hop back into bed. You want me to sit with you for a bit?

Kai nodded. Then took himself to the bedroom and climbed onto the mattress. A fan oscillated on the side table, pushing the hot, clothy air about. Keely sat at the foot of the bed. Kai fixed on him.

I'm right here, Keely whispered.

The fan droned. Somewhere in the thin-skinned building, a pipe flushed. A can rolled down the side street in the freshening easterly.

We're okay, Keely whispered, willing it to be the truth.

He woke in sunlight with Gemma standing over him. Before he could properly focus on her face and what she was saying, he saw the Bali poster over her shoulder, the waves of coconut palms, the wrongness of where he was. He hauled himself upright on the couch. Dawn light spilled onto the kitchen bench.

Shit. What time is it?

What're you *doin* here? she hissed.

I don't know, he said thickly before catching himself. Kai. I didn't —

He's got school, said Gemma. Jesus, he knows not to let anyone in.

As she leaned over him, whispering fiercely, he smelt sweat and coffee and cigarettes. He struggled to his feet. His back hurt.

Sorry, he croaked. He had a nightmare.

He went to your place?

Yeah. Well, no. He called.

Christ, he shoulda called me. What sort of nightmare?

Calm down, Gemma, it's alright.

You don't stand in someone else's place when you're not sposed to be there and then tell em to calm the fuck down.

Okay, yeah, I'm sorry.

Jesus. Just go, will you.

I think it's something he's seen on the telly. The war maybe, or some science fiction thing. He's alright. He was careful.

Careful be buggered. He knows the rules.

I meant to slip away, he said, busking it now. I just sat here a minute to make sure he was really asleep. I was worried about leaving him here alone.

He registered her flash of anger but before she could speak Kai was in the doorway, looking circumspect, wary of both of them.

Tom's just headin off, said Gemma.

Keely gave a little wave, but from the kid there was not a flicker.

Still woozy, and with a beach towel around his neck, Keely limped to the shed behind the laundromat. As a pair of welfare mums watched from the second-floor gallery, sharing a fag and a few laughs at his expense, he extricated his bike from the snarl of greasy wrecks and wheeled the old Malvern Star across the carpark at the rear of the building. He wobbled out onto the side street, rounded the corner and noted, as he rolled by the front of the building, his neighbours wan and silent heading for the bus, the train, the boss. The forecourt was baking already, and he was glad to leave the whole place behind a while.

On soft tyres he pedalled through the morning streets as they stirred, past discount stores, supermarkets, cafés, keeping where he could to the footpaths to save being mown down, and within a few minutes he was in the residential arc between the marina and the beaches, where he felt safe enough to tool along taking in the weatherboard cottages, limestone semis, peppermint street trees and vine-strangled verandahs. The old neighbourhood was a comfy mix of prosperity and bohemia, where the Kombi lay down beside the Beemer, and the little garden patches in front were either wistful references to Provence or a homely riot of hippified vegies and bougainvillea. The further south you rode, the more prayer flags there were strung from porches, the more bikes and dreads you saw, and the thicker the reek of patchouli became.

He pulled up a moment outside the old house. Its lovely window sashes were freshly painted. The jarrah boards of the verandah had been oiled. And there was a silver Prius gleaming in the drive. Alerted by the familiar creak of the front door opening, he stood on the pedals and teetered away.

Along Marine Terrace, tradies in idling utes sucked choc-milks and wolfed meat pie breakfasts as brokers pulled into the boatyards and dealerships in Mercs and Range Rovers. A few seedy live-aboards weaved in from the marina on their rusty jetty bikes, all deckshoes and earrings, abroad in search of coffee, sex and cheap labour.

Keely pushed on past the stockaded perimeter of the yacht club and on to the grassy apron behind the dunes. At the open-air showers a woman hefted a woolly mutt beneath the spray; holding the dripping pooch to her breast she looked blissful in a way that didn't bear examining. He leant the old crate against a casuarina and picked his way through the eternal dog shit to the water.

Stripped down to his Speedos, he plunged in by the rock groyne. The sand bottom was a creamy blur and the water delicious. But his limbs felt heavy and uncoordinated and it took a little time to find a rhythm. Eventually he settled into a long, reaching stroke and for several minutes thought of nothing at all except the feel of the sea. But by the time he reached the southern breakwater he was back to wondering what it meant for a child to dream of falling – not just flying, but crashing to his own death surrounded by faceless aliens. And what did having such a dream repeatedly say about Kai's mental health?

Keely couldn't get it out of his head, the plausibility of the kid's description – or was it more an intimation? – of the actual sensation of dying. Like a failing current: *no battery*. You couldn't ignore that; it was alarming. Though what could he do? He'd already overstepped as it was. And now the shutters had gone down. He'd pissed Gemma off. There was no mistaking her fury. He'd be back to keeping his sorry self to himself. And he should be glad.

He swam until the acid built up in his shoulders and his lower back began to tighten. Inshore, locals gathered in gossiping knots – long-shanked men, women with high, late-life bellies. They all hurled sticks for galumphing mutts, their sun-fucked faces shining with adoration. It was a village of cults, Fremantle, but of all the twisted sects it harboured, surely the dog folks were the hardest to take.

He waded ashore, breathless, mindful of where he trod, and as he retrieved his gear and towelled off, he felt restored, even modestly cheerful.

But of course when he got to the grass beside the casuarina, his bike was gone. No sign of it in the saltbush thickets nor the maze of trails behind the ti-trees. He scouted south towards the kiosk and the carpark where weed-dazed backpackers were only now beginning to spill from vans in the heat, but it wasn't there.

He trudged homeward alongside the rail line. The low fence was festooned with purulent yellow bags of dog shit. These daily offerings were part of the liturgical practice of dog folks. Who bagged their pooches' turds, tied them into gilt baubles and either left them on the sand or hung them here on the fence. As evidence of their good intentions. To be collected later. Which of course they never were. And after an hour or so the contents began to fester in the heat until they became objects of penitential contemplation for wayfaring pedestrians. Haste-making incense. The collect of the day. And Keely was, in the spirit of things, both hastened and incensed. He was impressed to the very limits of derangement. How could they be matched for devotion, these dog folks? What a spiritual service they did! Doubtless, good people and true. And yet smug and dozy fuckwits all the same. What else could these golden offerings, these buzzing prayer flags be except emblems of right-thinking, evidence that actions were but paltry moments of attachment? This wall of ordure said it all. It was *so Freo*.

Of course, he might be a little bitter. A tad jaundiced. And his day wasn't shaping up as he'd hoped.

He held his nose. Pressed on. Mocked by the wet slap of his thongs.

Fucked-fucked.

Fucked-fucked.

Fucked-fucked.

Yeah, very funny.

Googling aimlessly, sniffing the panic abroad, Keely wondered how Faith's rescue mission was faring. He hoped that whatever she was saving was worth the sweat. It was two degrees in London. Maybe not so much sweat.

Knew he shouldn't be looking. Letting himself be persecuted by the news cycle like this. Given what it did to him.

A noise outside. Someone scraping against the security grille on the way past. The door was closed. He was in full lockdown. Back to business as usual. Whatever happened out there did not interest him. He had to learn from the dog people. Rise above mere shit.

But there it was again. That sound. Like somebody saw-ing against the insect screen with a fingernail. Irritating. Hard to detach from. Given it made the hairs rise on the back of his sunburnt neck.

The screen door opening. Bloody cheek of it. The Mormons were in the building. Or worse, someone from the body corporate.

Then knocking. One-two-three. Tiny knocks, too timid to be official. Perhaps the lonely demoniac next door. Seeking garlic.

Keely yanked the door open. And there was Kai. In clammy school kit. Clutching a book to his chest. So small. So fair. Making his heart jump. It must be after three – God, where had the day gone? He struggled to reassemble his expression for the kid's sake. He had the face of a monster; he could feel it.

Kai, he said.

The kid blinked. The wind ran through his hair. His uptilted eyes were dark, his gaze was cautious, even apprehensive. Then averted entirely.

Where's your nan?

Kai tilted his head towards home.

She know you're here?

The boy pursed his lips eloquently.

Kai, I don't think she's very happy about last night.

Kai did not disagree.

She won't like you coming over without her knowing.

The boy held the raptor book face out, presenting it at arm's length.

What's up?

The kid peered past him to the roasting interior of his flat where the westering sun was having its way.

I don't think you better come in, mate.

I was here before, said Kai.

Yeah, you said.

The boy took the book in one hand and raised his arms from his sides. Keely's first thought was of a bird, that he was stretching his imaginary wings, but then he thought, Underpits. The kid was letting the breeze cool his sweaty underarms.

Maybe you should run along. Your nan won't be happy. This morning was my fault. I fell asleep.

It wasn't a osprey.

Sorry?

Kai opened the weathered book and pointed to a photograph.

It wasn't a osprey, said the boy, what we saw at the river.

Kai pulled the book to himself a moment and rifled through pages. He presented a double-page spread of two similar birds side by side. Pressed it against Keely's chest until he accepted the book, surrendered his attention to it. Over the page were diagrams and silhouettes. Tipped into the gutter fold was an old envelope with Kai's markings in felt pen. They were dihedral representations of a soaring bird, the first with upswept wings and the other with wingtips tilted earthward.

White-bellied sea eagle, Keely read from the text. *Hunts on the water. Doesn't dive under.* Did our bird dive?

The boy shook his head solemnly. Keely thought back. The thing had swept down off the bluff, smacked the surface of the river and hauled itself away.

Well, he said with a grin. Inconclusive. But you might be right.

Am right.

Okay, I stand corrected. Even so, this bird'll still take a rat, so I consider myself in the clear. But let's just say it, for the record. I was wrong and you, my friend, are right.

The kid didn't smile. Either he'd forgotten the rodent that set all this off or he didn't understand. Or perhaps he simply didn't care.

You've been looking closely at this.

Kai said nothing.

Hmm. *Preys on reptiles, other birds, mammals, fish.*

And carry-on.

Carry-on? he said with a grin. What's that, like, luggage?

The boy looked at him blankly.

What is it?

Carrion? Well, anything really. Creatures that're already dead. You know, lying there.

Carrion.

He'll sweep down, cart it off. There we go: *immature individuals often confused with the osprey.* Well, Kai, he said, handing the book back. You're a smart kid.

The boy chewed his lips.

What? asked Keely.

Kai averted his gaze.

Kai, what is it?

The boy drew the book to him carefully.

Is there something you want to say? You look worried.

You mad?

Mad? Keely asked with a dropping sensation.

At me.

Oh, he said with a sick grin. Of course not. Why would I be angry? How could I be angry with you?

Kai hugged the book, his shoulders tipped inwards, his gaze lowered. A screen door clanged up the way. The boy took a glance to his right and though he couldn't see her Keely knew it was Gemma. Man and boy stood silent, even apprehensive, in the seconds it took her to arrive, clacking down the gallery in hard shoes. She pulled up in something black and short and sleeveless. Her hair was raked back in a barrette and she wore truly high heels, shoes of a sort that could not be ignored, not even by a man like Keely who knew nothing about clothes and for whom women's shoes were an abiding mystery.

What're *you* lookin at? Gemma asked.

Nothing.

They're just shoes.

They were ridiculous shoes, porn shoes. They showed off her legs. Everything, now he let himself look. Felt a little nutbuzz despite himself.

Just shoes, he said, grinning.

Ignoring him, Gemma addressed the boy.

Told you to ask first.

That's a good idea, said Keely as much to her as Kai.

She was staring at him now, weighing something up.

What? What is it?

I gotta be somewhere.

Keely said nothing.

I can't take him, she said.

So lock him in. I'll keep an ear on him.

Well, he's here now.

And?

Can you look after him for me?

You really can't take him?

Forget it, she said, reaching for the kid who sidestepped her effortlessly.

Don't be daft, he said. Of course he can wait here.

I'll be twenty minutes.

Take your time.

Just keep him inside, orright? Keep him safe.

We'll be fine, he said. Won't we, Kai?

The kid didn't even shrug.

And then she was gone, clopping down towards the lifts, bum bouncing sweetly, dressed to impress someone else entirely. For twenty minutes. They stood in his doorway a while, Keely and the boy. He could still smell Gemma's cloying perfume. The boy gave off no sense of having triumphed. He just moved past Keely and went inside. Keely followed, pleased and slightly nervous.

When he looked around for something to feed Kai he saw that all he had in the place was a bowl of oranges. The kid didn't seem keen until he offered to peel one for him. Perhaps it was a juice thing, or not knowing how to get the skin off. But once the fruit was on a plate, bare and slightly furred with pith, Kai was all action. He was fastidious, almost obsessive, about breaking the orb into segments. He fanned them around the plate, anxious to avoid any juice-letting, and when everything was laid out to his satisfaction he took a piece and began to suck at its point with great care.

Keely did little more than sit back and watch. That round face, the silky hair, the paleness and self-possession. He seemed slightly damaged, and yet he was so bright. Keely knew nothing about kids but this boy was too sharp for his age.

I know all this, said the boy, pausing a moment to look around. I've been here.

Keely opened his mouth to speak just as a pair of doves fluttered onto the balcony. Kai flinched. After a moment, as if embarrassed, he recovered his affectless poise.

Doves, said Keely, getting up to wave them away.

Doves aren't smart.

They're supposed to be peaceful, said Keely. But they're always crapping everything up.

Birds are first, said the boy, the orange segment flaccid in his hand.

First at what?

First to die.

Keely was flummoxed. This fixation. How did he get straight to death from a pair of doves? What was happening in his head? A six-year-old. He was scary-smart, but he couldn't have read Rachel Carson. Perhaps he'd seen something on telly, a show about canaries and coalmines. Keely hoped to God he hadn't set this off himself with all his faffing on about seabirds.

Kai got up, looked at his bare feet a moment, as if arrested by a thought or a sensation, then stepped up to the sliding door to gaze out. He suckled at the crescent of orange and with his free hand he touched the tips of his sticky fingers to his thumb in steady alternations, like somebody recalling music or the lines of a poem.

I'd never lived up so high before moving here, Keely said. Strange, isn't it, being able to see so far – out and down.

Kai made no sign of having heard.

Isn't it weird, the way you *look* out there and you *feel* yourself going out at the same moment?

Kai turned and surveyed him and immediately he regretted saying it; this was not the sort of thing you said to a kid ten storeys up, especially not a kid with falling dreams – and, fucksake, not a kid who leapt off the balcony in your nightmares. What was he thinking?

You go out, said Kai, agreeing. But it's okay. It's just your eyes.

Exactly, he said, sounding in his relief like a dolt.

Keely had never had a thing about heights but some days up here it was too much to simply stand your full measure without being giddy. Talk like this was not helping. But he was fascinated by the kid, wanted to catch what he was seeing and thinking.

Kai pressed his brow to the screen, wheezing slightly.

So, what're we looking at down there?

Just me.

You're down there?

Sometimes.

Like a grownup? Walking around? You imagine yourself like all those people down there one day? You know, being in the big world?

The boy thought about this a moment. No, he said.

Where are you, then, what are you doing when you see yourself?

There, he said, pointing down to the paved forecourt.

What are you doing?

Laying down.

Resting? Asleep? Just lying there?

Kai sniffed, gave the slightest of nods.

Can you see it now? Kai, are you down there now?

The boy sucked his bit of orange with some fierceness, as if impatient.

Kai?

No, not now.

This is your dream, then?

Sometimes.

Wow, he said for something to say. That's pretty interesting.

Can I go out? asked the boy, pointing to the balcony.

No, mate. I think we'll stay here.

Do you have Scrabble?

Keely shook his head.

I know a tree with an owl in it, he said lamely.

The boy said nothing. Worked his way through the orange.

I gotta wash my hands.

Keely ushered him to the sink and when he'd dried his hands on the teatowel Kai picked up the book and headed for the door.

Kai? Maybe you should wait for your nan?

But the boy went ahead regardless. Keely trailed him along the gallery to 1010 where Kai was fishing a key from inside his shirt.

Kai? Shouldn't we wait for Gemma?

The boy went in and closed the door behind him. Only a few moments later Gemma came clomping down the walkway from the lifts. She'd been gone a lot longer than twenty minutes.

What's he up to?

I think he wanted to play Scrabble.

We don't have Scrabble.

Me either.

Keely didn't know how to broach the subject of the boy's strange fantasies. Gemma seemed preoccupied, anxious to get inside.

Listen, he said. Kai asked me if I was angry with him.

Are you?

Of course not. Why would he ask that?

Maybe the bird, she said.

What about the bird?

You had the wrong bird. He knows a bloke doesn't like getting showed up.

You're kidding me.

Never wrong, any of yez. But look out if someone calls you on it.

Oh, man.

You said it.

He sees things.

Tom, you dunno what he's seen. You got no bloody idea.

All he could do was nod, acknowledge it.

Okay, he said. I'm going back to what it was I was doing.

And what was that?

Not nearly enough.

I need a favour, she said. Can I come by in a minute?

Not a problem.

Jesus, she muttered, going inside. You gotta stop sayin that.

When she returned to rattle his screen door he was halfway through a grocery list. He'd already made his daily resolution to finally scrub the shower recess and then put it off until first thing tomorrow. He waved her in. She was barefoot. The dress was all but backless and he saw that she had a tattoo he'd not noticed before. The standard murky butterfly, in the middle of her back.

And down her arm, inside her left elbow, was a burn scar the size of a coin.

What d'you need? he asked, hoping to hell it wasn't money.

I don't like to ask, she said, sitting opposite, tugging the barrette from her hair. But there's no one else.

Kai's no trouble, he said hopefully.

Gemma turned a bracelet on her arm.

It's not that. He'll be at school then.

When's this?

Thursday, she said. I've gotta collect something from his father.

He waited.

And I was sorta hopin you'd come along.

Right, said Keely with a nervous flutter.

Won't be any aggro, she said. Shouldn't be. But some company'd help. Figured while you weren't workin.

Well. Fair enough. I spose.

You don't mind?

Not a problem, he croaked.

She leant over and kissed him on the side of the head. A flash of lust ripped through him. He laid a hand on her hip and it slipped free as she straightened.

It won't take long.

What're you picking up?

Just some stuff that's ours. I've put it off too long. It's not easy doin all this shit on me own.

No, it doesn't look like it is.

When we first come here, when the Housing people put us here, it gimme the creeps, this place.

A school for Kai. Right next door.

Yeah. And work, too. In the beginning at least. It's somewhere, I spose.

That's what I tell myself.

There's others with nothin after all, she said. And Kai likes it.

He's a nice kid.

He likes you.

Keely's heart gave a treacherous ping.

And his dad – there's not much contact?

Restrainin order.

I see.

Anyway.

Gemma reached into the front of her dress and his balls buzzed again. From inside her bra she drew out a key tied to a dark loop of wool.

Here, she said, getting up. This morning I got a fright, that's all. I'm sorry. I didn't know what to do. And then I fell asleep.

Just look in on him, willya? When I'm at work?

He nodded.

Other night.

Yeah?

You'n me. We were just lonely.

Yeah.

And I'd had a couple. You see?

Yeah, of course.

I don't want a bloke anymore, Tom. I haven't got it in me. But I could do with a mate.

Not a problem, he said too brightly.

Christ, will you stop *sayin* that? she said with an exasperated laugh.

Absolutely.

Thursday. Means you got time for a shave and a haircut.

You serious?

Wouldja mind?

She gave him a winsome, girlish grin of supplication that excited and annoyed him. But Keely thought about it, the itching nest his beard had become. What was it anyway, all this hair, but a kind of wallowing in defeat?

Honest, you're no use to me lookin like that.

Okay, he said, from longing more than friendship.

She kissed him chastely again and when she was gone he gathered the key and held the woollen loop to his face to catch her musky scent.

Conan the barbarian was harmless enough. Between spells in the locked ward the scrofulous, bellowing vagrant was a fixture on the streets in all seasons, and at his least offensive the locals were fond of him. He did a lot of unfocused seething and roaring, his great leonine head thrown back in rage or pleasure, and although he was an infamous and copious public defecator there was some charm in knowing he did this more for effect than from need. Conan was nuttier than Queensland batshit but he wasn't mad enough to underestimate the grander pleasures of performance; he laid it on with a trowel – and that wasn't always just a figure of speech. Wags in cafés said it was only a matter of time before he got an arts grant. In summer he liked to colonize bits of public space – a bus shelter, park bench, beach awning – where he could hunker down in his midden, snooze, scream and drink epic quantities of beer. He was entirely harmless. Unless you offered him money, advice or help of any sort. Keely, who had over the years done all three, knew that the best way to get along with Conan was to avoid him completely. For once you fell into his noxious orbit he liked to reward you with his attention, for hours, sometimes days, and this would entail blistering harangues, buttock display, and the trumpeting of your name in public as he pinched a loaf. All in the service of extortion, for the purpose of securing free lager, in bulk. And the wily bastard never forgot a face or a name. Which was why, next morning at the beach, rinsing at the spigot and feeling semi-decent, Keely was so studious about ignoring him.

He'd come straight up between the dunes in a sweet pain-shadow, mildly revived by his swim, and he was standing beneath the shower when he caught the glint of crushed beer cans around the awning. There was a denser mass of junk in the shade where it looked as if someone had backed a truck in and dumped a load of garbage. But the sight of two horny feet protruding from beneath a candlewick bedspread was all it took to know that overnight the beach shelter had become Conan's latest bivouac. Keely cut his ablutions short. Morning regulars jogged by, wincing as they caught whiffs of the old stager's ruinous miasma. Some raised a conspiratorial eyebrow and grinned circumspectly, with the sort of boho-bourgeois forbearance locals prided themselves on. As Keely towelled off he observed from only the very corner of his eye the mattresses, shopping bags, rags and cartons, the profusion of empties shining in the sun like footlights around the perimeter. He was seasoned enough not to gaze frankly but found himself caught up in documentary wonder all the same. You had to marvel at the havoc one man could wreak on a place in the space of half a day.

Conan was asleep. Or lying doggo. Maybe biding his time between eruptions. The dozing inferno. Keely was keen to be on his way. Feeling as tentatively fair as he did this morning, there was no point pushing his luck by staring recklessly into the maw of this Vesuvial force of nature. So he looked away, finished towelling off briskly and was gathering himself to go when his eyes wandered back treasonously. Which was when he saw it. Buried deep. But patently there. Camouflaged by sodden underpants, beneath hanging kelp and broken fronds of saltbush. His bike. Keely's spirits rose. Then sank again. Because just seeing this had complicated his day irrevocably. Conan was mad, not stupid. He loved to negotiate. Especially when he couldn't lose. Like a desert warlord in a hostage bargain, he'd choose the longest and most indirect path to the least pleasant outcome.

The Malvern Star wasn't worth suffering for. Its ransom would include an hour's foulmouthed argy-bargy and a carton of Emu Export at a bare-arsed minimum, not to mention having his woebegone name shouted up dune and down dale for a week. Keely hadn't even had breakfast yet. He had five bucks seventy in his pocket. He was supposed to be home cleaning the flat. Then to the barber to satisfy Gemma. These days the price of twenty-four cans of industrial-grade beer was no small thing. And it seemed so much steeper when you weren't drinking them yourself.

No, he thought. Bugger it.

And yet.

He needed the bike. It was, after all, his bike. And it browned him off, being robbed and stood over by a lunatic.

He was fresh from a swim. Fresh-ish. Damp flab. Headache in partial remission. Weak. But no kitten. He could dash in now, right now. While Conan slept the sleep of the unloved. Wrest the treadly from the grimy heap and bolt before the malodorous thief even stirred. Yes, dammit. He'd have it back.

Dry and dressed, Keely stalked towards Conan's camp, thongs clapping him on. I'll outrun you, mate, outride you, and you can take your pants-down, butt-slapping warrior dance elsewhere. It's my fucking bike.

Keely went all the way. He did not deviate. He strode right through the eye-watering frontier of Conan's encampment, head up like a man with a sturdy will, and actually had his fingers around the handlebars when a single basso fart sent him scurrying in search of an ATM, an early opener and a slab of Western Australia's nastiest.

The bloom was well and truly off the morning when Keely finally wheeled the redeemed Malvern Star into the cycle shop. He wanted a titanium lock. Immediately and forever. Yes, it was worth more than the bike and twice the cost of a carton of piss, but after what he'd just endured he needed to know there'd never be a repeat performance.

He was comparing two rival brands and muttering to himself when he heard her voice.

Tom?

Before he even looked up, he knew it was Harriet. She wore a black suit and blunt-toed shoes. Pushed back on her head, her sunglasses held up the dark tide of her hair. She looked flushed, even blotchy; he supposed it was the heat.

I didn't recognize you for a moment, she said. The beard.

Right. Of course.

So.

Right. Yeah.

So, um.

How's things?

Harriet did that slant thing with her mouth. It was hard. Lovely. Terrifying. To see her again after so long. A year? Fourteen months. There before him. Smelling of herself.

Thought you'd gone to Brussels.

She shrugged. Changed my mind.

Ah.

You okay?

What? Why?

You know you were talking to yourself?

Bullshit.

Whatever.

I have to buy a lock, he said, holding up the gizmos in their sealed packets. Bloody Conan.

The homeless bloke?

Homeless? He loves the outdoor life. Makes himself at home wherever he goes. Helps himself to whatever you have. Shits in front of old ladies.

So, okay. Right. The street bloke.

Keely recognized the tone of aggrieved patience. He waved abstractly and put the locks down in surrender.

Anyway, he said. Not a good start to the day.

They stood miserably a few moments, during which time Keely registered the fact that she'd put on weight. For a second he had the dimwitted and painful thought she was pregnant again. The things he did to himself. She was ten years his junior. But that glorious youthful gloss was gone. Which just made her more sad and lovely.

I was in town for a meeting. Always loved this shop. You know, she said, tilting her head towards the boys putting sleek machines together, bustling about in their dreads, talking nerdy bike lingo.

Yeah, he said, just to make a sound.

Thought I might even buy a new bike, she said. I'm chubbing up, as you can see.

Bollocks.

Thought maybe I could ride along the river before work. There's a nice path on the foreshore.

Keely nodded, a little lost. It was a lot of talk. Out of nowhere. Out of nothing. After such resolute silence.

Listen, she said. You want to get some lunch?

Us?

It's only food.

But. I mean. You think that's a good idea?

We're not savages, are we?

No. But.

A quick meal, Tom. Don't get —

Okay.

Right, then.

He looked down at his thongs, his damp shorts and T-shirt.

It's Freo, she said. No one gives a shit.

It was too hot to go in search of somewhere anonymous, so they ended up in their old regular, the Thai joint a couple of blocks away. Their entrance caused some confusion amongst the family staff who'd witnessed the dissolution of their marriage, enduring it week by week with sad discretion.

After a minute's skin-peeling banter with various members of the clan, Harriet ordered a bottle of semillon. Waiters came and went gingerly around their table. He was glad when the food came and they were free to do more than stare at one another indulgently.

You're living in Perth, then, said Keely despite himself. In the CBD?

It's odd. Like living in an industrial park. Bit of a shock, actually. They weren't kidding; it really is Dullsville.

I guess there's the river.

Yeah, there's that. The flat, shallow, brown bit.

And the food's better there.

If you fancy a fifty-dollar steak.

Are they good? The fifty-buck steaks?

She glared at him.

And work's okay? he asked with a grin of small satisfaction.

Corner office.

So you're a partner at last.

I live a block from the building. No wonder my arse is bigger than my tax bill. All I do is work.

Keely gulped wine, caught himself. He set the glass back and made handprints on the bare wood of the table.

So.

So, she said.

Is it still good work?

Righteous work, you mean? she said with a wry grin. Sometimes.

I meant is it stimulating, interesting.

I know exactly what you mean; you're a Keely.

He held his hands up in concession.

Harriet cracked a wan smile. Anyway, you know how it is.

Afraid so.

So, yes, they own my bones.

But it's interesting?

Of course. I'm in China once a month. Paying homage.

He nodded – what could you say?

You look shocking, Tom.

Thanks for noticing.

Sorry. That wasn't . . . But the beard – Christ.

The beard is not long for this world.

But are you okay?

He shrugged.

Are you seeing someone?

Harriet.

I meant, like, counselling.

He stonewalled with a mirthless grin.

I wish it hadn't happened, she murmured. Any of it.

Keely took a breath but she clarified immediately.

I don't mean the marriage. I don't regret that. Just —

Let's not, eh?

No, you're right. I'm sorry. Hey, is it true you're living in the Mirador? That's different.

You've been talking to Doris?

I'm always talking to Doris.

And she's talking to you.

Well, sometimes it's professional.

She never said.

She's a bloody legend, you know. Anyway, everyone still wonders what you're up to.

Sure they do.

Hey, I saw Freda from the EDO. She sees the WildForce crew all the time. Half the movement knows where you are.

And so few visits, eh.

Come on, Tom. You've left them in no doubt about where things stand.

So why ask? he said, pouring himself another glass.

I dunno. Worried, I guess.

Right.

People respect you. I know you don't feel it.

Stop.

And they're curious about what you'll do next. Both sides.

What is this, a bloody reconnaissance mission?

Sit down, she said. And don't be a wanker.

I mean, shit mate.

Let me rephrase —

Don't bother.

Sit down. Please. You're embarrassing me. Everyone.

Keely flopped back to the chair. Chugged his wine. Refilled. Went again. And Harriet sighed. The sound was so familiar he could have wept.

Sorry.

Me too.

But I mean it. A lot of people wish you well.

It was wasted. All that time.

The reef? The karri forests? Are you serious?

Fuck it, anyway.

Like I said, they wish you well. Wish you *were* well.

I'm fine, he lied.

So. The Mirador.

It's just a little flat, he murmured, noticing they'd almost finished the bottle already.

But it's okay?

Come and see, he said. If you're that curious.

Doris says you won't even let her up there.

No.

What's that about?

I don't even know anymore.

So why ask me?

I'm not planning to jump, if that's what you mean.

What?

Lure you up and jump. It wasn't on the agenda. I'm all out of romance.

What the fuck are you talking about?

Nothing. Sorry.

Jesus, Tom.

Well, don't just sit there looking guilty and buying me lunch. Say something interesting. Spice up my sad little life.

Try not to be a shit, will you?

Keely shrugged hopelessly and downed the last of the wine. He badly wanted to leave. To take her with him.

We should have had children, she said. I concede that.

Stop it.

I know that's what this is about. I know it's why you *went* like that. We were stupid, both of us.

No, just me.

Well, you were stupid and I was cruel.

I was shooting for cruelly stupid. Fell short, as usual.

I'm a ruined person, she said dully. I know it sounds melodramatic, but it's how I feel, even on a good day.

You're still young. You'll recover.

Not that sense of who I was. No. I don't think so.

What do you mean? How can you say that?

You know damn well how I can say it, she said, staring him down like he was a vexatious litigant. There's just part of me I don't believe in anymore.

Keely blinked. In recognition. It smarted.

You know, she said, I was proud, in a way. Proud to be me. I don't think I was conceited. I think I had good reason to be proud and so did you. We always did what we said, acted from principle. Couldn't be bought, felt like we were authentic.

Oh, that old crap.

Yes, that old crap.

Harriet, you're still the same person.

No. It's as if one betrayal unlocks others.

People screw up, mate. It's normal.

So banal, though. The office romance.

Yes, banal. That's what I thought. How banal.

Bad faith. It bends you out of shape.

Faith of any sort, I'd have thought.

Jesus, we shouldn't be talking like this.

Don't mean to harp on a costly theme here but —

Tom, I don't want to hear about your forgiveness.

But what about forgiving yourself? You're a good person. Good people do stupid things. Your entire life isn't defined by one mistake.

And *you're* trying to tell *me* that?

What I did was not a mistake, he said. It wasn't wrong.

Just weird wrong. Crazy wrong. As if you didn't understand defamation.

I understood perfectly.

Well, it wasn't much of a martrydom, was it?

I've loved every minute. Look at me. Rejuvenated.

Still, she said bitterly. You did get to retain your status as the moral cleanskin.

Yeah. Feels great.

And you've heard about the CCC, I gather.

Fuck the CCC, he said, feeling the penny drop.

What? she said in false protest. It's Tiny Town. Everyone knows already. Something's finally happening.

Keely looked at her. Wished he could tell her what was really happening. But he knew he wouldn't. He was a coward.

Sorry, she said. Didn't mean to bring it up. I'm just —

You don't have to be sorry. None of it matters. I forgive you.

Tom, we've covered this, she said briskly. In several fora.

Fora.

Stop it.

Keely saw what this was doing to her. She'd put herself in the same room as him and he was doing this to her.

Okay, he said, assembling himself with some effort. Let's just eat.

Don't you dare jump out the fucking window.

Listen —

You don't have the right to punish me. You have no right.

Harriet. I promise you, I promise.

She looked at him directly and her eyes shone with tears.

Really, he said. I don't want to punish you. And I promise. A Keely never breaks a promise.

Isn't that the whole trouble? she said with a smile rendered ugly by pain.

Love you, he murmured.

Please!

Sorry.

God, you're a strange man.

So I gather.

And loving doesn't help. Believe me.

But he couldn't. The evidence supported what she said. But that was one shred of faith he wouldn't let go of. Love had to help something, somewhere, otherwise he *would* just go ahead and launch himself off a balcony.

They ate for a while in wounded silence. Keely noted the air of covert surveillance from the counter and the kitchen door and it heartened him to think anyone harboured hopes for them, however fanciful.

Keely was as thirsty as a motherfucker but he didn't dare order any more wine.

You ever think of going back to teaching?

I couldn't do it, he said. Even *I'm* not that worthy.

So what will you do? You must be skint. You look it.

He shrugged.

Do you need money?

No, he lied.

Will you tell me if you do?

He smiled and she snorted a friendly surrender.

Your arse isn't big, he said.

Don't lie – you're no good at it.

Get the bike, he said. Buy it now, while you're thinking of it. You'll have fun. I'll ride it up the river to your place, save you the delivery.

No, she said. No visits. Besides, I drove. Maybe I'll put it in the boot.

You can't drive after this much wine.

Well, Jesus really wanted *you* for a sunbeam, didn't he?

I'm only saying.

And you're right, you scruffy prick. I'll get a cab.

They finished lunch. Harriet did not buy a bike. As her taxi pulled away he walked up to the barber on the next block and ordered a haircut and full shave. He fell asleep in the chair and woke to the news that he owed seventy dollars, which meant taking the bike lock back across the street for a refund.

II

Keely lingered a while in front of Cash Converters, scooting the bike back and forth beneath him, wondering what his laptop would fetch. By his calculations, unless he quickly got cash work or hocked something, he was a fortnight from destitution. It wasn't just Keely pride that kept him from the dole but the certain knowledge the perversities of Centrelink would crush him; he was neither fit nor mad enough to endure the welfare system. Even if he did sign up he'd starve by the time the first cheque finally appeared. Unless he stood in the street for soup and sandwiches with all the other lost souls. He couldn't touch his superannuation for another decade. He could sell the flat but it would take weeks or months to find a buyer and settle and in the meantime he'd have nothing. He had to cash up fast or come to terms with the idea of living with his mother like an addled invalid. Selling the dinghy would help. But even that'd take a week or two. The time for action was now.

He twisted the handlebars of his reeking bike. At the corner, tattooed thugs were sending their women into the loan joint, and pacing the kerb, flexing their roid-pecs.

He peered into the hock-shop. The store was the size of a big whitegoods franchise, the front window stacked with guitars, golf bags, chainsaws, the legacy of other reversals. What a display it was, this cargo cult. The entire window an altar to defeat. Which sounded a tad grandiose, but there it was. Blame the plonk.

Catching his reflection in the glass he was surprised by how old and dazed he looked. Surprised to be so surprised, truth be told; what did he expect from a seventy-dollar haircut and a shave – to suddenly look invigorated, to have excavated his inner George Clooney? When you felt as abstracted from yourself as he did these days, why not feel strange in your own face? How hard his chin felt, how creepy-smooth his cheeks. And there in the window, plain evidence of where his sorrowful beard had been. So much fresh white skin, he looked as two-toned as Roy Rene or Michael Jackson. High up on his face, where the sun had been, he was dark, especially around the eyes. A veritable boobook owl. Which struck him as funny. Maybe not funny enough to warrant laughter, but there he was anyway, causing passers-by to give him a wide berth on the pavement: a piebald cyclist, chemically augmented, kneading his own chops in a pawnbroker's window, indulging himself in his very own Knut Hamsun moment, chortling like a loon.

He shouldn't have been back in there, amidst the boxes of goon, the racks of gleaming bottles; he'd spent money he could not afford to be blowing and he'd regret it, regretted it already, but he wanted something decent, had a little glow on from lunch, and the front window of Cash Converters had kicked him off a bit and he couldn't settle.

He bought a couple of bin-end McLaren Vales that were crazy cheap, telling himself he'd saved twenty bucks on them, his luck was turning.

Keely had only been in a few hours before, securing the ransom cans, but now the bloke in the bottlo didn't recognize him without the beard. It was disconcerting at first, but then it struck him as possibly advantageous in a way he couldn't quite put his finger on just yet.

Stepping back onto the street he was nearly mown down by a cyclist whose expression morphed from irritation to delight in a heartbeat.

Tom!

Keely jerked upright, like a man accused. Just stood there hugging those costly bargains to his chest. The youth's face was distantly familiar but Keely couldn't place him. He had a downy soul-patch and girlish arms and his flash mountain bike was laden with wholesome produce.

Damien, said the boy brightly.

Ah, said Keely. The helmet and sunnies, I didn't . . .

Wetlands campaign, said the kid. And the mallee fowl thing, remember?

Yeah, of course, he said. You did good work, mate.

He knew the kid now and it was true. He was good value. Environmental science graduate with a real bird bent. Especially good on habitat loss. A straight shooter.

Your ideas, Tom. Your vision.

Didn't they hate us, though.

Truly. But like you said: if the suits don't hate you, you've wasted your time.

Well, jury's still out on that.

Wasn't it Gandhi saying first they ignore you, then they ridicule you, then they negotiate?

Something like that. Then you win. Apparently.

You've had a few wins over the years, Tom. Shouldn't forget that.

They let you win the odd skirmish, comrade. To make it look as if the game's fair. But the dogs bark, circus rolls on.

The youth offered a noncommittal grimace.

Who you with now? Keely asked.

The kid laughed skittishly.

Government?

Ah no, said the boy.

Keely didn't need to be told what that meant. He'd had his wild years, this kid, his Gandhi-quoting period. If the iron giants hadn't bought him it could only be oil and gas. These days they were co-opting them as undergrads, paying their tuition. Miners employed more ecologists, marine scientists and geology graduates than six governments. In order to smooth the way, before they literally scraped the place bare. All that harmless data owned and warehoused. It was brilliant.

Still, he said. Look at you, buying organic. Like a trouper.

It's only for a while, said the boy, stung.

Keely saw young Damien eye the brown bags cradled in his arm. Here was his old boss, ravaged and unsteady outside the roughest liquor store in town. Quite a picture. But the youth, plainly the better man, was charitable enough to refrain from comment. Keely felt like a shit.

He offered up a lame smile.

I know, I know, said the kid. A while's all we get.

You gotta stop quoting me, Keely replied, straining to relent, to show remorse.

Listen, I'm sorry to hear what happened.

Keely shrugged, graciously as he could.

You were right, you know. It's all coming out.

We'll see.

They were nuts to let you go.

I was probably nuts when they did.

Well, good luck to you anyway.

Maybe you could put in a good word at Woodside.

Mate, said the kid, missing the joke entirely, they'd snap you up.

He gave the boy the bravest smile he could manage and watched him wheel his righteous vegetables through the canyon of junk shops and manicure joints until he was gone at the corner. It was Wednesday – a day off, no doubt. He imagined the neat little cottage Damien was headed for, the sleek girl coming home to him tonight, the couscous he'd have waiting on the scrubbed-pine table. It was beautiful.

Enough to make you want to drink yourself a new arsehole.

He'd hardly made a dent on the second bottle when Kai appeared at the door, toting his schoolbag. For a moment the kid rocked on his heels as if he'd peered into the wrong flat. The look of alarm on his face was unmistakeable.

It's me, said Keely. I shaved my beard off, that's all.

But the kid was gone, his footfalls chiming in the rails of the gallery.

What was that about? said Gemma, suddenly filling the doorway. Christ, look at you.

He doesn't approve.

Of what – the haircut, or the fact you're pissed as a squirrel?

Why should he object?

You're a bloody idiot.

What, leaving the door open to the likes of you? Obviously an error of judgement. For which I need not seek forgiveness. But which I seek all the same.

Get stuffed. The five-dollar words, they don't make you sound any smarter.

Duly noted.

Christ, what a disappointment you are.

Refresh my memory, Gem. Did we get married at some juncture?

Juncture.

Is there some claim you have, something I signed that gives you the right to stand in my door and wave the nana finger at me? Maybe I nodded off during the ceremony.

Go fuck yourself.

I suspect. This evening. It may come to that. But I am. You might say. A dab hand already.

What is it with you?

I had my *bike* stolen.

Don't you dare come over tonight.

Here, he said, reefing her key from around his neck so hard he feared he might have sliced his own ears off. Gemma didn't even flinch as it bounced off the insect screen.

Pissweak, she muttered, giving him a parting stare he felt in the pit of his guts.

Correct, he said to the empty doorway once she was safely gone. He thought of the last great stand of tuart trees bulldozed and trucked away. Ripped earth as far as the eye could see, and homeless birds, black and wheeling. Cheap work. A Chinese construction deal cost millions in bribes. But here you could buy a new suburb for seventy thousand bucks. Small beans. Price of a Prado for a western-suburbs soccer mum. While she's waiting on the Audi. Small fucking beans. And still too big for the likes of him.

A few hours later she was there again in the doorway. Kitted out for work, bearing a foil-covered plate.

And another thing, he said, trying to be funny.

I'm off, she said. Chrissake eat something.

Is this the heart of gold shining through?

Be buggered, she spat. I need you tomorrow. Whatever's left of you.

Well, you're not fussy, I'll give you that. Couldn't you find some poor prick in the street? Offer him an inducement?

Just shut up before I clout you.

Your sister did once. More than once, actually.

And that's not all, I bet.

Nothing else. She never offered me anything but a thick ear.

And I'll bet she had her reasons.

Doubtless she did.

Fuckin slag.

Fair go, he said blearily. She was just a girl. Tryna find her way. Lookin out for herself. Never bothered much to protect me.

There was nothing Keely could say to this. It felt dangerous to proceed. He was too far gone. And the smell of food was making him queasy.

Kai alright?

He's fine.

Done his homework?

He's six.

Oh. Right.

In her pale-blue smock, her hair scraped back in a ponytail, Gemma looked like a faded, beaten-down schoolgirl. Sensible shoes, support hose. He was a little bit in love with her.

I didn't mean to scare him, he said abjectly.

You won't forget tomorrow?

All yours.

Two o'clock, orright?

Right you are.

Your teeth are all black.

I'll brush before two.

What happened to you, Tommy?

My wife had an abortion.

What?

I couldn't handle it.

Well, shit.

And it wasn't my baby anyway.

You kicked her out?

No, he said with a laugh that burnt like acid reflux. She asked me to leave.

What the fuck?

Kept going on and on. About the baby. Mourning. Just mourning.

Well, it's not bloody easy, take it from me.

Not her, he said, holding his hands in the air like a halfwit. Me. Gemma looked at him with a mixture of bewilderment and scorn.

I would have taken it. I didn't mind. I would have raised it. It was like my own child had died.

You're bonkers.

This is probably true.

I'm late, she said, turning for the door.

At the security screen she stooped to collect her key on its woollen noose. And after a moment's consideration she set it on the counter beside the giveaway newspapers and the leaflets for pizza bars and quick loans.

I have redeemed a bicycle, he whispered as the door clacked to. *That* is what I have saved. And what God hath joined together let no man . . . spoil, with a chunder.

He pulled the foil off the plate and smiled. Rissoles!

Jesus wept, she said when he opened the door at two.

Apparently.

You orright?

Fine, he lied into the blinding light of day.

You got some better clothes?

Better? Keely could only make out a shape, an outline, until she stepped past him into the dim fug of his livingroom and jerked the curtains apart.

More . . . formal. Like a suit.

A suit. Yeah, there's one in there somewhere. But is it really necessary?

Would I ask ya just to be annoyin?

He offered a smile as evidence of his doubts – all scrubbed

teeth and bleeding gums.

It's in a box, he said.

Great, she replied. You got an iron?

Somewhere.

I'll have to press it. Carn, let's fix this.

A suit, he thought. And why am I doing this? Because she's pretty, because she's blonde? Because she's little Gemma Buck the waif? Christ, his guts, his head.

Reaching deep into the wardrobe he fought a bilious shudder. You were rude to her, he thought, said something nasty you can't quite remember, and she cooked you dinner anyway. You'll do whatever she says.

I've only got an hour, she said. Kai gets off at three.

Here he said, digging the thing out and brandishing it as a single wodge.

Lovely, she said with full scorn. Dunno whether to press it or mop the floor with it.

As they walked through the back end of town with its sour smells, blasts of noise and pitiless rods of sun, Keely noticed, despite his nausea, that for all her hard-boiled banter Gemma was becoming increasingly edgy. She wore another small black dress that showed her figure. He recognized the heels from Tuesday, or whenever it was. Her hair was swept back in a black band that looked something like velvet and the dark vinyl satchel she carried seemed new. She looked like a real estate agent on the make, or the sort of defence lawyer who lived off a roster of 'colourful' clients. If he hadn't felt so rocky he'd tease her about it – or at the very least dawdle behind her for the simple pleasure of watching those legs scissor away deliciously. Right now he was focused on keeping his rissoles in place. Gemma hauled him by the sleeve, drawing savagely on a fag. He prayed she wouldn't blow smoke his way.

I'm coming, he said. Listen, where are we going?

Collectin some things, that's all.

From the bank?

No. Geez, were you that pissed? I told you. From his father.

The father. I knew that. So what's with the get-up? Both of us like pox doctors' clerks.

Try not to whinge, Tom. It's gettin on me nerves. Just tell me now if you're pikin out.

I'm here, aren't I?

Well, she said. A version of you, anyway.

A pale facsimile, he said.

Very pale.

And I'm sorry.

Well, beggars can't be choosers.

Keely took it on the shaven chin and sucked in hot air, anxious for this task and the rest of the day to be over.

Near the markets, short of the grand old pub at the corner, Gemma drew up at a familiar row of semis whose narrow verandahs were variously draped with footy flags, banners advertising Bundaberg rum, and the kind of cheap bamboo blinds that reminded him of his student days. The street gave off a swampy stink of frangipani, ganja, incense and rotting vegetables. There was broken glass on the footpath and music spilled from open doorways. Gemma took his arm and steered him towards a traffic bollard.

You stay here, Tommy.

Well, he said peevishly. You're the boss.

She angled towards the closest house, the seediest in the row, glanced back at him briefly and clacked her way up to the door.

Her bum rolling in its dark sheath, her hair flaring from within the shade of the porch.

The way she thudded on the door was more than emphatic; he felt the percussion ten metres away. She kept it up, applying the side of her fist, until finally the door was opened by a scowling girl of about seventeen. She surveyed Gemma, squinted past her at Keely, who folded his arms instinctively and Gemma said something he couldn't make out. After a long moment the girl slunk off in her tiny shorts and tanktop, and a minute later another figure loomed in the doorway. Gemma rose to her full height, seemed to exceed it. Her battle stance brought Keely to a new level of alertness.

The man was tall and wiry. His bare chest and arms were covered in the sorts of tattoos that hadn't yet found favour with the cooler cadres of the middle class. Keely figured he was in his late twenties. He had an aura of easy violence about him. He looked as sly and unknowable as a mistreated dog. As he leant contemptuously against the doorjamb, he took the opportunity to reach into his trackpants to huffle his nuts.

Gemma spoke. The man began to shake his head disdainfully, projecting ostentatious amusement. Gemma unzipped her document case and drew out a folder. She held up several sheets of paper in turn and then began to wave one right in his face. Keely caught the bloke glancing over at him. The dark flash of his eyes caused something to hitch in Keely's throat. The fellow licked his lips appraisingly, not breaking his glance as Gemma continued to speak. He seemed to consider his options. He glanced up the street, ploughed his fingers through his hair. Gemma's voice became audible, but the only word Keely made out was a shout: *Now!* Even at this distance, the young man's rage was evident. Keely knew this was the moment to step forward, to reinforce whatever point Gemma was driving home, but by the time he summoned the requisite courage the bloke had already turned in the doorway and disappeared.

Gemma swivelled and held up a hand, halting Keely's unhappy progress, so that he was left lurking there, mid-stride, stranded in the sun, awkward and shamefaced, about as threatening as a faded traffic cone.

Without speaking they waited a long couple of minutes. Down the row a dreadlocked busker was setting up outside the markets. Gulls wheeled above the street as a keg truck pulled up at the corner pub. A once-great drinking place. Now the haunt of Facebook hipsters and metrosexuals. Another lost cause.

When he returned, the young man dumped a cardboard carton on the porch at Gemma's feet. She stood her ground and held out a hand to receive something that was a long time coming. Eventually the punk handed over a small object, perhaps a key. Then he said something that set Gemma's head back. It was as if she'd been slapped. He closed the door on her with a sneer and after several seconds she stooped in her heels, took up the box and stalked unsteadily down the path.

What the fuck was that? he said, fumbling the carton she shoved at him in passing.

It took some effort to keep up with her and she didn't slow down until they were at the roundabout beside the football oval. She was white-faced and agitated, blinking back tears so fiercely he thought she might strike him.

Are you alright?

Shut the fuck up.

She blundered into traffic and he followed her, juggling the box and copping car horns and howls of abuse. When they were safely across and headed for the carpark in the lee of the old prison, she began blotting her eyes with a tissue. There was mascara down her face.

Gemma, what's the story?

Doesn't matter.

What's in the box?

Nintendo, she said, blowing her nose on the mottled Kleenex.

A computer game? All that back there was for a Nintendo? You're kidding me.

She broke away and he trudged behind her until they were amidst rows of parked cars baking in the sun.

Come on, Gemma, you're not serious.

He followed her up and down ranks of vehicles. The sun was vicious. He saw the dress glued to her back with sweat.

Finally she stopped in front of a battered little Hyundai. A thick sheaf of parking tickets fluttered from the wipers. Gemma sighed, swiped them up and unlocked the car.

It's Carly's, she murmured, pulling her hair free. Get in.

The superheated Hyundai stank of cigarettes and mould. Keely sat ankle-deep in burger wrappers and chip buckets, breathing oven air.

No petrol, of course, muttered Gemma. Let's find a servo.

Keely refrained for a moment but he couldn't help himself.

The charmer back there, that's Kai's father?

She turned the key in the ignition several times and eventually the engine came sluggishly to life.

Stewie. He's a turd. Christ, wind your window down!

He lowered it all the way and she stabbed at the aircon button, hissing through her teeth.

I don't get it, he confessed. All this get-up, all the drama.

It's Carly's stuff, Kai's stuff. Pictures, toys, clothes. What's so hard to understand?

Well, what was I there for? he asked, half knowing already.

There's bloody court orders and letters and he wouldn't give it up. Two years! I've had no car, nothing for Kai, and no one bloody follows through. Not the coppers, DOCS, no one. I'm payin for taxis just to get to work.

Didn't you say there was a restraining order?

There's a list of em, take your pick. Not worth the paper they're printed on.

And you went over there?

You saw me, why ask?

Because I didn't know what the hell I was getting into, Gemma. I didn't know what I was supposed to do.

I needed a bit of support, orright? Sorry to put a dent in your busy day.

It was so hot in the car, Keely was surprised to feel an actual flush of shame.

Anyway, she said, relenting. You looked the part. That's the main thing.

Thanks. I spose. Remind me, though, what part was I playing?

I was just messin with his head. Little arsehole couldn't decide if you were the bailiff or my bloke. He was twitchy as shit, wired by the looks. In the end I reckon he was wonderin if you might be my lawyer, or even a cop. I never said a thing about it and he didn't ask. I just left you out there – like a mindfuck, she said, beginning to enjoy herself. You do look pretty bad-tempered with a hangover. The beard wouldn't have worked, made you look like a hippy preacher with a hurtin heart.

Well, this is all very handy to know, of course, he said, grateful the car was moving; even a roasting breeze was better than none.

He's got parole conditions, she said, steering them towards the exit. The house musta been full of speed or something, cause he caved real quick.

What if he hadn't? What if he'd done something to you? Really, Gemma, what was I supposed to do?

I dunno, she said, lurching out into the traffic. Tell him love conquers all and punch him in the throat. I saw Nev put a bloke through an asbestos fence once.

That was probably a prayer meeting.

She laughed and he joined her.

He rooted through the carton as she drove. Apart from the papers and toys the only thing of use was the laptop. As a boxful, as a trophy of war, it wasn't much.

He's flogged everything else, she said as if reading him. Only reason he kept the computer and the Nintendo is to use himself. Maybe you could look at it for me, the laptop. Kai'll need it for school. They do everything on a computer these days and he's not gunna miss out. I dunno the first thing about the bloody things. Would you do that?

He nodded.

This thing's hers, she said, whacking the wheel, but it's registered in my name, so guess who pays the rego and the fines. I couldn't stand walkin past it every day knowin Kai and me're catchin the bus, it was eatin me up.

Well, you're game, I'll give you that.

Now and then you need a win, she said. Keeps you goin.

She veered into the BP. He thought of Prudhoe Bay; it was involuntary. British Petroleum, he thought – what a friend *they* had in Jesus.

While she pumped the fuel, Keely sat nursing the cardboard carton. In the end he felt silly enough to get out and stand on the greasy concrete. Across the vehicle, in a wavering tableau of heat shimmer and fume shadows, Gemma stood with one hand on her hip, the other gripping the nozzle. With her body cocked liked that and all her hair rippling off her shoulders, she was a sight in her little black dress. Keely felt a surge of admiration. She had more guts than he could hope for. Just looking at her made him happy all of a sudden, just for a moment, and when she caught his gaze and his dopey grin, she looked at him quizzically, and then became guarded, as if suspecting she'd been mocked.

You look great, he said.

Oh, get fucked, she said, grinning.

Despite the fact that Kai's school was on the same block as the Mirador, Gemma insisted on collecting him in the car. Keely's headache was luminous; he would have preferred to get out, cross the street and go up in the lift, but he didn't have the heart – or maybe the nerve – to leave her in this moment of triumph, so in the minutes before the bell rang, they idled in the sweltering line around the block behind all the other vehicular parents and guardians and afterschool carers.

He doesn't like surprises, she said. But he'll like this one.

Why the convent school? Is it just because it's close?

Well, duh.

I wondered if you might have gone Catholic.

Nah, just went to Sunday school with you and Faith. Whatever *that* was.

Like you said. A hippy preacher with a hurtin heart – Billy Graham meets Billy Jack. Singing 'Morning Has Broken' if memory serves.

They told us there was angels lookin out for us.

Well.

When I was livin at your place with Nev and Doris, it sorta felt true.

And now?

Angels move away, mate. They die. They get old. They leave you on yer own.

Still, he said. You're a tough bit of gear. No illusions. Just yourself.

Your *self*, she said with unsettling authority. Your self isn't enough.

Keely had nothing honest to offer her. How could you counter such a sense of abandonment? She really did carry with her a kind of desolation. It wasn't just his parents who'd vanished from her life, but their fierce saviour, too, their Great Defender evaporating along with them. That much he understood. He had a hole that size in him too; sometimes it was the size of him entire.

He gazed out at the retro Minis, the 4x4s, the muscle cars ahead in the line. Behold, the miracle of hire-purchase and lax lending. Clearly he wasn't the only one to feel empty. What a pageant of consolation this line of vehicles was, what a spiritual mystery conveyances had become.

He angled the poxy little A/C vent his way. This hangover wasn't just making him maudlin, it was bringing on mortal thoughts – not helpful. A blast of icy air would have been welcome. But from this triumph of Korean engineering? Not happening.

Listen, she said cautiously after a long silence. Now I've got the car, I'm gunna visit Carly.

That'll be nice, he said, sensing it coming.

Yeah, she said. I'm going up Saturday week.

Please, no, he thought – don't ask me.

I was gunna say. If maybe you wouldn't mind.

Keely averted his gaze. His temples felt scorched. He didn't want this.

It's way the hell out towards the hills, I know, she said.

Keely ran his dry tongue across his teeth. It was maddening, this obscure, relentless sense of obligation. It wasn't his fault they'd lost the house and moved away from Blackboy Crescent. You couldn't hold Nev responsible for a heart attack. Doris had her own children to see to; hadn't she done all she could? This was getting ridiculous.

He said nothing, gave her no relief.

I know you've never met her or nothin. But Kai's always funny about it. If you go he'll be orright. It's his mum, Tom.

He shifted in his seat, angry now.

Like I said, she murmured. Don't feel obliged.

Keely knew he didn't have the balls to say no. He wondered if she could see it in his face, if she'd known it all along. He drew a defeated breath, put a hand on her thigh from sheer opportunism and she didn't flinch.

Not a problem, he said with all the irony he could muster.

God love ya, Tom.

No chance of that, he thought, taking his hand away ruefully.

The bell rang. The schoolyard filled instantly with darting, leaping bodies.

There he is, he said too brightly.

Kai emerged alone from the mob with his distinctive stiff gait and air of self-containment. He was solitary, oblivious, preoccupied. When he saw his grandmother waving from the car window he halted and stared.

God, she said. I could eat him up. Look at him.

Hyundai, said Kai as he finally opened the rear door. Smaller than a Volvo.

And quite a bit cheaper, said Keely.

The boy looked at him warily.

I told you about the beard, said Gemma.

It was better before.

I agree, said Keely. But she made me.

Come on, you heathen. Get in.

The boy pursed his lips and slid in alongside the trash on the back seat. Hyundai, he said again. Hy. Un. Dai.

It's Korean for Nana, said Keely.

The message on the machine was curt. Doris sounded agitated, testy. He belted down some pipe-sick water and called her.

What is it? he asked, looking out across the sound as the southerly began to ruffle the sea.

The islands looked insubstantial as soufflés. The cement-works dredge ploughed on across the bank, pillaging shell for its lime, ripping sea grass up by the tonne, leaving a filthy plume in its wake. They'd recently secured another decade's lease. Surprise, surprise. And a few hundred metres inland their stack rained particulates on the roofs of five thousand homes. With an EPA licence, no less. Business as usual. Democracy at work.

Mum, what's the matter?

I was about to ask *you*, Tom.

You've lost me.

Faith called.

How is she?

You should know. You spoke to her last night.

Me? Last night?

She's upset. So am I.

Keely felt a twinge of dread, said nothing. He had not called his sister last night. After seeing Gemma in the early evening he hadn't spoken to anyone at all. Had he?

She said you were awful, said terrible things.

Keely had been sick all day. But not as ill as he felt this minute.

Tom?

I'm here.

What's happening?

I'll call her now.

She's on a plane. Leave her be.

Shit.

What's got into you?

I don't know, Mum. I'll fix it up.

She's your sister. She doesn't deserve this. You think because she works with money she doesn't have a conscience? She's a good person – you have no idea.

I don't remember, he confessed.

That she's your sister, that I'm proud of her?

Calling her, Mum. I don't remember calling her.

Which speaks for itself.

Keely leant against the wall, took the sting right through him. He deserved it.

Have you cooked yourself dinner?

It's three thirty-five, Doris.

Don't dare take that tone with me.

Sorry.

I've got some mussels. More than I can eat. I should know better, but when you look at them in the shop, you see the handful it takes to feed yourself, it looks pathetic, like it wouldn't feed a sparrow.

I know, he said. Cooking for one, it's science over instinct.

Dreary, that's what it is. No wonder all these Claremont ladies eat out. Divorce is the only thing keeping the hospitality industry afloat.

God, he thought in wonder. She's moved on already. Like some sort of moral amazon, she's sucked the poison from the wound, wiped her mouth and resumed the fight; it's bloody sainthood.

I'm sorry, he said. I'll do whatever it takes.

I'll be there at five, she said. I'll call you when I'm outside.

Mum, I'll catch the train.

No, I'll be there directly.

He put down the phone and ran the shower. His face in the mirror was ailing. His cheeks were lumpy with ingrown hairs, stippled in places by shaving rash. He thought he preferred the preacher with the hurtin heart to the feeble wonk looking back at him. Doris probably hadn't even bought the mussels yet; she'd be on her way to the Boatshed Market to get them now. What a rube he was; she was brilliant.

After he'd scraped his chin and dressed, while he waited for Doris to do her thing, he called Faith's landline, left a message on the machine. His apology was heartfelt but after a few moments he could feel himself rambling. He sounded like a drunk, a loon. He tried to wind it up. But lost his nerve and rang off mid-sentence.

The moment he hung up he wished he hadn't called. She'd think he was barking. He'd only made it worse. He stared at the carpet, felt the reflux of panic in his throat. When the phone rang he grunted and was relieved to hear it was only Doris.

Her back garden smelt of frangipani and citronella and in the evening light white cockatoos roamed in raucous packs above the treetops of the neighbourhood. On the sea breeze came the waft of cut lawns, barbecue smoke, leaf-blowers. The proximity of the river was like something on the skin, a pleasant clamminess that brought to mind tree roots, undercut banks, stranded jellyfish. The house's rear deck was deep and broad. The little table hardly occupied a corner.

Keely sopped up the last of the tomato sauce with crusty bread and sat back, conscious of being observed. There was no wine on the table.

It's a nice house, this, he said sincerely.

Still, you've always disapproved.

Not true.

In ten years you've never had a good word for it.

Working-class prejudice.

Oh, rubbish. That's middle-class anxiety.

Probably.

You had a place just as nice yourself.

True.

In a street of old lumpers' cottages – go on, say it, make the distinction.

Which cost about the same, I know.

Tom, love, you have such romantic ideas about the working class.

Oh, come on, Mum.

Really, it tickles me.

Annoys you, actually.

Well, yes. I'm not as sentimental.

You couldn't get out of Blackboy Crescent fast enough. Could you?

I didn't have a choice, if you recall.

Sorry, I didn't mean it to sound so judgemental.

Really? The further you got from Blackboy Crescent, the more you wore your blue collar on your sleeve. And I know that sounds mangled but you know what I mean.

Keely winced. Because he did. Also because it was true.

And don't tell me about mixed metaphors – I *am* one.

Just never thought there was any harm in being proud of my origins, he said. State housing, state schools.

But why wear it like a badge of honour? As if it's *your* achievement rather than the result of government policy? The way all these people here seem to think the state is swimming in money because they *invented* iron ore, planted it, watered it. It's sheer luck. And it's luck that got you to university free of charge. You're the product of an historical moment, a brief awakening. *Tom*

Keely: My Struggle – it doesn't wash, love. You were generationally privileged. You're just another sulky Whitlam heir.

Mussels were never so expensive, he said by way of concession.

I'm not saying you didn't work hard.

Mum, all I was actually saying, if you remember, is that you have a nice house.

Well, it's too big, and as you can see I can't keep up with the garden.

Geez. People'll think you're renting.

At this there was an indulgent silence between them.

Sometimes I wonder if I'd still be there, she murmured. Blackboy Crescent. If things had worked out differently.

Really?

I don't know. It was your father who was restless, not me. We would have travelled, I think.

Where?

Central America, the Philippines. The liberation theology thing – we were in that together of course. Couldn't you just see him as a worker priest?

An evangelical with a wife and two kids – why not?

Well, everything smelt different then. A sense of possibility. Vatican II and all.

Think of it, he said. Nev as a Catholic, Billy Jack takes the Pope's shilling.

They both laughed. It was good. Better.

Anyway.

It really is a nice house, Mum. You bought it with hard work, righteous work. There's nothing to be guilty about.

I know that. I'm comfortable with that.

Okay. Good.

I'm just worried about you.

I know.

And I suspect you've come to enjoy the rewards of defeat. Shopping in despair's boutiques.

The law degree I applaud, Doris. The psych thing has become a nuisance.

So I'm told.

He pushed his chair back. It growled across the boards.

I saw her yesterday, he said. Harriet, I mean.

Don't try to sidestep me, Tom. Last night, along with every other vile thing you had to offload, you told your sister you were already dead, and that they'd be steaming you out of the carpet for weeks.

Fuck, he said, despite himself. No way.

Perhaps she imagined it. Maybe she's lying.

He sat there.

And you don't remember, she said. Or you'd rather not recall.

The sun was gone. Night had fallen without him noticing. Keely gripped his knees and let mosquitoes nip at his ankles.

Tom, I think we should talk about this.

Gemma's got a grandson.

You said.

He lives with her. In my building. There's something about him.

Tom, I'm talking about you. Right now there's something about you, she said, sliding a business card across the sauce-flecked table. I'd like you to go and see someone. I've made an appointment. You can call my doctor in the morning and he'll give you the referral.

You've been busy, he said.

Want something done, ask a busy person. This bloke's good. No scented candles, no hand holding, no bullshit.

And, listen, thanks for paying the phone bill. I meant to say. You shouldn't have.

I prefer you to be contactable. And you're changing the subject. Will you go?

Look, I appreciate all these recommendations, Mum, but really.
I've fixed it. If it's the money you're using as an excuse.

Gemma's boy, he's very economical with his facial expressions.
Almost affectless.

Tell me you'll go.

I thought you were asking.

I am asking.

When an angel asks something of you, isn't it kind of like a
command?

What're you talking about? Angels don't have arthritis – or a
thing for Leonard Cohen.

So. Guided democracy – that's what it's come to in the People's
Republic of Keely?

Just tell me you'll go.

He nodded. He wondered if, strictly speaking, a nod was actual
consent, whether it constituted a promise.

They washed the dishes together and cleaned up the messy remains
in a wary détente. He could sense his mother stepping around
him tenderly, soothing him however she could, compensating for
her little moment of intervention. Keely tried to spend the inter-
vals between neutral passages of small talk ordering his thoughts,
attempting to unpick strands and settle upon one memory, one
idea, a single resolution, but there was a rising, teeming noise of
thoughts in him like the uproar in a rainforest at the approach of an
intruder.

This boy, Doris was saying. Gemma's grandson. How old is he?

Kai.

Kai?

I know, he said guiltily.

I spose he could be Jet.

Or Koby.

Listen to us, she said. What's he like?

Strange, really. Smart. Very self-possessed, a bit withdrawn.

How old?

Six.

Maybe somewhere on the autism spectrum? Or just bright and lonely.

I wondered. You know, Asperger's, something like that.

Or foetal alcohol syndrome, she said. But he wouldn't be so bright. His mother?

Bandyup.

Drugs, I imagine.

He nodded.

The boy'll have a caseworker, said Doris. He'll be in the system, poor love.

He's so serious.

So were you.

Yeah, and I turned out alright.

Has he fixed on you? This boy?

Imagine how it's been for him.

She nodded. Please be careful, Tom. For his sake. And yours.

I am, he said. I will.

Suds splurged and gargled down the drain. Doris looked at him bravely, almost all her scepticism hidden from view.

Up close, where the sunspots and loose flesh showed, you could see she was an old woman. It never ceased to come as a shock. All the girlish hair, the sleekness and gravity. You forgot she wasn't young anymore. She was older than, well . . . Julie Christie. And had she stayed in Blackboy Crescent she might have been a great-grandmother now.

Is she beautiful?

What?

Gemma. Is she beautiful?

Well, he sighed. You can certainly see she *was*.

Doris finished wiping down the benches and straightened the cloth too carefully for his liking.

Attractive, isn't it, lost beauty?

Mum. Honestly.

Men like it. Gives them confidence. Then there's the added *frisson* of damage. They can't resist.

Are we looting old tutorials here or speaking from experience?

She glanced at him as if she'd been struck.

I'll drive you to the train.

Keely got out of the lift, turned the corner and there along the gallery in a puddle of light outside his door was Gemma. He hesitated a second but it was too late. She'd seen him. And his moment of indecision. In cargo shorts and a singlet, she leant against the iron rail, sucking on a fag beneath a cloud of moths. As he tramped on towards her, she glanced up and scattered them with a savage jet of smoke.

Evening, he murmured.

She said nothing. Leant on her elbows and stared out towards the bridges. Her hands shook.

Everything alright?

On his doormat was the laptop they'd retrieved that afternoon. It felt like days ago. He gathered it up and unlocked his door.

Gemma?

Moths churned and wheeled above her. She blew them into disarray once more.

Keely went in, set the little Acer on the kitchen bench and opened the sliding door to catch whatever mucky updraught there was. He turned to see her stab the fag out against the rail and pitch the butt into the darkness.

You coming in or what?

She turned beneath her corona of moths, ran a hand through her hair and peered in at him. She came on in, but unsteadily. She was drunk. Or drugged. Or something.

Kai asleep? he asked.

I can't get him off that bloody Nintendo.

What d'you want me to do with this? he said, pointing to the laptop.

I dunno. Set it up or whatever for Kai? Dunno nothin about em.

You want a cup of tea or something?

She shook her head.

You're not working tonight?

What is this – quiz night? I called in crook, okay?

As she brushed by to flop into the armchair he saw how puffy her eyes were, as if she'd been crying.

Something's happened, he said.

Let's go for a drive.

Maybe you should tell me.

I feel like a drive, she said.

It's late, Gem. I'm knackered. And what about Kai?

He can come too.

He's got school. I don't think it's a good idea.

He's comin, she said hotly. Don't look at me like I'm some horrible slag. All I want's a bloody drive in me car – is that a crime? Come or don't come, I don't care.

She blundered back out onto the gallery and up the way. He watched her fumble at her own door.

Leave us alone! she yelled back at him before stepping inside.

Keely retreated indoors. Alert to the prospect of a stormy return, he left the door ajar and tidied the kitchen, but she didn't show.

He was brushing his teeth for bed when he heard Gemma's angry shout in the distance. A door slammed. He went out onto the balcony from where a child's wailing carried on the warm night air. Keely told himself it could be anyone's kid. Every window in the building was open as residents courted the tepid breeze; the place was as porous as a birdcage – sounds you swore you heard next door actually boiled up from several floors below.

He went inside, uneasy but determined to get an early night. But another door thudded shut and then footfalls rang along the gallery.

Do what ya bloody told! yelled Gemma.

Keely stepped out to see her hauling the resistant boy by the arm and the sight of them struggling out there between the wall and the railing sent a ripple of fear through him. When he reached them they were both flailing and tearful. A few doors down, from the safety of the darkness, someone threatened to call the cops. Gemma told whoever they were to get stuffed. But she gave up the car keys the moment Keely asked for them.

It wasn't until they were past the Old Traffic Bridge and the container terminal that the boy's rending sobs finally gave way to silence. Keely cranked down the window to let in a soothing rush of night air. He steered them along the coast, savouring the quiet, not knowing or caring where he was headed, his bewilderment and disgust gradually softened by the smells of limey sand, ocean air and saltbush. The road narrowed and wound through unlit bush reserves. The little car burped and rattled. There were sparks behind his eyes and that deep ache in his skull further back, but he tried to concentrate on the sweet feel of the wind rummaging through his shirt. In the mirror he caught the pale flutter of Gemma's hair, the swipe of a hand blotting tears. She sat in the corner of the back seat cradling the kid. Kai seemed to have subsided into sleep.

Swanbourne, Floreat, City Beach. Gulls orbited the orange sodium lights of the northern beaches and above them the sky was starless, inky. The waterside carparks were scattered with vanloads of backpackers and partying youths hunting shadows. Every rocky groyne bristled with fishing rods and the shadows on the dimpled sand looked like moon craters.

At Scarborough he circled the roundabout beneath the ugly clock and wound slowly through the old terraces.

Christ, she said.

I know.

Why here?

It wasn't deliberate, he said.

I'm just sayin.

I'm just driving, he said. I could be in bed, you know.

She said nothing and he caught a glimpse of her running a hand through her hair, gazing out at the old sights. Keely steered them past the tawdry strip of shops, the Norfolk pines, the kids sitting on the bonnets of their cars.

Saw a boy surfin a Torana here one night. The mudflaps were on fire.

I was there, he said.

Riot police and everythin.

Happy days!

Loved that show.

That too, he said, pulling up by the northern shower block where the coolest surfers used to hang and the stink of hash was often more pungent than the reek of piss. A couple of kids hacked up and down on skateboards. It looked desolate here now. But at this time of night perhaps it had always looked a bit bleak.

Carn then, she said. We come this far. Let's check it out.

Check what out?

You know what.

What happened tonight?

Five minutes, Tom. It won't kill ya.

Why?

Old times' sake.

Why now?

Cause we can. And I got the car, Tommy. I don't care what that little shit Stewie says. I got the car. I can drive where I like. C'mon.

The skater boys flipped their boards warily, waiting for the old folks to get out or drive away. With one of them in the front and the other in the back Keely knew they probably looked dodgy. He wheeled the car around and a minute later they were on the four-lane east.

I remember this, said Gemma. I remember when it was a lime-stone track.

Keely said nothing. He recalled it well enough. Wished she would shut up.

When he pulled into the old street he felt uneasy. Why couldn't he have tooled along the river, somewhere neutral? He hadn't been back in thirty-five years; he wasn't sure he wanted to do this tonight. Maybe another day – alone, on foot, in daylight. But he was here now. And he could smell wild oats and lupins from the empty lot on the corner. He remembered this, the smell and the patch of dirt, from all those long treks to school. He thought of bikes with banana seats, boys in desert boots, hot tar.

In the back Gemma twisted and gasped.

Christ, she muttered. They've changed the name. Grasstree Crescent.

Grasstree? he said as evenly as he could manage.

I'll bet it's to keep the Abos happy.

Keely let it go. But he felt the twinge of loss, despite himself. He eased down the hill in first, struggling to get his bearings. The road was the same; he remembered when this too had been limestone. The crescent curved down towards the swamp, so strange and familiar. But few of the old places were there anymore. The modest uniformity of the original neighbourhood was gone and with it the sense of egalitarian plainness, the peculiar comprehensibility it once had. The quarter-acre blocks had been subdivided, the small brick-veneer bungalows replaced by two-storey triplexes pressed together without eaves or verandahs. On nearly every roof sat an airconditioner and a satellite dish. Where there had been picket fences, high brick walls. No families out on porches watching TV, no cars sprawled across front yards, no lumpy aprons of buffalo grass.

Neither he nor Gemma spoke until they reached the swamp, now a recreation precinct of bicycle paths, pine-log gazebos and mown lawns under floodlights.

Fuck, she said.

Yeah.

Go back, she said. Chuck a u-ey.

A little dazed, Keely swung about and headed uphill at a crawl. Number 14 was gone. He idled out the front of a shrunken Tuscan villa behind whose wrought-iron gates stood a Chinese 4x4.

I don't care about ours, she said. But I wanted yours to still be there.

Well. It isn't.

A sensor light came on. He pulled away, heard her counting

houses. But in the end they didn't need to count. For there it was, unmistakeable.

Wouldn't it rip ya? she said quietly.

The old Buck place had every light on, curtains askew, music pounding from open windows. On the parched front lawn a slew of vehicles, some on blocks. A dog flew out, flashing its teeth. From the porch a woman called it back with a foul stream of imprecations.

That'll be why they changed the name, said Gemma. So more boongs could move in.

Stop it, he said, pulling away.

I wish we hadn't come.

Well, we did.

It's all different.

No, he said with pleasure. Your place is still the same.

Fuck you, she said lighting up a fag. Go fuck yourself.

He drove homeward in the stormy silence and as the lights of the container terminal rose before them he heard her weeping in the back.

Instead of settling for budget-brand muesli, Keely sat in Bub's and ordered his morning usual. While he was waiting he fired up the newly charged laptop for a casual look at what needed doing. And a single glance was sufficient. He slapped the thing shut with so much force a woman cried out at the next table and all he could offer was a grimace of apology.

Keely thought he'd seen porn but he'd never encountered anything quite like this before. When breakfast came he ate it blinking dumbly at the battered Acer which had suddenly taken on a radioactive aura. Between that and the nervous glances from the poor woman alongside him, he wasn't inclined to linger and the outing was an expensive washout.

Once he got the machine home he found the software was

registered to Carly M. Fairlight, but he doubted she was the gonzo-porn enthusiast. He spent the rest of the day dumping files and running clean-up programs. He wondered about Gemma's mood last night, whether she'd stumbled on this cache – or worse, found Kai with it. That was an ugly thought. But no. If she'd seen that shit she'd have pitched the thing off the tenth floor already, wouldn't she? Maybe he was a resentful puritan – wasn't that how the shock-jocks portrayed him? But that stuff was foul. He wished he hadn't seen it.

Eventually he got the computer running smoothly, and for good measure found he could pirate other folks' wireless networks right here in the building, and by way of exorcism or whatever sacrament applied to soiled machines, he wiped it down, inside and out, with antibacterial handwash.

In the afternoon he left the front door open but nobody knocked. He made a fiery and extremely cheap vegetarian curry and ate it at dusk in a virtuous sweat.

At eight the phone rang. He was expecting his sister or his mother, but it was Gemma. She was subdued; she sounded hoarse. Kai was being difficult. She had a shift to do. Would he mind coming over for an hour?

He met her on the gallery. She was dressed for work, made up a little too vividly. She looked wretched and spent.

You could have come by, he said.

I didn't think I should, she murmured shakily.

It's fine, Gem.

I'm just a stupid bitch.

What did he do, that bloke? What'd he say to you?

Somethin nasty. Somethin a bloke'll say.

You won't tell me?

She shook her head.

Last night.

It doesn't matter.

I just needed somethin nice, she said. Somewhere I could remember bein happy.

It took some absorbing. After everything she'd told him, everything he'd seen for himself, Blackboy Crescent was where she'd been happiest? He didn't say anything. She looked too tired.

Just sit with him, will you, Tom? Don't make him do anythin. Just be there.

He nodded. She gathered herself, pecked him on the cheek and went.

Inside 1010 the TV was off but the flat was a mess. Kai was in bed flipping through the raptor book. As if his being difficult were directed at Gemma alone. Keely greeted him but the boy did not respond. There were blue pools like bruises beneath his eyes. Keely resisted the urge to natter brightly at the kid. He did only what Gemma had asked, pushed her pillows against the wall and sat with him.

The boy closed the book and sank deeper. He tilted the thing up on his chest and surveyed the cover. It was a close-up image of an eagle's eye – black-rimmed, stark, the iris a web of yellow-bronze – and Kai wasn't merely glancing at it but peering deeply, chewing his lips, wheezing in fervent concentration. Keely tried not to stare but it was difficult. The kid seemed to mesmerize himself, sink into the interlacing layers of the bird's iris.

Eventually the boy's eyelids began to droop and flutter. He seemed to struggle against sleep as if stalked by it, and this skirmish went on for a minute or so, until the book began to waver. At the last moment, as if to save himself from falling, the boy reached aside and took Keely's arm. And was gone. Keely caught the book with his spare hand. Saw him down. Tried not to hold his breath. Watched him sleep.

He woke on the floor in his own place with the slider open to the baking wind and his legs stippled with mosquito bites. His face hurt, his mouth was woolly, but he didn't remember drinking anything. In the bathroom mirror he saw what amounted to a shiner. He had no memory of hurting himself. But there was still an eerie sparkle behind his eyes. A sequin fizz. It took a full minute to unscramble the label on the toothpaste.

In the café Bub raised his eyebrows but said nothing. Keely drank one coffee only and paid with shrapnel. He was turning to leave when Bub sent down a double-shot on the house. He waved in sheepish gratitude and tried to savour it. But he thought of the boy, his dry little hand on his arm. And the bird's yellow eye. And the troubling fact of the wide-open door.

After a few moments Bub emerged from the kitchen and slid a tall glass of apple juice onto the table.

Here, said the nuggety bald fixture. You look dry as a camel's cookie.

I am that. And thanks.

Tom, said Bub, smiling at the black eye, you're not the fighting type.

You think?

The kitchen bell chimed. Bub clapped him on the shoulder and headed back.

They gave him thirty bucks for the iPod and ninety for his laptop. He suspected that without the shiner he'd have gotten more, but he was content enough afterwards, trolling op-shops with cash in his pocket, looking for something to please the boy. He started at Save the Children, moved on to Oxfam, then the Vinnies. But they had nothing he was after. Then at the last stop, closest to home, he scored. He walked out of the Good Sammies with a perfectly serviceable game of Scrabble and change from a fiver.

At home, tucked into the grille of his security door, was a fair pencil rendering of a mudlark. He pulled it out and went on to Gemma's. At his knock he saw the tiny moon of the peephole flash a second. She pulled the door back on its chain and peered out warily.

Just me, he said.

Christ, what happened?

I walked into a cliché, he muttered.

I'm serious.

It's nothing. Really. And look, he said, holding up the battered box.

The whole Scrabble business was a mystery to Keely. Kai had the Nintendo, after all, and kids were supposedly addicted zombies after only a day or two's feverish toggling, but although the boy seemed to enjoy murdering thugs and aliens, and often shouted disconcertingly at certain leering villains, the excitement wore off after the first mad binge. He never completely forsook Super Mario, but tended to lose energy after half an hour or so and drift to the laptop whose charm lay in the keyboard as much as the screen. As far as Keely could tell, Gemma had never played Scrabble with him. Perhaps he'd seen something on TV – he didn't say and Gemma couldn't recall, didn't find the question nearly as intriguing as Keely did. The boy was in his first year of school and yet he could already read extremely well and write after a fashion.

Keely wondered who'd taught him. It didn't seem possible he could have absorbed it all himself. He got simple words arse-about, and certain letters as well. It was strange to watch him hunched at the computer, wheezing slightly, experimenting – building words with cautious pecks at the keys, consciously or inadvertently creating lists that plunged down the screen like ratlines.

Keely was excited at the prospect of teaching Kai to play, but he wondered how the kid would fare. It wasn't the raciest board game invented. But from the outset Kai seemed less interested in scores than in the words themselves. Games might begin in a spirit of boyish competition, but Kai seemed to fall into a trance, rousing now and then in a momentary shiver of recognition. Keely imagined the syllables emerging from chaos. He recalled his own childhood, how words hid as if aching to be found, transformed by his gaze, reaching out to meet him. He was fascinated by the way the boy handled the tiles, how he turned them over in his hands, running the tips of his thumbs across their faces as if tempted to slip them into his mouth like milky chocolates. His fingers twitched, tantalized, over the board, as he breathed upon his row of letters on their little pine plinth.

Kai was an exacting playing partner. He did not like tiles to fall out of alignment on the board. And there was no point making conversation or daggy jokes between moves because he'd stiff you. The only time he tolerated noise was during the initial shaking and shuffling of pieces in the box lid before the game commenced. Then he seemed like any other kid. He liked to rifle through the tiles like a miser with his loot – Scrooge McDuck in the vault – but once he settled down it was all sober concentration. He did not enjoy the letter Q. And blanks, letters that were mutable, seemed to cause him anxiety; they had to be marked laboriously with a pencil before he could accept them as real, and even then they troubled him, as if there were something untrustworthy about their nature. But defeat didn't bother him. And thankfully he was bored by the tedious endgame. Like Keely, he had no interest in plugging holes with two-letter words or suffixes, scrounging points in endless rounds of lexical puttying. Once the rich pickings were gone he began to fidget and Keely was only too happy to concede a comradely draw and start afresh.

They played afternoons and evenings all week; it became a routine. And apart from his morning swim this was soon the thing Keely most looked forward to. Something to digest, really, the knowledge that a game of Scrabble with a six-year-old had become the highlight of his day. But there was weird pleasure in it, something he'd been missing for longer than he cared to think.

Often as not Kai came straight from school bearing a new sketch – a wattlebird, a kingfisher, a heron – and Keely sent him home for his fruit and biscuits and lime cordial before he returned with the Scrabble box pressed to his chest. Around five Gemma came by to dragoon the boy into showering and Keely followed them up the gallery to 1010 where she'd already have the makings for dinner on the bench. Evenings settled into a pattern of school notes fixed to the fridge door, and reading before bedtime. Their conversation became desultory, as if the adults were partners in a faded marriage. It amused him, and he was grateful for it, but often he yearned for more. Not high conversation, nothing taxing. But he would have liked to know things, to press her for details, facts about her life and Kai's. He wondered about her sister, Baby. There were so many gaps, years and relationships, disasters and hurts he was left to infer. And there were moments, too, when Gemma's physical proximity caused him pangs.

Even so he felt that his life was different, that it had finally tilted towards something coherent. The headaches seemed more bearable. He could suffer Gemma's diffidence because of Kai. At day's end, he and the boy played their games of Scrabble and Super Mario, talked birds and habitat, rifled through the dictionary, googled odd facts in a long and pleasurable post-ponement of bedtime. The nightly challenge was to present the kid a story, like a cat dragging in a rodent. As Keely perched at the bedside, waiting for any flicker of inspiration, the boy noted the progress of his shiner as the contusion flared, morphed, and began, thankfully, to fade. It was kind of charming – flattering, really – having him catalogue every change of colour.

You like this shiner, he said to Kai.

No, said the boy. Just makin it go away.

The kid had tropes and sayings, things that stuck in Keely's head.

At the start of a game: Seven tiles, he said, almost chanting. Seven letters. Like seven days. 7-Eleven. 24/7. Always seven. Gotta be seven.

Then at bedtime: Wattlebirds. They eat spiders. If there's too much spiders there's too much poison. In the world.

When Keely's jokes wore thin: No, Tom. No falling.

At dusk: Look. The lighthouse. Counting the night.

During an episode of Friends: Eagles. They're killers. Do they get to go to Heaven?

In Keely's flat: Really, but. Where do words come from?

At home alone at night, he sat up late resisting all temptation, exhausted but unable to rest his mind. He tried re-reading *Catch-22* and marvelled that he'd found it so mordantly funny in his youth. Now it was too distressing. He wanted to shout at the novelist: no more, no fooling, no falling.

Mostly, though, he felt okay, more or less functional. Just bubbling with thoughts that kept him from sleep, watching the Parker Point lighthouse measure out the darkness.

He thought a lot about Kai. Especially the way he resisted sleep. As if it were something to fear, not a release. Except for those final moments, the slipping away, the kid avoided physical contact. Keely had to police himself, refrain from tousling the kid's hair or shoving him playfully in passing. As a boy he'd loved being monstered by Nev, rolled on the floor in a headlock, tickled until he was blue. He liked to be overwhelmed by him and then have at him with camel bites and knee jabs – just to feel and make himself felt in return. But Kai could find space where there seemed to be none; he could sidestep any well-meaning pat or squeeze, as if his body anticipated yours, as if he were monitoring your every movement.

The boy retreated into silences, reveries, fugues. During which he was impassive, unreachable. He could blink you away, delete you from his presence, and these silent lockouts sent Gemma into furies. There was so much Keely didn't understand. It was as if he'd stumbled into a play halfway through the show. And he wondered if he'd ever catch up.

But he adjusted to some things rapidly, even if he didn't know what they signified. Like the bedtime ritual, which he came to need as much as the boy. There was something about that period of potent, dreamy calm between the pair of them, the intimacy of the whispered story and the long silences that ensued. The way Kai drifted beside him in the shafted gloom, unmoored from the day and his defended self. Every night came that moment of panic before surrender when the boy made solid contact, seizing him, the arm shooting out like a baby's startle reflex, the hand gripping Keely's shirt as if he were steadying himself before finally letting go.

I knew you, said Kai one night. I knew you before you had a face.

I don't understand, he murmured. What do you mean?

But the boy was silent, perhaps asleep already, and Keely was left to turn it over in his mind, the thought that Kai had been waiting for him, lying alone in the flat night after night while Gemma worked, waiting for someone to keep him safe. The idea was intoxicating. It made a man feel enormous and substantial. That he might be necessary.

Towards the end of the week he noticed Gemma becoming increasingly fractious. Sent on an errand he bought the wrong brand of paper towels. He cooked with too much garlic and like Kai he left the toilet seat up. She was fed up with their nerdy boy talk, their birdy bullshit – and why was he always here in the flat anyway, taking up space? She didn't want a wife and besides he wasn't even paying his way, so why didn't he stop botting off her and leave them in peace?

On Thursday he gave Kai a quick game after school but sent him on home alone for dinner. Keely figured he'd make himself scarce a while. But on Friday evening she came by with a takeaway roasted chicken and reminded him of the prison visit next morning. She had the night off, she said girlishly. And for someone just back from the supermarket she seemed a little too carefully put together. She was giving him the willies.

Gemma left him the chook but he stayed away and jerked off miserably during the SBS movie. Later he thought of calling Harriet – she'd probably be still at work, the number wouldn't take long to find. He suddenly wanted to hear her voice, tell her about this boy who held his arm, but he wasn't mad enough yet to do it. She'd think it was either vengeful or pathetic. He'd make her cry and hate himself.

So as drunks rolled festively through the streets below, he carted himself off to bed. He couldn't think about tomorrow. Tried to hypnotize himself. Fox his way down step by step, turn by turn, avoiding all thought. And mostly failing.

He dreamt he was swimming, coursing towards the sea on his own, fleeing shadows, making himself tiny with fear.

It was a long, hot drive out into the valley. They had the drab entirety of Perth to traverse – every grey and khaki suburb, every baking industrial park, car yard and junk-food franchise on the ravaged plain. The Saturday-morning drivers were torpid and maddening. Heat rolled down from the ranges in waves. Although they began the journey with Gemma at the wheel she was so erratic from nervous excitement she had to pull over and surrender the controls to Keely. Almost as jittery as her, he followed her directions, submitting to her liverish commentary until he got to the outlands where droughted horse paddocks gave way to housing estates of heartbreaking ugliness.

In the back with his sketchpad and pencil case, Kai sat subdued to the point of complete withdrawal. The boy had been to Bandyup before but he would not be drawn into conversation about it. At home whenever Gemma mentioned his mother he rarely engaged. The whole thing gave Keely the yips.

His eyes hurt. His head pinged and throbbed. Smears of light caught on everything, gave his vision a nasty lag, like old-school video. It was the shits, feeling this bad after a booze-free evening. He hadn't even gobbed a pill for twelve hours and now he felt worse than if he'd been on a bender. For relief he thought of worthy analgesics: Panadeine Forte, Nurofen Osteo, Mersyndol.

When the turn-off finally came he missed it. Gemma slapped the dashboard in disgust. He pulled over violently.

For God's sake, he said, startled as much as angry. Just calm down, will you?

Turning around on the highway, he took his indignation out on the car, conscious of how unhelpful the histrionics were.

The women's prison was a squat brick campus set well back from the road. Except for the coils of razor wire it looked no nastier than the schools he'd gone to in the sixties and seventies. And yet his mouth went dry just rolling up the drive.

They were a few minutes early. He found somewhere permissible to park. Left the motor running for the sake of what paltry relief the aircon provided. Gemma opened and closed her handbag repeatedly. She checked her face in the mirror, tried to fold Kai's hair behind his ears. Other vehicles began to coast in around them.

I'll swing back at eleven, said Keely. Or if you'd prefer, I'll wait here – in case you come out early.

You're not comin in? she said with feeling.

Oh, he exclaimed dishonestly. I didn't realize.

Well, Jesus. You don't *have* to.

No, it's that I didn't —

I asked for Kai's sake.

Not a problem, he said. Of course.

Jesus.

Really, he said, turning off the engine.

See? she said to Kai, twisting in her seat. Tom's comin too. You ready to see your mum?

Kai shrugged.

Love! she said too brightly. She'll be *that* excited.

The boy packed up his things without expression.

When they opened the car doors, the heat was withering. Keely felt it shrink his throat and cause flares at the edge of his vision. Gemma took Kai by the arm and Keely followed. All the way to reception she prattled about shade and airconditioning but once they passed into the industrial chill of the interior there was surprisingly little relief. With its muddle of signage, its antiseptic smell and atmosphere of tamped desperation, the building could have been the annexe of any social service – the dole office, Homeswest, DOCS. This side of the glass attempts had been made to create a sense of normality, but the strain was palpable. The false cheer amongst visitors. The sideways looks. Keely felt a scalding flush in his cheeks.

He followed Gemma, did what she did, tried to seem relaxed. They joined a queue, exchanged thin smiles with others. But they'd barely begun the process of registration when Gemma turned and seized him by the sleeve.

Oh Christ, she said. They've brought the dogs.

What's that mean? he asked.

Down the line a uniformed officer and his eager mutt capered in and out.

Non-contact, said Gemma through her teeth. It's gunna be a strip search – Jesus! Tom, take him.

What?

Kai, she said. Take him out.

But why?

Just get him in the car, drive him around for a bit.

Gemma —

I'm not havin em touch this boy.

Are you sure?

Of course I'm bloody sure, just go – now!

Bewildered but galvanized, he steered the child back towards the entrance.

Everything alright? said the officer at the door.

Change of plan, said Keely.

Imagine so, she murmured a little too knowingly.

They stepped out of the refrigerated enclosure and into white sun. Keely felt it dig into the pits of his eyes and the pain travelled through his shoulders, elbows, hands.

He didn't know what to tell Kai. Then wondered if the boy needed anything explained anyway. Keely got them onto the highway for the sake of being gone, yet the moment he was free, giddy and slightly guilty for the relief of it, he was faced with the immediate problem of where to go and what to do out here in this desolation of overpasses and spiky bush. There was nothing: no shade, no houses, no shops. Enormous signs rose before them touting wildlife parks and tourist-trap wineries.

After a few minutes Keely pulled in at a semi-rural roadhouse where articulated trucks parked in lines at high-flow diesel pumps. Watermelons sat piled in crates. At the edge of the gravel apron there were trailers for hire and horse manure for sale.

You must be thirsty, he said to Kai.

Yes, the boy allowed.

Inside the place stank of fried bacon and scorched coffee. Homely smells after the prison. And the place was cool but not cold. Keely bought a Coke and a packet of chips for the boy.

Scruples be buggered – the kid needed some sort of treat. Got an apple juice for himself. He chugged it before he'd even drawn up a chair. Kai opened his drink and then his chips and set his sketch-pad on the table. Keely hadn't even noticed him bring it in. He watched the boy lay out his pencils.

Well, he said. That was all a bit awkward, wasn't it?

The boy glanced past him.

I'm sorry you didn't get to see your mum.

Kai selected a pencil.

Your nan will explain everything.

It's drugs, said Kai.

I see, he said haplessly.

A waitress sloped by on tender feet and informed them that if they wanted to sit inside they'd need to buy a meal. Keely couldn't face the heat just now and he was anxious to avoid any unpleasant-ness, so he ordered a BLT. Maybe the kid would pick at it.

Lucky you've got your nan, he said.

The boy chewed his lip.

What're you drawing?

Kai shrugged.

Can I see?

Kai rolled a pencil on the laminex as if weighing up the request. Then he pushed the pad across. Keely took it up and flicked through pictures of magpies, a Pacific gull and several failed attempts at a pelican. After this came a series of simple, almost stylized images that were not at all birdlike. It took Keely a few moments to under-stand what they were.

Kai, what's this?

Just me, said the boy, considering a salty crinkle-cut chip.

An outline?

Kai licked the salt off the chip. Keely looked again at the emphatic line, the splayed limbs. It was the classic pictograph of a dead body, the sort of thing you saw every night on TV.

What's it about? What's it for?

I draw it when I dream it.

When you *dream* it? You mean the same dream you told me about?

Where I land. I'm there for a while. Then I'm gone and that's all that's left.

This line?

The boy ate the chip, took a gulp of Coke, and burped quietly.

Are you sure this is a dream?

Kai offered a look of studied patience and did not quite meet his gaze.

Well, that's pretty interesting, he said, trying to disguise his alarm.

The boy retrieved the pad and thumbed through the pages.

Does it make you afraid?

Kai took up the pencil and commenced to roll it again.

Kai? Can you say?

The boy pursed his lips in a manner suggesting assent.

Keely pressed his thumbs into his temples, tried to think.

The waitress returned with a colossal sandwich. They looked at it, man and boy, and Keely saw that Kai wanted it but needed coaxing. He passed him a knife and fork.

Bet you can't finish that, he said.

Kai set aside his pad and pencils, drew the plate to him and went to work with his usual finicky precision. Keely could have watched him do it all day. The boy's fine blond hair fell across his face. He brushed it aside with a forearm and chewed methodically, eyes half closed in concentration.

Keely got up to buy himself more juice and at the counter he looked back at the kid working his way through another mouthful.

He's lovely, said the waitress, clearly mistaking this for a Saturday access visit.

Yes, said Keely. He is.

As Gemma got into the car she brought with her an acrid smell that suggested an electrical fire, and he saw by the cooked colour of her face that he'd kept her waiting in the sun for some time. For several minutes nobody spoke. The Hyundai's airconditioner buzzed impotently. And then at the freeway on-ramp Gemma began to blot her eyes with a tissue.

Sorry you didn't see her, Kai, she said.

Keely wasn't sure the boy heard. He watched him in the mirror as he gazed out at the traffic, licking his lips without expression.

Not your fault, Keely murmured.

No. It's not.

She hunched forward suddenly. She beat a fist against her brow in a ghastly, silent sob. Keely did his best to focus on the road and traffic ahead but he monitored the white flash of the tissue clenched in her fingers, the veins rising in her neck, one livid ear. She gave out a small, strangled sigh. And after a few moments she'd mastered herself.

The dog, she said at last. They bring it out when she's blown her privileges.

I don't follow you, he said, anxious about the boy.

She wouldn't say, of course. But I could see it right off.

I guess you've had practice, he said lamely.

You just know. When it's suddenly non-contact, when they strip you and put the dogs over you, means she's not clean. Christ, she coulda said when she rang, to spare the boy. She knows what it means. She doesn't even care *that* much. How can she let us go in there and have him felt up like that? Jesus, you're lucky they didn't follow you out and do a car search.

How could it matter? he asked. There's nothing here.

Mate, the dogs'd be howlin over this thing. You think this doesn't stink of what they're lookin for?

But we're not carrying anything, Gem.

As if that makes any difference. The dog gets a positive, they think you're supplyin. And suddenly it's all hands on deck. Big search, more bullshit.

But they'd see we're clean.

Jesus, you haven't got a clue.

Keely steered the car. Nauseated. Angry. Fighting blips of phosphorus he could taste now.

After a moment's silence she lit a fag and cracked a window.

This piece of shit, she said.

On the freeway he threaded through the citybound traffic.

I was only there ten minutes, she said. You know what she wanted to talk about? The car. She wants me to sell it, wants the money in an account. She wants the computer stuff sold. Can you believe that? She wants money. I've been down this road, I don't need it.

It's just the drugs, said Kai.

Yes, love. That's what it is. But she'll get better. We'll go again another time. When she's right again.

The boy said nothing. They rode home in silence.

He swam out to the pontoon in a languid Mersyndol crawl. Beneath him the white sandy bottom was ribbed and scalloped and the sheen from the surface spangled across the sand in pulsing bursts like brain waves. As he hauled himself onto the ladder squealing kids leapt overhead, spearing out behind him, their bodies sending shocks through the water. He clambered up and sat awhile, bracing himself against every lurch and jerk as the platform yanked on its chains and children launched and chased and goaded each other. He felt self-conscious there amongst the kids, but the water had brought him back off the boil, calmed him enough to enjoy their antic energy. Neither Gemma nor Kai had wanted to come and he was glad. The beach was a relief, a happy rippling mosaic of colour. Umbrellas, balls, lycra, bodies, hair. The desert breeze carried laughter, shouts and music across the water. He lingered, savouring it while he could. Up on the grass there was no sign of Conan at all. Keely was home free.

Afterwards he rode into the West End, took in an art show at an old Victorian warehouse. Just to feel normal again. But the gallery was hot, its whitewashed walls too bright for him. He moved on to a bookshop but lost his bearings. Found himself standing by a row of fashion tomes beneath the airconditioning vent.

Is there anything I can help you with? asked the tattooed young woman striding down from the counter.

He gave a witless smile and shook his head. There was nothing here he could afford. And he'd been there fifteen minutes, he now realized. Not even browsing. Just there. Like a post, an uncurated installation.

Late in the afternoon Kai came to the door.

Nan's got takeaway, said the boy.

Keely didn't fancy it; he could have done with a break from them, but he didn't have the heart to knock the kid back.

I'll be up there in a minute, he said.

Keely washed the salt from his face and looked for a clean shirt. When he got to the door the boy was still there. He wasn't sure if Kai had something to say to him or if he was simply being escorted. He didn't want to quiz him. Nothing was said.

Gemma dished up takeaway Chinese. Kai shoved a disc into the DVD player. They watched Shrek do his thing for the umpteenth time. No one said much. Gemma seemed faded. She bore an air of regret, of unspoken apology. Kai had eyes only for the green ogre and his mad japes; he loved everything about this movie except the musical routines, which bored him. Keely's mind kept returning to the boy's most recent drawings. Perhaps he'd seen these body outlines on a cop show. They bothered him. He should mention them to Gemma. Though maybe not tonight.

He's not happy, she said later, quietly at the sink.

It was a rough day, he murmured.

Will you stay with him? Just till he's asleep?

He nodded. Of course.

When you weren't here it didn't matter. Now you are – well, look at us.

He shrugged. It was hard to know what she meant.

Sometimes I wish she wasn't born.

Keely set a sudsy plate on the draining board without comment.

Her father was a shithead. I wish none of it happened.

Then you wouldn't have Kai, he said gently.

She nodded absently, blotting the plate with a towel.

Gemma?

I don't wanna talk about it anymore.

H e woke.

Gemma's. The couch. The boy standing over him.

Oh, he croaked. What's the matter? What time is it?

Four and twelve, said Kai. The boy's face was pale in the yellow light spilling up from the wharves.

You alright?

I have a question.

Ah, he said, cranking himself slowly onto an elbow. Right. Okay. Hang on a sec, just let me wake up a bit.

What's it like, getting old?

Keely hauled himself more or less upright on the couch, let his head fall back a moment to catch up with where he was. The bedroom light was on. Gemma was still at work.

Did you have a dream?

The boy said nothing. He was bare-chested in his shorty pyjamas. His breath was bitter, his eyes wide in the gloom.

Tom?

Kai, it's the middle of the night.

Are you awake?

Well, I guess I am now, he said. Have you had a fright?

Can you tell me?

Getting old? Is that the question? Keely's back was stiff. He wondered how long the kid had been awake.

It's just, I don't know what it's like, said the boy.

Mate, I don't know what to tell you.

But you're old.

Well. Older than you. And yeah, right now I feel pretty old, that's the truth.

Can you say?

What it's like, you mean? What it feels like? Keely scratched his stubble, kneaded his cheeks a moment. The thing is, he said. Thing is, you hardly notice. It happens so slowly. You look different in the mirror, but inside you feel pretty much the same. You're just a kid with an old man's body, that's how it feels. Same for everyone, I guess.

The boy shook his head.

I try and see it. But I can't.

Well, I spose it takes a lot of imagination.

I have a lot of imagination. Mrs Crumb said. Father Crean said.

That's good. That's a big compliment. You want to sit here a moment? he said, patting the cushion.

But it's not *there*, said the boy, ignoring him. Still standing. Looking past him.

Sorry? What's not there?

Old.

Keely peered into the boy's face.

Kai?

It won't happen to me.

Getting old? Happens to all of us, mate.

No, he said sadly. Not me.

Keely reached for the boy's arm but Kai eluded him.

Kai, listen. You don't have to worry about things like that.

Are you like your dad?

Mate, what's bothering you?

Keely struggled to his feet and the boy made room for him. At the sink he found a glass and filled it with water. He drank it off and filled it again.

I'm not like my dad, said Kai, resting his chin on the counter between them.

My dad's dead, said Keely.

I know. But maybe you're like him. When he was alive.

And what makes you say that?

Nan said.

Well, said Keely. I'd like to be. But I don't think I am. Sadly. I'm older than him, now. Isn't that weird. Listen, what did she tell you?

Are you going to be my dad then?

She said that?

Kai shook his head.

Oh. Well, no. You already have a dad.

Yes.

But I'm your mate, okay?

Okay.

Really. I'm your friend. You can tell me anything.

Kai considered this.

I know things, the boy said, spreading his hands across the

laminated counter.

I believe you.

He saved people.

Who?

Nan said.

Who saved people?

Your dad.

At this, Keely felt a peculiar flush of grief. Hotter, fresher, harder than he'd felt for years.

Is it true?

Well, if your nan says.

But sometimes she says stuff. To be nice. He's not just a story?

Keely set the glass down and looked at Kai's hands. He felt ensnared.

Listen, why don't we go in and lie down, eh?

Is it true? Like, he saved people? They called out in the night and he came?

Well, yeah. I guess.

There's this bad dad, said Kai. It's dark in the street. He's real mean, he does all the baddest things. And the kids are crying. They hide in the toilet. Run in the shed. They go in the garden, and call out for help. But no one comes cause they're scared of him. Nobody 'cept your dad.

Well, yeah. I think that's true.

And he saves them.

He tries.

He fights him, said the boy, warmed to his own telling. He saves the kids. He's big and he's got a motorbike. And big hands.

Let's talk about it in there, Keely said, pointing to the bedroom.

He's real big, said the boy, allowing himself to be steered. Like a ogre. Like Shrek.

Maybe, said Keely, thinking on it. Maybe a little bit.

He got the boy into bed. The easterly was moaning in the balustrades and window sashes already. The sheets were cool. They smelt of woman and child. Kai's hair fanned back against his pillow. He steepled his fingers on his pale chest.

I wish he wasn't dead.

Yeah, said Keely, lying back on Gemma's pillow. Me too.

He would come. He would save me.

Keely searched the kid's face.

This nightmare. I think it's really bothering you.

The people aren't bad, Kai said quietly. There's eyes and no faces. But they aren't bad.

So there's no one hurting you?

No. The hurting gets smaller. It's kind of sad. Like . . . Like everything goes away, turning off. But I don't want it to. Everything goes off like the end of the day.

Like going to sleep?

He shrugged.

And can you see yourself?

Sometimes I'm smaller. I can see from here.

And that's what you draw?

The boy yawned.

Kai, have you told your nan about this dream?

The boy wheezed a little.

Kai?

He didn't get very old either. Your dad.

You'll get old, mate.

And a beard, said the boy sleepily. And big hands.

There was a long silence, as if Kai were picturing the big man of legend and savouring some detail before offering it up.

Keely felt the little hand on his arm, the moment's panic, and then the boy was off, overtaken by fatigue.

They were still there, side by side, the boy asleep, the man awake, when Gemma's key scratched into the lock at dawn.

At midday the hot streets were crammed and the Strip was a freakshow. He angled his way off the main drag but even Bub's was full. The place reeked of bacon, coffee, garlic, but beneath that comely fug were the contesting deodorants, unguents and perfumes of Sunday.

Gawd, he muttered at the door. Spare me days.

By the looks of you, said Bub, bussing his own tables, it's breakfast rather than lunch.

Keely nodded bleakly and looked about for somewhere to settle but there was nothing.

I had the Minister in here an hour ago, said Bub.

Which one?

You know which one.

Shoulda poisoned him.

Clowns I'm hiring, I probably did. Pig and bumnuts do you?

Perfect.

The sheeny-domed proprietor set him up at a stool beside the servery and his tall apple juice and double-shot appeared soon after.

You're limping, Tommy.

Crook back.

Shagger's back.

Not likely.

Keely picked up a pre-loved paper despite himself. Flopped it on its ugly face to see what fresh recruiting disasters the Dockers had gotten themselves into in the pre-season. But it was all cricket. He threw it down as his breakfast arrived in the arms of a lovely goth in a kilt and fishnet singlet.

Cricket, he said. What's that about?

Money, I guess. And blondes. Who could resist, eh?

Keely smiled and she set his plate down with an ironic flourish. As she sashayed away he caught a glimpse of the dish station through the swing door where a buzzcut kid wrestled the gooseneck amidst a pile of trays and pans. His acned face was flushed and miserable and their eyes met for a moment before the door swung to.

Bub's had always been their morning joint. Him and the Wild-Force crew. It was a modest place, decent but unfussy. During the week it was a haunt for seedy locals, policy wonks, coppers and fishermen. Once upon a time half the NGOs in town began their day here, back when a coffee and a good bitch session passed for a briefing. Since his messy exit old comrades and rivals seemed to have moved on to other establishments. Which left a few dejected humanitarians who ignored him from either pity or fear of contagion.

Bub never mentioned his public blow-up. He had the discretion or perhaps the indifference of a bloke who'd torched a few bridges himself. Today he seemed particularly harassed. The Sunday crowd required a different level of energy – a lot of fluffy milk to make, for one – and he looked short-handed.

I know what you're thinking, said Bub, passing him with plates of pasta. You're transparent.

Keely worked at his eggs and bacon and as Bub returned he raised his head.

Actually I was thinking about you, you poor bugger. You want some help?

Piss off, Bub said good-naturedly.

I'm serious.

You look like a bent nail.

I'll be right.

Eat your breakfast, said Bub, heading for the kitchen.

Keely watched him and the girl in the kilt blow to and fro, sweating and harried.

Really, he said, catching him on the next pass. I could help out. You need another dishpig?

Bub took his plate and wiped the counter.

You actually serious?

I'm broke, mate. Today I'll work for love. Any other day I'll do it for money.

Fuck me.

Is that compulsory?

Bub looked across his shoulder towards the kitchen. It's settling now anyway. But thanks. You need a few bucks?

Only if I can work for it. Without actually having to, you know, deal with the general public.

Well, it'll be weird. But I could do with the hands. Every other prick's at the mines and the backpackers are all heading home to save what's left of Europe.

I'm serious.
Thursday. Come by at seven.
Hey, thanks.
That's *a.m.* And don't be late.

Stepping into the lobby after the white heat of the streets, Keely was momentarily blinded. He hesitated. The doors slid to behind him and he took a second or two to get his bearings in the much weaker light. As he turned the corner for the lifts, he clashed shoulders with someone he hadn't seen coming.

Look out, ya dumb cunt, the bloke said hoarsely, pushing past without a pause.

Geez, mate, said Keely, flattened hard against the wall. What's your problem?

You, said the bloke over his shoulder. Fuckwits like you.

Listen, sport —

But the doors rolled back and the little oaf was gone, lost in the welding flare of afternoon. Nobody he recognized. Not that he got a proper look at him. Just the impression of somebody small and dark-haired with a whiff of sweat about him. Keely hoped he wasn't a resident; his heart sank at the prospect of regular encounters. What a charmless turd. The Mirador wasn't exactly genteel – there were all sorts of characters pressed in floor upon floor, some of them less than lovely – but people mostly managed a kind of strained civility. This sort of default-setting aggro was not promising.

A lift opened. Keely stepped in, rubbing his shoulder. On the ride up he let himself reclaim some satisfaction about the job. It wasn't much. In fact it was work for teenagers and halfwits. But he'd come away from Bub's with a little buzz on, just a faint glow of self-respect at the idea of having made a start. It didn't matter that Bub was embarrassed. Keely had to work. And he'd made something happen. This was a good thing.

Up on the gallery he pulled out his key but hesitated at the door. It was silly – mortifying really – that he should want so badly and suddenly to share his news. Maybe Gemma wouldn't see the funny side or even the flicker of hope it gave him, but he had to tell someone. He rapped on her kitchen window and something crashed in the sink.

I've got a knife! she bellowed. She was muffled by the glass and obscured by the curtain. Get the fuck away!

Keely recoiled.

You hear me? I said a week.

Gemma?

Come near me I'll use it, I swear.

Gem, it's me – Tom.

The nylon curtain lurched askew. A flash of face, hair. She looked raddled, mad even. And she wasn't bluffing about the knife; it was an evil steeled-out boning piece.

Just me, he said.

The curtain fell to and he heard the door-chain in its slot. His skin tightened with apprehension. As the door heeled open he retreated instinctively and felt the rails against his spine.

Gemma's face was flushed, her skin mottled. There was snot on her lip and tears clinging to her chin. She held the knife at her side.

Gem, what're you doing? Is everything alright? Where's Kai?

In the bathroom.

Something in Keely's gut turned over. He stepped up and peered in through the screen. She was shaking.

Is he okay?

Hidin.

The knife, he said carefully. How about we put that down. You're freaking me out here.

Oh, she said, looking at it.

Is that alright?

She turned aside and set it on top of the fridge.

Can I come in?

She nodded.

As he slipped past he felt the heat coming off her. She closed the door behind him and he nabbed the knife while she had her back turned. He headed for the bathroom, calling the boy as he went.

Only me, he said to the locked door. It's just Tom, Kai. Are you okay in there, mate?

The handle rattled and the door opened a crack. The boy's face was white but he looked unharmed.

Kai?

Did you get him? said the kid. With that?

What? Keely saw it was the knife he was referring to. No, I didn't get anyone. Who are we talking about? What's happening?

Keely stared at the boy a moment. The kid looked confused. Keely took the knife back through to the kitchen and tossed it onto the bench. Perched on an arm of the couch, Gemma flinched at the clatter.

Just tell me what's going on.

The flat smelt of grilled cheese and burnt toast. The TV lay on its back, flickering away. Things were in disarray everywhere he looked. Gemma tried to light a smoke but her hands were shaking badly. He strode over and lit it for her.

What's happening?

He hauled the TV back onto its stubby base. Judge Judy soundlessly dishing out rough justice.

Gemma?

I can't talk with him here, she said in barely more than a whisper.

I told you he'd come, said Kai.

Well, he came too late, didn't he?

Hey, Kai, said Keely as sunnily as he could manage. How about you set up a game for us?

The Scrabble's at yours.

Well, here's the key.

He's not goin anywhere, said Gemma. He's not leavin this flat.

Well, maybe we could step outside?

She shook her head.

The balcony?

She sucked in a chestful of smoke, raked her hair angrily, got to her feet. Keely grabbed the TV remote and cranked up the sound. There was cricket, soccer, a fat-person show. Judge Judy would have to do. He turned to Kai.

Mate, I think there's still some icecream in the freezer. Get yourself a big bowl, much as you like. Here, I'll do it for you.

He dragged out the tub and scooped icecream into an inviting mound. Put the bowl in the boy's unsteady hands. Kai glanced at it, then looked to his grandmother. She nodded, tried a washed-out smile of reassurance but it didn't carry.

We'll just have a chat out there, your nan and me. We'll be right here.

The boy blinked and chewed his lip. Keely followed Gemma out onto the sun-blasted balcony and slid the glass door to. They stood at the rail in the roar of traffic and cooling stacks. The broiling updraughts tugged at his hair, his shirt.

Tell me, he said.

She pulled hard on the fag, squinting in the gritty wind. Her tanktop was soaked with sweat. She wiped her face on the hem and sighed.

First of all, what's the knife about?

He wants five grand, she said.

Who wants five grand? Five grand for what?

The car.

This is the father? He called you?

Didn't even have the guts to show up himself. Sent some filthy-faced prick around to do it for him.

Just now?

Christ, I shouldn't have even opened the door – I thought it was you. How bloody stupid is that? Before *you* come along I had it together. I wouldn't have just opened the door like an airhead, would I?

So it's my fault?

What? Have I hurt your *feelings*? she said scornfully.

Gemma, just tell me. Someone was here. Who was here?

Christ, I dunno. Stewie's dopey little ferret. I can't remember his name. They've found out where we are. Fuck, I told the Welfare this was too close, I said it in court, I begged em. The judge, the cops, the suits – no one listened. I'm just another dumb bitch with a junkie daughter, what would I know?

But it's supposed to be secure here, he said. There's a swipe card.

People follow you through the lobby every day, Tom – wake up.

And he's come to the door? Here?

And like a dill I've left the chain off and his foot's in the door and the little shit's up in my face, pushin me back inside.

Did he touch you?

Of course he fuckin touched me – what are you, dense or somethin?

And where was Kai?

Right there. At the table.

He saw all this?

Saw enough.

Shit.

He's just standin there, this little turd, grindin his teeth, stinkin the kitchen up. They want money. Otherwise they'll fuck us up.

What is this, television? What does that even mean?

Gemma ditched the fag, didn't look at him. You were a woman, she said, you'd know what it means.

Okay, he said, chastened.

You never seen a meth-head off his chops?

He shrugged.

He says his piece and then he's just hangin there, givin off the fuck-yous, like sayin nothin for a bit, thinkin he's standin still. But he's fidgetin, bouncin like – I dunno, like a boxer. Eyes on him like he's not even human anymore. And then he looks out the window, out here. And I could see it straight away. I'm thinkin, Look here, you little shit, look at this, think of me, not him, not Kai.

Oh, Gemma, this is insane.

Cause you could *see* the little shit – the idea arrivin in his head. You know – Kai, the balcony. He's smilin. Like it's brilliant. His big idea to get me to pay. And he sees me knowin it, you know, watchin it sink in. And it's like he's just won Lotto. All's he had to do was look out the fuckin window and we both knew.

And Kai?

Jesus, I dunno. But he knows what trouble smells like.

Gem, this is just bravado, it has to be. Kai's father isn't going to have someone kill his own child.

You know what Stewie calls him? Gump. The retard. The girly-boy.

But he's not going to kill him.

You still wanna know what he said to me the other day?

Not sure I do.

Said all he needed was five minutes, said he'd been thinkin about it for years, even when he was with Carly.

Five minutes, said Keely.

To fuck me in the arse so hard I'd cough up shit for a fortnight.

Oh, God help us, he said aloud, holding hard to the rail. Dear God. Please.

You think he won't kill his kid? Maybe you're right. Maybe his little mate just thinks it's funny to dangle a boy by the ankles, ten floors up. Like that'd be a hoot. Wouldn't that rock, eh? she said, kicking the blighted geranium across the balcony. Wouldn't that be a fuckin scream?

The pot glanced off his shin. Keely staggered back, sat on the milk crate by the door, felt something crack under his weight – a scorched saucer whose service as an ashtray was at an end.

Gem, this is serious, he said, pulling the shards from under him, rubbing his leg. We should go to the police. Right now, this minute.

I can't.

You have to report it.

Tommy, I just. Can't.

This is bad. This is scary.

You think I'm not scared? You think I'm just stupid?

What'd he look like, this bloke?

What does it matter what he looks like?

Please. Just tell me.

Small, orright? Black hair. Somethin gold in his teeth. Anyway, I've seen him before.

So you can tell the cops.

No.

Just say what happened.

Oh, Jesus.

C'mon! Just call them.

Tommy, Jesus!

Keely thought of the thug getting out of the lift. He'd missed it all by a minute. And if he'd been there in time what could he have done? Really, how would he deal with somebody like that?

Shitheads, she said bitterly. He tried to hug her but she jabbed him away.

This is all about the car?

I spose. Sort of.

Gemma, that thing's worth about five hundred bucks if you're lucky.

I know that. You know that. Probably even they know that, the fuckin drug-addled idiots. But now I've made it worth something, haven't I, like a fool. I've called him, AVO and all, and I've gone around there thinkin I'm real smart, like they'll reckon you're a cop or a lawyer or some bullshit, and all he's seen is I've got a new bloke and I'm in a nice dress and he thinks, Right, she's got money. He needs money, he's got ugly debts. And now they've found where we are.

How does this *happen*?

What're you talkin about?

The authorities, the DOCS people, the courts – don't they make sure the kid's somewhere safe and private?

Dream on.

Could these guys have followed you home?

Or you.

Me?

Stewie knows what you look like.

Right, he thought. Terrific.

And I've got the car parked down there, obvious as you like. What a blockhead. For a stupid little car. What a brilliant idea that was.

Well, you had a right, he said lamely.

I can keep the car – that's what he said. But I need to pay up. Five thousand bucks, she said with a hopeless laugh.

When?

I told em I needed a week.

Do you have it?

What d'you think?

If you did it wouldn't be the end of it anyway.

I know that.

Keely glanced back and saw Kai still standing with the bowl on the other side of the glass. He wasn't eating; it didn't look as if he'd even taken hold of the spoon.

Well, he said. There's a week, then. At least there's that.

Gemma leant against the rail, her features darkened by a new thought. She blinked repeatedly, pulled herself upright.

When were we at Bandyup? she asked. Yesterday?

Yeah, he said. What is it?

Christ Almighty.

Keely saw some dread realization travel through her face.

Jesus Christ Almighty, she said. She was already askin about the car. They're in it together. Carly and him. That's who they are. That's what Kai is to em.

She held her head, as if she could not trust it to contain the noxious reactions this thought had set off. Her eyes widened. The hot wind whipped her hair in every direction. She looked like a woman hurtling, falling backwards.

He tried to go to her but she batted him away again, tears tracking crazily in the wind. He caught her arm, drew her in, took the blows and when she gave way he held her to his shoulder for some gesture of comfort, some hopeless promise of safety. And there was Kai at the window, alert and afraid.

Keely let her cry. He did what he could to show the boy he meant no harm. Her face burnt through his shirt and her sobs were awful. He tried to master his panic but his mind capered perilously. This business, these threats – it was all probably junkie bluster. No one in this town would be shaking a six-year-old off the top-floor balcony for five thousand dollars. But he didn't have the stomach to wait around and test the proposition. The state of her, the fear in the boy's face.

He couldn't just leave them. And even if Gemma did go to the cops, she and Kai couldn't stay here in the building.

The wind tore at him. The boy's icecream melted.

Keely didn't know what to do. But he knew he had to do something. Today. Now. Without hesitation.

Keely stood at the sink washing flour from his hands as Doris spun a lettuce beside him. From the kitchen window he saw Kai wading through fallen plane leaves. Gemma leant against the verandah rail, smoking pensively, alone. She'd been out there two hours; she'd hardly spoken all afternoon. Since the unsettling drama of their arrival – all that clutching and weeping in his mother's arms – she'd withdrawn. As if she regretted the chaotic outpouring of need, the words, the mewling. And now she was shaky, remote, somehow defiant.

Do you have a plan? his mother asked.

No, he said. Not really. I'm sorry. I just . . .

It's okay. See them safe first. Figure it out later.

Yeah, he said ruefully. That sounds like a plan.

Chip off the old block, then.

He saw her gracious smile, did what he could to respond in kind, but he knew she was just trying to steady his nerves.

So you didn't witness this exchange, hear threats uttered?

He shook his head, told her about the encounter with the little thug in the lobby.

Doris seemed diffident, even sceptical.

She was a mess, he said. They both were.

Over a fifteen-year-old Hyundai.

You don't believe her?

My instinct is always to believe her.

But?

Doris set the broken lettuce into a big majolica bowl and wiped her hands on her apron.

Well, my instincts haven't always been infallible. I wasn't there, Tom. I don't know these people. I don't have enough information to make a judgement. I've learnt some things the hard way.

Forty years ago you'd have taken them in without question.

Tom, love, I *have* taken them in without question.

Yes, I'm sorry. I'm just . . .

Caught up. It's normal.

My head's still reeling.

Doris took a cucumber and a jar of olives from the fridge.

You know she should be at a police station. Laying a complaint, making a statement.

She won't go. I've tried.

Keep at her.

I can't. She just shuts down on me.

Are you involved with her somehow?

Why do you ask?

To get some idea of the situation. And because of the way the boy watches you.

Kai? How?

As if he's waiting for something. I don't know. Waiting for you to take her off him? Waiting for you to do what men have done before? Who knows? He's just very watchful.

He's had a pretty crap day.

No doubt. Seems a lovely boy.

He is.

And she's a very attractive woman.

Doris.

You didn't answer my question.

I don't know how to answer it, he said. And I don't know why I should.

Fair enough, she said. As long as you're still able to ask it of yourself.

Mum, I just couldn't stand by and do nothing.

Of course not.

And I don't need any ulterior motive to help them out.

She dipped her head in assent and rattled away at the cutting board, glancing up now and then at Gemma and Kai in the fading light.

Strange, isn't it? she said. Seeing her again – a woman, a grandmother.

Strange doesn't even get close.

I think my head's spinning a little, too.

Full house again.

Doris smiled broadly, her pleasure finally evident, and just then Gemma turned and saw them. She looked guarded, even disgruntled, as if suspecting their smiles had come at her expense.

Thanks for this, he said.

Get the girl a drink. And run a bath for Kai.

Dinner was every bit as quiet and chary as the afternoon that had preceded it. Kai was silent. Keely and his mother did what they could to lighten the mood, but Gemma was shy, almost childlike with Doris. She hadn't come inside until dusk, when Doris had gone out to coax her in. She was nervous with her cutlery, visibly anxious about the house and its furniture. To Keely she appeared sullen. Doris seemed to take it all in her stride. But he could see Gemma was already having second thoughts.

They ate the fish he'd fried and passed the salad around. After five minutes or so, having eaten very little, Kai withdrew to stalk the livingroom. Gemma ate in silence for a while and then pushed her plate back as if she had neither strength nor appetite to finish. Doris laid a hand on Gemma's.

You've done a good job with Kai, she said. You're a brave girl.

Gemma brightened, rose from her hunched posture, stretching in a manner that struck Keely as feline. She leant in towards Doris, actively seeking contact, and it gave him a queer feeling. She didn't say much. Just gave that bashful, pleased smile as Doris stroked her hair and petted her.

In the livingroom Kai moved from shelf to shelf in his PJs, peering at the contents of every bookcase and cabinet, glancing up at the ochres and oils on the walls. He stopped before a Wandjina. Stared at that big mouthless face. The owlish eyes. The storm-power radiating from its head in thick brown rays. He turned and for a moment their eyes met – his and the boy's – and he wondered what he made of it, this ancient depiction of the Mighty Force. But with the women having their moment it didn't seem the time to ask him. They were watching him themselves.

He's a delightful child, said Doris. A credit to you.

Does he remind you of me? Gemma said in a teeny voice he'd never heard before. When I was little?

That hair, said Doris sadly.

Keely wondered if Gemma could detect the melancholy in his mother's voice. It unsettled him. He didn't know what it meant. Wondered if he was jealous. Which was absurd.

But Gemma looked pleased. She kept smoothing down her dress, smiling at her hands.

The boy opened the atlas on the canted shelf. Keely finished up his fish. It was red emperor, would have cost Doris a bomb, and in the end only he'd eaten it.

Does Kai look like his mum? asked Doris.

No, said Gemma. She's different.

They stretch us. Our kids.

And that's just the start, said Gemma with a conspiratorial grin, in a voice more like her own.

Doris laughed knowingly and Gemma's smile was suddenly warm and womanly, as if she'd declared herself. Maybe this would work after all.

I might go for a walk, said Keely. Let you gals compare gynaecological notes.

Look, said Doris. He's set to bolt already.

Blokes, said Gemma.

I could show Kai how close the river is. Let you two ladies catch up.

Listen to him, said Doris. He's gone all Mister Darcy on us.

He needs puttin to bed, said Gemma.

The kid turned a page of the atlas.

I'll give you a hand, said Keely.

Gemma can handle it, said Doris.

Right, he murmured. Course.

All our stuff's in binbags, said Gemma. I gotta find me work clobber.

You think you should go in tonight? he asked.

Yes, said Doris. We should go and make a report.

It'll take bloody hours. I'll be late.

I'll come with you, said Doris. Maybe speed things up a little.

I've took sick days off already, said Gemma. They'll give me the flick if I don't show.

We'll write a letter, said Doris.

I know how the bosses think. Tell em what's happenin, you sound like trash, like a crim. Gives em the excuse they're lookin for to sack ya and put in some cheap Chinks.

Gemma —

I need the job. I can't lose the job.

Maybe tomorrow, then.

Have to think. Get Kai to school.

You think that's wise?

It's all he's got. Gotta keep him in school. School's the most important thing, isn't it?

Keely caught Doris's look of misgiving. He felt as useful as a hip pocket on a singlet.

Okay love, said his mother. You do what you think's best. Now, I've made up a bed in the spare room. And there's a mattress on the floor for Kai. I thought he'd prefer to be in with you for a few nights.

Gemma nodded abstractedly.

Will that be okay?

Gemma turned the handle of her knife back and forward across the plate. Funny, isn't it? she said.

Funny?

Weird.

Doris patted her arm.

Forty-four and still bunked down at the Keelys'.

Yes, said Doris. Life's a surprise.

It's the shits, really. Scuse the French.

No, said Doris. You're right. It is. You've got to work, you have a boy to care for, and a home you have every right to live in without feeling you're under siege. If that isn't the shits, then I don't know what is.

We'll sort it out, said Keely, conscious of how lame he sounded.

Perhaps we'll talk about our plans in the morning, said Doris, getting up, drawing things to a close.

There's only a week, said Gemma.

A week's a long time in Stewie's world, said Keely.

You'd know, would ya? Gemma said with a flicker of disdain.

I'm just saying.

If I had five grand, Tom, he'd be dead. That's all it costs.

I think we can all leave it at that, said Doris frostily.

Keely turned in his seat and saw Kai in the doorway, taking it all in.

While Gemma showered, Keely and his mother did the dishes. Doris was taciturn. The set of her mouth was grim, almost disgusted.

Doris, he said in the end. What is it?

She shrugged and rattled her bangles. I don't know, she murmured. That poor little boy.

He's watching telly. I'll put him to bed in a minute.

Let her do it, Tom.

Okay.

He set a brush to the pan, scoured it of its ghostly outlines of fish.

He's seen too much, she said.

No question.

The weight of it, she said. You can see it on him.

Keely didn't know what to say.

You know why I can't give her money.

She's not asking you for it. Neither am I.

Keely scrubbed the pan until it glowed. He hadn't been completely forthcoming with Doris. He'd been vague about the threat to Kai. And she was right, he hadn't witnessed it. Not that he didn't believe Gemma. She was scared. It was natural she'd be afraid for the kid. In her position you'd take any sidelong leer as a threat, wouldn't you? But he hadn't wanted to send Doris into overdrive right from the outset. He also needed to process what was happening, get his mind into gear. It was just that his head was so boggy and slow. As if his software were old or compromised.

Tom?

The pan shone where he hadn't even applied the brush. Around the rim was an aura. The pan replicated itself on the tile-work, the window; it gilded his hands and made his head swim.

What are you doing? Tom?

He saw he'd braced himself against the windowsill. I'm alright, he said as much to himself as her.

You don't look alright.

Thanks.

You're exhausted. Here, let me finish this.

No, he said. I'm good.

I know you're *good*, she said. What I'm wondering about is whether you're well.

Too late in the day for a grammar lesson, Doris.

Well, she said, summoning all her matriarchal indulgence. Don't drown in my sink. I like to keep a tidy house.

He grinned. But she was right there. Watching. Like that Wandjina painting. Owl-eyed. Taking him in. Him. In his freeze-framing jerks of consciousness. Washing. Sticking. Coming free. Grinning. Holding onto the sink like a geriatric.

Gemma drove herself to work in the accursed Hyundai. Before leaving she put Kai to bed with the door open and a lamp burning.

Keely watched it all happening as if he were outside the house looking in. He had to concentrate to keep up and there were constant jerks of energy coursing up his legs as if his body were repeatedly recovering from stumbles.

He sat in the kitchen trying to look casual. Doris retreated to her room, face ominously untroubled. Keely knew the boy was still awake. From along the hallway there was silence, only the light slanting from the door, but he knew Kai well enough to be certain he'd be restless. He hauled himself upright. Ghosted down the passage like a dirigible. Saw the kid lying in there beneath his sheet, examining his hands. He knelt beside the mattress.

Kai looked up, unsurprised.

This'll only be for a few days, Keely said carefully.

Kai said nothing.

Are you comfy?

The boy surveyed his palms.

I know it's a strange house. I mean, a different place all of a sudden. But it's safe here. Doris is here in the next room. I'll sleep in the lounge tonight. I'll be right there, right along the hall. You can see me anytime.

Kai chewed his lip.

You want to tell me anything?

The boy breathed, wheezing slightly.

You want to ask me something, Kai?

There's a letter, he whispered.

A letter? Where, mate? Who from?

No, said the boy impatiently. Here. Look.

He held out his palms.

Em.

Sorry?

It's a em. See?

It took a moment to understand what the kid meant: the ragged letter M formed by the creases of his hand.

This one, too, said Kai. Em.

Well. Yeah. Look at that, eh?

I have a question.

Fire away.

Like, is it the same? For you?

Keely looked at the boy a second, then at his hands. He held them out. At the end of his arms his hands looked alien, improbable. The boy blinked and the sound of it was like cutlery chinking.

Not really, said Keely. Mine are a bit. Different.

Kai took a little while to digest this.

But what's it for? he asked. M for what?

Well, M for whatever you like, I spose. They're your hands, sport.

But what does it mean?

I don't think it means anything, mate. It's just a . . . just . . . just crease.

But only me?

Like a fingerprint, maybe. Yeah. Only you.

The boy settled on the pillow and reached for his arm. He wasn't even close to sleep. And Keely couldn't feel the boy's fingertips. He was rattled.

You're safe, he whispered prayerfully, needing it to be true, wanting to believe.

When Keely opened his eyes Doris was there, her silvery hair spilling over his chest.

Are you with me? she said.

Keely saw the ceiling rose behind her head. The pendant light-fitting like a halo.

Tom, love, are you with me?

As opposed to what? he replied. Against you?

Her hands on his neck and face were greasy. He knew the smell from childhood. Oil of Olay. Clearly Doris hadn't heard about the animal testing. And now maybe wasn't the right time. He was on the floor in the livingroom, and his limbs were treacherously slow, but he felt so alert. His mother clanked and rattled over him and he felt the boards under his arms, the Afghan rug prickling at his back. There was no getting around it. He'd checked out momentarily. He knew he should be terrified but right now he felt too embarrassed to be afraid.

I gather it's not morning, then.

No, she said. It's just after ten.

I wonder if that fish was alright.

It was fine, she said.

I must have tripped on the rug.

Maybe, she said, unconvinced. I was about to call an ambulance.

Call it what?

You're squinting.

Am I?

Tom, are you taking something?

I wouldn't steal from you, he said with a grin. Check my pockets.

Don't worry, she said. I already have.

Through the jarrah floor he felt the fridge cycle off, shaking itself like a pup. A clock dripped. He felt the sound on his tongue.

Love, is there something you need to tell me?

I don't think so, he said, levering himself by seven stages into a sitting position.

Doris sat back on her haunches. He looked at the big, saggy T-shirt, her bare legs. His mother went to bed in a Midnight Oil tour shirt. He never knew.

I fancy a shower, he said gamely.

Are you up to it?

It's just water, he said.

I think I should call someone.

No, he said. Not tonight. You can't do that now.

Doris pursed her lips.

I'll be right in a moment.

Tom, we need to talk about this.

Look, he said woozily. I'm up. It's fine. It's these bloody Afghans, they're all trying to kill us. That's a joke.

If you say so.

He surfed the hallway to the bathroom. There was a towel, a spare toothbrush. Dear, dear Doris, he thought. Always two kicks ahead of the game.

Afterwards, cleaner, clearer, he stood in her doorway. She was on the bed cross-legged with a book in her lap. She glanced up a moment and turned the page. On the dresser a little desk fan turned its head to and fro. He leant against the architrave with a nonchalance Doris wasn't buying.

What're you reading?

A biography, she said. Dorothy Day.

On the bedside table there were more hardbacks. From here he could see something about Paul Robeson, a Brian Moore novel, the Bill McKibben he'd given her at Christmas.

Feeling better?

Yeah. Good.

What was that about, Tom?

He shrugged. I don't know.

You just fell down.

Tired. I guess. Bit of vertigo.

Nothing you want to tell me?

He offered a counterfeit laugh. I haven't even slept the night yet, Doris. You're starting in early.

Has this happened before?

He shrugged again and she pushed her specs impatiently back into her hair.

It's nothing, he said.

The sleepwalking. You asked me about sleepwalking.

Let's just drop it. There're bigger things on.

Do you have headaches?

Just an ear infection.

You never said anything about —

Ages ago. And, look, I haven't been sleeping too well. It's nothing.

I'm worried you'll fall in the bathroom, somewhere else.

I won't fall.

But you're big, love, she said, at the verge of tears. I can't lift you up.

Mum, you won't have to.

He went in and held her. She was cool and trembling. He could feel her. And his arms burned a little.

Really, he said. You're making this into a big deal. And no, I'm not on heroin. Budgetary reasons, mostly.

She sniffed, suffered the embrace a moment, then pressed him away. He sat on the bed, guilty, mortified. She reached for a tissue and blotted her face with fierce detachment. The book lay face-down between them, wings out like a fallen bird.

It's fine, he said.

If you say so. But Gemma and Kai. They're here now.

Yes, he said, sensing a corner having been turned.

Doris straightened herself.

And now, to an extent, they're my business too.

He nodded, waiting for it.

So you better listen to me.

All ears, Mum, he said, trying to match her tone.

I know you haven't got a plan.

No, I'm just —

That's fine. I understand.

But.

In the absence of a plan, you need a stance at least.

Stance.

A considered position. An act, as my younger clients like to say. You need to get an act. Even your father figured that much out – too late, I'll admit.

What're we talking about here?

Your own survival, for one thing.

Oh, Mum, I don't think the situation's *that* fraught.

Don't be so literal. Just give yourself a bit of distance. That's all I'm saying.

You mean from them? Gemma and Kai?

Doris nodded.

Geez, he said. You're a surprise.

You're trying to do the right thing, I know. It's how we raised you, the both of you. But you save yourself first, Tom. That's something I do know, it's what I've learnt. You save yourself, then you look to the others.

Keely was confounded. He took a breath but she cut him short.

Perverse, isn't it, how we could teach you that in the water but not on land, in life. We didn't see it. We were such innocents.

You've lost me.

Swimming lessons, Tom. Lifesaving. How you approach a swimmer in distress.

You're kidding me, aren't you?

Feet first, ready to fend off.

Okay, he said, shaking his head. Wise as serpents, innocent as doves. Tick that box.

Tom, I'm serious. To save a drowner you need to be a swimmer. Remain a swimmer.

You've really thought about this.

For thirty-five years, she said with a heaviness that flattened his scorn.

Keely ran his hand over the dark dimples of her book. He slipped the page-marker back into the gutter, closed it and felt its heft.

You think you'd still have him if he'd been more of a swimmer, had an act?

She sighed and reclaimed the book.

Who knows, she said. When somebody burns that hot you don't really expect a long haul.

But he never did have a sense of professional distance.

Not when it might have served him best. Nev was so bloody impulsive.

Being careful, though. After a while it grinds you down.

I'm not talking about your job.

Feels like submission, Doris. Being careful.

I don't think you know as much about submission as you'd like to imagine.

But wasn't I always too careful? Hasn't that always been my problem?

Presently, I wouldn't see it as your chief problem.

I didn't want to make the same mistakes. Nev was like a bull in a china shop.

He was a giant surrounded by moral pygmies.

I'm not saying he wasn't. I just wanted to be smarter.

Smarter?

More effective.

There's no virtue in saying you're not like Neville Keely, so don't sit on my bed and talk bullshit, it's insulting.

Sorry, he said, angry, humiliated, confused.

And don't kid yourself, Tom. Your father was transparent. I could read him like the form guide. You're not so different.

Keely got to his feet, anxious to disentangle himself.

How are you getting Kai to school tomorrow?

Gemma's off at five, he said meekly. So there's the car.

Right, Doris said, taking up her book. The car.

Chastened and bewildered, he took himself off to the couch and the livingroom and the long night ahead.

From the wind-ripped walkway on the tenth floor, Keely heard the school bell toll. He paused at the rail to watch the stragglers sprint indoors with their backpacks and folios and soccer balls.

He thought of Kai settling at his desk, examining the puzzle of his own palms as the teacher tried to launch the school day. The kid had been subdued all morning and silent on the drive down to the port. Keely didn't dare mention the wet bed. Or the way he'd curled in beside him on the couch sometime before dawn. At breakfast Keely saw the sheets out on the line. The boy was already showered and dressed. Doris had him eating toast and staring at the sudoku on her phone. The Hyundai was in the driveway. Gemma asleep. His mother was quiet but there was conspiracy enough in her sunniness for him to know she'd dealt with everything seamlessly, as if nothing had happened. Doris had an act. She knew who she was and what she was doing. And he loved her for it.

At breakfast Kai said little, but he watched Doris assiduously. Just as he had last night at dinner. Perhaps he was trying to match this trim old bird and her noisy bangles with the young heroine in Gemma's stories. Keely feared the legend had gotten out of hand. Blackboy Crescent. When moral giants strode the earth. But Kai didn't seemed disappointed. Children fell in love with Doris. As a boy it shat Keely to tears, but this morning the spectacle revived him. If only he could project such calm authority.

He'd stirred for a second in the gloom, feeling the boy settle on the couch beside him. He savoured it briefly before falling away again. Only when he saw the washing line did he know he hadn't dreamt it. And now, at the gallery rail, looking down at the schoolyard, he was ashamed of his self-absorption, his unctuous little moment of paternal fantasy. What about the kid? What's it like to wake wet and frightened in a stranger's house, to spare your grandmother and crawl in beside some old guy you hardly know? A sudden rage rose in him. At everything ranged against this boy. He had to do something.

He unlocked the flat and changed his clothes.

He wondered if he could convince Gemma to go to the police. She'd be awake just after midday; he had until then to make a compelling case. Failing that? There was Stewie. Maybe he'd negotiate. But Keely had no more persuasive arguments this morning than he'd had last night. And as for dealing with Stewie, he hadn't the first clue how to parley with a bug-eyed speed freak. He had nothing.

He shaved. Brushed his teeth. With his own brush. He made his bed, straightened the place, and checked the fridge. Some piss-weak bit of him wished he could just stay. But he couldn't leave

Gemma and Kai to Doris alone. She had to work. There was the school run. Gemma's shiftwork to deal with. He'd just have to suck it up and endure the couch a while. Until he thought of something. Or it all went away of its own accord.

He packed a few clothes, a couple of books and snatched up his pillow. He decided to swing by Gemma's place. There'd be things she'd want to collect but he didn't know what she required, felt squeamish about going through her stuff. He could bring her back this afternoon when they collected Kai from school. Needn't do it now. But he'd check it out anyway. Satisfy himself.

At Gemma's door a bit of paper flapped in the security grille. Just a yellow square, ruffled by the desert wind, a Post-it note held captive by the steel mesh. There was nothing on it but a solitary dollar sign scrawled in biro.

Keely looked about anxiously and stuffed it into a pocket. He was turning to leave when something else caught his eye. Behind the mesh, on the inner door, a second yellow slip. He pulled Gemma's key from around his neck and unlocked the screen door. He snatched it up. Same adhesive note, same symbol.

Trying to stay cool he examined the flyscreen but it was undamaged. Short of unlocking the grille, there seemed no other way of depositing the second slip there. He knocked on the door, feeling like a fool but fearful of walking blindly into something. Like what, an ambush? Keely turned the key in the lock and eased the door back slowly.

The flat still smelt of cheese and toast and smokes. He could smell Gemma and Kai. But it was hard to read the place. Everything had been a mess when they left, chaotic where that shithead had kicked things about, after which they'd tossed stuff into rubbish bags and fled in a panic. Food on a plate. Clothes on the floor. The TV where Keely had set it back upright. There was no sign anyone had been in since yesterday. Not that he could see. But somebody had definitely been by outside at least. And maybe in here as well. That note inside the locked grille. Keely thought of the Mirador's supervisor, a bloke who'd taken against him for his brusque refusal to engage all these months. No point asking him if he'd let someone in. Besides, this wasn't even Keely's flat. How could he explain his interest? Gemma's business and his would be all over the building inside an hour.

He wondered if Gemma had come by last night before work. Or this morning after her shift. To collect something. But why would she take the risk? Had someone followed her into the building, waited until she was inside and left both notes while she was in the bedroom grabbing what she'd come for? Why not confront her then? Make their little threats in person. Seemed more their style. Unless they'd had cause to think someone else was in here with her. A bloke. Him.

He locked up. Jumpy. Freaking at his paranoia. Wondered if he should even tell her.

Down in the gated carpark he found the Hyundai where he'd squeezed it between a Kombi and a scrofulous Commodore. He was in the car before he noticed it on the windscreen.

He couldn't see anyone – not in vehicles, nor around them. The bike shed looked deserted. There was a spill of suds emerging from the laundry door.

He started the car and waited a full minute, his pulse going feral. But no one. He buzzed the gate and rolled out into the narrow street. Under the jacaranda a Chinese kitchen hand smoked in his stained tunic. A smooth-cheeked hippy girl coasted by on a bike.

Bastards, he said aloud. You little shitheads.

All thoughts of a swim and a coffee evaporated. He had to get this vehicle out of town. Warn Gemma. Maybe the supermarket could give her work in a franchise a bit further out in the suburbs. Even if there was nothing more than bluster behind all this, she couldn't stay here. He'd ask Doris about a refuge, support services.

He turned into a side street. Idled down the quay, checking his mirrors all the way. He wound slowly along the river and saw nothing but mid-morning traffic. But by the time he pulled into his mother's drive, his hands were shaking.

Doris's Volvo was gone. Conscious that Gemma would be asleep, Keely unlocked the back door and entered the house discreetly, but as he crept through the kitchen he heard the shower running. It was too early for her to be up. She couldn't have had five hours' sleep. He filled the kettle, set it on the stove and tried to steady himself.

The couch had been straightened. His pillow and folded sheets lay over one arm. There was no sign of Kai's bed linen and pyjamas on the line outside. In this heat they'd have been dry hours ago. Doris had covered her tracks before heading off to work. She'd left a newspaper and a sprig of basil in a jar on the dining table. The kitchen sink was empty.

He sat a moment, listening to the kettle, trying to think. As the water ran and ran in the bathroom, nothing sensible came to mind.

He got up. Made a pot of tea. As he set the canister back on the shelf he reached for a couple of mugs with one hand and fumbled. Caught the first. But the other mug hit the floor and smashed.

The shower stopped running. He cursed himself and grabbed the broom. Handle looked fuzzy. Felt smooth in his fingers.

Who's there? called Gemma.

Just me, he said, sweeping the shards into a pan.

Fuck, said Gemma in the doorway. I thought I was on me own.

Sorry, he muttered.

Geez. I nearly shat meself.

Broke a mug.

She'll be happy.

Doris won't care.

She rested her wet head against the doorframe, settling her nerves. Wrapped in a fluffy towel, she'd drawn a cloud of soapy steam into the kitchen. How could he tell her things were worse, not better? Was this the moment to say she should quit her job and move?

Couldn't sleep?

In your little boy-bed. Feels wrong.

You should try the couch, he said.

He get off orright?

He nodded.

Lunch?

Could hardly fit it in his bag. Mum saw him right.

You sure it's cool us bein here? I'm gettin a vibe.

It's fine. It's Doris.

I should make some other plans. But I don't have any ideas.

Have a cuppa, he said. We'll think of something.

Should just piss off up the coast – Carnarvon, Exmouth, Broome.

I think that would be smart, in the circumstances.

But, what about Kai? They'll cut off me benefit. Won't they? I'm not even declaring half me wages. And I won't have a job.

Not right away.

Maybe go to the mines? But I can't take a kid.

I dunno.

They'll take him off me. I know it.

Gemma.

Put him into fuckin Care.

Here, sit down. It's not that bad.

Keely got her into a chair, poured some tea and finished sweeping up the remains of the mug. She looked jittery.

Gotta be somethin, she said.

Yeah. Just need to think it through. You're not on your own here, mate.

He found shortbread, got himself another mug and sat with her. She steadied a little, ate the biscuits quickly, with infantile greed.

Not exactly the old place, is it? she said.

No, not really.

Did you like it here?

I never lived here. She bought it about ten years ago.

Old. But fancy.

It's a nice house.

She's changed.

Well, she's an old lady now.

Not that, she said. All this stuff. Way she talks. Kai, he's *such a delightful child.*

He shrugged. Doris's accent was as broad as ever but it was true, the vocab had moved up a peg or two.

When I was little I wished she was *my* mum. Pretended she was, sometimes. Like her and Nev were me oldies. She let us think it.

Think what?

That she loved us. Like we were family.

Keely didn't know what to say. Because that was how he remembered it. And it had irked him, as a kid. Not that much had really changed. Last night Doris had nursed her like a frightened child. Hadn't he seen Gemma luxuriating in the attention? So what else had happened that he hadn't noticed? Probably nothing. Gemma had endured a long, dull shift, an entire night in which to mull over every detail, letting any tiny change become a disappointment.

She's still Doris, Gem.

Well, Kai thinks she's the duck's nuts.

Yeah, he murmured. But you've filled his head with all these stories.

They're true.

Only up to a point. Neither of them was a superhero. They're just people.

Maybe she's just puttin up with us.

Oh, mate.

Like we're gunna break somethin, mess her house up. Ask her for money.

I don't think so.

And now you think I'm not grateful.

No, he said. It's a wrench. The sudden move, being in someone else's place.

It just wasn't what I expected.

Keely wondered what it was she had been expecting. He thought Doris had done pretty bloody well with only thirty minutes' notice. Okay, maybe she wasn't quite so ardent as she'd once been. But Gemma was a grownup now, not a little girl. And there was the boy, taking it all in. Of course Doris would be a bit more circumspect. Anyhow, she was an old woman. All this was out of the blue. On her doorstep. In Mosman Park.

It's strange, he heard himself say. You know, seeing someone again after so long.

Gemma shrugged. Almost pouting. He felt a twinge of annoyance. Then talked himself down. The trauma. You couldn't expect something as petty as good manners.

What if she doesn't want us here?

If she didn't want you here, you wouldn't *be* here. She'd have written you a cheque the moment you arrived. To get rid of you.

Gemma blinked, considering this, but she seemed unconvinced.

She didn't mind me when I was little. When I was cute. Didn't have a girl in Bandyup then, did I?

Gemma.

She thinks I'm rubbish.

Oh, that's just bullshit.

You don't know, Tom. You're like a kid.

I'm like a kid? he said, flaring up.

I'm not stupid, she said.

No one's saying you're stupid.

She knows you fucked me, Tom. She can smell it.

He let out a mirthless laugh. Not literally, I hope.

Look at you, gone all red. You can't even think about it in your mum's house, can you?

Don't be daft.

Look at you.

Why are we even discussing this? There's stuff we have to deal with.

Come on. Why don't we do it now? Right here on her kitchen bench.

Why're you doing this?

Frightened of his mum.

I thought it was respect, he said.

Same old goody-two-shoes, she muttered, sinking in her chair, tightening the towel across her breasts as her animation subsided.

He got up and tipped his tea into the sink.

I need a fag.

Not in the house, he said dully.

Don't worry, Tommy. I'll take me filthy habits outside.

He let her go, watched her out on the verandah as she fired the thing up and sucked on it angrily in the hot, dappled light. He wished he could reassure her. Wished just as fervently there was somewhere else she could go.

He saw her mug on the table and, thinking it was empty, snatched it up. Tea flew everywhere. Before he'd even found the dishmop the stain was deep in the wood.

It was one of those late-summer days when the river, blown hard against the lee shore by the easterly, smelt rank. Like something left too long in a pot. The thin stews of his early teaching days that languished on the stovetop, half fermented overnight. The sun drilled through his skull and he was glad when they reached the shade of the cypresses beneath the bluff.

Gemma hadn't spoken since they left the house. She'd come along at his urging but dawdled and sulked enough to make him regret it. If only he'd brought a pair of Speedos. The sloughy riverbend was hardly inviting, especially now the wind corralled the jellyfish against the bank. The water was brown and chunky as a dishful of steeping mushrooms. He imagined hauling himself through it, all those slick domes sliding down his chest and thighs. Not pretty. But even that would have felt like a few minutes' reprieve.

He sat out under the limestone crag where the grand old marri reached across the water. And there it was. The bird's wingbeats were effortless. It banked and soared on an updraught, turned and eased away, keening. It looked weightless, as if the heaviest thing it carried were that plaintive, querulous call.

Your idea of a good time, she said, lighting another fag.

He surveyed the tangled bush, the dancing insects. A bit of remnant wildness. It reminded him of the swamp. Faith and him. The ragged gang of Blackboy Crescent kids plodding single-file through the melaleucas.

Used to be yours, too, once, he murmured.

She said nothing. Blew a jet of smoke that ripped away in the wind like a current with its own angry energy. She flicked ash.

Listen, he said. I'm happy to pick him up this afternoon.

You don't look good, she said.

I'm fine.

She bit her thumb, tilted the cigarette away from her face. And glanced at him.

There's something wrong with you. Doris can see it. I can see it. Everyone 'cept you can see it.

I think it's better if I get him today.

And why's that?

He pulled the little yellow Post-its from the pocket of his shorts and flattened them on the rock beside him. Out here in the dappled shade they weren't nearly as unnerving.

Cunts, she said wearily.

Does Stewie have a key? he asked.

Course not.

And Carly?

She shook her head.

303

I think they know someone, he said.

In the building?

Seems like it.

She looked sceptical.

So, I figured it was smarter for me to collect him.

Like, because you're smarter'n me. That it?

Of course not.

Cause you're the big fella.

Keely tore at a clump of sedge.

Fuck em, she said. It's my car. He's my responsibility.

Okay, but listen —

Anyway, they really think I've got the money.

What possible difference can that make?

I drive me own car. I pick up me own kid. *They* don't decide what I do.

I understand the sentiment, but —

You don't get it, Tom. If I hide, it looks like I haven't got the money.

Wouldn't it be better if they knew you haven't?

Now? Are you jokin? They'd go nuts. They think I'm good for it.

Shit, why?

You, ya fuckwit. Isn't hard to google it, or whatever the fuck people do. You were all over the telly, in the paper, ya must have money.

That's how these dickheads think?

It's how anybody thinks.

So glad I had that shave, he said bitterly.

Well, sorr-ee!

We're all bloody sorry now.

The moment he said it he could have torn his own tongue out. He sat there with the hot wind baking his face, yanking at his sleeve.

I've got a week, she said. Six more days. Because they think I've got it. I'm half a chance of lasting the week if they still think I'm good for five grand.

I don't understand the logic.

It's not about logic.

She ditched the fag into the water. Got up and picked her way back down the track.

Keely snatched up the little yellow notes. The adhesive edges had lost their stick. They were dusted with limestone grit, a couple of addled ants. He held them up, let them flutter in the easterly. By way of standover action they looked pretty low-rent. But maybe she was right. What did he know? The whole thing still seemed melodramatic. And yet there it was, that sick, falling sensation. Sitting here on a rock, safe in the shade. With something dark and hot rushing at him like so much wind.

Doris came in at three and tossed her satchel on the kitchen bench. Keely looked up from the table, whose surface he was still rubbing with oil.

Where's Gemma?

Doing the school run.

Do I detect a certain atmosphere?

I spilt tea on your table.

I'll live, said Doris, pulling open the fridge door. But I see neither of you kids has thought to do any shopping for dinner.

I'll go in a minute.

Perhaps I should've pinned a note to your shirt, she said grinning. She went through to her room and came back in a faded sleeveless summer dress that showed how thin her arms had become. She stood at the kitchen bench a moment. Divining the situation, it felt like. She took an orange from the bowl beside her.

Good day? he asked, getting in first.

Not bad. Luxury of being a part-timer.

Anything interesting?

Nothing cheerful.

Try me.

Just documents for the Ward inquest.

Oh. God.

Indeed.

And?

Even seeing the medical reports – it's beyond belief. They cooked that man alive, basically. In the back of a prison van. Fifty-seven degrees, that's how hot the metal got. What's that, 130-something in the old money? He was in there half a day, nearly a thousand kilometres, and neither guard thought it was a big deal that he was without airconditioning.

I forget what he was even arrested for.

A traffic offence, she said, beginning to peel the orange. If that man had been a sheep there'd be people marching in the street. But he's just an Aborigine.

What about charges?

My guess, she said, toiling arthritically, is that neither guard will be convicted.

And the private contractor?

She looked over her specs at him and he saw the answer in her cocked eyebrow.

Business first, he muttered.

So, not a sparkling day. I thought by now I was unshockable.

You want me to help you with that?

I can still peel an orange.

Sorry.

Anyway, she said, how's Gemma?

He shrugged.

Does she cook?

Well, yeah. Of course.

We'll let her cook tonight, she said before biting into the orange.

What d'you mean? Why?

Doris pulled a paper towel from the roll to blot the juice from her chin. Don't give me that look, she said. It's not a test. I thought it might help her settle in, give her a sense of control, bit of normality.

Okay. See your point.

She's not helpless. Doesn't want to feel helpless.

Please don't say the word, Doris.

Empowerment? That word? If I had to see you on the news every night calling an ecosystem a precious *asset*, or a tourism *icon*, then you can suck eggs and let me say the E-word.

Keely raised his hands in surrender, glad she smiled.

I'll be gone at seven, she said. Tickets for the Vaughan Williams.

Oh, he said. Who you going with?

Well, she murmured, pausing to swallow a mouthful, I had hoped you'd come. But since I booked it, things have developed somewhat.

Ah. Damn. Sorry, but I can't leave Kai.

No. Of course not, she said. I wouldn't let you.

Bum, he said. I love Uncle Ralph.

I know that.

Which piece is it?

The oboe concerto.

Ouch.

Yes, it's a shame, she said, rattling her bangles and then straightening all of a sudden. Listen, why don't you go anyway? I could stay with Kai.

But you love Vaughan Williams.

Doris shrugged and took another bite.

Mum, I couldn't.

We'll see if Kai's comfortable with it. If he's iffy I'll leave him with you.

Thanks, he said, looking hopelessly at the watermark in the jarrah. Really. But you go.

Come on, then, she said. I'll finish this on the way to the shops.

There was a peaceable languor to Doris's riverside quarter where the shady streets smelt of cut lawns and lavender. They walked in equable silence, eking out the orange, segment by segment. An Audi slid by sedately and when they saw the personalized plates they both erupted in laughter. MINE, it said in powder blue. And in that moment of lovely wordless understanding he thought of what he'd lost and all there still was to hold onto.

The little retail enclave was bustling. He followed, like a boy shopping with his mum, mortified by how quickly he subsided into the role. But it was worse than that, weirder than just his own submission, because after a few minutes he could see that Doris was not so much shopping for their dinner as parading him through the cluster of neighbourhood businesses. She twirled her plaits in the butcher's and jangled her ethnic hardware in the fruit and veg shop, chatting with those she passed and everyone who served her, and as the glances of cashiers and floral dears became ever more obvious, his irritation mounted. Clearly people knew and liked Doris. Their curiosity about Keely was palpable.

Well, she said when they were back on the street. You caused a stir.

Oh? he said. I didn't notice.

I don't think they quite believe you're my son.

Well, he said. Sometimes I find it hard to credit that myself.

I always said I had a son, she said loftily. But maybe I sounded like a lonely old duck spinning yarns.

Okay, Doris, he said. Point taken. You've had your fun.

Heading downhill, they sought the mottled afternoon shadows of the planes trees that lined the street.

What are you thinking? she asked.

Nothing, he lied. He was wishing he'd been more forthcoming about the situation with Gemma.

Kai's a curious little boy, she said, steering him into a backstreet of heavily pruned peppermints.

He doesn't really remind you of Gemma at all, does he?

No, she said. Apart from the situation, the damage. Gemma was only cunning. Kai's bright.

Cunning?

She had to do what she could to survive. You had the sense she'd endure. Suffer, Doris said bitterly. But endure. Kai seems more fragile.

He doesn't believe he'll ever grow old, he said, hating himself for letting it out, relieved he had. He thinks he'll die young.

Well, she said without emotion. That's upsetting.

It kills me. Hearing him say it.

Maybe he's a realist.

What do you mean? he said, horrified. What are you talking about?

You've met his father, I gather.

Seen him.

Can you imagine *him* growing old?

Keely thought about that. I guess the odds aren't great, he said.

And where are all the other men in his life? she asked. Maybe there just aren't any examples of a benign old age. How can he conceive of what he's never seen except on TV? Gemma's father's dead. She hasn't mentioned her daughter's father.

She doesn't talk about it, he said, still troubled. You think she's *cunning*?

Was, I said.

Still, you sound —

Does he ever give an indication of hurting himself?

Kai?

Does he talk about it, give you that impression?

No, he said, unable to bring himself to mention his sense of dread, the pernicious image of the kid standing at the balcony rail, leaping. It was always there now, like a dark thought, something shameful he could suppress but not expunge.

No, he said again. Not really.

Well, that's something.

Yes, he said, unconsoled.

How to express his fear that the kid was enchanted by something obscure and awful, some terrible certainty? Because it was as if the boy were leaning out towards it, resigned to meeting it, only seeking what lay in wait for him. How could he tell her that? What would Doris hear except confirmation of his own mental unravelling?

Keely knew he should tell her about the boy's dreams, at the very least. The drawings, the outline he seemed to have already filled with his own body. But Doris was so vigilant. He could feel himself beginning to fall to pieces under her gaze. And he could see it now, his mother stepping in, catching him, relieving him of responsibility. Half of him wanted that, to be found out, sent home, set free.

But this squalid little skirmish was all he had now. He was in it with them. Wasn't he? He had to be. Even if he was shitting himself. Not quite present and accounted for. Pressed into service.

But this was his chance to mean something again. He'd do whatever it took to keep them safe. Wondered if Doris could sense the wildness teeming beneath his skin.

They walked a while in silence. To break the sense of clinical observation, Keely relieved his mother of the shopping. He was shocked that he hadn't even noticed her carrying it all until now. Made a lame joke at his own expense but was upstaged by crows as they fluttered down to heckle and strut on the grassy verge ahead, voices high and boastful.

Listen to them, said Doris. Like jockeys before a sauna.

You didn't really answer me before, he said, emboldened. About Gemma. You said she was cunning.

It's not an indictment, Tom. Kids use what they have, to survive.

But what do you make of her now? Honestly.

She's a battler.

A battler.

I know. Sounds patronizing. But she's got more starch than her mother. She's woken up to blokes. And she's done okay with Kai, all things considered. But of course it'll never be plain sailing. She's a damaged girl and he's a troubled boy. She's not a person of boundless resources. She's doing what she can, what she thinks best.

Is it me, or are you a little wary?

Doris kneaded her hands. The bangles clunked and chimed at her elbows.

We always had such low expectations of Bunny.

I wasn't really talking about her mother.

Bunny had a rough trot, no doubt about that. But, looking back, I wonder if she wasn't a bit dim and lazy as well. She got used to being helped, being absolved of accountability. I think, despite ourselves, we got caught up, Nev and me, making her the victim, only ever seeing her as, I don't know, prey. She was passive enough to begin with. We didn't expect enough. We didn't really help.

Well, you were about saving the kids, I guess.

Yes, she said. From her, as much as him, truth be told. All that sixties optimism, love. We infantilized the poor woman, indulged ourselves. At her cost, I think, and our own.

So what're you saying?

Gemma wants me to be her mother again. To pretend I am. And I won't do it. I can't. I'm hard-pressed as it is – being yours, Faith's.

So that's it – a professional distance?

It's not my profession, Tom.

I never thought of you as dispensing kindness with quite so much calculation.

I suspect Gemma's a little confused by kindness.

Jesus!

Don't speak like that.

You should bloody talk!

Tom, people sometimes confuse simple decency with investment. You help them, therefore you must love them, require something of them, desire them, need them. And then you're expected to forsake everyone else for them.

What's this, Social Work 101? *Ayn Rand in the Antipodes*?

No, Tom, it's half my life.

Well, he said. You sound like a jilted lover.

Doris offered up a saintly, suffering smile and the birds lifted testily from the grass.

Sorry, he said. That was mean.

True enough, though. In a way.

I can't – Mum, I don't understand.

Listen, I was young. Vain. Idealistic. Of course I adored Gemma. Because she was adorable. I favoured her, tried too hard to compensate for what she'd missed. And a lot of that came at Faith's expense.

She's never mentioned it.

She's not a whinger, said Doris. Faith's smart. She never had to be adorable. But she was always generous with Gemma. Took her cues from us, poor thing. These other kids had needs greater than hers or yours. From Faithy we expected too much.

And from me?

Tom, you never shared your room, your clothes, your dolls. You weren't cannibalized so thoroughly in the name of charity.

Fair enough, he said, all the more irritated because he knew it was true.

So, what is it?

Nothing, he lied.

Not true.

He walked beside her a few moments and then just said it. You sound so cold-blooded, that's all.

And you seem unwilling to face what's real. Gemma made herself loveable in the way some needy kids do. To survive they cultivate you. They want so badly and they take compulsively. They learn to manipulate you. No one can blame a little girl for seeking comfort. But I think I crossed a line somewhere, flattering myself, thinking I really could be her mother, that she could be one of my own. It's a wonder Faith ever forgave me.

You mean you've talked about this?

Tommy, it's our grand theme, the pea under our mattress!

She never said.

Maybe you never listened.

They came into her street and Keely looked through the treetops to the broad reach of the river glittering in the afternoon sun. He wished there could be a settled interval, just an hour or so when he could let himself believe he knew what was what. Nothing was solid anymore, nothing felt safe or ordinary.

So you regret all that? he asked. Everything you and Nev did?

No, she said. I just wish I hadn't been so romantic about it, so vain. I wish we'd known more, that we'd done a better job.

A horn sounded behind them. Gemma's car rattled by and turned up into the drive.

Remember, she's changed, too, Tom. Like I said, she's not her mother. And neither am I.

On the way into central Perth, piloting the Volvo around the river's edge beneath the bluffs and the park, he wondered if Doris had given him the ticket simply to get him out of the house. To have some time alone with Gemma. Take stock. Perhaps even take charge. He still felt awkward leaving Kai with her on only the boy's second night in a strange house. It seemed flaky. But Gemma had no objection and Kai seemed indifferent. Maybe it was just Doris bunging on the charm and rattling the Scrabble box. All the way down Stirling Highway and into Mounts Bay Road he'd worn himself ragged with second-guessing, until his head felt like a tinful of bees. Why couldn't he just take his mother's offer as a gift? Why make so much trouble for himself? Some things were what they appeared to be.

At the concert hall he slunk down the aisles feeling underdressed and pitifully unaccompanied. Took his seat beside an elegant old couple. Peered at the program. Anything he'd learnt about classical music was picked up second-hand in Doris's slipstream. Delius, Elgar, Britten. The Brits, for God's sake. God's little joke on their prickly republicanism.

He caught the older woman beside him glancing surreptitiously. Felt himself wither. Rescued by the dimming lights and the soloist striding onto the stage to warm applause.

Keely's pulse quickened. A stab of apprehension. He was the same at any live performance, suddenly anxious for the players. So stupid; these people were professional musicians. But the way his throat narrowed they could have all been kids at a school recital. His kids.

And before he knew it, before he could get his thoughts under control, the concerto was up and running. From the soloist's first brazen thrust he was captivated by her impish confidence. Such a naff instrument, really, the oboe, but she went at the thing like a jazzer. You could feel the ripple of indignation roll across the hall. Maybe it was the woman's bebop stance, the way she appeared to goad the rest of the orchestra. Keely sweated on the sense of resistance in the room, the squirms and clucks. All this wild fingering, he felt it could come apart at any moment, yet he was swept up in it, fraught and amazed by the soloist's reckless brio as she began, sally by wheeling sally, to win first the stage, then the auditorium and finally the piece itself, looking all the while like someone glorying in the peril she'd exposed herself to, beating the odds with a smile in her eyes and a hip cocked against all comers. She was nailing it. Surfing it. Riding the storm into the aisles, past their greying heads and through the bars and braces of their ribs, skating home on the glory of having dared and won. Bravo, he thought, fucking *brava*, whatever. He was filled, overcome. And like an idiot he began to weep, silently at first and then in tiny, shaming huffs that were drowned, thank God, by the roaring ovation. The air felt too thin. Keely could not applaud; it was too much. He held his knees as if his legs might fly off, sobbing like a village fool until the silver-haired woman alongside him, a dame of some provenance if posture counted for anything, placed a neatly folded tissue in his lap as if he were an ancient bridge partner whose little weaknesses were old news.

There's the Elgar yet, she said.

I'll never make it, said Keely.

Come on, she said. No guts, no glory.

Doris was still up. Her hair was out and her bifocals shone as she closed the biography and stood. He dropped the keys in the bowl on the bench. It was too warm in the kitchen. Something about his mother having gotten to her feet seemed off.

So? she said with only a thin smile.

Unbelievable, he murmured. I'm wired. I'll never get to sleep. Kai alright? What is it?

Gemma had a call, said Doris. Before work.

He stood there with that falling sensation.

Something unpleasant. A kind of threat, I think. She wouldn't say.

Shit.

She took the call outside, said Doris. We were having a nice evening. Up until then.

Was Kai in bed?

No.

She didn't say who it was, what they said?

No, but whatever it was, it wasn't nice. She was upset. And then Kai was agitated.

And she still went to work?

That was what she said she was doing.

I'll call her.

Her number's there beside the fruitbowl if you don't already have it.

Keely snatched the cordless phone from the bench and thumbed in the digits. A recorded message.

She never turns it off at night, he said. In case Kai needs her.

But he's here with us. And she won't need any more calls like the one she's had.

Can't she screen them?

You've never had calls like that.

I've been threatened, believe me.

Don't be ridiculous.

Okay, I'm just saying. I don't know what I'm saying. But, hell. I think I'll go down and check on her, he said, grabbing up the Volvo's keys again. You mind?

Would it matter?

What's that? he said abstractedly.

Tom, she's at work. How will you check on her? They won't let you into the supermarket.

I don't really know. I just need to make sure.

What you need is to think clearly. She needs to go to the police.

She won't go, he said. No cops, no refuge.

Just sit down for a moment.

I can't, he said.

Stay, she said. Go to bed. Please.

Mum, I can't, he said, pulling the door to. I just can't.

Traffic into Fremantle was light. In the distance the Jurassic container cranes of the port loomed like some sort of lurid arena spectacle. Keely had no idea what he was doing. This aimless driving about. But anything would feel better than lying awake half the night at Doris's.

He crossed Stirling Bridge. Turned away from the harbour and headed inland a little on Canning. Bitsy clumps of retail. Traffic lights. Car yards. The Cleo.

Pulled into the empty parking lot in front of the shopping complex on the hill. Sat idling a moment beside the concrete bunker where Gemma worked. No sign of her car. No vehicles anywhere except those flashing by out on the four-lane. And then it occurred to him. Basement entry. He eased up to the end of the building, angled onto the ramp and crept down the steep decline. But halfway down he came upon a boom gate and was forced to reverse out. Parked the Volvo on the street and walked back down.

The underground carpark was well lit and so much warmer than the night above. Foetid, even. Over by the lifts, slotted in behind a Subaru and a couple of unloved Corollas, was the blue Hyundai.

He pushed the call button for the lift and waited but the doors didn't open. He tried again and a crackly voice spoke from the pipework overhead.

Sir, if you're not an employee, you'll have to leave.

Keely looked up, saw the sinister dome of the CCTV camera.

Sir? said the voice. We can escort you out if you're lost.

Keely grinned like an imbecile, showed the camera his palms and left.

He lapped the block in the Volvo and pulled into the alley behind the supermarket. Refrigerated trucks chuntered against the loading docks but the big roller-doors were shut. He fished out his phone and called her, but got the same message. Maybe it was enough to know the building was secure, that there was surveillance. Because if she was at work she seemed to be safe.

So why didn't he feel reassured?

He rolled back down Canning towards the bridges. The wharves with their penumbra of yellow against the dark sky. The streets into town were empty. Even the drunks in the park next to Clancy's were gone. The East End was desolate. A few gulls squabbling over food on the pavement outside the Woolstores. Disposable cups, newspapers in gyres against graffiti walls.

Rolled by the old Mirador. Counted lights on the top floor. Nothing at his, nothing at hers. All clear.

He drifted along the Strip with the windows down. The midnight news came on the radio. He switched it off. The street-sweepers were not yet trawling the alleys but the pubs were closed and the last evicted drinkers were plundering kebab shops and hailing cabs. There were modest altercations at the kerbside but this was a long way from the standard welter of puke and broken glass that graced the precinct at weekends. A few cafés were still open to service the late-shift bohemians and confused old men. On the Market Street corner a couple of Euro-hippies strummed and bojangled at pedestrians, whose indifference did not deter them.

South Mole. Victoria Quay. The old passenger terminal. Crossed the tracks again. The warehouses, backstreets. Round House, the Roma.

Everything familiar. His town. Doing what it did in the week-day wee-hours. Nothing to be agitated about. Riding around like a bored hoon.

Just before one he buzzed himself into the Mirador carpark.

Rode the lift to the top floor. Along the gallery the usual night noises: thudding bass, scrambly TV atmospherics, gurgles of plumbing and conversation.

The flat was hot and closed up. Out on the balcony the air was cooler. The cranes of the port flashed and lumbered. Closer in, on the pavements below, there was nothing moving but blown trash and gulls that looked like blown trash. Gloom, tranches of deep darkness, spills of light. He could feel the pending, aching near-ness of something about to happen. The streets, so familiar, now a maze as much as a neighbourhood. Their very emptiness made him uneasy. Caused the roof of his mouth to itch.

A horn sounded. Freight train wending its way around the water to the old bridge. Rumbling, squealing on the bends. White quills of masts bristled on the marina. The sea beyond winking out measures of distance and depth, flashes of warning.

Gemma's balcony was dark. All well. Not feeling it.

Before locking up he rolled the knife drawer out and snatched up a few cards of medicine. Just to get him through the next day or two, while he was gone. Found a Coles bag and stuffed them in. Necked a couple of the Valium for a steadier.

Out on the gallery the wind caused the plastic bag to rustle against his leg. And the moment he turned from his door he could see something hanging from the grille at Gemma's. It hadn't been there when he arrived. Or at least he hadn't noticed it.

From a distance it looked like an out-of-season Christmas

decoration. Up close it was a leprous teddy bear suspended by one leg. Keely swore and yanked at it. The bear tore free but the snared leg hung twisting in the easterly, leaking sawdust and lint that blew in his face and caught in his eyes. He pulled at it madly, broke the dirty packing string and got it off, but by then it was little more than a hollowing scrap of fabric. He stuffed this and the mutilated bear into the shopping bag and headed at a trot for the lifts. Halfway along the gallery he caught a brief flare in the street below, as if someone were lighting a smoke.

The lift down was ponderously slow. No one in the lobby. Nobody outside the laundry. He shoved the bear into the garbage skip. Couldn't see anyone in the carpark, but the lighting out there was patchy.

Got to the Volvo without actually breaking into a run. For a few moments sat peering out. In the side street, a flicker of movement. Someone there. Definitely there. So he started the car, buzzed the gate open and rolled down the ramp without lights. As he swept into the street he snapped on the high beam and saw them. Beside the stranded shopping trolley, the parked bike, the yellow-topped recycling bin. A tall, white-haired bloke in pinstripes. And a smaller figure in a tracksuit. One smoking. The other busy on his knees.

Keely took the corner too fast to be safe. Launched out onto the main street wildly. Like a fool. Like a man who couldn't tell if he was relieved or ashamed. Traffic lights. Side street. Esplanade. Rail lines. The shimmer and open space of the marina.

The sardine dock was deserted. He pulled up and got out shakily. The tarmac glittered with scales. He strode out to the planked jetty, feeling the sparks in his fingertips, pacing under the jaundiced lights until he got his breath back and trusted himself to think again. Underfoot the reeking timbers bore all the hallmarks of night-owl anglers – bait bags, beer cans and stomped blowfish.

A few gulls worked through the scuzz of pollard and bait scraps. Out in the pens, boats nodded at their moorings and light flecked the water.

He leant against a wooden pile. It still had the warmth of the sun in it.

Wondered if he should have kept the teddy bear. For proof, evidence – he didn't know what.

He had to bring this matter to a head. Another kind of man would have had it sorted by now. No use hiding and hoping these nasty pricks would go away. No point reasoning with them. What this situation required was swift and sudden violence. Stop them in their tracks. Disable them. But that just wasn't in him. He could imagine it easily enough, fantasize. But he'd never do it.

So whatever happened to *whatever it takes*? That bit of steely resolve had lasted all of an evening.

God, why couldn't Gemma just go to the cops? Or pack the car, take the boy and drive north? What the hell was he supposed to do? And why *him*, anyway? How long could he live like this, waiting for the hammer to fall? Wouldn't it be better to just bring it on, spare himself and the others the misery of anticipation and make something happen? That's what the old man would have done. And, okay, there was often carnage in his wake. But that wasn't all carelessness. Shit happened. Keely knew how merciful it could be, a decisive nature.

He needed a bit of that huge, headlong, loving force. Kindness with a backbone – wasn't that Nev's mantra? Why was it so hard to summon? Why wasn't it simply there, bubbling up instantly the way anxiety did, the way this festival of second-guessing did? Couldn't blame that on too much school, too much soft-handed generational success. It was something lacking in him. Something in the shape of him. This empty thing he'd become.

He ran his hands over the soft grain of the jarrah post. Rested his forehead on its edge a moment. Drew himself back. From torturing himself with Nev, making the poor old bugger some mythic paragon again. Like the superhero Gemma had turned him into for Kai's sake. This business would not be resolved with an honest bit of biffo and some sorrowful Kumbayah. It was going to take more. Worse. Better. Cleverer. No point wounding them; they'd be back. If you couldn't get them arrested you'd have to kill them. And you weren't killing anybody.

What you needed was a few minutes' confidence. Not the sort you got from being built like a brick shithouse, but the kind you got by being convinced. Determined. Wasn't it hot, hurting conviction that had fuelled you all those good years? Didn't you have some warrior in you then, when things were only as hopeless as they'd ever been, when despite that you still went at it like a good and faithful servant? With only your backbone to lean on. And the pride of still giving a damn. You could have stood before Nev then, him and his Mighty Force. With your head up.

This is it. The bounce off the bottom.

You want to walk away. But you don't walk away.

Because here you are. Shining in the dark. Poisoned head radiating power. Parked two blocks from the problem. Smarter. Bursting. With nothing left to lose.

Across from the decaying row of houses, a spare parking bay. He backed into it and switched off the ignition. There was a light on upstairs and music audible even at this distance. Although it was nearly two, it was evident that neighbours were well-enough acquainted with Stewie's nature to refrain from complaint.

Keely thought first about a molotov cocktail. Simple procedure. But you couldn't set fire to a house adjoining so many others. You couldn't set fire to a house full stop. That wasn't smart. Just thuggish. Cowardly.

But he was here now.

And now was the moment. Whatever he was going to do would happen now.

He restarted the Volvo, pulled out, floated around the block.

There was no alternate point of access, no rear lane. Unless he could scale a wall and scuttle over the tin roofs of the markets and leap down into Stewie's backyard. And then what? Be caught like a wharf rat in a kero tin?

Outside the football oval, in the shadow of the weatherboard grandstand, he parked, killed the engine and switched on the interior light. No. There would be no scaling of walls, no window-breaking. No fire, no charging in full of piss and vinegar. He wasn't dealing with a neighbourhood drunk here. This was a snaky, drug-addled sociopath. Who required something a little weird, something asymmetrical. Immobilizing. Paralyzing. Keely would never pound a man's head in, but he could surely fuck with his mind. Knew a bit about that, didn't he?

Reached for the glovebox, inspired.

There was a ballpoint, of course, and a pocket torch, a tube of hand-wipes, a notepad. Dear, dear Doris – ever prepared. Wedged into the pad was a blank and sun-faded postcard. Rio de Janeiro. The monumental statue on the mountain was all blotchy, the colour chemicals on the card were failing, but the image was plain enough – Cristo Redentor. Photographed from above, across the figure's shoulder. And beyond the great head and the Redeemer's outstretched arms, the teeming city below. Roiling chaos at his feet. The watchful Saviour. It was perfect. Christ the Redeemer, why not? Enough Nev in that to make you smile.

The ballpoint was dry and the ink a little lumpy at first but with the notepad as backing, he got his message written quickly enough.

> Jesus loves you, Stewie.
> Which is just as well.
> Because we are watching you.
> All day. All night.
> All eyes.

Then he took the notepad and began to draw. Words wouldn't be necessary. But it was hard work, trembling as he was, suppressing the spasms of laughter that welled up in his neck. He couldn't believe he was doing this. He felt bloody fabulous.

He tore each picture free and laid them on the console beside him. Yes. If they wanted to play funny buggers, then this was a start.

There was no one in the pedestrian mall. As he strode beneath the frangipanis that overhung the limestone wall of the row, he felt adrenaline sparking in his lips and teeth and fingertips. The stone was rough underhand, as alerting as a cat's tongue. Up ahead, the music was an approaching headache. The urge to laugh evaporated. He willed himself on.

The wooden gate to Stewie's place was only slightly ajar and without the churning bass from upstairs the noise from the hinges might have been disastrous. Keely picked his way up the path onto the junk-strewn verandah and bent carefully to slip the postcard beneath the flywire door. There. Jesus on the doorstep.

Then he took the first sheet of paper. Threaded it into the ruined flyscreen.

As he turned for the path, he reeled momentarily, seeing spots. The sudden welter of smells around him pressed in. Wood rot, the inner soles of shoes. Dry mortar. Sea air. Incense. Clove cigarettes. Hash. Sweat. Sardines. Garam masala.

And.

And.

For a couple of seconds he thought he'd puke. Found the verandah post in the dark. Hung off it a while. Staring back at the red glass of the fanlight over the door. Pulsing in time with his blood. That colour. The angry music.

He felt a nail in the post rake his palm and the pain pulled him up. He impaled another sheet on it.

Then he launched himself clear of the verandah, plunged down the path and glanced off the open gate, reeling into the street to rub his hip and get his breath. He was two doors down before he felt the last sheet in his hand. He hesitated. And went back. Shoved it bloodied into the letterbox beside the gate.

And ran like a maniac.

Clambered up from the couch with a start. Fuck. It was ten o'clock. In the a.m. Mouth tasting of rusty nails. Doris's house. Hot. Bright. Silent. And his hand smarting. A divot gouged from his palm. Felt worse than it was.

A terse note on the table. From Doris. Saying she'd given Kai his breakfast and driven him to school herself. That the boy's sheets were on the line. And please bring them in before Gemma wakes up.

He leant against the bench with a groan.

Crept into the bathroom. Stood beneath a cold bolt of water. Drying off, he caught a whiff of tobacco smoke.

Gemma was sitting at the kitchen table with a coffee and a fag.

I woke you, he said. Staring at the note in her hands.

Bloody hot, she said. I dunno how you can sleep in it.

Pfizer, he said.

What?

Merck. Aventis.

What're you talkin about?

Nothing.

He crossed to the livingroom in his towel. It was awkward rifling through his cabin bag for clean clothes, dressing in plain view: underpants, shorts, T-shirt.

Gemma wore nothing but a stretched and shapeless singlet. Her hair was crushed, damp with sweat. He noticed the points of her nipples, the back-curving thumb as she held the cigarette aloft, elbow in hand.

He's wettin the bed, she murmured. And no one tells me.

I guess we didn't want to make you feel any worse, he said, pouring himself a coffee.

She squinted through the smoke. We?

I know, he said. All this.

No shit.

Why don't you go back to bed? he asked. You'll be knackered tonight.

I told you. It's too hot.

I gather there was a call.

Doris. Does it all, does she?

He let it go. He didn't feel well. The coffee was thin.

Where were you? she asked. Last night. When I was at work.

The concert. Remember?

After.

Why?

Why not tell me, Tom? I want to know what you've done.

Done? he said carefully.

She nodded slowly, regarding him through the haze she put between them.

Just drove around, he said.

In your mother's car.

Like being young again.

He got up, tipped the coffee down the sink.

I think we'll go home, she said. Me 'n Kai.

He glanced back at her but Gemma's eyes were averted. She twitched the fag with her thumb and sniffed.

Something's happened?

I'm over it, she said. I want me own things, me own bed.

But it's not safe, he said.

It'll have to do.

What about Kai?

He's not happy here.

But you said it yourself: he loves Doris.

Home with me he doesn't wet the bed.

Keely drew a breath, but said nothing.

Have you got a gun?

A what?

You heard me.

No, he said.

She drew on the fag. Blew smoke at the ceiling. Didn't think so, she said. Couldn't even afford to buy one.

I don't want one, he said.

You're broke.

I told you I was.

Thought you were exaggeratin. But she says you haven't got a pot to piss in.

So now you know for sure.

Look at ya, she said with a scornful grin.

What?

Never been skint before, have ya?

He spread his hands on the table.

You're soft, Tom. That's the thing.

You wouldn't know, he said.

Believe me, she let out with a laugh. I know.

Tell me what he said.

Who?

You know who. On the phone.

It's bloody hot, she said. Let's go for a swim.

He's texting you.

Carn, it's hot as hell. Let's swim.

I thought you were moving back to the Mirador.

Thinkin about it.

How does he have your number, anyway?

Where's close?

Gemma, how does Stewie have your number?

She gave it to him, orright? Carly. The silly little bitch gave it to him. She'll never fuckin see me or the boy again.

You don't mean that.

I want a fuckin swim.

The river's close.

Stinks, she said. Fuckin shithole.

Okay, he said, with puffs and sparks behind his eyes.

Fuckin jellyfish and brown water.

I *said* okay, alright?

Don't shout at *me*, mate! I'll bloody go on me own and you'll be walkin.

Fine, he said, retreating to the lounge and the crackly bag of pills.

Bad thought, but the water was like novocaine. So cool at first, delicious and silky, stalking him pore to shivery pore before the numbing warmth sank in and clumsiness took hold. He felt heavy beside her, annoyed by her sudden playfulness, shamed by the hard-on he got the moment she clung to him. Steadying herself.

Gemma was no swimmer. But the way Keely felt today it was just as well. He looked about. After the shabby free-for-all of South Beach, Cottesloe was a total scene, a kind of flesh pageant.

The pair of them bobbed tiptoe on the sandbank, ducking modest waves. Laughing a little. Well, *she* was laughing. Keely squinted and held her hand and felt the weight of water roll by. Today a real swim was beyond him. The sun too bright. Sand in his veins.

Your wife, said Gemma. Doris loves her. Reckons she's beautiful.

Says she's smart.

Ex-wife, he murmured. But yes, yes.

Screwed another lawyer.

Don't want to talk about that.

And you dropped yer bundle.

Told you that already. Keely rose to his toes as a swell pushed past.

This before or after they sacked you?

I said I don't want to talk about it.

Don't mind talkin about my shit, but, do ya?

Before, he said. All happened before.

But Gemma seemed to have lost interest. She'd turned to survey the amphitheatre of sand and grass, the fatuous tearooms, the preening oilers and cruising hipsters on the terraces.

Makes ya sad, dunnit? All them young, beautiful things.

Why?

Doesn't make you think of bein young? she said, grabbing an arm and hanging off him.

Didn't notice, he said.

Liar.

What are you talking about?

What do you call this, then?

She brushed a hand across his shorts and laughed. He couldn't tell what was scorn and what was simple exuberance.

I'm going to swim, he heard himself say.

He broke free and struck out through the surf to deeper water but every turn of his head sent his brain spilling like unsecured cargo and it crashed against the bulwarks of his skull until he could take no more. He rested a moment, floating on a sudden pulse of nausea. His hand stung. Starbursts went off behind his eyes. He sculled back gingerly. Whole ocean curving away beneath him. Shining hard and horrible.

Staggered to shore.

Down a long barrel. Gemma. On a towel. In the sun. Golden. Breasts pooled against her ribs. Startled. Snapping her phone shut. As he reeled up, dripping, at the other end of the telescope.

Christ, she said. What's wrong?

Nothing. Just. J-j-j-just . . .

Steadied himself. Hands on hips. Gemma sat up. Shielding her face from the bursting sun. Her limbs shone. Smoothed by water, light. Belly soft. And a glow hung over her every movement, flaring and trailing white as if some kind of phosphorescence were upon her. Felt he was standing too long. Looming over her. Saw he didn't know her, not really. Wondered if he even liked her. Wished she'd just shut up, leave him alone. Wanted to say it, but they bounced in his head, the words. Clotted his jaw. Ground it shut. Till his teeth went into his soft, glowing brain.

Why couldn't he sit down?

Tom, you're starin.

Head, he said. H-h-ha.

What? What're you sayin?

Car, he said.

What about the car?

Ahr, he said.

Staggering through shelters. Volleyball games. Across towels and glistening, leaping limbs. Towels. And scowls. Howls of outrage. The light rode right through him; through his eyes, his throat, into his belly and balls. At the steps he stumbled. Stuck. And someone caught him by the arm. Canting there.

Christ, she said. All I wanted was a breather.

Rippling steps. Leaning trees. Hot tar. The horizon lurching, oceanic. The car. The ground turning as he fell into the roasting interior. Round in circles, tighter loops and whirls. Gemma drove fast, spinning him into the roof, his lap, the green furze of golf links, screaming, slapping his belly through the cowling of his head.

Hours after the room stopped spinning, Keely lay on the couch, eyes tightly closed, throat burning, his fingers sore from holding on, unable to believe it was over. The house stank of disinfectant. A fan oscillated nearby, but he couldn't think about oscillation or rotation of any sort, not now the vertigo had finally wandered away like a storm seeking carnage farther afield. The floor pulsed slightly, as if there were still a swell running. But the turmoil was gone.

A car door slammed. Then another.

Don't wake him up, said Gemma near the back door.

The fridge opened, closed with a rattle of bottles and jars. Keely dozed a moment, woke to the slight give in the cushion beside him. Heard the boy's wheeze. When he opened his eyes Kai was there, studying him. Shirtless, pigeon-chested, his arms pitifully thin.

The car really stinks, said Kai.

Sorry.

Do you still feel crook?

I feel a bit better now, Keely croaked. Where's your nan?

Kitchen. Look, said Kai, holding a book of some sort too close. It's you.

Keely pressed the boy's arm back gently and struggled to focus. It was an old clipping glued into a scrapbook. And there was his grinning face beside a startled Carnaby's black cockatoo.

Where'd you get that?

The lady. Doris. It's a whole book on you.

That's a special bird, he murmured. Not many left.

Says it's dangerous.

No, said Keely. Endangered. Means they might all die out.

Extinct.

That's it.

The boy twitched the scrapbook back in order to peer at it again.

They mate for life, said Keely. They're all left-handed.

Habitat, said the boy, quoting from the headline.

That's the big problem.

For birds.

For all of us.

The boy drew his gaze from the clipping slowly. He examined Keely's face, blinked.

Habitat, he said. Seven letters.

Extinct, said Keely. Also seven letters.

Kai peered at him, counting.

You think you can beat me? Keely said. Just cause I've had a bit of an ordinary day? Just because I'm not right in myself?

The boy lost command of his face a moment. His shy grin betrayed him.

Despite Doris's best efforts, dinner was a subdued affair. Keely couldn't tell whether Gemma resented having to cook or if she was simply nervous. The food was fine, but Keely had no appetite. He was still getting over his complete failure at Scrabble and Kai seemed crestfallen, even resentful. Things had started out normally enough, but a few minutes in Keely began making elementary mistakes. He couldn't distinguish an E from an F. Ds and Bs confused him. Kai seemed to suspect him of playing dumb and looked more and more affronted, but for minutes at a time the letters of the game became inscrutable to Keely and it was difficult to tamp down his creeping panic. The call to dinner had come as something of a relief.

When the meal was finished, Gemma excused herself and

retired to the bathroom and Kai sat on the couch to watch television. Keely got up to help with the dishes and caught Doris's eye as she took up a saucer and tilted it his way discreetly before tipping butts and ash into the bin. He shrugged.

She's not well, he murmured.

Oh, it was her that was sick?

Yes, he lied.

Faith called. She's home safe.

Pulled the bank out of a nosedive, has she?

Some foundation in Geneva is asking about you.

They contacted her?

She bumped into someone. In London.

She's touting for me?

She was approached.

I doubt that.

A climate change thing.

Now, there's a defeat I haven't suffered yet.

I looked them up, she said. They seem good.

Who was this person?

She can't say.

It's Harriet, isn't it?

No, it's not. I wrote down the number.

And the name?

Apparently you just call the number.

What is this, Secret Squirrel?

I'm just passing on the message.

Why couldn't she call me herself? he said, setting down a plate with more force than he'd intended.

You need me to explain that? The fact she's even bothering to do this for you seems angelic to me.

Keely did not respond. He was puzzled. What could be bugging Faith?

Tom?

Yes?

Did you hear me?

Yeah, he said. It's good of her.

You won't call anyway.

Probably not.

Well, she said, wiping her hands and cracking the freezer door. No need to trouble you with details, then.

The shower thundered through the wall. It seemed to get louder the longer the water ran. Doris stood at the sink, appeared to hesitate over the hot water tap.

Perhaps we'll wash these later, she said.

Okay, he murmured. Think I'll just go for a walk.

You don't remember, do you?

Remember what?

Faith. Your behaviour.

He made for the door.

It was still light outside and the air was hot and motionless. Gemma's car stood in the driveway, all its doors and windows open. The interior reeked of vomit and disinfectant. The street hissed with sprinklers. The sky was a starless blue and the ground felt firm enough underfoot.

All the local shops were closed. He walked on out to the highway and found a big servo where they sold hot food, car parts, homewares and stationery. On a rotating stand he found a promising selection of postcards. He bought one of every kind. The surfing koala, the colour panorama, the arty black-and-white, a wildflower, a shark, the body beautiful, and the sleazy double entendre. He sat at a table with a Coke and a felt pen and as punters came and went from the pumps on the tarmac he went to work. The eye. The memorial cross. The Luger pistol. On the last card, the one featuring a Great White with gaping maw, he wrote a message: *Coning soom . . .*

He returned them to their packet and walked back to Doris's as darkness fell.

Gemma was in the drive, wiping out the car again. She gasped as he stepped up behind her.

Jesus Christ, she said. As if I haven't had enough today.

Sorry, he said, copping a little spray from the bucket as she tossed the rag down in disgust.

Bloody useless.

Stewie, he said. What's his surname?

That scumbag. Who cares?

I just need to know who I'm dealing with.

Knowin his name won't help.

Just tell me. Please.

Chrissake! Name's Russell. Wish I'd never heard it, meself.

And you remember the address?

What are you, thick? You were there.

I know the house, he said. But the number.

I don't remember. Four, six. Somethin like that.

Okay, he said. The name'll do.

You're in enough shit already, she said, closing the passenger door.

You think?

Doris found your stash.

Stash of what? he said.

Your pills.

Oh, he said. That. I get these headaches, that's all.

Tipped em down the toilet. I shoulda known. Figured you were just a boozer.

It's not like that.

I'll bet it's not.

It's complicated.

Yeah, mate. They all say that.

I spose they do.

I mean, Jesus, Tommy. I thought I could trust you.

You can.

Yeah. What choice have I got anyhow?

He set Gemma down outside the glass doors of the super-market and waited until the uniformed guard arrived and let her through. She went in without turning or waving. Keely sat there a minute or two. Trying to reassemble the plan in his head. Had to concentrate. To keep it clear. It was exhausting. But it was still there. He had it.

So he drove on in to Freo. The Mirador. Into his flat for a couple of those bigboy codeines. Quick scout around. Over to Stewie's. Rolled past, to the next block. Got out and walked back. Casual. Copped the house number. Six. Shoved a card into the letterbox. Said the number to himself over and over, all the way back to the car. To calm himself. To remember the number.

Pulled in beneath the big old ghost-wall of the empty prison.

Wrote it all out. Steady as he could manage. Then headed east. Canning. Great Eastern. Flashes of river. Towers across the water. Glitter in the far hills.

Halfway to the airport he remembered his promise. Pulled into a servo. Did what he could with the steam-cleaning gizmo. But he'd never used one before. Began to think it was making things worse. Had some taxi driver watching him, shaking his head. But just ploughed away until Gemma's money ran out. Him being short. And Doris not feeling magnanimous tonight.

Climbed back into the swampy pig of a thing and rode on inland with the smell revived and the damp seeping into his clothes. But it sharpened him. That smell of bile. Kept him focused.

Driving into the hot, dry western night with all the windows down.

He put it together. Made the run he'd mapped out for himself. Well, not completely to plan. Got lost a couple of times. Distracted, really. But he got it done. With the pain backing off he rode them all out, those cards in their motley envelopes, stamped and addressed in every variation he could make of his own handwriting. Which was none too steady tonight, hard for even him to recognize, truth be told.

Posted the first at a street box in Midland, the second at the Inglewood post office, another outside a 7-Eleven in Cannington. By the time he reached the northern suburbs the Hyundai's interior was nearly dry but the carpet still had a whiff to it. He tooled around a huge, empty shopping complex in Morley until he found a mailing point. There was a box near the aquarium at Hillarys and as he headed back south there was another by a glass-strewn bus stop along the wilds of Marmion Avenue.

It was late when he coasted down the hill at Blackboy Crescent. For some reason he had trouble finding it tonight. He skirted the restored wetland and idled along the edges of the park where once he'd kicked the footy with neighbourhood kids every evening until dark. The bounding silhouettes, mothers bellowing, the ball hanging in a spiral climb against the sky. The memory skin-close. And strangely consoling. I was happy here, he thought. The world made sense. All of us together.

He drove down the coast feeling buzzed. Another salvo gone. Every card a mind-bomb. From all points of the compass. Encirclement.

And he yelled through the open windows. Blowing down West Coast Highway, lane to lane, light to light, light from true light.

Our name is Legion, Stewie! For we are many!

The thought of it. That little tweaker. Getting all these cards. Day after day. All with different postmarks, styles, messages, pictographs. It buoyed him. You're surrounded, Stewie. Outnumbered. Just see the little numbskull turning them over, licking his lips. The girl there, too, probably others, passing them across the table, scoffing, anxious, eyes like schooling fish, searching out any hint of alarm in the others, the paranoia beginning to smoulder. Fuckheads.

Keely had no need of violence. He was smart. Black-ops. He'd always been good at this shit.

Had a tenner left from the steam-clean. Which kind of confused him. But he angled into a servo anyway and found a spinner rack. Bought a few more cards.

And then he was walking along the gallery. The Mirador.

Quite suddenly there.

And there was nothing hanging from Gemma's door but the last wafting bit of string. He unpicked it carefully and shoved it in a pocket. His own place was stale but with the slider open it cleared soon enough.

There were messages on the machine – an odd one from Faith and something terse from Doris. He didn't want to call her but the tone of his mother's voice alarmed him. Jabbed in the number.

What do we need, Tom? she said the moment she picked up. And he saw it was late. Very late.

Tell me, she said. Do we need a neurosurgeon or just detox?

I'm fine, he said. I'm home. It's alright. I'll be at yours in the morning.

You need help, love.

I've got work, he said. Need sleep.

Work? Why lie to me?

But it's true.

What are you really scared of?

I just need to sleep. I'm really sorry.

He hung up and stood alone in the little flat a minute. Thought of the trail of sand and spew he'd left through her house, the bag of pills she'd found stuffed in a corner of the couch. Within reach of the child. Not good.

Time for bed. But he was too stirred up.

Then he remembered. Tomorrow wasn't Thursday. So, no job. Just Gemma to collect at dawn. As promised.

Set the alarm. For five.

Slumped into the chair, turned on the TV. More fat-people shows, cooking shows, forensic investigations, Jeremy fucking Clarkson. Flicked it off.

Fished out the latest cards. Spread them on the kitchen table. Every last one of them a tit joke – something to behold. He found a pencil, a biro, a felt marker. Worked his way through the icons: eyes, gun, cross. In the knife drawer there were envelopes and stamps. In beside his last sheet of Temazepam lay the boning blade he'd taken off Gemma.

He lined up the cards, addressed the envelopes and sealed them. There were stamps enough. He'd make another run tomorrow. Keep it up until Stewart Russell was a blithering mess.

Grainy half-light. Sky green-grey above the desolate carpark. The glass doors peeled back. The bloke in uniform stepped aside to let a dozen workers out onto the sick-lit pavement. In their pastel tunics and smocks they were variously festive, weary, sociable, anxious to be on their way. Gemma and a tall, lithe young man lingered in the supermarket entry. His hair was long and fair and his movements outsized and antic enough to make her laugh and push him away playfully. She turned and caught sight of Keely parked across the deserted tarmac, and as she came on, stepping from the kerb, clutching her shoulder bag, she spun girlishly and shot the bloke a wave.

She opened the passenger door and flopped in, smelling of deodorant and tobacco and something sugary.

Snake? she said, shoving a cellophane bag his way.

Keely glanced into the snarl of bright colours. Recoiled at the cloying whiff of industrial additives.

Buckle up, he said.

Yes, Dad.

He passed her a takeaway coffee and she grunted. Refrigerated trucks pulled onto the street and the sky was bronze already. He steered them down the promenade of car yards and furniture warehouses, out across Stirling Bridge and up the four-lane towards Doris's. Gemma lit a fag and reefed her hair free of its band.

You been busy, she said, sniffing.

You have no idea.

Feet're killin me.

But you seem happy enough.

That new bloke, she said. French or somethin. Like a bloody TV show. Talk about laugh. Been there a week now. He won't last.

She sighed and angled smoke out the window.

Kai orright? she asked.

I slept at mine, he said.

Gemma hoisted herself up in her seat. You shoulda said.

Yeah.

Well, that's bloody ordinary.

I spoke to Doris. It's all good.

Says you.

So, it's okay to leave him in the building on his own, but leaving him safe with my mother's not on?

Don't try and lecture me. No position.

Fair enough. I should've called. But your phone's off.

Well, duh.

Okay.

Where'd you go, then?

Just for a drive.

She blew smoke and gulped the coffee. He saw the red splash of a post box and veered into the forecourt of a deli.

What're you doin?

I just need to post something.

He reached behind him, pulled out a plastic bag.

Jesus, what's all that? What're you up to?

Nothing, he said, turning the addresses away from her. Just business.

Business, she said. Don't make me laugh. What kind of business would you do? Second thoughts, don't even tell me, I don't wanna know.

Suits me, he said, getting out.

At the box he shoved the cards through the slot, wishing he'd waited and spread the postmarks again for the fun of it, for the chance of further bafflement, but having them on him had become a little nerve-racking; it was better to send them off before he mucked anything else up. As he turned for the car, Gemma tossed the paper cup onto the bitumen. He picked it up without comment and dropped it into a bin.

As Gemma took another of her interminable showers Keely sat in the yard beneath the noise of stirring birds. Almost fully light now and the morning easterly stirred the trees. Beyond the aimless trails of rustic paving the grass was unkempt and snarls of bougainvillea had colonized the hibiscus and frangipani. The big motley plane tree rested hard against the fence and last year's leaves lay everywhere like the remains of a betting plunge. Parked in beside the leaf-shingled shed, the dinghy gave him a pang. He'd been putting it off but he knew he had to give it up, job or no job.

A blur of movement at the corner of his eye. Kai's face at the window. He waved.

The boy came out onto the deck in just his pyjama shorts. Hesitated, then came on down to join him.

I went looking, said the boy. I didn't see you.

This weekend, said Keely. Let's put the boat in the water, go see that bird again. What d'you reckon?

The boy nodded.

Can I get in?

Now? Sure.

Keely strode over, hoisted him up. There were deep, heart-rending dimples above his shoulderblades. Kai clambered to the rear thwart, reached for the tiller, and the moment he assumed the posture of skipper his solemnity failed him. Such a grin of pleasure. Transformed. And Keely felt a vicious sweep of feeling. If anyone should touch this child. Anyone.

At breakfast Doris was brisk. She moved at such speed there was no spare moment in which to pull her aside, make an apology, explain himself, give undertakings. He wanted to reassure her but she hurtled by, citing a meeting at eight, her only breaks in momentum the little fussing pauses over Kai that seemed like in-jokes between her and the boy, brief but lavish gestures of affection that Kai drank up. Doris was hurt. Keely could see that. And angry. Now she was moving in on Kai. Making the save.

She crashed out the door in a dark suit, her satchel and handbag clutched to her hip.

In the wake of her departure, with Gemma already in bed, he waited as Kai dressed himself for school. Saw his own pillow and folded sheets on the couch. Protruding from beneath them, a sheaf of papers. Too neatly collated and placed to be accidental. When he riffled through he saw they were sheets from a legal pad. But this was not Doris's work. A list of words.

MAN

    MACE

    MAGUS

    MAUL

    MENTAL

MERCY

    MITE

    MIST

    MONK

    MOON.

MAGPIE

    MALLARD

    MINER

    MONARCH

    MOPOKE

        MUDLARK

    MUTTONBIRD

On the sideboard, beside the ancient Scrabble set, was a dictionary – the Concise Oxford.

Traffic was slow on the highway. Kai sniffed furtively now and then but was not talkative.

So who won last night? Keely asked as they sat in a snarl by the rail crossing.

Doris.

She's a terror for those little words at the end.

The boy nodded absently.

You working on your M-words?

Kai leant forward, opened the glovebox, rummaged through. Keely saw a hairbrush, a jar of Vicks VapoRub.

M is a good letter, said Keely.

Three points, said Kai.

And there's only two of them. Isn't that right?

The boy flipped the glovebox shut and held out his hands. For a moment Keely thought it was the preface to a game, some joke Doris had taught him. And then he saw the creases in his palms.

Two, said Kai.

Driving by Stewie's again was tempting fate. He knew it, but couldn't resist. After all, what did he expect to see – doors and windows thrown open in panic, speed-freaks tearing at their hair, a taxi being loaded with binbags?

As it happened, the place looked undisturbed. Office drones trudged by, a bloke hosed the pavement at the pub on the corner, hippies coasted past on bikes in the direction of the Strip.

He drove to South Beach, swam a ginger lap. Watched a bloke with his granddaughter building a sandcastle at the water's edge.

Outside Stewie's again, later in the morning, in the shade of a casuarina, he waited for the postie to swing by. Nuts. Being there, lurking in that blighted car. But he wanted to *see* something. So badly needed to witness some action, evidence of an outcome, a stirring of the pot. Oh, to see the look on Stewie's canine face. Yes, he wanted that. Next time he'd send a parcel, a courier. Ramp this thing up. Lay siege. Full campaign.

But nothing was happening. No postman. No movement at all.

He drove back to Doris's. Keyed up. Frustrated. Crept about in the cool refuge of the kitchen. Made himself a sandwich. Felt all his mother's oil paintings watching, unblinking, expectant. It welled up in him. This urgent desire to see something happen, make it happen.

Stalked carefully down the hall. The door to the spare room was ajar. Gemma lay asleep in a singlet and undies, a hip and thigh exposed, one arm dangling from the bed. The soles of her feet were yellowish, heels cracked. The top sheet was rucked into a wedge where she'd kicked it down. On the floor beside Kai's mattress were a few books, his laptop. Keely snuck in, grabbed the Acer.

Out on the kitchen table he booted the thing up, hooked into Doris's wireless network. And keyed in the name.

It was too good to be true. He had to stifle a bark of delight. The little turd was on Facebook. There were several Stewart Russells and even more Russell Stewarts, but here he was, plain as dog's balls, Stewie himself. Mista Gangsta. A wall of crim poses and tattoo displays. Arms across the shoulders of vamping molls in titty tops. Likes to PARTAAAAY. Approves of Black Eyed Peas, Wu-Tang Clan, Funkmaster Flex and a solid block of names that meant nothing at all to Keely. Has twenty-seven friends, lucky lad. What a cohort. What a boon to the culture.

And there she was. Carly. The girl from the happy snap in Gemma's kitchen. A sexier, stringier version of that young woman. With kohl-ringed eyes and a fuck-you snarl. Still friends. Still in contact.

Keely sat back. Head spritzing.

Should have thought of it sooner. Because it really was tempting.

All it would take was a new email address. A girl's name. And a slutty photo to go with it. Some lame story he'd spin to Stewie about having bumped into him at a pub. Then, pretty soon, after a bit of Liking and Friending he'd be rattling around in Stewie's hood. Talking shit. Sharing pics. Mixing in. Like a shadow-self. Just biding his time. Until he started lobbing a few grenades into his world. All he'd need was a bit of footage from a phone. Say, Stewie at his front gate. Doing something apparently harmless. But with an inflammatory caption. Along with his street address. Something impossible to ignore. Didn't need to be true. Better if it wasn't. KIDDY FIDDLER IN OUR MIDST. Some mad vigilante thing. And – click – upload it to YouTube. Flick it to all Stewie's friends. Blam. Out there. Wildfire. It'd be a frigging riot. In five minutes it'd be viral. Pestilential. Exactly the sort of no-holds-barred guerrilla campaign he'd never let the kids in the movement unleash, regardless of how often they pleaded for it. Couldn't happen to a nicer fella. Surround him with phantoms. Grind him to a gibbering pulp.

He shut the machine down. Crept back to Gemma's room, set it beside the boy's mattress.

Food for thought. But he'd need money. And a little help. Post-cards were only going to get him so far.

After school Kai ran to the car. Buckled himself in, cranked up the window and locked the door.

Not such a good day, then?

The boy slid down in his seat and said nothing.

Fancy a swim?

Kai shook his head.

Right, he said. Back to dear-dear Doris's. I'll give you a game.

The boy gave him nothing.

How about a kick? There's gotta be a ball somewhere.

Silence.

What about the boat, Kai? We'll squirt out on the river, eh?

Kai looked sceptical. They settled in for the grinding crawl up the four-lane. Keely got nothing more out of him.

When they walked into the kitchen, Gemma was up and Doris was home, still in her silk blouse and skirt. There was a cheerful air in the room that seemed to falter the moment he arrived. The women fussed over the boy, who was still out of sorts but suffered their attentions with patience.

Any requests for dinner? he asked.

Doris's bought steak, said Gemma. And there's spuds and salad.

Okay, he said. Excellent.

Doris deftly avoided his gaze. He cancelled all plans to quiz her about the day. When there was frost on the lawn all you could do was wait for things to thaw. He went outside. Raked leaves half-heartedly until dinner.

At the table the women got to reminiscing.

We used to say you looked like some movie star, said Gemma.

Bollocks, said Doris, dragging her hair free from its workday bun.

Nah, it's true.

What about yourself? said Doris. Who were you – Bo Derek?

Women, he thought. What a marvel they are.

He washed and dried the dishes as they kicked on, laughing and sledging till nightfall.

At eight, when Kai was in bed, Keely announced he was heading out for a stroll.

Gemma ironed her work smock. Doris was thumbing messages on her phone. He caught his mother's glance at the bowl on the bench: the car keys.

Just a walk, he said with a bland smile.

I need some air meself, said Gemma, her rare animation undiminished.

Haven't you got work? he asked.

Not till nine. It's a stroll, not a hike, right?

Keely shrugged. He would have preferred to go alone but now he was snookered.

Doris paused a moment, stared at the tiny screen of the phone, as if it really were the focus of her attention.

You mind, Doris? asked Gemma.

Go ahead, said his mother. I'm not going anywhere.

By the river the air was still and thick. Gemma prattled excitedly. There was no relief from the heat, his sense of entrapment. Under the trees the foreshore smelt of fallen figs, cut grass and dog shit, and from the narrow beach came the sweaty low-tide odours of brine, algae and stranded jellyfish. The moon hung above the towers of the city. It shimmered on every bend and reach of the river.

She does look like an old movie queen, don't you think? You probably can't see it cause she's your mum.

Whatever you reckon, he said.

And what about me? Who did I look like?

I don't remember.

Bullshit, she said.

The mown grass was soft underfoot. Tiny waves lapped and sighed onshore.

Mate, I'm not really in the mood.

Come on, she said, who did I remind you of? Would it kill you to say a name?

Fine, he said ungraciously. I thought you looked like Farrah Fawcett.

Gemma gave a little moan of satisfaction.

I guess I wanted every girl to look like her, he said. It was a long time ago.

But Doris still looks like Julie Christie.

Keely sensed he was expected to say something here, pay Gemma some courtly comment, but the idea irritated him. He didn't understand why her happy mood should irk him so.

The grassy riverbank ended at the limestone bluffs. In the moonlight, the pale fingers of stone shone through the shadow-patches of trees. The track was narrow but white enough to be distinct. They wound on through the undergrowth.

Nico says I look like Brigitte Bardot.

And who's Nico?

New bloke at work, the French one. He's a real card. They're gunna sack him for sure. He opens stuff, food packets. Like chocolates and things. Last night he's trying to get me to eat em, says I deserve it, says he wants to build me up, says it makes him feel good watchin me eat. There's cameras everywhere and he's got me duckin down behind the shelves and the trolleys, and he's stuffin things in me mouth, the dirty perv. He's like twenty-eight or somethin.

I guess you'd better be careful, then.

Tired of bein careful, she said. Where are we goin, anyway?

Keely said nothing until they were beneath the great silver trunk of the dead marri. Under moonlight it was stark, smooth, impossibly beautiful, like a stylized theatre prop. It looked dreamy there amidst the dark presences of living trees. The way it glowed. Cantilevered over the water, owning the night. Hard to imagine an ordinary bird alighting on it.

He sensed her beside him, craning to stare. He felt her hand in his.

It's not there, he said, almost relieved.

She yanked on his arm. He remembered then, she was on at

nine. But she dragged him further into the bush, away from home. Was suddenly facing him, stepping in to pull him close. Her tongue was hot in his mouth.

Hey, he said. You've got work.

There's time.

For what?

I need to draw you a picture?

No, he said.

Carn. I'm goin fuckin mental.

She kissed him fiercely and took handfuls of his hair. Their teeth clashed and she laughed.

But there's nowhere, he said.

She lifted her skirt and guided him down urgently. The stones bit into his knees and a dog barked somewhere as he nuzzled deep between her thighs. She twisted her fingers in his hair and pulled him away and he knelt there, looking up uncertainly into the pale cascade of her hair.

Say somethin nice, she panted. Nothin dirty, just somethin nice.

But Keely could barely speak at all. He was breathless, mindless with lust.

Christ, she said too loud. They used to beg me. Couldn't you say I'm pretty? Is it so bloody hard to say?

You want me to stop?

You think I'll let you stop now? she said, stepping out of her pants.

I'm sorry. I wasn't expecting anything.

Just shut up, she said, grabbing his hair again.

He didn't dare pull away. He stayed where he was until his knees felt lacerated, until she cursed him and whimpered and smacked the back of his head and began to sob.

Gemma wasn't long gone when Doris emerged from her room to fill the kettle and set it on the hob. Keely was still at the table. Stuck. Just following his hands. Watching the jangly pattern of his own fingers. Pressed them down in the end, those hands. To manage the tremor.

Hot, said Doris.

Keely felt his mouth move. But nothing came. He didn't want this. To be here. In this bloody tangle.

You okay?

He nodded.

Such a shame, she said. She was in such good spirits at dinner. Felt like we'd – I don't know – broken through, a little.

He clamped his hands together. And then Doris dropped

something onto the table. At his elbow. Kai's sketchpad.

We need to talk about this.

She opened it about halfway though. The kid had been busy. There were a lot of new drawings organized in crude panels like storyboards. Each sequence featured a rudimentary superhero, a bearded, bear-like colossus. Fists swinging against all comers, legs planted wide, his boots black as his whiskers.

No prizes for guessing who our hero is, then, he said.

And this later one, the fellow with the sword?

Doris leant close. Turned a few more pages. She smelt of coconut shampoo. Tapped the page with a gnarled finger. And there he was himself. A man with a black eye. Like a half-masked Zorro. Dishing out the same rough justice as Nev. With a weapon, no less. The boning knife had become a scimitar and pools of blood lay about, black as Keely's cartoon shiner.

He showed you these?

Let's just say they came to my attention.

You don't miss a trick.

Don't even start me.

Mum, I don't know what to do.

Perhaps you should think about why you're doing anything at all. Whether you're a fit person. In any sense.

What're you talking about?

I think you know exactly what I'm talking about.

No, he lied.

Oh, Tom.

I told you the situation.

Which situation?

Well. Gemma's situation.

Even with that you can't be straight. You think I enjoy saying this, seeing you do this? Wake up, Tom. Look here. Right in front of you. This anxious little boy. Just look at his pictures.

What the hell do you want me to do? What'm I supposed to do to fix this?

You could start by paying attention.

Jesus. I'm fighting for this kid, Doris.

I think your mind is elsewhere.

That's a disgusting thing to say.

Maybe after you've been to the bathroom and washed your face you'll come back and still feel the same way.

Keely lurched back from the table and as he stood the chair capsized behind him.

Don't, said Doris as he headed for the door. Please. We need to discuss this.

He was past listening. He wanted darkness. To be unseen. But there was moon out in the yard, light in the street, the sky bulging at him like a milky eye, and he just kept walking.

Still scratching his bites, Keely rode the six-thirty to Fremantle.

He'd woken radioactive on the back deck with Gemma squatting beside him. He knew how it must look. Him lying there on the boards in last night's clothes. As if he'd gone out and got trashed. Then been locked out by Doris. But it wasn't like that. He didn't think so. Because although there were gaps he knew there'd been no booze. No pills. He had no money, for one thing. He'd just been walking. Barefoot. Along the river, the leafy streets, under drooling lights. Moth trails. Electric flashes of sky. Until his legs gave out. And then he was in warm sand by the river. Ferry lights, red and green. Then some bastard kicking him awake. Shitheads sporting with him in the cold glare of high beams. Running through gardens. Dogs. Patches of wild bush. He fell, lay a long time. Awake. In the wailing air. And when he finally tottered up the steps to the back door he found Doris had locked it. Prudent, that; he wasn't taking it personally. He didn't dare bang on the door. Just lay on the warm deck, waiting for morning. To die. To sleep. Dreaming of dogs streaking from the dark. And waking there, sore, stiff, mozzie-flogged, flayed like a Filipino penitent. With dawn in the wings. Gemma there. Confusing, the way she stroked the thin shell of his head. Like a girl with a horse about to be taken out and shot. She produced a tissue. Blotted his eyes.

What? she whispered. What?

Panadol, he croaked.

It was Thursday. His first day of work beginning in less than two hours.

He reached the café on time. Actually he was early. And Bub seemed surprised, as if he'd forgotten the offer or expected a no-show.

Second adolescence, comrade? Bub said, pointing at the lumps on his face and neck.

Bites, he murmured.

That's all we need, he said. A malarial dishpig. Come on.

Bub led him through to the greasy fug of the kitchen. Gave him a cursory briefing of the racks, the machine, the flow of the benches and sinks. He pointed out the hipster over by the stoves, a bloke in a chef's jacket and pirate bandanna, scowling at his knife-roll as tongues of flame rose from the hobs behind him.

Steer clear, whispered Bub. Psycho in clogs. Thinks he's a genius.

What is he really?

A third-rate cook trying to stay off the gear. Why else could I afford him? Why else would he be doing breakfast?

Keely took down an apron. There were pans waiting already and trays of glasses, coffee cups, saucers queued up in front of the old Hobart. His feet hurt. The drum-and-bass on the stereo was torturous. Bub slipped back with a double-shot and a slice of apple cake. Then he left him to the fifteen-bucks-an-hour reality of scraping scum and scouring glassware.

At two he limped in ruins to the Mirador.

Day one, he told himself. Fresh start. And feeling so damn fresh, too.

Rode the lift up alone. So far past tired he felt tipsy. Began to giggle.

After a tepid shower he sat on the balcony to let the sea breeze cool his feet. And the sudden respite brought the whole weight back down on him. The look on his mother's face. The gnawing fear in those missing chunks of evening. And these savage impulses twitching in him.

Things weren't going to work at Doris's. Not now. Best he moved back here. Maybe Gemma would stay. Doris could brood over Kai like Yahweh over the formless deeps. She could make herself a neat little intervention, call in the kiddy squad. She knew what she was doing. And any fuckups that followed would be her fault.

He took a couple of mother's little helpers and lay on the bed, breeze rifling through him.

The building clanked and gurgled. He felt a moment of kinship. Here we are, he thought, beige and past our prime, haggard but hanging on. He sniffed at the chicken fat and lemon detergent in his puffy fingers. Caught himself drifting. But he had Kai to collect at three. Having promised Gemma. Promised himself. He sat up quickly, so fast there were bubbles and specks behind his eyeballs and the room spun and for a second he thought it was the vertigo returning. Went hand over hand to the armchair. Fell in. Let the air settle. He was okay. All safe. All good.

A dove alighted on the rail of a balcony along the way. It lifted its shoulders, twitched and fell.

He thought of Kai's little storyboard. His cartoon self. Brandishing the scimitar. Wished he'd never seen it.

At the school gate the boy stopped in his tracks, obstructing the path. You could see him register the absence of a vehicle. Not dismay; he was too blank-faced for that. But the hesitation was eloquent enough. He was shunted aside by kids at the rear. Stood there until Keely went in and extracted him.

Your nan's got the car today.

There's a Volvo, but.

Doris needs it for work. We'll take the train.

I can't.

It's easy.

The kid crowded him, pressing so close Keely almost stumbled.

Can you see? said Kai.

I'm fine, mate. I just need room to walk.

Is he looking?

Here, said Keely. Give us your bag.

He was there, said the boy, taking a handful of shirt.

Who? One of your mates?

I come out and he's there.

What? he said, stopping at the corner, looking down onto the crown of the boy's head. Who?

The kid's hair fell forward, he pressed his brow to Keely's side and pulled on his shirt. Wouldn't lift his head; it was maddening, but a chill flashed through Keely.

Kai? Who are we talking about? Who's there? Who's watching?

Can we go? said Kai.

Keely cupped the small head against him and swivelled to scan the street. The boy's limbs snarled against his, almost tripping him. He felt impatience and alarm in equal measure. Just couldn't get free enough to move properly. It was a crowded side street. Purring vehicles. Adult faces. Darting, chirping children. No one he could distinguish as a threat. And yet Kai clutched him, trod on his feet.

Please? said the kid.

The word resonated against Keely's belly. He swept the boy up and hoisted him onto his back. Threaded the little bag onto his arm. And made for the station. The kid's nose pressed hard to his neck, Keely broke into a shambling trot.

When they got to the platform the train doors were chiming. He bullocked his way aboard and nearly sat on the kid as he fell gasping onto an empty seat. Kai turned his head away from the window. The train pulled out of the terminus.

For a couple of minutes Keely let him be. He was too breathless anyway. They rolled along the quays, rode the giddy span of the bridge over sheep ships, car carriers, containers rising from the deck of something blocky and orange. And then they left the harbour behind. The derricks and funnels quickly gone.

Keely sat against the graffiti-clouded glass. The boy retained a fistful of his shirt, scanned the carriage again. The train smelt of feet and bubblegum. The aircon was freezing but the afternoon sun scalded everything it touched.

Kai, he said again. You can tell me.

Is this the way home?

This is it, mate. We're on our way. We get off in a few stops and walk to Doris's.

Is there a taxi?

No, mate. We're walking. What is it? What's bothering you?

Kai stared at the high-schoolers cavorting down the carriage, the raw-boned Christian Brothers boys poking and sledging each other. The sulky state-school chicks thumbing their phones, buds in their ears.

The sea flashed by in silver glimpses. Keely unpeeled the sweaty little hand from his shirt. Took it in his.

C'mon, Kai. Just say.

He's watching.

Who?

At school.

Not a kid? A teacher?

No.

A stranger?

Clappy.

Clappy. That's a man?

Kai dipped his head. Retrieved his hand. As if from habit he turned it palm up and scanned it.

Someone called Clappy, said Keely with a pulse in his throat. And he's watching you.

The train slid into the station at North Fremantle. The boy

nodded, stiffened as the doors opened, scoped the carriage while the train got under way again.

This only happened today?

Kai shook his head, gaze averted.

And not just after school?

The boy pressed his lips together.

Where does he watch from?

Across.

And you know him? You've seen him before?

Kai studied the grimy floor of the carriage.

It's okay to be worried. And it's okay to say it. I'm right here. Tell me, how do you know this bloke, what does he look like? Is he tall or short?

The train pulled up at Victoria Street. The boy blinked and dropped his head again, his face obscured by hair.

Just one thing at a time, said Keely, backtracking. Tell me how you know this fella.

The doors chimed. Rumbled shut.

Kai? This is the bloke who came to the flat. Isn't it?

Kai took another fistful of Keely's shirt.

Keely stared down into the pale blur of the kid's hair. A cold feeling in his gut. Too familiar. And he knew. It had been coming. This carnage. Since before he even knew this child. It was this all along, not destiny but a chance.

The train stopped. Got going again.

No need to worry anymore, he said.

He tried to turn the kid's head his way but Kai resisted.

They pulled into a station. Girls in straw boaters got on. Christ, this was Claremont. He'd missed their stop.

By the time Doris came in, Kai was sprawled before the TV, as closed off as he'd ever been. And Keely was finishing the Margaret River chardonnay he'd found in the fridge. He'd filched a couple of Panadeine Forte from his mother's bedside table. Should have felt calm. But it was six already and there was still no sign of Gemma.

Well, said Doris, setting down her satchel and slipping off her jacket. Just help yourself.

He didn't acknowledge her. Thought about Wally Butcher. Now there was a bloke who'd been handy in his day. No shortage of stories about him fighting his way out of a corner. But Wally was in his seventies, fat as a fart and in serious need of a hip replacement. Wal wasn't going to be any use to him.

Have you eaten? asked Doris. Either of you?

Kai's had a sandwich and some fruit juice.

That's all?

He's not hungry.

What about Gemma?

No idea.

And where did you go today?

Work, he said.

What work?

I wash dishes. At Bub's. It's very fulfilling.

And every day's payday, by the looks of you.

Sorry, he said. I was planning to leave. Go home. But something's come up.

You've had an argument?

Haven't seen her. But I need to speak to her. Before I go.

Where did you get to last night?

Doesn't matter where I went. I wasn't drunk, okay?

But tonight's another night.

So it seems.

Doris busied herself at the fridge and pantry. She brought out garlic, tomatoes, capers, anchovies. The makings of a puttanesca, from what he could see. She slid a pan onto the stovetop and drew a knife from the block.

You've got your work duds on, he murmured. Let me do it.

Pass me that apron, she said.

Mum, really.

You'll end up taking a finger off.

He handed the apron across. You know anyone with a caravan somewhere? he said in little more than a whisper. Somewhere discreet?

No one in this town has a caravan anymore. And if they did they wouldn't take it anywhere discreet. Where've you been the last ten years?

What about a beach house?

I've already asked, she said. Stephanie gave me the keys.

Stephanie who?

Does it matter?

You've organized this? He heard how stupid he sounded. Where is it?

Eagle Bay.

Legal Bay, he said before he could catch himself.

The heavy knife thudded against the bulb of garlic, perhaps a little harder than strictly necessary.

That's good of her. Good of you. Thank you. It's the best we can do. I wonder if I could do it tonight?

Do what? asked Doris, chopping, filling the kitchen with the heady reek of garlic. Drive three hours in your condition?

I wouldn't have to drive.

But you'd need to be competent.

So, maybe I'll wait till morning, he said, colouring. I'll be right in the morning.

Provided Gemma agrees, said Doris, lighting the hob. After a few moments the smell of caramelizing anchovies rose about them. She should be calling the police, she said in a fierce whisper.

I know, but she won't. Could you do it?

And tell them what, a story at third hand? I haven't *seen* anything.

You know cops, people from agencies.

There aren't any signs of physical injury. I don't have any evidence, Tom, there's nothing I can tell them except a few things unlikely to go in Gemma's favour.

What about – I don't know – something more informal?

Send the boys around, you mean? Illegal, and it doesn't work, believe me.

I don't mean the local cops.

I'm not paying to have anyone kneecapped. Forget it.

Of course not. I understand.

What do you think I've become, the sort who'd write a cheque to make this poor girl, this whole thing, go away?

No. No.

Tom, I'm not that person.

I know. I see that.

I doubt it.

So, I'll just report it myself.

Yeah, go in drunk. That'll really help.

Okay, okay.

Besides, said Doris, as if she needed to say it for her own reminding, Gemma has to make this decision herself. And hard as it is to resist overstepping, it's her call to make. We can't just wade in uninvited.

Not even for Kai's sake?

Doris said nothing. He could feel the torment in her silence.

The beach house, he said at length. It'll do for the moment. It's good. It's a start. But where the hell is she?

Kai needs to shower, said Doris. And you need to calm down.

I'm fine, he said.

I'll have this ready when he's out. And you might want to think about freshening up yourself.

Doris, dear, I think *that's* a case of overstepping.

Yes, she said, slipping capers into the pan. I'm sorry. Somehow I keep forgetting you're a grownup.

They were eating when Gemma came in. She tossed keys on the bench, dumped her bag on the floor like a high-schooler and lifted lids from pots on the stove. Keely noted Kai's watchful gaze. He saw his mother follow Gemma's movements without actually turning to look. Doris jangled, lifting her glass, sipping soda water.

Looks good, said Gemma, as if saying so cost her something.

Plenty there, love, said Doris, glancing at Kai.

Gemma wore the little black dress she'd confronted Stewie in, the day they seized the car. Her hair was in a chignon that had gone awry and been flattened with sweat. Still in her heels, she dredged some pasta into a bowl, pulled a fork from the drawer and began to eat listlessly at the sink, her back almost completely turned. Keely saw her reflected face in the kitchen window and knew there was trouble.

He picked at his food. Felt the crackling energy in the room. After a long pause the boy spoke up.

Where'd you go?

Out, said Gemma.

Shoulda said.

What? Are you the boss now?

The boy glowered at his plate. Gemma turned. Her eyes were red, her face looked boiled.

You don't need to know everythin.

Doris laid a hand on the boy's arm and the gesture seemed to inflame Gemma.

Let him be, she said fiercely. You'll make him soft.

Soft isn't so bad, love.

Look where it gets you, she said, hitching her chin towards Keely.

He felt his mother's indignation before the insult even registered. He looked at his food, glanced at Kai's clouded face.

What say we finish our meal and have a talk afterwards? said Doris with a steely lightness.

What say we all mind our own beeswax, said Gemma, shoving her bowl along the bench.

Gemma, he said. I need to talk to you.

Talk? That's all you're good for.

Has something happened, love? asked Doris.

That's my business.

Kai, said Doris brightly. Maybe you and I could finish our dinner out on the deck.

Instantly there was fear in the boy's face.

He can stay where he is, said Gemma. I'm sick of being told what to do.

Sweetie, I'm not telling you what to do. That was a suggestion.

Pig's arse.

You're upset. Kai and I could leave you two to talk things over, that's all I'm saying.

You make it sound like butter wouldn't melt in ya mouth, Doris, but you're still telling me what to do. Kai, get ya stuff.

Don't be ridiculous, said Keely. Just settle down, will you? Kai!

Kai, maybe you should tell your nan about Clappy, said Keely.

But the boy shook his head. There was tomato sauce on his chin and then tears on his cheeks.

Who's Clappy? said Doris.

Jesus Christ, said Gemma. I'll fuckin kill him.

Doris stroked the boy's hair but he slipped from his chair and ran to the spare room. Tom, she said, there's a key and a map on the sideboard. I'll go and sit with Kai a minute.

What the fuck? said Gemma when Doris was gone.

Keep your voice down. Please.

Tell me.

He says Clappy's watching him, said Keely.

Shithead! What'd he do?

Nothing. He's just there. Stands across the street from school, out in the open. Like he wants to be seen. Gemma, you have to go to the cops.

I told you.

Then there's a place down south. Doris made some calls.

Fuck Doris!

You have to protect him, Gem, he said despite his fury. You have to think of him.

They'll take him off me – that's what's gunna happen. I *am* thinking of him – you haven't got a clue.

No one's going to take him off you, mate. You're just rattled, that's all.

They're crazy, she said, picking up her bag and heading through to the livingroom. Fuckin mad dogs, that's what.

Keely followed as she collected things he hadn't even noticed – folded laundry, celebrity magazines. She pitched them into a plastic washbasket.

They've got debts. And now they're jumpin out of their skin cause some other joker's movin in on their business. Like someone's declared war. They want the money right now.

So tell the cops, he said, reeling.

Stop sayin that! Fuckin look at you.

Then go tonight. The key's here. You heard Doris. Go away for a bit.

There's no goin away, don't you understand? No one's gunna pull these pricks in. Even if they do and some copper gets lucky or fits em up with a bit of gear, they're out on bail. Just down the road there. Even if a charge sticks there's only jail.

Then at least they're locked up.

What planet are you on? Nothin stops em from in there.

Keely felt for the couch, braced his knees against the frame, pressed his hands on the curve of its back to keep himself upright.

So what are you saying?

We have to find money, she hissed.

But this'll just go on, Gem.

Not for them. They won't get a cent.

I'm not following.

We need money to pay someone else. To fix this, stop em.

He took her arm, led her out to the deck. Slid the door to behind them. She shrugged him away, scowling.

Gemma. Paying someone else. What're you talking about?

You gunna stop em? You're a fuckin softcock, mate.

Well, thanks a lot. But Keely knew she was right. All he'd done was make it worse. He'd indulged himself, thinking he was so bloody clever.

I don't need your pissfartin about, I need this sorted. And it costs money.

What, like some kind of standover man? This is insane.

Properly. Professional.

No.

No choice.

It's wrong, Gem. It's his father.

I don't care. I've made me mind up.

Jesus, Gemma. You can't pay.

I'll pay.

How.

She looked at him. In the light her face was cold with resignation. He'd seen that look before. Just seeing it made him ashamed to be a man.

And then Doris was approaching from inside the house. Her heels thudding on the floorboards. She slid the door open.

Tom, can we speak for a moment?

I'll go pack, said Gemma.

You'll do it, then? asked Doris. You'll go south?

No, she said. We're goin home. Thanks for havin us. Sorry it's such a bloody mess.

You're always welcome, love, said Doris sorrowfully, stepping aside to let her pass. Catching the kiss on the cheek she wasn't expecting.

I'll go, too, he said.

I wish she'd go to Stephanie's.

Me too.

Look after them, Tom. And yourself. Please.

I will, he said hopelessly.

We'll talk.

We will.

In the Mirador carpark he tried to jolly the kid along a little but Kai was unresponsive.

I shoulda stayed, said Gemma in the lift.

You're here now.

He looked at their things stuffed into shopping bags, a plastic laundry basket. The kid's schoolbag.

The door cranked back at the tenth floor. There was no one on the gallery. No sign of anything wrong at either flat.

I can sleep on your couch, he said in her doorway. Kai went straight in to bed.

No, she said. No need.

Really.

I'm late for work.

You're going?

Of course I'm goin.

What about him?

He's got your number. He'll stay here now.

What about school?

Not until it's over.

She shut the door on him.

His flat smelt stagnant. He flopped into his armchair and thought of Kai. Heard Gemma leave for work a little before nine. Sat up. Waiting. He'd do it all night, stay awake until she was safely home.

But somebody was pounding at his door. And it was dark. Well, half dark. And when he groped on the floor beside the chair there was no plausible weapon to hand.

He snapped to his feet and felt the sickening lag as if half of him hadn't made it there yet. Thumping at the door.

His name.

They were yelling his name.

Clawed the wall. He was bare-chested. Lurched to the bedroom. For a shirt. Absurd, but he needed a shirt. To do this, confront what awaited him. Wondered if he had the balls to do anything more than cower behind the door. The room was dim. He groped for the cupboard. And almost trampled the kid. Curled in his jarmies. On the carpet, at the foot of the bed. Stirring now as Keely stumbled around him.

Open the fuckin door, Tom!

Keely wheeled back into the livingroom at the sound of Gemma's voice. Only Gemma. He was fine. Everything was fine. He plucked at the door-chain.

Right now!

He leant against the fridge a moment. Things were blurry.

You hear me?

The door jumped in its frame; she was kicking it. He turned the lock. Hauled it open. And she had the force of dawn behind her. It was like having his head staved in.

Where is he? Jesus Christ, Tom, what the fuck?

Keely sagged against the fridge, fists against his temples. She pushed past him.

You, she said at the boy grinding sleep from his eyes in the bedroom doorway.

Gemma grabbed him up fiercely and Keely caught Kai's glance across her shoulder as she hugged him.

Keely pulled himself around to face the kitchen clock. It was 6.52. Which meant he was supposed to be at work in eight minutes.

What're you fuckin doin? she hissed. What happened?

Nothing happened. I think he let himself in.

Gemma rounded on him. You don't even *know*?

I only just saw him now. He was asleep on the floor.

Jesus Christ, she said, lowering the kid to his feet and hauling him towards the door. You didn't even hear him come in? You let him sleep on the floor?

He looked at Kai, saw the key on its shoelace against his pigeon chest.

He's alright, Gem, he's safe.

No thanks to you.

All I did was go to sleep in my own flat.

Pissed as a stick.

No, he said.

She dragged Kai past him and out onto the gallery.

The boy looked back hopefully. Keely tried a reassuring smile but the kid was not fooled.

At Bub's he was a man hauling his own corpse through a swamp. The air in the kitchen was miasmic. He felt the grease settling on his skin and he drew it hot into his lungs with every breath. He was queasy, lightheaded, sore and clammy, so unsteady others had to jostle and dodge him. Kids, most of them. Taking the piss. He saw their mouths move, their eyes roll. Sound seemed to come and go intermittently. Everything around him – light, noise, space itself – felt sliced and diced. The morning towed him along a little way, sluiced past him, washed back to get him. Time was choppy. Fitful. Endlessly interrupted. Like a broken signal. Dirty coronas hung over every passing object. He worked, aping his own movements, head fluffy as the suds rising in his face. Bub looked disgusted. The chef – that squirrelly hipster with all the earrings and the pirate get-up – had the shits with him. Scowling, flashing his ruined teeth. Keely stayed at it all morning, digging deep; he was determined. But the Hobart cabinet had racks backed up beside it and the benches against the sink were head-high with pans and trays, everything, clean or dirty, glistening horribly. And then in the prep-hour before lunch he found himself just hanging against the trough, hands jerking in suds. Vertical. But useless.

Suddenly the chef was screaming. Something he couldn't hear. The bloke was brandishing a cleaver at him from across the room and next moment Keely was on the reeking mats amidst a forest of clogs and legs. I've been struck, he thought. That idiot's actually thrown the thing at me, cut me down. No sound at all. And then, like an approaching cataract, a rush of noise overtook him – laughter, cutlery, music – and he was wrenched to his feet.

Fuckin plonker, said some kid.

Go outside and get yourself what you need, said the chef without a hint of camaraderie. Ten minutes. Or piss off now.

Keely sat on a milk crate in the reeking alley as a waiter and a kitchen hand played hackeysack during their smoko. Bub appeared beside him, squatting on the step.

Everything alright, Tom?

Yeah.

Sure?

Soft, mate, that's all.

Bub glanced at him sceptically. Keely's younger workmates propped and kicked and giggled amidst the weeds and the flattened cartons.

Geez, mate. You must need the money.

I need something, Keely thought. But all he could manage was a thin grin.

Go home, said Bub. God's sake, go to bed.

I'm fine, said Keely. Sorry about the fuss.

Behind them in the kitchen a tub of plates smashed. It was like a mortar blast between his temples, but he got up, wiped his bacon-greasy hands on his apron and watched Bub go.

Hey, he said to the kids with the hackeysack. You know a speed-freak called Clappy?

The kitchen hand shrugged and stooped to pick up his little beanbag.

Ask Gypsy, said the waiter.

Nah, he's off the gear, said the kitchen hand.

Still, he'll know.

Gypsy? said Keely. Are you serious?

The waiter sniffed and the kids resumed their game.

The morning chef's studied machismo wasn't just irritating, it was silly. It was as if he'd worked up an act to imitate the celebrity bad boys of New York and London. The pirate scarf, the earrings, the sea-leg swagger. Gypsy might have been a good-looking dude in his time, but he was ravaged. Probably in his early forties. Looked a lot older. Even before the stunt with the cleaver Keely hadn't liked him. It wasn't just the posturing, it was the sourness, the lack of generosity. As if a roomful of people scurrying to keep things afloat deserved to be shat on.

Yesterday, after his shift, the chef had sat out at a street table in his checks and clogs, necking espressos and passing comment on women as they swept by. And he was there again after lunch today as Keely stepped out into the shade like a man delivered.

The day was over. Thank Christ.

There was an old bloke with Gypsy, an Italian gambler he recognized from around town. The chef shook his hand and the geezer cranked himself to his feet and gimped off. Keely hesitated, then sat down uninvited.

Ah. The fainting dishpig, said Gypsy. That had to have been embarrassing.

I guess it was.

This is my table.

I think it's Bub's table.

And, what, you've come to apologize for being a pussy?

I wanted to ask you about a couple of blokes.

You look familiar. Which bothers me.

Maybe we were in Sunday School together.

That'll be it.

Tom Keely.

That your name, or the bloke you want me to tell you about?

No, it's me.

Hang down your head, Tom Keely, sang Gypsy. Hang down your head and cry.

Bloke called Stewie Russell – you know him? He's got a mate called Clappy.

The chef's eyes narrowed.

Why would I know two little shits like that? Shitlets. Small pieces of ordure.

So you do know them.

Never said that, said Gypsy. Fellas you met inside, are they?

Here? I don't think so.

Fucksake.

Oh. *Inside.*

The chef uttered a sardonic laugh. Christ.

No. Nothing like that.

Figured you for a lag. Bub giving an old mate a second chance. He does that, bless his cheap little heart.

I need some information.

Mate, if you're looking to score you're talking to the wrong bloke.

I just wanted some advice.

A bloke looking as fucked as you, talking about shits of a certain species, sounds like you're in the market for advice I don't give anymore. Wake up, mate, clean yourself up. Leave me out of it.

I wanted to clarify something. A situation.

Tom Dooley. In a situation. Who'da thunk it?

I need to know who I'm up against.

Gypsy circled the espresso cup on its saucer, shunting it round with a be-ringed pinky.

There's just something I have to deal with, said Keely. For someone else. I need to know how dangerous they are.

Smaller the stakes, the nastier the fight, Dooley. Morons. And what could be worse?

How d'you mean?

Nitwits with nothing to lose. They're not people you *deal* with. You walk away. Or find some mates to fix it for you. And if you've got those sort of mates don't talk to me anymore, I don't wanna know. I'm not shitting you. Don't even come near me. These little cunts are only ever a few weeks from fucking up. They'll be banged up in Casuarina soon enough. Your 'friend' needs to cash up or keep his head down. Now move on, Dooley, you're frightening the ladies.

Kai was fidgety, restless from being cooped up in the flat all day. Their Scrabble game felt desultory. The kid was not really interested.

BARGS isn't a word, Keely told him. At least he thought that's what it said.

The kid shrugged. He'd been distant before, but not this sullen.

What about Mario? We could play that.

Kai sniffed disdainfully.

What is it, mate?

You cried.

What?

Last night. When you was sleeping.

Oh, said Keely with his spirit sinking – something else; it was endless. Did I?

I got scared.

The kid ran his hand through the lidful of unused tiles.

Why were you scared?

The boy looked away.

Kai? Why were you scared?

I dunno. Just the bawlin.

Kai pushed the tiles around the board – the game was toast now.

Is that all? Really? Honestly?

The boy shrugged. He looked at his palms.

Was I sleepwalking or something? Did I do something strange?

Cryin, that's all.

Well, blokes cry too, you know.

The kid's scepticism bordered on contempt.

But we do, he said. Even if we have to do it in our sleep.

Kai lifted the board and funnelled the tiles back into their box.

My dad, said Keely. He cried, you know.

The boy pressed his lips out sardonically.

True story. He wasn't some action hero, mate. He didn't spend all day biffing bad guys. He was a minister, like a priest. Just a bloke. I'm just a bloke too.

Can I watch TV?

I spose, said Keely.

He stood behind the couch awhile, watching the boy thumb through the channels. In fifteen minutes the school bell would ring.

Gemma came in, blotchy from the heat. She set down the bags of groceries and opened the fridge. He stood close, so Kai wouldn't overhear.

Nothing, she said.

I might take a look.

What's the point? Kai's not even down there.

Just to know what this little prick looks like.

Stupid bloody car, she hissed.

He peered down from the gallery. The side street was gridlocked with parents in vehicles. People of all shapes hung at the chain-link fence and smoked outside the seedy restaurants and shops across the road.

He wished he still had binoculars. He wanted to see faces but from up here people were only figures, bodies whose postures he couldn't read. And the longer you stared, the less innocent they seemed. Everyone began to look sinister. Lurking, plotting, in gaggles of colour and movement, indistinct behind the rippling hot updraughts. But they were just folks, parents, aunties, older siblings, waiting to collect their kids, walk them to the pool, the airconditioned shops, cricket training, dance lessons. He had to let them be people. Even the bloke at the corner. In the beanie. Black tracky-dacks, blue singlet, reflector shades. On a day like today. A woollen hat. Pity's sake. Folding his arms. One leg cocked against the wall. A small bloke.

Keely pulled the door to behind him and headed for the lifts. Probably wasn't him. But he needed to know.

As the lift door peeled open he startled an Indian granny emerging with a fully laden supermarket trolley. He stepped aside, smiled like a cretin and caught the door before the lift set off again. The school bell echoed up the shaft. At the fourth floor two emo kids tried to squeeze a desk and an office chair in, and after a few moments of trying to help them, he got out and took to the stairs.

By the time he got to the ground floor he was blowing and his spine felt as if it had been hammered up through the base of his skull. He bowled through the lobby and out into the hot light, shuffled breathless to the corner, but at street level everything was different. A blur of moving bodies, the sun glancing off vehicles as they purred by. Shopping bags blowing free, snagged in jacarandas. Hijacked supermarket trolleys abandoned in every alley. Spilt drinks, gobbets of food on the pavement. Gulls feasting, fleeing, banking back for more. A truck in reverse, all beeps and diesel fumes. And kids, hundreds of them still fanning out everywhere. He wondered how many had noticed Kai's absence today, whether there was a single girl or boy in this spreading mob who'd actually missed him, who'd even notice if he never returned.

He wheeled around, causing mothers and infants to clutch and cower. He climbed onto a street bench to scan the crowd. There were single men, blokes in suits, tradies in hi-viz, but no solitary lurker he could distinguish from the endlessly moving parade, no leering thug in tracksuit pants and gamy runners, no fag, no tatts, no beanie. He was too late.

He pushed back through the crowd, conscious he was bothering people now, frightening them a little. He was a fool to have come down. He'd left Gemma and Kai up there alone and whoever he'd seen wasn't just gone – he could be anywhere.

The lift wormed its way uncertainly up the shaft. He willed it on, shuffled in agitation and the Sudanese woman with the little girl in cornrows avoided his gaze. He knew what he looked like – there were others in the building: you saw them jounce and fidget every day, sweating and panting by the laundromat. Keely smiled at the woman reassuringly, but it only seemed to alarm her more.

He took the gallery at a trot and his knock on Gemma's door was too emphatic. He saw the momentary flash of the spyhole before the chain slid back.

Oh, Tommy, she said. Go and take a shower. You bloody stink.

They ate dinner together. Gemma cooked, almost defiant about it. Keely had no appetite but he knew better than to leave food on his plate. Things felt strained enough between the three of them as it was.

He was at the sink afterwards, trying to find something amusing about being elbow-deep in suds again, when Gemma's phone chirped on the bench behind him. Kai was in the shower. He heard her cajoling him from the bedroom. Tonight her fractiousness had a hint of wear in it, as if she were running out of fight. Maybe she'd go south after all. He'd call Doris.

It was just a single chirp, a message.

He reached for a towel and dried his hands. When he opened the phone there was no text, just an image. One of three.

Kai at the school gate. That round face, the unguarded gaze, the white hair to his shoulders. The second pic was the teddy bear. Horrible and yellow against the door grille, hanging as he'd found it, dangling from one leg. And the third was Gemma. Walking in the street. Carrying her shopping. Taken this afternoon.

He sensed her in the doorway before she spoke.

The fuck you doin?

Close the door, he said.

Bloody tell *me* what to do.

Please, Gemma. Close the door.

She glowered but pulled it to. The water ran on in the bathroom. He gave her the phone. He didn't know how he was going to tell her about the teddy bear, the fact he'd found it and said nothing. Best he didn't go there. Her face was instantly wild.

Get him into bed for me, will ya?

What're you doing?

Makin a call, she said, moving past to the sliding door. She stepped out onto the balcony and closed it behind her. He rapped on the glass. Watched her a moment until she turned and glared. She motioned for him to leave her alone. He went through to the bedroom, called to Kai to wind things up in there, that it was time for bed.

Kai and he were paging through the raptor book without much pleasure when Gemma appeared in the doorway.

Be out for a few minutes, she said.

Where? he asked.

I'll be back for work.

Stay here, Gem, he said, conscious of Kai's attention. Really. I mean it.

Just something I forgot, she said. A girl thing.

He got up from the bed and followed her to the door. Gemma, I'm serious.

Don't forget the chain, she said, averting any attempt at discussion.

And she was gone. He went back in and sat on the bed. It was a while before Keely noticed the boy surveying his sun-damaged hands. Kai drew his own from beneath the sheet and turned them over, examining them. Keely laid a hand on the boy's palm. Kai seemed uncertain about this. He lifted it a moment as if weighing it. Then he ran a finger across the veined back of Keely's mitt, the lined knuckles. Keely's hands were pulpy from hot water and looked a little swollen. He had no idea what the boy was thinking. He let him turn his hand over, trace the creases in Keely's palm.

You'll get big old blokes' hands like this one day, said Keely.

I wake up and I'm the same as you, said Kai. Like, I'm dreamin. Then I *am* you.

See? That's imagining. You're seeing in your head what it's like in the future, to be a grownup, to get old.

No, said the boy, giving Keely back his own hand. That's not it.

Gemma came in at eight-fifty. She was shaking and glassy-eyed. She smelt bitter but had no time to shower before work.

Where'd you go? he whispered, pulling the bedroom door to.

I told you, she said, shucking her dress and pulling a tunic from the plastic laundry basket on the coffee table.

What happened?

Don't ask me, it's a lady thing.

I don't believe you.

It doesn't matter what you believe, she said, zipping the tunic and stepping into her shoes.

Don't go, call in sick.

I can't, she said, tipping a compact and brush onto the kitchen bench. Not tonight.

Keely watched Gemma assemble herself. It was a mystery to him that a woman could arrive as a ruin and reconstitute herself in moments. There was still something shaky about her as she smoothed herself down and checked her reflection in the sliding glass door but she had assumed an armour that hadn't been there a few minutes before. He didn't believe she was going to work tonight. But why the uniform?

Can you stay? she asked, turning for the door. Will you be here?

Of course. I'm on at seven.

Okay. Good. I'll be back in plenty of time.

Whatever it is, Gem, don't do it.

Just work, she said.

I don't want you to.

She shot him a game smile as she pulled the door to and after she was gone he puzzled over the false note it struck.

He sat up till midnight. He felt the urge to call Doris, to speak to Faith, but he didn't know what he could say that wouldn't sound as if he were coming to pieces. But he was okay tonight. He was straight, sober, making himself useful. He had a job to go to in the morning. He was not mad.

The Mirador gulped and whistled. He paced the unblemished carpet of Gemma's livingroom, he watched the channel lights, the low constellations of tankers riding out in Gage Roads.

It was only night, just an ordinary darkness, and he was still and merely himself.

There was a weird vibe in the kitchen at Bub's. A sort of repelling field, a fraught space that nobody would enter. After yesterday's little fiasco it stood to reason. But it gave Keely the creeps the way the hackeysackers surveyed him in sideways glances, exchanging round-eyed looks and shrugs. Gypsy offered nothing but scowls and glares. The volume of the kitchen music was hellish, as if the chef had dialled it up for purposes of punishment or mastery.

Bub seemed fine, if somewhat distracted. Saturday mornings the joint always got smashed and Keely knew he needed all hands, even him at a pinch. The work was hectic and unceasing, a wave they all rode for fear of being overtaken.

The first lull didn't come until ten. Keely made himself a heart bomb – a four-shot espresso that filled a tumbler – and he was perched on the back step when Gypsy's spattered clogs appeared beside him. Keely made space for him to pass but the chef squatted close by, gazing out across the blighted little yard, all rings and fingernails and greasy curls, rubbing the burns and scars along his hands and forearms.

What the fuck, Suds?

Sorry?

Are you insane?

I hope not. Have I done something?

Well, that's cute.

Just give me time to get this down and I'll come in and fix it up, he said chugging his coffee.

Hardy-fuckin-ha. What've you got, a death wish?

I'm not with you, said Keely, wiping his mouth on his sleeve, properly rattled now.

The events of last night. Ring a bell, Suds?

Keely shook his head, set the glass down on the step beside him.

You're a smartarse, mate. I don't like it.

Maybe you could explain the problem.

Chrissake, mate, don't insult me.

I actually don't know what you're talking about.

A bloke gets dragged from the water last night at the sardine wharf.

Okay. I'm listening.

And just after midnight someone *I* know sees someone *you* know rolling by on a gurney in the A&E. All wet and untidy. Both his legs broken.

You're shitting me.

I don't need to be shitting you, mate. You need to be shitting yourself. You fucked it up.

Keely swam to his feet. He gazed over Gypsy's head to the flashes of movement in the kitchen, a rectangle of fluttering shadows, momentary visitations, blurs more abstract by the second.

You think so?

Well, Jesus, even this little scumbag's got friends. The cops'll be heartbroken he didn't drown, but now they'll have to show some kind of interest in who mowed him down.

In a car?

Ran him down. Into the water.

Nothing to do with me.

So why do you look like you're about to pass a fucking kidney stone?

Keely had nothing to say; he was too busy chasing his own thoughts.

This is a bloody small town, said Gypsy. A village of village idiots. People talk.

So let them.

Those kids in there. They know you were asking about a certain couple of dipshits. And they sent you to me. But I need to stay sweet with old Bub. I can't afford any trouble. So I'm not happy, Suds.

Fair enough.

You asked me, I didn't know who you were talking about. Right?

Alright.

You're just some derro off the street, I don't know you, we only spoke the once.

Keely shrugged.

And if I were you I'd piss off. Or take steps.

What kind of steps?

Mate, I'm not even here, said Gypsy, getting to his feet and dusting himself off like some sort of potentate regaining the dignity of his station.

Keely stood out in the yard. He stared at the coffee glass on the step, the jam-tin of butts, the row of fat drums, the wheelie bins, the big plastic skips.

He wondered if Bub would let him go early, whether this in itself might attract attention. He had four hours to get through. Gemma and Kai would be locked in the flat, that was something. But he had no idea who was in traction and who was still out on the street. Whoever had gone into the drink last night had likely consented to a meeting, with someone known to them. Neither Stewie nor his noxious mate was likely to give the cops anything. They'd want to fix this themselves. But money would hardly be sufficient now. From here on this would be about revenge.

He dug in behind the apron and pulled out his phone. His fingers were slippery and unsteady but he found the number.

What is it? she said.

You have to ask?

No idea what you mean, she said.

Kai alright?

Bored, she said. I bloody hate Mario.

Have you thought about . . . travelling? The key is still at my place.

Thinkin about it.

Don't go anywhere till I get back, alright?

Keely thumbed through a few sites. He had his own ideas about pissing off, but the other alternative – the taking steps business – that was another matter.

He was halfway across the town hall square, heading for the Mirador at something just short of a trot, when he saw the figure in the shadow of the Moreton Bay fig. The man stood with his hands in the pockets of his trackpants looking busy doing nothing, the way some blokes could, and there was nothing out of the ordinary in the blue singlet, the Adidas pants, the lizard eyes or the tatts. There were always charmers here lurking to sell or floating to buy between the figs and the date palms. But this character gave off a malevolent interest that didn't seem accidental. The twinge of fear quickened Keely's pace a moment before he reined himself in, and then he was as angry as he was afraid.

At the far edge of the square he stopped and turned. It seemed to him the man's face was still angled his way, at this distance little more than a pale disc.

Keely raised a hand in the unmistakeable shape of a pistol. Saw the man's hands leave his pockets in alarm. Took aim. Mimed the discharge and recoil of a weapon. Blew imaginary smoke from the end of his index finger. Saw the stranger's arms fall to his sides in shocked relief. Turned for home. Did not run.

The lobby was empty. He went straight through to the rear door and into the carpark, scanning the rows until he found the Hyundai wedged in the farthest corner. There was no point searching for any obvious signs of collision because every window was smashed and from front to back no panel had escaped a stomping. Three tyres flat and on the front hood, coiled like an adder, a human turd.

He hurried to the relative shelter of the bike shed and called her. It was hard to keep the panic from his voice.

Have you seen the car?

What part of the car?

Shit, Gemma.

What?

Well, travel just got harder. There is no car. It's trashed.

Fuckin Clappy. How does he even know?

How do you think?

Oh, Jesus Christ.

Call the cops, he said. I'm begging you.

You know that's not gunna happen. Tom. Jesus. Help me.

Stay there, he said. Don't open the door to anyone. I'll be back in an hour.

He climbed down from the bus and oriented himself at the truck-snarled junction.

It was brutally hot. Houses fronted by concrete lions gave way to factory units, discount furniture stores and machinery dealerships. He trudged east a hundred metres, still in his greasy shirt and half-dried pants, until he saw the window with all the steel bars. He wiped his palms against his sleeves and pushed on the door.

When he stepped inside a buzzer announced him and he saw the surveillance cameras. The tinny smell of light oil greeted him. For some absurd reason it reminded him of his mother's ancient Singer sewing machine. And then of the old man's Triumph, up on blocks in the shed.

Ah, g'day, said the red-bearded bloke rising behind the glass counter.

Yeah, said Keely. G'day there.

Not since he'd stumbled into a sex shop in Amsterdam had he felt so self-conscious in a retail space. There were many more pictures of guns on display in this place than actual weapons, but as he approached the modest array in the case before him he felt a bilious mixture of shame and menace.

Help you with something?

Well, I dunno, he blurted. I was thinking about a pistol.

Revolver or semi?

Ah, semi, say.

Just joined a club, then? the man asked indulgently.

Club?

Well, you don't strike me as the farming type. Or enforcement, given we're talking sidearm.

Sorry, I'm not with you.

Mate, you can't bowl up cold and buy a pistol. Not in this country. Need to be a registered member of a club with six months' standing, for one thing. After that, you need to apply for a licence from the cops and have your record vetted. But at least you're over twenty-one, so that's a start, eh.

Keely blushed and offered a colicky grin.

Yeah, he said at last. Point taken. I guess I was just after an idea.

Of what they look like, or what they cost?

Well, both, I guess.

Research, then.

Yeah, said Keely.

Don't spose you've heard of Google?

Well, it's just different, isn't it? When you see them.

It must be.

Anyway, I think I've satisfied my curiosity.

Well, said the gunsmith by way of dismissal. Glad to be of help.

He caught the bus back to town, got out at the lurkers' park beside the big pharmacy and went op-shopping. At the St Vincent de Paul store, in a box of used toys that reeked of disinfectant, he found a plastic Luger. Two brick-faced matrons at the till smiled kindly and sent him on his way with a recycled shopping bag and a few God-blesses. He made straight for the hobby shop. Bought a tin of Airfix paint the size of a cotton reel. Paid for it with his last shrapnel and made for home.

The lift yawned open. He rode to the top, stood outside her window until he saw the boy's head pass behind the nylon curtain. He tapped the glass softly and Kai peered out. Keely gave him a thumbs up and the kid waved hesitantly, as if anxious about being discovered. When Keely made a silly face the boy produced a wan grin and let the curtain fall to.

The faded red Luger — burred at the butt where some infant had gnawed it — was just a water pistol with a missing bung. He spread newspaper on the kitchen table and painted the thing blue-black and when he finished the job, set it aside and stood back, he saw it would never work. What the hell had he been thinking? Another hour wasted. He had to get them out of town. Tonight. As far as he could make out, Gemma or someone she knew had deliberately run a man down and pushed him into the harbour; that was no small thing. She'd do time for it, so there wasn't a chance she'd go to the cops now; it'd mean relinquishing Kai to foster care.

He dialled Doris but rang off before she answered. Then he called Gemma who picked up but said nothing.

In the background the noise of the TV or the computer game,

the squeal of tyres. Then the faintest sound of her weeping.

I'm here, he said, for something to say. It's only me.

Christ, Tommy, she whispered.

Whatever occurred last night, he said, there were reasons. You could explain it. If you went in and told them what's been going on, it'd go in your favour. Doris could get you a kick-arse lawyer. And if anything . . . well, if it was necessary, even if it's only a few days, we'd look after Kai, you know that. They'll have you out on bail. Whatever happens we'd look after him, both of you.

I can't, she said. I fuckin *can't*.

We'd look after him, Gem.

She's an old lady, she hissed. And you think they'll let *you* have him? You haven't even had the job for a week. You're a mess, Tom. I've seen you lookin at me. I know what you think. But you know what? Compared to you I'm doin orright.

Yeah, he said. Apart from the fact that you can't leave your flat and you're wanted by the police.

If you fuckin dob I'll tell Clappy where your mum lives. I'm not kiddin.

Keely sat down. He gazed at the sunset. It was unbearably beautiful.

You hear me?

You don't mean that, he said as if saying it might convince him. Blood's thicker than water.

No.

I'm serious. What else can I do?

Well, you can think of your friends, he said. Because if blood's thicker than water, you're fucked. And so's Kai.

He hung up and stared at the stupid little toy on the table.

The phone buzzed.

Tommy, I'm sorry. I didn't mean it. I know you won't tell.

But now you can't be sure, he said.

No, she said. I trust you.

He didn't speak. It shamed him, hearing her say it. Scoured him no less than being told the truth, that he was not a fit person to be entrusted with the care of a child. What had she put her trust in but a falling man?

Do you think Doris will have us back?

Yes, he said, knowing it was true.

Keely thought of the Volvo. Doris would give her the car, get her away, and bugger the consequences.

Christ, Tommy.

The sun flattened itself against the limpid sea. The sky was magnificent.

I feel sick, she whispered.

Pack some stuff. I need to talk to Doris. I'll come by when I have something organized. Don't call anyone.

He hung up. And when he headed to the sink for a glass of water, one leg was heavy. His hands shook so much he had to set the tumbler down and rifle through what remained of his supplies. Needed something to iron him out. Rattled and faffed through sheets and packets. Everything shining evilly. Shook out what he could, gobbed a party-coloured handful, whatever it took.

And then he packed a bag. Tried to be methodical.

Time to call Doris. And also Bub. Wished his hands would settle down.

Drank some more water. And nearly dropped the glass. He was rushing, too frantic. Needed to sit a moment. Get clear.

And then he looked seaward and the sky was dark.

Yes, he'd ask Bub for whatever he was owed, take him up on his offer of a loan. Go to Doris's – no, call Doris. Maybe hitch the boat to the Volvo, sell it for cash at a yard along the highway. Use the money to buy a van. There was a line of them outside the station where backpackers offloaded them to get home. He had the keys to the place down south. Or Doris did. She'd collect them any minute. Be surprised to see the flat after all this time. She'd come through, and they'd slip away, stay south a while, keep going. He'd go with them or not go with them, he didn't know yet. Better he got them away first. Couldn't think past that, couldn't think past the lowering dark. Really. Just couldn't really. Think.

The phone. It rang. And rang. From so far away.

And after some time he got himself upright. But it had stopped.

Then, on the floor beside the chair, the mobile began to flash, buzzing and shivering. He reached for it as if through moving water. Chased and seized it. Felt it buck like a fish. But let it breathe and wheeze against his ear. Like the sound of his little sister. He smelt Airfix paint, thought of the Spitfires and Typhoons he'd glued together in his room at Blackboy Crescent. The lanolin reek of a damp footy jumper, the Syd Jackson poster on the wardrobe door. If he closed his eyes he'd be there again. And he wanted to. Yes. Faith in the next room. Doris and Nev talking quietly out on the porch. Everything good, all safe.

Tom? Is it you?

Yes, said Keely with a croak. And only then did he understand that it wasn't Faith but Kai.

Are you awake, Tom?

Yeah, he said, though everything felt and sounded dreamy. Yes, I think so.

But where are you?

I'm here, he murmured, trying to straighten in the chair. At home.

We didn't know. We waited.

Where's Gemma? he asked, still confused. Because it was dark, so late.

Sleeping, said the boy. She was cryin. But now she's asleep.

Good, he said. That's good.

She said you wouldn't run away.

And Keely remembered the packed bag. The trip south.

Tom? Are you really there? Can I see?

What's wrong? Is something happening?

Just, I had the dream. And I'm scared of falling back to sleep.

But you must be tired. Hell, I'm tired. It's only a dream, mate.

The boy wheezed quietly. And there was a rushing noise behind him, as if he had the TV on; it sounded like static.

It's only a dream, Kai. It can't hurt you, mate. It's just a thing running through your head. It's not real.

Are you real?

Of course, he said. But Keely no longer felt real.

You're really there? Can I see? Can you come out?

Out where?

Outside.

Keely felt a jolt of fear and suddenly he was alert. Kai, where are you?

On the balcony.

Keely flailed at the air, found his feet. His head was water-logged, precarious on his neck. He hauled the slider open and tottered out. Three doors up, there he was, in the milky spill of city light, pale and bare-chested.

Kai!

I can see you, said the boy, waving.

Go inside now. Please.

Kai moved, but only to the rail. The bars divided his figure into vertical strips. One hand rested on the horizontal. And Keely's gut fluttered. He was back in his own nightmare.

Can I come over? Tom?

Really, mate. I just need you to go inside before we do anything else.

But Nan.

We'll whisper, alright? Let's just get you inside and you lock the door and lie down on the couch and we'll talk.

Okay, said the boy.

Keely watched him go in, saw a sheen at the rear of the balcony as if the door had moved.

Have you locked it?

Yes, whispered the kid.

Why don't you lie down, aren't you tired?

Yes.

Just lie on the couch and I'll stay on the phone. You can go to sleep if you want. I'll just be here, listening.

In my ear, said the boy softly.

That's right, he said, subsiding into the chair.

Like Father says? Says it's in your ear, the Holy Spirit.

Well. I guess that's one way of thinking about it, yeah.

Father's not a father, but.

Um, no. Not in that way, no.

Not allowed.

No.

Are you allowed?

Yes, he whispered. I think so. But I think it's too late for me.

There was only breathing for a while.

My dad isn't good, said Kai. But I don't want him to die.

No, of course not. He's your father.

You didn't do anythink bad. I know.

I make mistakes, Kai. Your mum and your dad they just made mistakes. People get stuck. They need help.

It's you. I knew you was real.

Still here, mate.

You're the one.

Shh.

I seen it.

Try to sleep, he said, unable to stifle a yawn.

I'll get old, Tom. Like Doris.

Yeah, like Doris.

But it's sad.

Nah.

We saw the bird.

That's right.

And the bird saw you.

You sound sleepy.

Yeah.

It's okay. I'll be here. And then I'll be —

In my ear.

Alright.

Bye, Tom.

Goodnight, mate.

Keely felt close enough to hear sleep overtake the boy. There was no hand in his shirt but Kai's breath was in his ear, right in his head. Something sweet and benign finally inside him, like a bulwark. He sat a few minutes and listened to the holy wheeze of the kid asleep.

Didn't know how long it was before he stirred again, still connected. Climbed up. Took the mobile into the next room. Blinked at the suitcase on the bed. He knew Doris would come if he called. But he was too blurry just now to get going and stay going. Needed to be competent.

Felt the mattress subside beneath him. Clutched the phone close. Sound of the living boy. Just for a moment, until he was clear.

Then they'd go south. To forest, white coves, granite boulders like beasts resting before the silver sea.

Then, in a moment, it was light. Something ground into his skull like a fist, like the muzzle of a gun. And a voice was in his ear, screaming, pleading. When he rolled over the phone fell squalling to the floor but the demonic noise was everywhere in the building, out on the gallery, at his shuddering door.

He was up, still dressed. She was calling.

And when he reefed the door open the little man exploded from the searing flare of sunlight and had him stumbling against the fridge before he could even speak. Both of them careered into the kitchen bench, and Keely felt the grip on his throat, saw the flashes of sari and opening phone as someone ran past the open doorway. Clappy trapped his free hand, forced his head back so hard his neck felt it would tear free of his shoulders, and all he could do was clamp the bastard's forearm to keep from choking. The edge of the countertop bit into his spine and buds of light began to open behind his eyes.

You fuckin idiot arsehole, said Clappy.

Keely's jaw was pressed shut. There was no way of answering. He did what he could to brace, neutralize the pressure, ease the pain, and he felt a brightness awaken in him. He was not afraid. Just angry. He watched the whiskery runt down the length of his nose. He was all pupil. The beanie was navy-blue. The earrings looked like fish-hooks, couldn't be fish-hooks. Mackerel eyes. Sour, chapped lips. His breath stank of ruined teeth and battery acid. There was something about the moronic grin that riled Keely. It was a performance. This was Clappy's act, a routine learnt from the telly. Dosed to the gills, he'd talked himself up, convinced himself he could be mighty, prevail, satisfy himself and whatever darkness ruled him. And it was kind of pathetic. He was half his fucking size. Malnourished, twitching, puny.

A laugh boiled up in Keely's throat and it caught them both unawares. Clappy snarled and jabbed his knee deep into the softness of his thigh and it was as if there had been no real pain before this moment. After which Keely was sober. He saw his mistake. Here was havoc, after all. Despite his size, performance or no, Clappy was dangerous. He pressed Keely back with renewed vigour, twisting his vertebrae, wringing his throat.

Fuck *us* about, he hissed. Try that shit on. You don't know what I can do, you dumb fuck. Finish with you I'm in *there*, mate, with those two, and then the fun really gets goin.

The strain on Keely's neck was unbearable. He couldn't draw away, but managed to ease himself sidelong a half-step before the little prick gained on him again and the second's respite was enough; he saw how high his assailant was reaching to maintain pressure; Clappy was dancing on tiptoe. And the bench was breaking Keely in half. He could feel his windpipe beginning to collapse. Knew he couldn't hold position for much longer. There was no help coming. But he could feel the other man's arms trembling with the strain. Saw his eyes flick away, past Keely's shoulder, to what – the view, the table? Shit, the table. The newsprint, the paint, the gun.

It was just a flicker, an instant of lost momentum, as if Clappy's fevered mind had snagged a second. His eyes widened. He blinked. And Keely jerked sideways, felt the little bloke lose his footing and release a hand to steady himself. Keely spun free and saw him stagger then recover, an arm's length away.

You dumb cunt, said Clappy.

Keely went for him. Felt the boyish thinness of his flashing wrist. And heard the knife before he saw it.

The blade clattered to the floor and Clappy stooped a moment before drawing back, glancing again at the table behind them. Keely grinned at him. Clappy blinked, chewed the air a second and then fled, crashing out onto the gallery, leaving Keely with a hot flush of relief coursing through his guts.

Somewhere in the building there was singing. Eggs were being fried. Next door his neighbour chanted metrically, musical as a nursery rhyme. As he staggered out onto the walkway the east wind rose in his face. It tasted of dust, of crops, the great country. He heard a siren. Every fingertip began to spark. He felt lightheaded with overcoming. He was larger than himself. His legs shook.

And now, in nothing but a T-shirt, Gemma came running his way.

Where's Kai? he said.

Up here, she cried. He's safe.

Go back, he said. Get inside.

Lie down, Tom. They're coming. The cops, the ambo. God's

sake, you need to lie down!

He heard her calling, left her behind on the gallery as he set off. I'm the one, he thought. This little prick hasn't seen the last of me. I am the one.

He didn't bother with the lifts. He surfed down the stairs, thudding through every steel-railed right angle with the wind in his ears. Pursued by his own gathering momentum, he felt stronger and faster by the second. He was peaking. He felt power in his teeth, a great force pressing for escape.

At every floor the lift trundled ponderously earthward in the shaft. Clappy like a rat in a box. And Keely was close, in touch, nearly there, ready.

In the lobby, he crashed against the closing glass doors, saw the dark figure sprint across the forecourt into impossible light swarming with dim figures that surged away, crying out in consternation. The glass drew back and he was out there in the white world, in a field of stars and specks, of dancing sun. Faces loomed and bodies twisted aside as he ran on squelching feet. Ahead on the street there was a howl of braking tyres. Screams. And then people. So many people. Coming. Surging in, a gathering flock of heads and legs. Whatever was out there on the road, whatever had happened at the kerb, it was waiting for him, just within reach. He swam the hot air, reaching, clawing the breeze towards the flare of turning faces, open mouths, buffeting against the empty space of morning, puzzled, happy, still reaching.

So why the pavement, sudden and hot against his face? Palms scorched. Cold feet slippery-wet. He rolled to a shoulder, fell back strangely breathless to see the purling sky and the pink finger of the building above him. The world flashed outside him, shuttering light, stammering sound. A circle of dark heads in hoods enclosed him, offering moments of merciful shade.

Sir?

Dark-skinned noses, black eyes, pieces of face through the letterbox slits of cloth.

Sir? said the pair of spectacles, the swatch of human shape behind. Sir, are you well?

The veiled faces retracted uncertainly and Keely understood. He'd fallen. He saw the tower beyond and the tiny figure of the boy safe on the balcony. He smelt salt and concrete and urine. Saw lovely brown thumbs pressing numbers, cheeping digits, reaching down. The edit was choppy. The boy's face a flash – or was that a gull?

Sir, there is bleeding. Are you well?

Yes, he said with all the clarity left to him. Thank you. I am well.